Praise for Graham Hurley

'Hurley is a giant of British police procedural novels, and with *Western Approaches* we find an author on top of his game'   *Crime Time*

'Another cracker from Graham Hurley . . . This is a very good opportunity to climb aboard and savour this writer's very addictive series. Brilliant'   *Crimesquad*

'Hurley's devastating account of the breakdown of Suttle's marriage is one of the best things he has done'   *Daily Telegraph*

'Skillfully combining murder mystery and police procedural drama with a West Country travelogue, this is a satisfying read'   *Sunday Mirror*

'Hurley never disappoints and here proves his standing as one of the UK's finest crime novelists'   *Independent on Sunday*

'There is no doubt that his series of police procedural novels is one of the best since the genre was invented more than half a century ago'   *Literary Review*

'Hurley's decent, persistent cop is cementing his reputation as one of Britain's most credible official sleuths, crisscrossing the mean streets of a city that is a brilliantly depicted microcosm of contemporary Britain'   *Guardian*

'It's a mystery in itself why Hurley is not better known as a crime writer. His Joe Faraday police procedural novels are spot on – well-written and plotted, utterly convincing and . . . g . . . An excellent and com-   *Daily Mail*

Belfast Telegraph

Graham Hurley is the author of the acclaimed Faraday and Winter crime novels. Two of the critically lauded series have been shortlisted for the Theakston's Old Peculier Award for Best Crime Novel. His French TV series, based on the Faraday and Winter novels, has won huge audiences. An award-winning TV documentary maker, Graham now writes full time. He lives with his wife, Lin, in Exmouth. Visit his website at www.grahamhurley.co.uk

By Graham Hurley

FICTION
Rules of Engagement • Reaper
The Devil's Breath • Thunder in the Blood
Sabbathman • The Perfect Soldier
Heaven's Light • Nocturne
Permissible Limits • The Chop
The Ghosts of 2012

DI JOE FARADAY INVESTIGATIONS
Turnstone • The Take
Angels Passing • Deadlight
Cut to Black • Blood and Honey
One Under • The Price of Darkness
No Lovelier Death • Beyond Reach
Borrowed Light • Happy Days

DS JIMMY SUTTLE INVESTIGATIONS
Western Approaches • Touching Distance

NON-FICTION
Lucky Break? • Airshow
Estuary • Backstory

WESTERN
APPROACHES

Graham Hurley

An Orion paperback

First published in Great Britain in 2012
by Orion
This paperback edition published in 2013
by Orion Books,
an imprint of The Orion Publishing Group Ltd,
Orion House, 5 Upper St Martin's Lane,
London WC2H 9EA

An Hachette UK company

1 3 5 7 9 10 8 6 4 2

Copyright © Graham Hurley 2012

The moral right of Graham Hurley to be identified as the
author of this work has been asserted in accordance with
the Copyright, Designs and Patents Act 1988.

All rights reserved. No part of this publication may be
reproduced, stored in a retrieval system, or transmitted,
in any form or by any means, electronic, mechanical,
photocopying, recording or otherwise, without the
prior permission of the copyright owner.

All the characters in this book are fictitious,
and any resemblance to actual persons, living
or dead, is purely coincidental.

A CIP catalogue record for this book
is available from the British Library.

ISBN 978-1-4091-3554-8

Typeset by Deltatype Ltd, Birkenhead, Merseyside

Printed and bound in Great Britain
by Clays Ltd, St Ives plc

The Orion Publishing Group's policy is to use papers
that are natural, renewable and recyclable products and
made from wood grown in sustainable forests. The logging
and manufacturing processes are expected to conform to
the environmental regulations of the country of origin.

www.orionbooks.co.uk

In memory of Deb Graham, 1972 – 2012

The sea has never been friendly to man. At most it has been the accomplice to human restlessness.

Joseph Conrad

Prelude

He awakes, as usual, at 03.55. For a second or two he lies in the clammy darkness, trying to work out what's gone wrong.

The last couple of days a thick tongue of high pressure has pushed up from the Azores, exciting weather forecasters all over northern Europe. He's listened to the headlines on the short-wave radio: 32°C in Amsterdam; hotter still in Paris; 35° expected this afternoon in London.

Christ, he thinks. London.

He searches for the T-shirt he carefully folded two hours earlier, checks with his fingers that it's not inside out. His mouth tastes of the tin of sardines they'd shared last night and he knows that his breath stinks. Sardines on Ryvita. Again.

He runs his tongue along his teeth and tries to pinch the darkness from his eyes. Something's definitely wrong. He knows it is. But, still groggy, he can't quite fathom what.

He pulls on the T-shirt. The last week or so, before the high pressure arrived, the weather and the ocean have been brutal. Sheer concentration has kept exhaustion at bay, but now, in the eerie calm, he feels totally wiped out. Yesterday he spent hour after hour checking their progress on the GPS, a habit – in Kate's phrase – that has become a nervous tic. But he can't help it. Without the suck and gurgle of a following sea, no matter how hard they pull, they seem to be going nowhere. He's sure of nothing except the heat of the day, a thick blanket that presses down on them, bringing everything to a halt: conversation, energy, belief, even the small comfort of a decent horizon. The ocean, poster blue, shimmers in the heat. Everything has become a blur. And now, as dawn breaks, this.

He struggles into his shorts, wincing with the effort. He has a couple of boils on his arse, incredibly painful. He checks them with a mirror when Kate's not watching. She's squeezed them dry as best she can and made him start on the antibiotics against the infection but he can feel, or he thinks he can feel, another one coming.

He's on his side now, up on one elbow, waiting for his arse to settle down. He can feel tangles of hair hanging round his shoulders and his head nudges against the roughness of the cabin roof. Ten days ago, riding out yet another storm, he'd popped a bottle of cooking oil in this khazi of a cave and everything still feels sticky to the touch. They lost a jar of coffee too, same storm, and the granules are everywhere. They melt in the sweat from his body and he's yet to emerge from the cabin without the telltale smears of brown all over his face. Kate, who seems immune from Nescafé Gold, has taken to calling him Coco the Clown. He thinks she means it as a joke but there are moments, especially recently, when he's not altogether sure.

The alarm on his wristwatch begins to ping. Four o'clock. He's learned to hate this sound with a fierce passion, the way some people react to the whine of a nearby mosquito. It means he has to move, gather himself together, face another day.

His fingers find the stainless-steel latches that keep the hatch in place. At last, thicko, he's realised what's wrong. The boat isn't moving. He can't hear the regular splash-splash of the oars, can't sense the faint tug as the boat inches forward. He feels nothing but the gentle sway of the ocean.

Anxious now, he fights to open the hatch. He knows how much Kate loves the slow drama of sunrise, that hour or so when the huge orange ball eases itself free of the ocean. Yesterday, she told him, was the best ever. Today, just maybe, might be better still.

Kate is keeping a record of everything. As the last latch comes free he can picture her squatting midships, her face to the rising sun, steadying her Nikon for yet another shot.

Daylight floods the chaos of the tiny cabin. He blinks at the familiar tableau of boat, of lashed-down gear, of sea, of the rich yellow spill of the new day. He wriggles his upper body through the hatch and rubs his eyes again, looking round, trying to find his wife.

But Kate has gone.

This, at least, was the way he explained it in the first of several interviews with Devon and Cornwall CID.

One

Nearly a year later, D/S Jimmy Suttle stumbled downstairs, knotting his tie, his mobile wedged against his ear. In theory, this was a precious weekend off. In theory, he should still be in bed.

'Where did you say?'

'Exmouth Quays. Sus death. Mr Nandy wants to blitz it. Asap, Jimmy. Do I hear a yes?'

The line went dead, leaving Suttle in the chaos of the tiny kitchen. In these situations, D/I Carole Houghton seldom bothered with anything but the barest of facts. That way she was already on to the next call.

Suttle gazed around. The tap he'd promised to fix this very morning was still dripping onto the pile of unwashed plates. Two empty bottles of cheap red and the remains of yet another Chinese takeaway were stuffed into the lidless waste bin. Even the cat, a tormented stray Lizzie had rescued from down the lane, wasn't interested in the curls of battered fish in gloopy sauce.

Suttle found it next door in the sitting room, crouched behind the sofa. Here, the carpet stank of animal piss and a fainter smell that signalled a more general neglect. In one of her blacker moods Lizzie had christened the cat Dexter in memory of a nightmare boyfriend at her long-ago Pompey comp. Now, his back to the wall, Dexter would do anything

4

to defend his patch against all-comers. Suttle, wondering why he hadn't swallowed more ibuprofen last night, knew exactly how he felt.

Upstairs, he could hear Grace talking to the mobile over her cot. This, he knew, was a prelude to the full lung-busting wail with which she greeted every new day. Normally it would be Lizzie who got up and answered the summons, leaving Suttle with a few snatched extra minutes in bed. Last night, switching off the light, he'd promised to sort out his daughter himself, giving Lizzie a lie-in. Now, looking for his leather jacket, he was trying to remember whether the car had enough fuel to get him to Exmouth.

Grace began to howl. Pulling on his jacket, Suttle headed for the door.

Exmouth, an old-fashioned low-rise seaside resort with a reputation for kite surfing, birdwatching and lively Friday nights, lies nine miles south of Exeter. Exmouth Quays is a marina development built around the basin of the old commercial docks, a quieter frieze of expensive waterside homes in various shades of New England pastel. Suttle, who'd been here before, had always regarded it as a film set, not quite real, a showcase destination for people who wanted to make a certain kind of statement about themselves.

He parked the Impreza beside Houghton's Vauxhall estate. Her dog, a mongrel terrier, lay curled on the back seat. A couple of uniforms had already taped off an area of walkway beneath the biggest of the apartment blocks, a towering confection with a faux clapboard finish and stainless steel trim.

Suttle crossed the bridge that spanned the dock entrance, flashed his ID at the uniforms and ducked under the tape. The apartment block was called Regatta Court. A banner draped across the fourth floor warned that only three apartments remained for sale while an accompanying poster asked WHY LIVE ANYWHERE ELSE? Why indeed, thought Suttle, eyeing the body at the feet of the grey-clad Crime Scene Investigator.

He'd worked with the CSI on a job in Torquay only last month. Difficult guy. Ex-marine. Mad about R & B. Lost his left leg after stepping on an IED in Afghan.

'Houghton about?'

The CSI was making notes on a clipboard. Suttle was trying to remember his name.

'It's Mark, if you were wondering.' The CSI didn't look up. 'And she's talking to Mr Nandy.'

Suttle was still studying the body sprawled among the puddles on the wet paving stones.

'So what happened?'

'He has to have fallen.' The CSI glanced up at last. 'We're thinking the top apartment. Big fuck-off place. Number 37.'

'The guy's got a name?'

'Kinsey. According to a neighbour.'

'Anything else you want to share?'

The CSI gave him a look. Wet weather made his stump ache.

'Some arsehole's been spewing round the corner if you want to take a look.' He nodded at the sea wall at the end of the walkway. 'Apart from that? No.'

Suttle was circling the body, examining it from every angle. The guy was on the small side. He was wearing a pair of Nike track pants and a red singlet. A crest on the singlet featured a pair of crossed oars. His feet were bare and there was something awkward in the way the body seemed to change angle around the neck. Blood from both ears had pooled on the paving stones and more blood had matted in his thinning hair. Guessing his age wasn't easy but Suttle thought around forty. His eyes were open, the lightest blue, and the last seconds of his life had left him with an expression of faint surprise.

Suttle knelt to examine the big Rotary on Kinsey's left wrist. The impact had smashed the face of the watch. Four minutes past three. Suttle's eyes strayed to the name beneath the crest on the singlet: *Jake K.*

6

'Has Mr Nandy asked for the pathologist?'

'Here, you mean?'

'Yeah.'

'No.'

'Why not?'

'He thinks there's no point. And he's probably right. A fall from that kind of height you're talking head first. If there's anything else, it'll show up at the PM.'

'You think he jumped?'

'I've no idea.'

Suttle nodded. His early years as a uniformed probationer in Pompey had taught him everything he ever wanted to know about the way the weight of the human head can turn a jumper upside down. Twice he'd had to deal with deranged adolescents who'd turned their backs on the world, or on a fucked-up relationship, and stepped off the top level of the city's Tricorn car park. Fall dynamics was a phrase he'd never grown to like.

He turned to the CSI again.

'CCTV?'

'There isn't any. The nearest cameras are in the town centre. We're talking nearly a mile away.'

'None at all?' Suttle was amazed.

'Zero. *Nada*.'

'Right.' He nodded. 'So how's Mr Nandy?'

'Manic. Argyle lost again yesterday and he thinks they're stuffed.'

Suttle turned to go. CID-wide, Det-Supt Malcolm Nandy was recognised as the king of lost causes. Trying to defend his empire against the marauding cost-cutters at force HQ was one of them. Plymouth Argyle was another. His beloved Pilgrims were on the edge of bankruptcy, and among the Major Crime Team Nandy was rumoured to be bunging them the odd fiver, doing his bit to help them stave off oblivion.

Fat chance on both counts, Suttle thought, ducking under the tape again.

Lizzie knelt beside the fireplace in a third attempt to coax a flame from the pile of damp kindling. Grace stood in her play-pen by the sofa, shaking the wooden bars in a bid to attract the cat's attention. Her morning bottle and a modest bowl of porridge had at last put a smile on her tiny face.

'Daddy?' she gurgled.

'He's at work, my love.'

'Daddy gone?'

'I'm afraid so.'

Lizzie abandoned the fire. Even the balls of newsprint beneath the kindling, the leftovers from last week's local paper, seemed reluctant to light. She pulled one out and flattened it against the cracked slates on the hearth, wondering if she'd missed anything. PENSIONER'S HANDBAG LEFT ON BUS went the headline. Breaking news in Colaton Raleigh, she thought. *What the fuck have I done?*

She was still taunted by dreams of her last day at work and the get-together in the pub afterwards. Starting her maternity leave in Portsmouth, she'd had every intention of one day resuming her job at the Pompey *News*. As the favoured feature writer, she'd cornered the market for the plum interviews and the occasional foray into serious investigative journalism, and she'd loved every minute of it. She'd scooped one of the big provincial awards for a feature on racial tensions among the city's Kosovan community and there'd been a couple of flattering calls from one of the national tabloids, inviting her to send a CV and a representative sample of her recent work. But then came Grace, and nine months later Jimmy had managed to score a promotion of his own. By this time she'd begun to know a different Pompey composed of fat mums at the health centre, ever-partying student drunks down the road and a manic neighbour – heavily tattooed – who claimed to have once met the Pope.

She remembered the morning the letter from Exeter had

arrived only too well. That night she and Jimmy had celebrated with champagne and blueberries with lashings of double cream. It had never been part of her career plan to move to Devon, and she'd never realised that her husband had fallen out of love with Portsmouth, but seeing the grin on his face as they emptied the second bottle she realised that she and Grace had no choice. Jimmy had grown up in the country, a straggly little village on the edge of the New Forest, and now he couldn't wait to introduce her to what he called the sanity of rural life.

Chantry Cottage had been his idea. His new employers – Devon and Cornwall Constabulary – had wanted him to start rather earlier than he'd expected, and he'd headed west without taking the extended leave he'd promised her. The Major Crime Investigation Team he was joining put him through a two-week force induction programme which gave him a little spare time at the end of each working afternoon. Within days, a trawl of the Exeter estate agencies had produced half a dozen potential buys. All of them, in Lizzie's view, were way too expensive. Property prices in Pompey were beginning to sink and mortgage companies were starting to demand ever bigger deposits country-wide. Jimmy was disappointed – she could hear it in his voice – but a week later she was looking at yet another set of estate agent's particulars. Chantry Cottage, according to Jimmy, nestled in a fold of the Otter Valley. It had half an acre of garden, mature fruit trees and space for a garage. The estate agent was the first to admit the property needed a little work. Hence the giveaway price of £179,000.

Needed a little work. Lizzie understood language, made a living from it, knew the multitude of blemishes a well turned phrase could hide. *Needed a little work?*

She lifted Grace from the playpen and wandered through to the kitchen to put the kettle on. She'd first seen the property back in high summer last year. It was a beautiful August day with real heat in the sun, and driving down the Otter Valley from the quaintly named Newton Poppleford even she had to admit that this little corner of England was hard to resist. The way the greenness of the valley cupped the water meadows beside the river. The silhouette of a lone buzzard circling high over a waving field of corn. The lumbering herd of cattle that brought them to a halt a couple of minutes later. Grace had kicked her little feet with excitement. She'd never seen cows before.

The cottage lay about a mile outside the village. According to the estate agent, it had once been a chapel, but on first glance Lizzie thought this highly unlikely. Grey slate roof. Red brick construction. Ugly metal-framed windows. The broken gutters were brimming with moss and there were water stains down the exterior walls. The estate agent's photo had been taken from the back of the house, the view artfully framed by shrubs and a fruit tree. On this evidence, and her husband's obvious enthusiasm, Lizzie had been expecting something that would grace a calendar. Instead, she found herself looking at a run-down property that might have belonged on one of the more distressed Pompey estates.

Inside, it got worse. The moment you stepped inside, the sunshine vanished. The place smelled of damp and something slightly acrid that she couldn't place, and there was a chill thickness to the gloom that made her physically shiver. You went in through the kitchen. The units, obviously home-made, were chocked up on wooden blocks. One door had lost a hinge and a couple of drawers were missing. Ancient loops of electrical wiring hung from the walls and the walls themselves were wet to the touch.

Next door, in the tiny living room, the floorboards moved underfoot beneath the scuzzy carpet. One of the windows didn't close properly and there were gouge marks in the metal frame where someone had tried to get in. The open fireplace looked promising but on closer examination Lizzie found neat piles of mouse droppings on the cracked stone hearth. When Jimmy – still wrestling with the window – finally managed to get the thing open, the draught down the chimney carried a thin drizzle of oily soot.

Under-impressed, Lizzie had tried to get her thoughts in order, tried to puncture the bubble her husband had made for himself, but he was already leading her through the chaos of the garden towards the tiny stream at the bottom, his daughter in his arms, fantasising about the life that awaited them in this new home of theirs. Walks on the common up the road. A cat or two for company. And evenings around the barbecue he'd install on the refurbed patio, toasting their good fortune in cheap red from the village store.

In the end, that evening, she'd said yes, not really understanding his passion for this horrible house but knowing how much it mattered to him. He'd already negotiated a £15K discount on the asking price, which brought the place within their budget, but the work she insisted had to be done right now would be down to Jimmy. No problem, he said. His dad was handy. He'd get him across from Hampshire the moment they exchanged contracts. Between them, they'd sort the electrics, install a new kitchen, do something about the bathroom, give everything a lick of paint and generally clean the place up. He might even be able to tap his dad up for a loan to cover new windows. By the time Lizzie and Grace were ready to move out of Pompey, the place would be unrecognisable.

None of it had happened. Jimmy's dad fell off his moped and ended up in hospital the day contracts were exchanged. Jimmy himself had made a start on a couple of the jobs, but the pace of life on Major Crimes was unforgiving, and by the time Lizzie had sold their little terraced house it was nearly November. Stepping into Chantry Cottage, she recognised the smell and the damp only too well, realising why Jimmy had been so keen to keep her away. His apology had taken the form of a huge bunch of lilies, beautifully wrapped, which he'd propped up in the cracked sink in the kitchen. It was a sweet gesture, and she'd done her best to smile, but she'd hated lilies ever since.

Now, with Grace still in her arms, her mobile began to ring. She went back into the living room and deposited Grace in her playpen before stepping outside to take the call. Mobile reception in the valley was patchy at best. Another nightmare.

'Lou? It's me. How are you?'

Lizzie closed her eyes, glad – at least – that the rain had finally stopped. The only person who called her Lou was Gill Reynolds. The last thing she needed just now was an hour on the phone with an ex-newsroom colleague eager to tell her what she was missing.

'I'm fine. Busy. You know ...' Lizzie tailed off. As ever, Gill had no interest in listening.

'Great news, Lou. The buggers have given me a couple of days off. You remember that promise I made to pop down?'

Lizzie tried to fend her off, tried somehow to wedge herself into the conversation, tried to explain that this wasn't the best time to make a flying visit, but in her heart she knew it was hopeless. Gill would be down on Tuesday, around teatime. Directions weren't a problem because she'd just blagged a new TomTom off the paper. They had loads to catch up on and room in her bag for something nice to kick the evening off. Stolly or something else? Lizzie's call.

Lizzie opted for Stolly. Under the circumstances, she thought, vodka and oblivion might be an attractive option. Gill was still giggling at a joke she'd just made about some guy she was shagging when she rang off.

Lizzie watched the rain returning down the valley. Over the winter life seemed to have physically penned her into this godforsaken place. She'd become someone else. She knew she had. Through the open door she could hear Grace beginning to wail. For a moment she didn't move. A fine drizzle had curtained the view. She lifted her face to the greyness of the sky and closed her eyes again, knowing she should have thought harder about trusting her husband's judgement. Underfoot, she could feel the paving stones shifting with her weight. That was another thing he'd never done. The bloody patio.

Jimmy Suttle found Nandy and Houghton in the apartment that served as the Regatta Court sales office. Houghton stood by the window, staring out, her phone pressed to her ear. Nandy occupied a seat at the desk, eyeballing an attractive middle-aged woman who evidently looked after the development. Her name was Ellie. She'd just put a call through to a local firm she used for work around the apartment block. They'd have someone down in ten.

Nandy glanced up, seeing Suttle at the door. He did the introductions.

'Ellie's whistled up a locksmith,' he said. 'We're talking number 37. Fifth floor. You OK with a flash intel search? Mark needs to meet this locksmith guy before he sorts the door for us.'

Suttle nodded. As ever, Nandy was moving at the speed of light. Thirty years in the Major Crimes game had taught him the investigative importance of the first twenty-four hours of any enquiry. Pile all your pieces on the board, give the shaker a good rattle and pray for a double six.

'So what have we got, sir?' Suttle asked. 'What do we know about this guy?'

Nandy threw the question to Ellie. Suttle sensed she was enjoying the attention.

'You mean Jake Kinsey?' she said.

'Yes.'

'He's been with us ...' she frowned '... a couple of years now? Nice enough man. Lived alone. Kept himself to himself.'

'What did he do for a living?'

'I'm not quite sure. I think he may have been an engineer at some point. He was never one for conversation but we once had a fascinating little chat about alternative energy sources.

Some of the residents were wanting to install solar panels and he told me why they'd never work on our kind of scale. Then we got on to wind turbines. He knew a lot about them too.'

Nandy glanced at his watch. He was sharp as a tack but famously impatient.

'Is there anything special about number 37?' Suttle again.

'Yes. It's the biggest apartment in the block. It's huge. I like to think of it as the jewel in our little crown.'

'How much?' Nandy this time.

'Space?'

'Money. How much did he pay for it?'

Ellie paused. The bluntness of the question seemed to trouble her. She looked briefly at Suttle, one eyebrow raised, then returned to Nandy.

'One point four five million.' She smiled. 'As I recall.'

'A rich man, then?'

'Not hard up, obviously.'

'You checked him out at the time? When you agreed terms?'

'Of course we did. Not personally. But yes.'

'Did he raise a mortgage? Some kind of loan?'

'I can't remember.'

'Can you check? I'd be grateful.'

Ellie nodded and reached for a pad to scribble herself a note. Nandy had got to his feet and was feeling for his watch again. A lean man in his early fifties, he wore the same grey suit regardless of the season and in situations like these reminded Suttle of Samuel Beckett. Recently Lizzie had taken to reading *Krapp's Last Tape* in bed, and Suttle had clocked the author photo on the back. Nandy had the same hollowed-out face, the same shock of iron-grey hair, the same unforgiving eyes. This was a guy who brought an unyielding sense of mission to every enquiry, every exchange. Suttle rather liked him. There was madness in those eyes. Stuff had to happen quick-time and Nandy was there to make sure it bloody well did.

Houghton was off the phone. Nandy wanted to know whether she'd secured a slot for the post-mortem.

'Tomorrow morning,' she said. 'Half nine.'

'Best they can do?'

'Yes.'

'Pathetic.'

'I agree.'

Nandy headed for the door. He was off up to the local nick to commandeer a couple of offices where his team could camp out. The enquiry already had a name: Operation *Constantine*.

Houghton and Suttle paused a moment, then followed him out of the door. Nandy was halfway across the car park, heading for his Volvo. Houghton and Suttle exchanged glances. Houghton was a big woman with rimless glasses and a blaze of frizzy silver-blonde hair. She had huge hands, a live-in partner called Jules and spent a great deal of her spare time riding horses on the eastern edges of Dartmoor.

'I'll field the locksmith and liaise with Mark,' she said. 'I'll bell you when we're ready for the flash intel.'

'And me?'

'Talk to Ellie.' She nodded back towards the office. 'She likes you.'

Suttle did her bidding. He'd worked for D/I Carole Houghton for more than six months now and had developed a healthy respect. The steadiness of her gaze told you a great deal. This was someone you'd be foolish to underestimate.

Ellie offered him coffee. The kitchenette was next door. It wouldn't take a second.

Suttle shook his head. He wanted to know more about Jake Kinsey. And about what he might have been up to last night.

'That's easy.' Ellie was smiling. 'He was in the pub.'

'Which pub?'

'The Beach. It's just across the way.'

'How do you know?'

'Because we were there too. My partner and I.'

Kinsey, it turned out, had been in the middle of some kind of celebration. Saturday night the pub had been packed. Kinsey had turned up around eight with a smallish bunch of guys in tow. Ellie hadn't recognised any of them but there had to be some kind of tie-up with the local rowing club because they were all in badged training gear, and Kinsey had made a big play of the silver cup he was carrying. Ellie was vague on the details but thought they must have been taking part in some competition or other and had won.

'He bought champagne over the bar,' she said, 'and that doesn't happen often in the Beach.'

Kinsey and his mates had stayed for maybe an hour. They'd all had a fair bit to drink.

'What happened then?'

'They left. Like you do.'

'Where did they go? Do you know?'

'Not really, but my guess would be home, Kinsey's place. There was talk of phoning for a takeaway. I suppose Kinsey lived the closest so that's where they went.' She looked at the phone. 'There's a Mr Smart who lives in one of the flats below. Nothing gets past him. Do you want me to give him a ring?'

Suttle shook his head, making a note of the name. Organising the house-to-house calls would fall to D/I Houghton. He'd pass the intel on.

'This rowing of Kinsey's. How does that work?'

'You get in a boat. It has oars.' Ellie was flirting now. Suttle knew it. He was thinking of the badge on Kinsey's singlet, the crossed blades.

'Yeah ... sure ... so is there a club?'

'Of course there's a club. I just told you. ERC. Exmouth Rowing Club. Pride of the town. There's someone else you ought to talk to. She's the club secretary. Her name's Doyle, Molly Doyle.'

'You've got a number?'

'I'm afraid not. Look on the website.' The smile again. 'Nice woman. Fun. Everyone calls her the Viking.'

Houghton kept her laptop in the back of her estate car. Still waiting for the locksmith, Suttle borrowed the keys, woke the dog up and made himself comfortable in the front passenger seat. It was raining again, harder than ever, and the CSI had draped Kinsey's body with a square of blue plastic sheeting before taking cover in the Scenes of Crime van.

Suttle fired up the laptop and googled 'Exmouth Rowing Club'. The website was impressive. The home page had an eye-catching banner featuring a crew of young rowers powering a boat towards some imagined line. This giant collective effort made for a great picture. Their mouths open, their backs straight, their faces contorted, these kids were exploring the thin red line between pain and glory, and Suttle lingered on the image for a moment, wondering how an experience like that might have triggered the celebration in the pub.

From the front of Houghton's car, he had line of sight to the scene of crime across the entry to the dock. The warmth of his body had misted the windows but he wiped a clear panel with his fingertip, gazing across at the hummock of blue sheeting, trying to imagine the sequence of events that had linked several bottles of champagne to this inglorious death four or five hours later. Was the guy a depressive? Had he got so pissed he'd done something stupid and gravity-defying and just toppled off his own balcony? Or was the story more complex than that?

A keystroke took Suttle onto the contacts page. Molly Doyle's number was listed under 'Club Secretary'. He made a note and was fumbling for his mobile when Houghton appeared beside the passenger door.

Suttle wound down the window. The locksmith had arrived.

It was still barely nine o'clock by the time Lizzie got Grace washed and changed. Despite the weather, she knew she had to get out of the house. Jimmy had taken the car so the only option was yet another walk.

She watched Grace tottering towards her, then scooped her up, hugged her tight and strapped her into the buggy. During nearly two years of motherhood Lizzie had often wondered about this new role of hers, but there were moments when they seemed bonded, and this was one of them. She wouldn't wish a rural winter on anyone, least of all her own daughter, but apart from the odd tantrum and a recent talent for ignoring the word no, Grace seemed to have weathered the discomforts. Lizzie put this down to her husband's evenness of temper. She'd never met anyone so tolerant, so easy-going, and it had always been a surprise – back in Pompey – to talk to his mates in the Job and learn how relentless and proactive he could be. So why hadn't some of this can-do spirit spilled into their own little lives? How come she still had to wrestle the back door open because the wood had swollen with the incessant rain?

She pushed the buggy along the lane, keeping to the right, splashing through the puddles in her wellington boots. One of the early lessons she'd learned about the countryside was how difficult it was to find anywhere decent to walk. From a car, or an armchair in front of yet another episode of *Countryfile*, it was all too easy to imagine a world of endless outings, mother and child spoiled to death by this magnificent landscape: crossing fields, pausing beside rivers or streams, watching the first of the spring lambs, glorying in the freedom and the fresh air.

The reality, alas, was very different. Everywhere you looked turned out to be someone else's property. Everything was badged: PRIVATE, NO ENTRY, BEWARE OF THE DOG, TRESPASSERS WILL BE PROSECUTED. And if you finally managed to make it through the long straggle of village and down to the river, chances were that the footpath was ankle-deep in mud from the last downpour.

The rain came often, blowing in from the west on the big Atlantic depressions. Early on, before Christmas even, Lizzie had learned to read the sky, recognising the telltale wisps of cloud that promised the arrival of yet another frontal system as the light died, and it wasn't long before her battle with the weather became intensely personal. She hated the wet. She loathed having to dry everything in front of a one-bar electric fire. She spent hours every day trying to hoover mud from that horrible carpet in the sitting room. And night after night she lay awake, trying to distinguish between a multitude of drips. Water came in through the roof, spreading patches of damp across every ceiling in the house, and leaked from a crack in the back boiler behind the fireplace.

Worst of all was the dribbling tap in the kitchen. Jimmy, as ever, had been oblivious to her pleas to do something about it, and after months of listening to the slow drumbeat of water in the stainless-steel sink she'd caught the mobile library, found a book on DIY and tried to change the washer herself. She'd attacked the thing with an adjustable spanner she'd managed to borrow from the man who ran the village store but had given up in tears when water threatened to fountain everywhere. That evening Jimmy had found her tight-lipped, curled up in bed, Grace asleep beside her. He'd fetched ibuprofen from the bathroom cabinet, filled a hot water bottle, suggested a slug or two of Scotch, convinced she must be heading for a cold, but only later – once he'd reappeared with a plate of pasta – did she tell him the truth. I'm going mad, she said. This place is driving me fucking insane.

In more positive moods, increasingly rare, she'd tell herself that this husband of hers was doing his best. There was no money for a plumber, or a roofer, or a crew of fitters to turn up with a vanload of double glazing. There was also, it seemed, precious little time for Jimmy to have a go himself, or organise his dad to make good on the promised help that had never happened. And so, instead, they'd retreated to separate corners of their new lives, increasingly withdrawn, pretending that everything was OK, or nearly OK, or OK enough for the spring to finally arrive and take them somewhere sunnier. But even by mid-April that hadn't happened. On the contrary, the weather seemed fouler than ever, taunting her optimism, snuffing out the last flickers of hope that kept her going. No wonder they call frontal systems depressions, she thought. Even *Krapp's Last Tape* beat life in Chantry Cottage.

She trudged on, wondering whether to put a call in to Jimmy, asking about the wreckage of his day off, about how he was getting on, reaching out for a little company, a little comfort, but then she paused in the road, fumbling for a Kleenex to blow Grace's nose, knowing there was no point. For reasons she didn't begin to understand, she'd ended up in a prison cell of her own making. And whatever happened next, she knew with growing certainty, was absolutely down to her.

The locksmith turned out to have a duplicate set of keys for Kinsey's apartment. He pushed the door open and then stepped back. Mark was wearing a one-piece Scenes of Crime suit. The locksmith and Suttle had left their shoes at the foot of the stairs. Later, the CSI would do the full forensic number on the landing and the flat itself. If Nandy wanted the lift boshed too, no problem. But for now it was down to Suttle to do a quick trawl through the apartment, scouting for obvious indications – bloodstains, signs of some kind of struggle – that would turn an unexplained death into a likely murder.

Suttle stepped into the apartment, astonished and slightly awed by its sheer size. He'd no idea how much living space a million and a half quid could buy, but nothing had prepared him for this. The hall alone seemed to stretch for ever, and at the far end lay a huge living area. Lounge? Playground? Romper room? Viewing platform? The biggest kitchen-diner in the world? Suttle looked around. The flat occupied the entire width of the building. Everywhere else in the block, according to Ellie, this space would have accommodated two apartments, but Kinsey's money had bought him a view like none other.

Glass-walled on three sides, even in shit weather like this the flat's trophy room offered a panoramic view on the very edge of the estuary.

Suttle walked to the nearest of the huge windows. It was half tide, and the water was sluicing out through the harbour narrows. Beyond the narrows lay a long curl of sand fringed with grass. To the right, trawlers and yachts tugged at their moorings, and through the curtains of rain, on the other side of the river, Suttle could just make out the grey swell of the Haldon Hills, shrouded in mist. To the left lay the long curve of Exmouth seafront, the beach already exposed by the falling tide, while the whaleback of an offshore sandbank had appeared, a long ochre smudge in the murk.

'Are we doing this or what?'

Mark, the CSI, was Exmouth born and bred. He'd probably lived with this view most of his life but Suttle found it difficult to tear himself away. *If I had that kind of money*, he thought, *I might just live here myself.*

The CSI had disappeared again. Suttle could hear him padding around in one of the other rooms. He reappeared a minute or so later, shaking his head.

'Fuck all. Someone's had a party but we can't nick them for that.'

Suttle nodded. The hugeness of the lounge was under-furnished. A shallow crescent of sofa had been placed to suck in the best of the view and there was a free-standing plasma – not large – for after-dark entertainment. To the left, Kinsey had positioned a desk and executive chair beside another of the windows. Within reach of the chair was a big brass telescope on a wooden tripod with a scatter of charts on the floor beneath. One of the charts covered the south Devon coast, and Suttle paused a moment, gazing down at it, wondering precisely where this belonged in the story of Kinsey's final days. Beside the chart was a set of tide tables for Dartmouth, open at the month of April. Saturday the 9th had been ringed in pencil. High tide at 09.03. Was this where Kinsey had been yesterday? Some kind of race? Might this have accounted for the champagne in the pub?

Suttle looked round. A room this big and this bare could swallow a multitude of sins, but the evidence for a serious post-pub party was remarkably modest. An area at the back of the room housed a kitchen so spotless it might never have left the showroom. Suttle noted a couple more bottles of champagne, both empty. There were six glasses neatly lined up on the work surface beside the double sink, all washed, and a collection of crushed tinnies – mainly Guinness – in the swingbin. The bin also yielded the remains of a sizeable takeaway.

Mark limped across and took a sniff. 'Chicken jalfrezi.'

Suttle accompanied the CSI to the master bedroom. It was a decent size, nothing huge, with a view of the river beyond the rain-pebbled glass. The en suite bathroom had the usual goodies – recessed lighting, slate-tiled floors, big jacuzzi – but there was nothing to suggest violence.

In the bedroom the CSI had found a silver cup on the floor beneath the window. Suttle stooped to inspect it, remembering the chart beside the telescope. They were celebrating in the pub last night, he told himself. This has to be why.

The CSI was looking at the bed. The duvet had been thrown back, along with the top sheet, and the bed appeared to have been slept in. Given that this was the master bedroom, it was reasonable to suppose that the bed's occupant had been Kinsey.

So what had got him up and taken him to his death? Suttle returned to the lounge. There were twin balconies on the right and the left of the view, flanking the front of the apartment. Access to both lay through big sliding glass doors. Kinsey's body had been found by a local walking his dog. It was lying on the harbour side of the apartment block, directly under the left-hand balcony.

The CSI was inspecting the latch on the big sliding door.

'Here ...' He beckoned Suttle closer.

The latch was unsecured. Under his gloved hand the door moved sweetly open. Suttle stepped out. The rain was lighter now, no more than a thin drizzle, and he went across to the rail, peering over. The blue shape of Kinsey's shrouded body lay directly below, and Suttle stared at it for a long moment, trying to imagine how a fall like that could have happened. Kinsey was on the small side. Mounting the rail and throwing yourself off would have required a definite decision, not something that could have happened by accident.

Suttle looked up again, trying to work out whether anyone might have witnessed what had happened. The balcony overlooked the entrance to the dock. According to the CSI, this was where fishing boats and water taxis and the ferry that crossed the river tied up. There was a line of working units on the dockside, rented by fishermen, with a terrace of 1960s-looking flats beyond. To the left, looking out over the basin of the marina, another row of properties had line of sight on Kinsey's balcony. Suttle made a mental note, fixing the view in his head. He estimated at least thirty front doors. More priority calls for the house-to-house teams.

He took a last look round. Kinsey's watch had stopped at 03.04. At that time of the morning, of course, it would have been dark. He needed to check the harbourside illumination and whether the throw of light would reach up as far as Apartment 37. He sensed that a lot of these properties would belong to retired couples, wealthy enough to buy a share of a view like this. People that age often had trouble sleeping. Someone might have seen something, a flicker of movement, something unexplained. Worth a try.

He stepped back inside, wiping the rain from his face. They already knew that the front door had been closed on the latch but not bolted inside. Now he wanted to know about the interior lights.

The CSI shook his head. 'Everything off.'

'Including the bedroom?'

23

'Yes.'

'Right.' Suttle nodded. 'So the guy gets up in the dark, comes through here, opens the exterior sliding door, finds himself on the balcony. Yeah? Is that what the scene tells us?'

'Spot on.'

'Then what?'

'Fuck knows.'

Suttle took a look at the other rooms. There were two other bedrooms, both en suite, and one of them appeared to have been used as an office: desk, filing cabinet, whiteboard on the wall. There was nothing on the whiteboard, and apart from a PC and a phone there was nothing on the desk either. This bareness extended to the rest of the apartment, and as Suttle did another walk-through he got an overwhelming sense of emptiness, of a life somehow on hold. When it came to furnishings and decor, this was a guy who'd stripped his surroundings down to the bare essentials. The stuff was functional, well made, served a purpose, but there were no pictures to brighten the bareness of the walls, no framed faces of friends or family, no hats doffed to any kind of private life. Even the fridge yielded nothing but a one-litre carton of milk, half a pound of butter, a Tesco fillet steak and a stalk or two of broccoli.

Beside Kinsey's desk, the CSI was checking the answering machine. Suttle threw him a look but he shook his head.

'Nothing,' he said.

D/I Carole Houghton drew the *Constantine* team together at 10.07. Ellie had volunteered her office, plus a supply of coffees, and Houghton sat on the desk, letting her anorak drip onto the carpet.

So far she'd managed to rally eight D/Cs. Nandy was looking for a couple more but they lived out of the area and wouldn't arrive for at least an hour. In the meantime, she said, D/S Suttle had conducted a flash intel search of the apartment and drawn up a priority list of addresses for house-to-house. The duty Inspector at the local nick was preparing three rooms for *Constantine* and all of them would be operational by lunchtime. Depending on initial inquiries, the investigation might or might not transfer to the Major Incident Room at Middlemoor. At the moment, she stressed, the jury was out on Kinsey's death. Nothing in the flat suggested anything but a man who had fallen off his own balcony. If the truth proved otherwise, it was up to *Constantine* to find out.

There were very few questions. Houghton wanted the D/Cs working in pairs. She divided the house-to-house calls between them and sent the most experienced team to the Beach pub. She wanted a full account of Kinsey's visit last night, plus names and addresses of fellow drinkers for follow-up.

By the time Ellie returned, the detectives had gone. Houghton eyed the tray of coffees she was carrying and offered her apologies. Ellie put the coffees on her desk.

'That nice young man I was talking to ...?'

'He's gone to meet the club secretary.'

'Ah ...' Ellie failed to mask her disappointment. 'The Viking.'

Molly Doyle opened the door on Suttle's second knock. She was wearing a scarlet dressing gown, loosely belted at the waist, and her hair was wet from the shower. The blush of colour on her face, plus the muddy Nikes on the square of newsprint inside the porch, suggested recent exercise. He'd phoned ahead but she'd failed to pick up.

'I've been out on the seafront.' She was still looking at Suttle's warrant card. 'My Sunday treat.'

After a moment's hesitation, she invited him in. It was a neat house, warm colours, comfortable, lived-in. A line of family photos on the mantelpiece suggested a sizeable brood of kids and already, from somewhere upstairs, Suttle could hear a stir of movement.

'So what's going on? What's this all about?'

Suttle explained about Kinsey. The news that he was dead

froze the smile on her face. She looked visibly shocked.

'Dead?'

'I'm afraid so.'

'But how can that happen?'

'I've no idea. That's what we have to find out.'

Suttle wanted to know about yesterday's race. Kinsey, it seemed, had won himself a cup.

'He did. He texted me. The Dart Totnes Head. First proper race of the season. His guys did well. Better than well.' She frowned, knotting her hands in her lap. 'Dead?' She stared at Suttle, wanting him to change the story, to apologise, to explain that it was all some kind of joke.

Suttle pressed for more details. 'You've got names? This crew of his?'

'Of course. Our events secretary is having a baby. I did the race entry form myself.'

'You've got contact details?'

'For the crew, you mean?'

'Yes.'

'Absolutely. That's my job.' She hesitated. 'You want me to get them?'

Suttle shook his head. He'd collect the names and addresses before he left but right now he was more interested in Kinsey. What kind of man was he?

'He was ...' she frowned, unhappy with the past tense '... different.'

'How?'

'Hard to say.' The frown deepened. She seemed affronted as well as upset. Who was this man to barge into her house, into her precious Sunday morning, and throw everything into chaos?

'The man's dead, Mrs Doyle. And at this point in time we don't know why.'

'Christ, what else are you telling me?'

'I'm telling you nothing. And that's because we know

26

nothing. Except that he probably fell from his own balcony in the middle of the night and ended up dead. There has to be a reason for that. Which is why I'm here.'

'But you're suggesting ...?'

'I'm suggesting nothing. You used the word "different" just now. What does that mean?'

'It means that he wasn't – you know – one of the usual crowd. We're a club. Quite a successful club as it happens. How much do you know about rowing?'

'Nothing,' Suttle said again. 'Tell me.'

'Well ...' She gathered her dressing gown more tightly around her. 'It's a sport, obviously. It's pretty physical, and it can be pretty challenging too, in our kind of water. People love that. It becomes a bond, a glue if you like. It sticks us together. When you're out there you have to rely on each other and that can build something pretty special. Not everyone races. A lot of our guys are social rowers. But I guess it boils down to the same thing. The sea's the sea. You don't mess with it.'

'And Kinsey?'

'He was never a social rower.'

'Meaning?'

'Kinsey was a competitor. In everything. Winning mattered.'

'And that's unusual?'

'To his degree, yes. This is me speaking, my opinion, but – hey – you did ask ...'

She offered him a bleak smile. She believed him now. Kinsey was dead and gone. No more cups. No more glory.

Suttle let the silence stretch and stretch. Footsteps hurrying overhead and then the splash of water in a shower.

'Did you like him?'

'*Like* him?'

'Yes.'

'Why do you ask?'

'Because these things can be important. I'm getting a picture here. People like Kinsey can be uncomfortable to have around.'

'That's true.'

'So was he liked? Was he popular?'

She looked at him for a long moment, then shook her head. It had been obvious from the start, she said, that Kinsey was rich. Not just that, but he was arrogant too. Wealth, like winning, mattered.

'He came to us from nowhere. Just walked into the clubhouse on a Sunday and signed himself up.'

'Had he rowed before?'

'Never. He said he'd watched us out of his window when we rowed up the river. That was important.'

'Seeing you row?'

'Telling us where he lived. That huge penthouse flat. It wasn't just pride. It was something else.'

'Like what?'

'He needed us to know the kind of guy he was. Rich. Successful. All that nonsense. Ours is a funny little club. We get all sorts. But money never comes into it. In a boat on the sea you are who you are. Kinsey never seemed to quite get that.'

Coaches at the club, she said, had taught Kinsey the basic drills. After a couple of outings, like every other novice, he'd sculled with an experienced crew, one oar in either hand, and hadn't let himself down.

'Was he good?'

'Not really. Some people are naturals. You can see it. Their body posture is right. They pick up the rhythm, the stroke rate, really quickly. They know know how to turn all that energy into real power. It's a bit like dancing. Either you have it or you don't.'

'And Kinsey didn't?'

'No. Don't get me wrong. He was OK, he was competent. But he got into bad habits from the start and never really listened to people who wanted to put him right.' The smile again, hesitant, almost apologetic. 'Am I making sense?'

Suttle nodded. He could hear a radio now from upstairs.

Heart FM. The last thing he wanted was one or other of the kids to stumble in through the door and bring this interview, this conversation, to an end.

'Tell me about the racing,' he said. 'How many other cups did he win?'

'None. Yesterday was their first outing. That was why he was so chuffed.'

About a year ago, she said, Kinsey had bought the club a brand new quad.

'Quad?'

'Four rowers and a cox. This was a sea boat. They don't come cheap.'

'How much?'

'Eighteen thousand, including the bits and pieces that go with it.'

The extras, she said, included oars, safety equipment plus a couple of trailers for the road and for the beach. The club had never had a windfall like that but Kinsey soured the gift with a major precondition. He and his crew always had first claim on the boat, regardless of who else might be in the queue.

'And that was unusual?'

'Absolutely. And it didn't stop there.'

Kinsey's crew, she said, was hand-picked. These weren't a bunch of mates he happened to get on with, like-minded souls with a taste for exercise and a laugh or two, but serious athletes he cherry-picked from the club's membership.

'It was like he was playing God. It put a lot of backs up. Here was a guy from nowhere, a virtual stranger, buying himself into the top boat. And no one could lift a finger because he was happy to pay for it.'

One of the crew, she said, wasn't even a club member. His name was Andy Poole. Kinsey had come across him on some business deal or other. It turned out Andy had been in the Cambridge blue boat two years running and had nearly made the national squad before a move west brought him to Exeter.

'Don't get me wrong. Andy's a nice guy. He's a bloody good rower too. We've been lucky to have him. Even on Kinsey's terms.'

Kinsey, she said, had enrolled Andy Poole in the club, paid his annual membership and designed a training programme around the guy's work schedule. The other guys in the crew had undoubtedly learned a huge amount from Andy's tuition, one reason why the crew had swept to line honours in yesterday's race, but the whole point was that access to this kind of coaching was strictly limited. Only Kinsey and his crew ever laid eyes on Andy Poole. To the rest of the club, he was Mr Invisible, the big man with the Mercedes who popped down from Exeter to do Kinsey's bidding. There were even rumours that Kinsey had paid him start money to make sure he turned up for yesterday's race. Not that Andy Poole was short of a bob or two.

'And that upset people?'

'Big time, if you let it get to you.'

'You're telling me he had enemies?'

'I'm telling you he was unpopular. And, to be frank, a bit of a joke.'

'Because he was so naff?'

'Because he was so crap in a boat. Some people called him The Passenger.'

'And he knew that?'

'I've no idea. But even if he did it wouldn't have made any difference. To be honest, he was the most thick-skinned person I've ever met. This is the kind of guy who takes what he wants and turns his back on the rest. He thought money could buy him anything.' The smile again, even bleaker. 'And – hey – it's turned out he was wrong.'

Footsteps clattered down the stairs. The door burst open to reveal a girl in her mid-teens. She was wearing a blue tracksuit and pink runners. Ignoring Suttle, she tapped her watch.

'Shit, Mum, I'd no idea. I'm supposed to be down there for ten. Tansy'll go mental.'

'They won't be launching today. It's a south-easterly, 4.3.'

'I'm talking Ergo, mum. You know what she's after for the 5K? After a night like last night? Twenty dead. I'm gonna be toast. See you.'

As suddenly as she'd appeared, she'd gone. Suttle heard the front door open and then slam shut again. Ergo? 4.3? Twenty dead? This had to be rowing talk. Had to.

Molly Doyle was on her feet. Like her daughter, she was tall and blonde. Hence, Suttle assumed, her nickname. Under the circumstances, the Viking thought coffee was a good idea. In the meantime, Suttle could help himself to the details on Kinsey's crew from the files she'd got upstairs.

'They went back to his place,' she said. 'After the pub last night.'

'All of them?'

'Yes.'

'How do you know?'

'He texted me an invite. Silly man.'

It had finally stopped raining by the time Lizzie got to the village church. It lay on the road that led down to the river, a sturdy plain-looking structure with a bulky tower that seemed out of proportion with the rest of the building. She opened the gate and pushed the buggy up the path towards the half-open door. Lizzie had never been a practising Christian and had avoided worship for most of her adult life, but this morning, for whatever reason, she felt the need to quieten herself, to find somewhere she might find a bit of privacy and a little peace.

Until she stepped into the gloom of the nave, it didn't occur to her that the church might be in use. *Shit*, she reminded herself. Sunday.

Heads turned, all of them old. There weren't many people, twenty tops. The nearest face looked familiar. She lived down the road, Mrs Peacock. They'd talked a couple of times in the village shop. She'd become the village's self-appointed chronicler and archivist, contributing badly punctuated articles to the parish magazine on various episodes in Colaton Raleigh's long history. It was May Peacock who'd confirmed the estate agent's belief that Chantry Cottage had once been a Nonconformist chapel, and – in the depths of winter – it was Mrs Peacock who'd battled through the snow and posted some additional information through Lizzie's letter box. There was some kind of tomb, she'd written, at the bottom of the cottage's garden. It had been constructed hundreds of years ago and was rumoured to contain the bodies of two children.

At the time Lizzie had dismissed the story as a figment of Mrs Peacock's imagination. This kind of legend was the currency of village life and Mrs P was obviously a big spender. Lately, though, as the damp walls of Chantry Cottage pressed closer and closer, Lizzie had begun to think more about the story. Anything to revive the numbness that used to be my brain, she'd thought. Anything to stop me becoming a complete vegetable.

Now, aware of Lizzie's hesitation, Mrs Peacock was beckoning her into the church. She had a long, slightly horsey face and wisps of white hair curling from her chin. Come in, she seemed to be saying. We won't bite.

Lizzie found a perch on the end of an empty pew. Grace, mercifully, seemed to have gone to sleep. At the altar a line of elderly worshippers waited to take communion. They were all women and most of them used walking sticks. Watching them as they shuffled painfully towards the altar rail, Lizzie found herself wondering what had happened to their menfolk. Were their husbands at home, sorting out the midday roast, or had the retirement years in Colaton Raleigh finally throttled the life out of them?

She had no way of knowing, of course, and as Mrs Peacock threw her another smile and struggled to her feet to join the communicants, Lizzie remembered the morning she'd taken up the carpet in the sitting room. Back then, in December, she'd still had the energy and the self-belief to pit herself against the challenges of Jimmy's little find. Chantry Cottage, she'd told herself, was simply bricks and mortar. She could make a difference; she could roll her sleeves up and have a proper sort-out.

The previous occupant, according to Jimmy, had been a lifelong hippy who'd read a couple of books about some Indian guru and become a yoga teacher. Living on virtually nothing, she'd tried to bypass the electricity meter with the aid of instructions from an anarchist site on the Internet but she'd screwed up badly and nearly burned the place down. This seemed to explain both the lingering sourness Lizzie caught from time to time, plus the sooty patches on the living room ceiling, but the latter, according to Jimmy, had come from the candles the woman had burned every night. This was someone who'd evidently lived by candlelight for most of her life and saw no reason to change. Quaint, he'd said. And very Devon.

It was at this point that Lizzie had decided to turn the year on its head and go for an early spring clean. The following morning, once Jimmy had gone to work, she moved Grace's playpen into the kitchen, shooed Dexter into the garden, cleared the tiny sitting room of furniture and began to roll up the carpet. For once the sun was shining. She'd strung a rope between two fruit trees and intended to give the carpet the beating of its life. With luck, she'd thought, the rest of the house would listen and take note. Pompey girl on the loose. Mend your ways.

In the event, though, the house – yet again – had won. The carpet had seen better days. Years of abuse had larded it with every conceivable spillage – grease, candle wax, coffee, wine – and when she took her gloves off to get a firmer grip it was sticky to the touch. That was bad enough, but as she began to roll the carpet back, she found herself looking at layer after layer of newsprint. These were papers from the early 60s. Headlines about the death of JFK. Feature articles asking why the Brits had to suffer yet another sterling crisis. She started to go through the papers story by story. This was a treasure trove of living history, she told herself, something to spark conversation when Jimmy came home. But then her interest flagged, and she stopped turning the pages, only too aware that Chantry Cottage had the feeling of a morgue, of time arrested under her very feet, a malevolent force dragging her unaccountably backwards, into a darkness that first alarmed and then depressed her.

That night, with the carpet in all its squalor back down on the sitting room floor, she'd tried to voice a little of this to her husband. She and Grace were still newcomers to the countryside. They'd been living here for barely a month. But already she could feel a sense of near-despair beginning to seep into her life. In some dimly remembered past she'd been the one pitching stories, conducting interviews, writing copy, dreaming up headlines, earning herself the beginnings of a serious reputation. Now, as the days implacably shortened and yet more rain blew in from the west, she felt totally helpless, a creature without either direction or worth.

Jimmy, as ever, had tried to understand. The winter was bound to be tough. They'd both known that. But the seasons would roll round, and spring would come, and then they'd all have a chance to take stock. At work, he said, they still think I'm great. He'd made sure that word of his last job in Portsmouth had reached the ears of his new colleagues, and there were still moments in the MCIT offices when he could feel the warmth of all that reflected glory. He'd been the key to the undercover operation that had potted Pompey's biggest criminal. If there'd been a medal struck for the death of drug baron Bazza Mackenzie, it would have had Suttle's name on it.

Lizzie loved her husband in moods like these. He'd always been a blaze of auburn curls in her life. With his freckles and his easy grin, he had an untiring optimism, an almost visible sunniness that was the very bedrock of their relationship. She'd always fancied him, and there were times even now when she still did, but she knew that her depression had begun to affect him as well, yet another reason to hate her new self. Evenings at home were beginning to be difficult. There was too much stuff that was better avoided – the state of the house, Lizzie's sheer isolation – and once Grace was tucked up, they both settled for silence or the telly rather than risk another row. But deep down, where it had always mattered, she suspected that Jimmy was right. Stuff comes and goes. You have to walk tall on life's road. But how on earth was she going to get back to the person she'd once been?

Thinking suddenly of Gill Reynolds, she watched the communicants returning to their pews. The last to take her seat was May Peacock. Lizzie gave her a little wave, hearing Grace beginning to stir, knowing that she had to get out of the church before the service came to an end. Her dread of conversation extended to pretty much anyone. She'd lost the knack of talking to people. She was no longer able to get the right words in the right order. Better therefore to keep the world at arm's length and pray that something, anything, turned up to make things better.

Suttle phoned D/I Houghton from his car. He had names and contact details for Kinsey's crew and knew that these would be priority interviews for the *Constantine* squad. When Houghton at last picked up, she told him to come to Exmouth nick for half eleven. Mr Nandy had sorted a couple of offices before departing for another enquiry in Torbay and he wouldn't return until mid-afternoon. By half eleven, she was expecting feedback from the house-to-house calls. After which she and Suttle could plot a sensible path forward.

Suttle checked his watch. Nearly eleven. Exmouth nick was round the corner, a two-minute drive. With time in hand, he fancied a little detour.

Molly Doyle had given him directions to the seafront

compound which served as the base for Exmouth Rowing Club. Suttle found it tucked up a wide alley behind a building that belonged to the RNLI. A wooden fence enclosed a patch of scrubland beneath the looming shadow of a half-completed leisure complex. A raised Portakabin served as a clubhouse and one of the sagging doors was an inch or two open. Suttle picked his way between a litter of abandoned rubber bootees, pausing on the steps to check out the ERC fleet.

In the compound he counted five big sea boats, all of them red and white, readied on launching trolleys beneath the spreading branches of a huge tree. Someone had attached a plastic owl to the roof of the Portakabin. Suttle was looking at the boats again. If the owl was a bid to keep the gulls off, it had failed completely. There was bird shit everywhere.

Suttle pushed at the door of the clubhouse and stepped inside. Neon tubes threw a cold hard light over the sparseness of the interior. Lighter boat shells hung from racks on the walls and a pile of ancient yellow life jackets occupied a corner at the back. There was an overpowering smell of sweat and effort, and among the handful of faces on the rowing machines he recognised the Viking's daughter. Even now he didn't know her name but he responded to her nod of recognition, wondering whether news of Kinsey's death had yet to reach this far.

A coach was squatting beside the nearest rowing machine, monitoring the performance readout on the tiny heads-up screen. The last thing Suttle wanted was a conversation, but the guy got to his feet and asked whether he could help.

Suttle shook his head. It was way too early to extend the investigation this far and in any case the circumstances were all wrong. He needed four walls, a desk, a couple of chairs and a door to ensure a little privacy. Not this place.

'You're interested?'

'I'm sorry?'

'In rowing. Only we do taster sessions for novices. Think of it as three free goes. If you like it, you become a member. If you don't ...' He shrugged. 'No harm done.'

Suttle looked around. It seemed like the place was falling apart: the sagging doors, the piles of abandoned kit, the bird shit. Yet at the same time there was no arguing with the buzz. These kids were really going for it.

'So anyone can turn up?'

'No problem.'

'When?'

'Sundays are best. As long as the weather's not too evil, you'll find us on the beach.'

The coach turned back to the rowing machine and checked the readout again. Suttle couldn't resist a look: 4,567 metres. In 19.03. The rower, a young lad of maybe seventeen, was cranking up for a final push. Sweat darkened his T-shirt. His face was contorted with effort, and every time he pushed back against the footstretchers the effort squeezed a grunt from his gasping lungs.

Suttle caught his eye. 'This is *good* for you?' he murmured.

The boy had the grace to muster a smile.

'Fuck off,' he mouthed back.

Exmouth police station occupied the middle of an otherwise picturesque square on rising ground beyond the main shopping centre. An undistinguished 1960s building, it had a slightly alien presence. An apron of parking contained a handful of cars and the clock on the church opposite had stopped at twenty to four. Suttle, already struck by the slightly retro feel of the seafront, regarded this as somehow symbolic. Exmouth, he thought. The town that time forgot.

Houghton was putting the finishing touches to the smaller of the two offices commandeered for *Constantine*. Three desks: one for Nandy, one for Houghton, the third for Suttle. A poster featuring a Thai beach occupied one wall. A second poster warned uniformed coppers that FIRST IMPRESSIONS COUNT.

'This used to be the sergeants' locker room,' Houghton grunted. 'You should feel at home, Jimmy.'

Suttle tallied the names of Kinsey's crew he'd picked up from Molly Doyle. Eamonn Lenahan, he said, served as cox. He lived up the river in Lympstone. Andy Poole, who turned out to work for a hedge fund partnership, had a flash apartment in Exeter. Tom Pendrick, who rowed in the seat behind Poole, was listed with an Exmouth address. While a guy called Milo Symons evidently dossed with his girlfriend in a caravan on farmland near Budleigh Salterton. She'd been at the party too. Her name was Natasha Donovan.

Houghton had scribbled down the names. Kinsey's body, she said, had been removed after the Scenes of Crime photographer had done his work. A Crime Scene Manager had joined the CSI and they'd made a start on boshing Kinsey's apartment. Documents from the desk that served as his office and from a filing cabinet in one of the spare bedrooms were waiting for Suttle's attention, and Kinsey's computer had been bagged for full analysis.

'The CSI also pinged me this.' She beckoned Suttle closer. 'He found it on the man's Blackberry.'

Suttle read the text on Houghton's iPhone. It read, 'V. We stuffed them. The whole lot. Decent time too. The Krug's on ice. Usual place. J. xx'.

Houghton wanted to know who V might be.

'The Viking. Her real name's Doyle. Molly Doyle. She's the one who gave me the crew names.'

'"Usual place"?'

'Yeah. Interesting.'

'You sound surprised.'

'I am, boss. The woman's no fan of Kinsey.'

'Are we sure?'

'Of course not.'

'But?'

Suttle shrugged. He honestly didn't know. Molly Doyle, in

his judgement, had her finger on the pulse of the club and her description of Kinsey had sounded all too plausible.

'The guy muscled his way in,' he said. 'No one liked him. He thought money could buy him anything.'

'Including her?'

'I doubt it.' Suttle made a mental note to check the lead out.

Houghton nodded, then updated Suttle on the house-to-house calls. Gerald Smart, who occupied the apartment below Kinsey, confirmed that his neighbour had entertained guests last night. He'd heard laughter and music and a bit of stamping around but not much else. Getting on for midnight, everything had gone quiet and after that he and his wife had retired to bed.

'Nothing afterwards?'

'No.'

'What about the other properties? Line of sight?'

'Zilch. The guys aren't through yet but we seem to be talking a particular demographic. These are retired people. They're older rather than younger. I get the feeling they party early, get pissed and go to bed.'

'How many of them knew Kinsey?'

'Very few. There's a residents' association which is pretty active but it seems he could never be arsed. Most of these good folk knew him by name because of the property he'd bought but that's pretty much as far as it went. You're going to ask me whether he was popular but I don't think it's that simple. When it came to socialising and all that, he just wasn't interested. Apparently he didn't even have a Facebook account.'

Suttle nodded. This is exactly what Molly Doyle had told him. *This is the kind of guy who takes what he wants and turns his back on the rest.*

'Mr Loner,' Suttle muttered.

'Exactly.'

'What about the pub?'

'The landlord was pretty helpful. Turned out to be an

ex-marine. His line on Kinsey was pretty much everyone else's. The guy very rarely made an appearance and when he did stuck to fizzy water. Last night seems to have been a one-off. Three bottles of Moët? The landlord couldn't believe it.'

'And the crack? The chat? Anything there?'

'Not so far. The landlord was too busy to listen in but he's given us the names of some regulars who were in last night in case they picked up a clue or two. I've scheduled the follow-ups for this afternoon.' Her eye strayed to the list she'd made of Kinsey's crew. 'These guys need sorting. Where do you want to start?'

Eamonn Lenahan lived in a rented cottage in Lympstone, a waterside village a couple of miles upstream from Exmouth. Suttle's first call had been Tom Pendrick, but his attempts to raise an answer on the phone or in person had come to nothing. Before leaving Exmouth nick, he'd run all six names – including Kinsey – through the Police National Computer but drawn a blank. No previous convictions. No one ever charged or even arrested. Model citizens, all of them.

Lenahan's cottage lay in a tiny cobbled street with a glimpse of the river at the far end. Clouds of gulls swooped over the rooftops and Suttle could hear the soft lap of water on the pebbles that fringed the tiny harbour. He knocked again, wondering if Kinsey's cox was still sleeping off last night's piss-up, and then stepped back from the door and offered his face to a sudden burst of sunshine. The weather had brightened from the west, and standing in the quiet of this little village, listening to the gulls, Suttle realised that he was beginning to enjoy *Constantine*.

Most of the jobs that came to Major Crime were, to be frank, tacky. In Portsmouth he'd lost touch of the number of pissed retards who'd ended up battering a friend or a stranger to death. There was no mystery, no challenge, to enquiries like these, and even the drug scene – a dependable source of more interesting work – was riddled with lowlife. Heading west, he'd somehow assumed that he'd be stepping into a different world, classier, more sophisticated, but crime hot spots like Torbay and Plymouth were as squalid and mindlessly violent as anywhere in Pompey. To date, he'd worked on two murders and an alleged stranger rape. In all three cases the real culprit had been cheap vodka and the girl reporting the rape had turned out to have been as pissed as the rest of them. These were lives in free fall, tiny domestic tragedies played out against a landscape of crappy bedsits, cheap drugs and increasingly elaborate benefit scams.

Constantine, on the other hand, already looked a great deal more promising. An alleged millionaire with no apparent reason to end his days plus five partygoing crew mates who may or may not have wished him well. Molly Doyle had painted a picture of each of these people. These very definitely weren't lowlife. Eamonn Lenahan was a medic. Andy Poole worked in hedge funds. Pendrick was an electrician. These people had jobs, education, prospects. Booze had undoubtedly played a part last night, but it was a relief not to be looking at SOC shots of fat battered women lying dead on yet another stretch of fag-cratered orange nylon-pile carpet.

Suttle was about to knock for the last time when the cottage door opened. A small figure in a pair of black boxers was rubbing the sleep from his eyes. He'd found a pair of pink slippers from somewhere and hadn't shaved for a while.

'Mr Lenahan?'

'The same. Who the fuck are you?' Irish accent. Inquisitive smile.

Suttle offered his warrant card. He'd appreciate a word or two.

'No problem, my friend. Always a pleasure.' He stooped to retrieve a pint of milk and stood aside to let Suttle in. The house smelled of burned toast. Lenahan blamed his fellow tenant.

'Sweet wee girl. Off out early, she and her lovely friend.

How can I help you?'

The sitting room was tiny and dark – a single tatty armchair, a battered sofa and a trestle table in the corner loaded with books and a copy of yesterday's *Guardian*.

Suttle took a seat. There was a row of framed photos on the opposite wall, randomly hung. Somewhere hot. A village setting. Some kind of open-air market in the background. A crowd of black faces mugging for the camera, many of them kids.

'Sudan.' Lenahan had found a T-shirt from somewhere and a pair of trackie bottoms. 'Know it at all?'

'No.'

'Shame. We all need a bit of Sudan. Keeps you fucking sane.' He perched on the sofa, his legs tucked beneath him. 'So what have you got for me?'

Suttle explained about Kinsey. The news that he'd been found dead sparked no reaction whatsoever. Lenahan just looked at him.

'You're not surprised?' Suttle asked.

'Nothing surprises me.'

'You're not ...' Suttle frowned, hunting for the right phrase '... upset?'

'Never. You go, you're gone. That's pretty fucking final. Dying would have upset yer man, for sure. Kinsey was one for the options, you know what I mean? That's how he operated. Always. Options. Possibilities. That sweet little opportunity no other fucker ever spotted. Dying's a terrible option. And you're talking to an expert.'

Suttle blinked. He'd been right. This definitely wasn't Torbay. Lenahan hadn't finished.

'Under that apartment of his, you say?'

'Yeah.'

'So you're going to want to know about yesterday, about last night. Am I getting warm?'

'You are.'

'OK, so here's the way it was. We need to start with the race. The race is everything. And why's that? Because the race, my friend, is where it begins and ends.'

Yesterday's outing, he explained, was a head race, nine and a bit miles down the River Dart from Totnes to Dartmouth, pretty as you like, acre after rolling acre of God's fucking England. The boats start every thirty seconds and the trick is to knock them off, one by one.

'Knock them off?'

'Pass them. That's the trick, that's what we're there for, that's what Kinsey wants us to do. Fastest boat wins. And if you pass every other bugger, you're home safe.'

Off the start line, he said, they were towards the back of the fleet. Lenahan is in the cox's seat face to face with Andy Poole. Andy is stroke. He sets the rate. Lenahan's known Andy for ever, rowed with him for years on the Thames, won oodles of fucking cups. Between them, they'll boss the race.

'So we're half a mile down the course, a long straight bit before the first bend, and already we've reeled in the boat ahead. The guys doing the work have no idea what's going on because they're all looking backwards, but I haven't said a thing so far because it's good to toss the guys the odd sweetie, and so I'm nudging towards the right bank for the overtake and you know what? It's Kinsey, the man himself, who's up there in the bow, he's the one who susses what's happening and steals a little glance over his shoulder, just a little look now, one of his trademark looks, and here's the point, here's what I'm trying to tell you. As we step on these guys, as Andy pumps up the rate and we go surging past, *racing* past, I get to see the expression on Kinsey's face. He's creamed them, he's fucking *buried* them, and the sweetness of that knowledge, that big fucking jolt of adrenalin, puts this nasty little smile on his face. He's top dog. He's up there with the angels. The heavenly fucking chorus is giving it full throttle and every last cell in his body tells him he can do this for ever. He doesn't feel a whisper of knackeredness. That man's got the world by the throat. All the nausea we've gone through in training, all the money he's spent, all that has paid off, big time, in spades, and all he needs now is more of the same. One bunch of muppets crushed. Eleven to go. And you know what? Yer man's right to think that. Because that's called winning.'

Lenahan shifted his weight on the sofa and offered an emphatic nod, driving the point home. There was a moment of silence and Suttle wondered whether to applaud or not. Was Kinsey's prize cox like this all the time? Or was the performance strictly for Suttle's benefit? Either way, he needed to find out more.

Lenahan was cranking up again. By the time they got to Dartmouth, he said, Milo and Kinsey had hit the wall and even the last couple of overtakes couldn't mask their pain. But they still crossed the line in 58 minutes 27 seconds, an easy win, and an hour or so later they're in the Dartmouth clubhouse on the right side of a couple of pints and they're scooping up the trophy and milking the applause and feeling thoroughly pleased with themselves when Kinsey starts again.

'Starts what?'

'Post-race analysis. That's his fucking phrase, not mine. My friend, you need to make an effort, you need to *imagine* it. We've won. We've done the business. We're all getting happily bladdered and Kinsey starts banging on about *post-race analysis*. Where we got things wrong. What we could do better next time. How we need to sharpen up on the catch or the extraction or changes of rate or any fucking thing. Can you believe that? We've pissed all over the opposition. We've come close to setting some kind of course record. And he's talking about *rate changes*? The man's an eejit. Was an eejit. And that's being kind.'

Suttle wanted to know what happened later, back in Exmouth.

'This is last night, right?'

'Right.'

'OK. So we tuck the boat away in the club compound and kiss it goodnight and then we go to the pub. This is a proper pub that's stayed scruffy and real and for once in his life Kinsey uses it the way you should. Maybe Andy's had a word. Maybe Andy's told him to lighten up, enjoy himself, tie a couple on. That's probably the way it was because Andy's the only one Kinsey ever listens to. The freemasonry of the minted, right? Both these guys have got money, real money, and so Andy deserves a hearing. The rest of us? We're just bad-arse drinkers, also-rans, trophy fodder for the man's fucking ego.'

At the pub, he said, they were joined by Milo Symons' partner.

'Now this girl is a piece. Her name is Natasha – Tasha if she knows you. She's late thirties, maybe older, good nick, works out, blonde, describes herself as a resting actress. Way back in the day she probably did it for real on some crap telly series, but we've been around her for the best part of a year now and I can't remember catching a single fucking gig, not one. But fair play to the woman, she's still got it, she's still good-looking, and she's funny and sexy in the way that those two words often go together, you know what I mean? She rows with us sometimes when one of the other guys can't make it, and while she'll never win any prizes for technique she makes us laugh. She's also taken Kinsey's fancy big time, which is funny in itself because the guy's a midget and she's way taller than he is. Not that little me can talk.'

'So how long were you in the pub?'

'An hour, tops. Kinsey's ordered champagne. In the end we do three bottles, no problem, and then Kinsey orders us all back to his apartment round the corner for a nightcap or two, and at that point it's Tasha's idea to sort out a curry because that woman eats for England. So she takes orders and gets in her little car and then the rest of us halloo round the corner to Kinsey's place.'

Suttle tried to imagine this little knot of revellers making its way through the windy darkness. Kinsey, it turns out, has more champagne in his fridge but no Guinness. Pendrick thinks that's a shame and so Milo gets on the mobile to Tash and tells her to pick up some resupplies.

'Tash has gone for the takeaway by herself?'

'Yep. Now I'm with Pendrick on the Guinness. Excellent fucking call. So we're all lying around Kinsey's pad, helping him with the Krug, and then Wonder Woman turns up with a whole load of takeaway plus an armful of tinnies. Me and Pendrick split the tinnies between us and we're drinking toasts to how fucking *invincible* we are and all the time the temperature's dropping because the sliding door to one of the balconies is open and then it occurs to us that Kinsey's out there chucking up over the rail. You can hear the *splat-splat* on the promenade below. Nice.'

Suttle made a note, remembering the CSI telling him about the puddle of vomit on the other side of the apartment block round the corner from the body. Then he looked up again, asking what had happened to Kinsey. It was Pendrick, it seemed, who'd sorted Kinsey out, taken him to his bedroom and tucked him in. Meantime the rest of the crew were getting stuck into the curry, which turned out to be a big disappointment.

'Splodge, you know?' Lenahan pulled a face. 'No theme. No story. Nothing to remember it by. It's one of those nights you pick at the best bits but our hearts aren't really in it. A lounge that big isn't the cosiest place in the world and the truth is we've all had enough. Nine hard miles? Our collective fucking bodyweight in Guinness and champagne? Definitely time for bye byes. So Tash dumps the curry in the waste bin and does the washing-up. She's got the little sports car for her and Symons but we need a cab so she makes the call. The guy's there within five minutes. He has to do a bit of a circuit to drop the three of us off. Andy lives in Exeter so he'll be the last man standing but you know what yer man does? He gets a price from the driver and then takes a whack from each of us before we even get in the bloody car. That's how you get rich, I guess. That's the kind of stroke Kinsey would pull.'

Suttle wanted to know more about Kinsey. Was he still in bed at this point? Or had he got up again?

'Still in bed. Yer man's spark out. This guy and alcohol are strangers. He doesn't know what's happening to him. But that's not the point. The place has got three en suite bathrooms and we're still all thinking why hasn't the eejit used one of those if he wants to be ill, but it's Pendrick who puts his finger on it. Guy's a dog, he says. The man has to leave his smell everywhere.'

It was a neat phrase. Suttle scribbled it down. Later Lenahan would have to volunteer a formal statement, but in the meantime – as precious background – this stuff was gold dust.

'So you left ...' Suttle suggested.

'Sure we did.'

'Time?'

'Gone midnight. Ask the cabbie.'

'And you pulled the door shut behind you?'

'Yeah. We do that grown-up stuff really well.'

'No one else around? No one you saw? Inside the building? Out by the marina?'

'Didn't see a soul.'

'And no calls when you were up in the apartment?'

'Nothing. Just us.'

'But a couple of hours later the guy's dead.'

'So it seems.'

'Don't you find that odd? Being a doctor?'

The word doctor brought the ghost of a frown to Lenahan's face.

'How do you know I'm a doctor?'

'Molly Doyle told me.'

'Ah, the Viking.' The smile was back. 'And did she tell you what kind of doctor?'

'She said you worked abroad a lot. Médicins Sans Frontières.'
Suttle nodded at the photos on the wall. 'I take it she's right.'

'She is. Fine woman.' He studied his hands a moment, then
his head came up again. 'You really want to know about death,
my friend? Then let me tell you. It's getting towards sunset.
It's hotter than you can believe. Even the lizards are getting
fucking stressed. But yer family are desperate and so they bring
little you into the clinic. They've probably walked ten miles
to get you to where it matters, and a journey like that hasn't
done you any good at all. So there you are on the knackered
old trolley we use as a bed and after your last ten breaths your
breathing stops and then you're gone.' He nodded, his voice
soft, his eyes never leaving Suttle's face. 'You're a couple of
years old, maybe younger. Your mother screams and leaves the
room. All the relatives outside, dozens of the fuckers, start to
wail. Your father squats on the cracked old plastic chair which
is the only one we've got and puts his face in his hands. A nurse
cleans you up, removes the IV, swabs all the fucking blood and
mucus away and then drapes something half clean over your
face. Then your dad ties your big toes to keep your little legs
together and wraps your feet and puts your hands together and
binds your thumbs like this.' He mimed the action, showing
Suttle. 'Then your dad lifts you onto a piece of coloured cloth
and wraps you for a final time and takes you away. Me? I'm
watching all this. It's something I've got used to. It happens
maybe five times a week. It's like a little piece of theatre. The
gennie's fucked again and the lights are flickering on and off
and you stand there in the dark and you listen to make sure
they've all gone. You have absolutely nothing to say. You
padlock the drugs cupboard and then step outside. With luck,
you're alone. You have a cigarette, you look up at the stars,
and you wonder if the rest of the guys back in the compound
have left any beers in the fridge. But on no account do you
allow yourself to think. No way. Never. Why not? Because
that's the truth about death. It's ugly. It's unsparing. And it's

48

fucking everywhere. So from where I sit, Kinsey probably had it easy.'

There was a long silence. Gulls again, more distant this time, and a stir of wind in the street outside. Suttle, for once in his life, was lost for words. He wasn't sure if any of this stuff served any evidential purpose but it was hard not to be touched.

'You're going back? To Sudan?'

'Sure. And to Uganda and to Somalia and to all the other fucked-over places.'

'So what does it do to you? Long term?'

'I dunno. I guess that's a treat to come.'

'Are you worried?'

'Sure.'

'Do you think it damages you?'

'I hope so.'

'*Hope so?*'

'Sure. Because it's real. Because this is what's waiting for us all, some place down the road.' He stirred again in the chair, his hand reaching for a packet of Gitanes on the floor. Suttle shook his head at the offered cigarette, watched Lenahan light up and suck the smoke deep into his lungs. 'Look at it this way,' he said finally. 'You go to some fancy dinner party. It happens a lot around here. You're heading for the cheese course and everyone's still talking about house prices or private schools or which four-by-four is best for towing jet skis or the horse fucking box, and then comes a bit of a lull, because there's always a bit of a lull, and you sense it's your turn. But what the fuck can you offer by way of conversation? Have any of these people got a clue about Sudan? About cholera, malnutrition, pneumonia, kidney infections, measles, meningitis, gunshot wounds, snakebite, sepsis after female fucking circumcision? Has any one of them ever heard an infant's heart stop? No fucking chance.'

'So who do you talk to? Who understands?'

'Is that a serious question?'

'Yeah.'

'Then it has to be Pendrick. This is a guy who lives in a dark part of the forest. He lives in the shadows. He lives in his head. But he's good, bloody good, and he's done a bit too, one way or another. Jesus, has he …' He tailed off, took another drag, expelled a thin line of blue smoke up towards the ceiling. 'If you want the truth, we talk about it a lot. Once you've been out there, I tell him, once you've seen it, lived it, been part of it, been *swamped* by it, you're ruined. There's a gap between you and the rest of the world. Nothing's real. And nothing matters. You knock at my door and tell me Kinsey's dead and you know what? I couldn't care a fuck.'

'You think he killed himself?'

'I don't know.'

'You think he fell by accident?'

'Maybe.'

'What else might have happened then?'

Lenahan's eyes drifted to the copy of the *Guardian,* then he was looking at Suttle again. He was smiling.

'You tell me.'

Suttle was with Houghton by half past twelve. One of the other desks was occupied by a young D/C trying to raise someone in the marina. Suttle pulled a chair towards Houghton. Boiling down Lenahan's account to the kind of brisk summary the D/I favoured was beyond him so he stuck to the essentials.

'The guys all left in a taxi around midnight,' he said. 'We need to check out the booking and statement the driver, but I've talked to the girl Lenahan shares with and she confirms he got back around that time. There's no way he could have got up and gone out later because the girl's best mate was kipping on the sofa downstairs and the front door opens straight out into the street.'

'Not Lenahan, then.'

'Not if we're talking murder.'

'And what's your view on that?'

'I haven't got one. Not yet.'

'And this guy Lenahan?'

'He says he's agnostic.'

'Meaning?'

'He thinks the jury's out. He says Kinsey was too self-interested to end it all, and too sensible to put himself in harm's way.'

'Kinsey was pissed,' Houghton pointed out.

'Sure. But he'd thrown most of it up. I'm not saying he was sober. Just that he'd probably have stayed in bed.'

Houghton nodded, said nothing. Then she glanced over her shoulder at the adjacent desk. The young D/C's name was Golding. He'd just spent half an hour in Exeter with Andy Poole.

'So how was he?' Suttle adjusted his chair.

'Same story, Sarge. They won the race. They had a bevvy or two. Kinsey got rat-arsed. The girl sorted a taxi. End of.'

'But how did he take it?'

'Take what?'

'Kinsey dying.'

'He was gobsmacked. He couldn't believe it. Neither could his missus.'

'She's alibied him?'

'Yeah. She was still up when he got back, watching some DVD or other. They talked a bit about the race then they went to bed.'

'She knew Kinsey?'

'Not especially well but I think they'd all socialised a bit. Poole couldn't get his head around it. At one point he was wondering whether he ought to have stayed in the apartment last night, kept an eye on the guy, stopped him doing anything silly.'

'As if.'

'Exactly. That's what his missus said. Sanest man I ever met. Direct quote.'

'Because he was the go-to guy?'

'Because he was rich. Because he had it all. Because he'd just won his first race. Because he had everything to look forward to.'

'And Poole?'

'Agreed. In spades. Apparently he'd helped Kinsey map out a whole load of these regatta things, pretty much every weekend over the whole summer. Money was obviously no problem. They were going everywhere. The big deal was to get into the South Coast Championships. On yesterday's evidence, Poole thought that might be possible.'

'Even with The Passenger aboard?'

'The who?'

Suttle explained about Kinsey's nickname around the club. The D/C consulted his notes.

'Yeah. Poole had just found another old mate who'd really strengthen the crew but Kinsey was obviously there for the duration.'

'So who was going to get dumped?'

The D/C went back to his notes again. 'A guy called Symons. Apparently he's really good for a novice, but Poole knows this other bloke will row the arse off him.' He looked up. 'Milo Symons? Name ring any bells?'

Lizzie was back at Chantry Cottage in time to give Grace her lunch. The prospect of Gill's visit had begun to weigh heavily on her and she was wondering whether she might dream up an excuse and put her off. They'd been mates for years, fellow journos on the Pompey *News,* and they'd ended up forging a friendship that owed more to Gill's pushiness than anything else. This was a woman who always needed a best friend, a mother confessor, someone she could rely on to share a drink or two and an account of her latest conquest.

Last in a longish line of failed relationships had been with a Major Crimes D/I called Joe Faraday, much respected by Jimmy, who'd brought his life to an end with three packs of painkillers and a bottle of decent red. Gill had regarded Faraday's suicide as a personal tragedy, hers rather than anyone else's, although her claim to a special place in her new beau's life had never stood up to serious scrutiny. Jimmy had discovered that his boss had shagged her just twice before locking his door and taking the phone off the hook.

The real problem, in Lizzie's view, was simple. Gill Reynolds had never mastered the knack of letting a relationship develop at its own pace. She had a bad habit of crowding her man from the off and never understood why thigh-length boots and a dab or two of Chanel wouldn't guarantee the love affair of her dreams. In this respect Lizzie suspected that nothing would have changed and wasn't at all sure whether she could cope with a couple of days of heavy-duty angst. Gill never arrived at any meeting without an agenda. Taking an interest in anyone else's life was beyond her.

But what could she say? And wasn't company – of any description – a brighter prospect than yet another wet afternoon banged up in Chantry Cottage?

The endless rain had made the front door stick again. She turned the key and gave it a kick at the bottom before stamping the mud from her wellies and wrestling the buggy indoors. For some reason she'd left her mobile in the kitchen. Half-expecting a text from Jimmy, she took it out onto the back patio and fired it up. She wasn't wrong about a text, but oddly enough it came from Gill. She'd had to change her plans. Instead of descending on Tuesday she'd arrive tomorrow in time for lunch. 'Lucky us,' she'd texted at the end, 'Can't wait.'

It was mid-afternoon before Suttle got to Tusker Farm. *Constantine* had yet to be upgraded to a full HOLMES 2 enquiry and in the absence of a statement reader, Houghton wanted Suttle to sort out the scraps of feedback from the marina, which were beginning to fatten into something more substantial. The house-to-house teams, while failing to unearth the bankable evidence that would turn *Constantine* into a fully fledged murder enquiry, were reporting widespread resentment of Kinsey and his behaviour.

According to one resident, a mainstay of the Exmouth Quays development, this was a guy who'd never had any time for his neighbours. He openly flouted some of the by-laws by having midsummer barbecues on his balcony and riding his mountain bike around the marina basin. He never turned up at the community fund-raising events – Canapes on the Quay, Carols on the Quay – that had become such a feature of waterside life. He never put his hand in his pocket when appeals were launched for a commemorative bench or a fighting fund to battle a nearby development, and when she'd confronted him, knocking on his door and trying to shame him into writing a cheque, he'd told her to go away and get a life.

None of this, of course, suggested grounds for dumping the guy off his own balcony and leaving his body to cool in the rain, but it confirmed a wider irritation. The landlord of the Beach pub, re-interviewed at his own request after the Sunday lunchtime drinkers had drifted away, confirmed that Kinsey had also upset a fair number of locals in the town, firstly by writing to the local paper and complaining about early-morning noise from fishermen putting to sea from the dock beneath his apartment, and later by mounting a vigorous defence of a bunch of developers planning yet another multi-storey block of flats within shouting distance of the marina. To upset these two very different groups of locals – working trawler men and middle-class worthies – took some talent, and in the view of the landlord Kinsey definitely had some kind of death wish. The interviewing D/C had underlined the phrase, bringing it to the attention of Houghton when he got back to *Constantine*'s temporary home.

Suttle was thinking about it now, as he bumped the Impreza into the farmyard. Houghton wanted him to develop the intel picture on Kinsey – the kind of guy he'd been, the risks he'd run, the people he'd upset – and barely hours into the enquiry he was already tallying an ever-longer list of potential enemies. Paul Winter, a Pompey D/C who'd taught him everything he needed to know about the darker arts of CID work, had once told him that money, serious money, carried a smell of its own. At the time Suttle hadn't really understood what Winter had been getting at, but his years on the tastier Major Crime jobs had wised him up. Money puts you in the bubble, he thought. And that's when you're truly vulnerable.

The farmer's wife answered Suttle's knock. Molly Doyle had been wrong about a caravan. Half a field away, tucked beside the shelter of a hedge, he could see what looked like a mobile home.

Suttle introduced himself. He said he was looking for a Mr Milo Symons. The farmer's wife was still studying Suttle's warrant card.

'In trouble is he?' She didn't seem surprised.

'Not at all.'

Suttle asked whether she'd been at home last night.

'Of course I was. We both were.'

'And does Mr Symons come in this way? Through the farm-yard?'

'No. They've got a separate entrance up beyond their place. It's a gate we use to get the tractor into the field.'

'So would you hear anything when they come and go?'

'Depends.'

'On what?'

'On the wind. And Bess.'

Bess, it turned out, was their sheepdog. Ears like a bat.

'So last night?'

'She heard nothing. Nothing that I can remember.'

'Around midnight? Maybe later?'

'Nothing. But the wind had died so she probably wouldn't.'

Suttle brought the conversation to an end. Symons and his

fancy woman had evidently been renting the mobile home for a couple of years. So far the farmer's wife had no complaints. The woman dressed like a tart, but these days that was so common you barely noticed.

Suttle thanked her and set off up the field. The grass was still damp underfoot but the sky was cloudless and there was a definite hint of the coming summer in the golden drifts of buttercups. Several fields away, Suttle could see lambs worrying their mums to death and he found himself thinking of Grace. There were lambs on a hobby farm up the lane from Chantry Cottage. Maybe Lizzie had wheeled their daughter up there for a look. Maybe.

The mobile home was bigger than he'd expected. A line of washing was flapping in the breeze and a sodden cardboard box beside the door was brimming with crushed tinnies. Behind the mobile home, invisible from the farmhouse, Suttle found a white Transit van. The van was pocked with rust around the sills. There was paperwork all over the passenger seat, and half a cup of something that looked like tea was balanced on the dashboard. In the well beneath the glovebox, a litter of empty crisp packets.

Suttle had phoned ahead, making sure Symons was available for interview. He'd wanted to talk to his partner too, but it seemed Tash was elsewhere.

Symons came to the door. He was tall and thin, dark complexion, single ear stud, a mane of jet-black hair tied at the back with a twist of yellow ribbon. He was wearing jeans and a black T-shirt under an embroidered waistcoat. With the gypsy look went the hands of an artist: long fine-boned fingers, delicate wrists.

'Come in. Yeah. Good.' Symons dismissed the proffered warrant card with a wave of his hand. Already, he seemed to be saying, Suttle was some kind of mate.

On the phone Suttle had been vague about the reason for his visit. Now he told Symons about Kinsey.

'*Dead?* Shit. How did that happen?' His amazement seemed genuine.

Suttle said he didn't know. In the circumstances it was his job to put together Kinsey's last movements and try and understand what might have led to his death.

'But the guy was cool with everything. Why ...?'

Suttle was looking around the space that obviously served as a living room. There was a built-in sofa that probably doubled as a spare bed and an Ikea rocking chair that had seen better days. The far end opened into a galley kitchen and Suttle could smell fresh coffee. But what took Suttle's eye was the PC on the desk in the corner. An image hung on the screen, two bodies on a bed. One of them was Symons. Straddling him was a woman. The long fall of hair down her naked back was a violent shade of mauve.

'That's Tash.' Symons laughed. 'You want to see the rest?'

Without waiting for an answer he stepped across to the desk. A single keystroke brought the sequence to life. Tash was moving very slowly, barely lifting her arse, her hands cupping her breasts. Symons' eyes were closed. These people have been at it a while, Suttle thought. Years and years. Perfect control. Lots of practice.

'Then this.'

Symons bent forward. Tash seemed to be almost immobile, waiting, poised. Then, seconds later, she arched her back and grunted and the shot cut to a stretch of sand, black with birds erupting from their roost. White flashes from a thousand wings filled the screen, a dizzying explosion of movement as the camera held them in frame, slowly panning across the gleaming expanse of the estuary. Suttle was transfixed. He'd seen exactly this landscape only this morning. From Kinsey's apartment.

'This is some sort of movie?'

'Yeah. It's a rough cut. You want to see more?'

Suttle shook his head. He had business to transact, questions to ask. Luke Golding, the young D/C who'd talked to Andy

Poole, thought that Kinsey had backed Symons on some kind of project by bunging him money. Maybe this was it.

'Tell me about yesterday.' Suttle took a seat on the sofa. 'Talk me through it.'

Symons, sprawled in the rocker, described the race. They'd been great. It was his first ever race. 58.27. Total result.

'And afterwards?'

'Afterwards was great too.' He described the pub. Toasting themselves in champagne was definitely a novelty. It was good, he said, to see Kinsey so relaxed. He deserved it. And so did everyone else.

Suttle wanted to know about the impromptu party afterwards. Had Kinsey shown any signs of stress? Had Symons noticed anything that might account for what happened later?

'The guy threw up. Then he went to bed.'

'And the rest of you?'

'We pushed off. Tash organised a cab.'

'For everyone?'

'No. She'd driven over. It's a sports car. It's only got room for two. The rest of the guys went off in the taxi.'

'Leaving Kinsey by himself?'

'Yes.'

'So what time did you get back here?'

Symons thought about the question.

'After midnight,' he said at last. 'Then we crashed.'

'Anyone else see you?'

'I doubt it.'

'And this morning?'

'I ran Tash up to Honiton and dropped her at the station. It's her mum's birthday. Normally you can get a train to Yeovil but on Sundays there's a coach service. She was well pissed off.' He grinned. 'Back tonight though. I'm driving over to pick her up. You know Yeovil at all? Evil place.'

Suttle shook his head and scribbled himself a couple of notes. There was something slightly childlike about this man. In ways he couldn't quite define he reminded Suttle slightly of J-J, Joe Faraday's deaf-mute son. The same hints of vulnerability. The same feeling that bits of the wiring didn't quite connect.

'So how did you come across Kinsey?'

'I didn't. It was Tash who met him first. Someone told her about the club after she'd seen the boats when she was out jogging and she went down to find out more. Kinsey was on the beach. He was still a bit of a novice himself in those days – he hadn't bought the new boat – and they sort of shared notes. He bigged himself up from the off, did Kinsey, told Tash all about his penthouse apartment in the marina, how he'd watched the club boats from his window going up the estuary, and how he'd fancied getting involved. They went out together that morning, same boat, half experienced guys, half novices, and it was funny because Tash came back and told me how crap he was, completely out of time, always ahead of the stroke. Stick insect she called him.'

'You were a rower then?'

'No. It was Tash who got me into it. That was a bit later. She said it was brilliant and she was right. She's like that, Tash. She's the one who sorts me out. Always has done. Ever since the off.'

They'd first met, he said, when he was in his early twenties. All his life he'd lived beside the river up in Topsham, but after leaving school with pretty much nothing to his name he'd bailed out of Devon and signed up for a film course in west London. Too much dope was doing his head in, and after a near-terminal bust-up with his dad he knew he had to get his shit together. The film course included a chance to work with professional actors and one of them had been Tash.

'We'd spent the afternoon shooting a whole load of stuff in some studios in Hammersmith. Afterwards we went to the pub, a place in Chiswick down by the Thames, and I was telling her about my own river, and what it meant to me, what it's always meant to me, and how hard that feeling was to express, and she said film, you need to make a film about it, you need to dream up a story, or make something associative, an image-based thing, something that does justice to this feeling of yours. And you know what? That was the most wonderful thing I'd ever heard. It was like a door opening in my head, or maybe somewhere way down in here ...' He touched his chest, leaning forward in the rocker, trying to draw Suttle into this story of his. 'Tease it out, she said. Take it in your hands. Nurture it, understand it, shape it, *treasure* it. Why? Because something's calling you. Maybe it's the spirit of the river. Maybe it's something else. But either way you're lucky. Because that kind of thing doesn't happen very often. So be aware. Stay in tune. *Listen* to the river. And *do* it.' His eyes found the PC on the desk. 'She was right, too. And it's worked.'

Suttle smiled. He could imagine a conversation like this. It sounded more like therapy than idle pub chat. Symons was a good-looking guy, no question, and Suttle could picture this new woman in his life, probably older, undoubtedly wiser.

'And this film has a story?'

'Sure. It's about the river. Actually it's more than that. It's a story about the river and a story about a love affair, about two people who live *on* the river, who are *part* of the river, who maybe *are* the river, its mirror image, its other self, the river made flesh. They live on an old barge. The barge sits on a mooring up off Dawlish Warren. That's where the tide flows strongest, where the river talks loudest. These two people, the man, the woman, they have no names. They just *are*. They're part of the river, part of each other. The word Tash uses is flux.'

'Flux?' Suttle was lost.

'Yeah. Wonderful word. Perfect. *Flux*.' Symons grinned. 'Partly this is about geography. Here, let me show you. This is Tash again. Her idea. Her trope.'

Symons unfolded his long frame from the chair and rummaged around behind the desk. Seconds later Suttle found himself looking at a framed map of the Exe estuary. Symons knelt beside him, visibly excited at this sudden interest in his life.

'OK, so what I'm wanting is a narrative, a story that does justice to the river, that captures its essence, its soul. The framing device is the affair. But the affair, this relationship, has to be shaped by the river itself. And here's what Tash came up with.' One bony finger settled on the river upstream of Exmouth. Then the finger tracked slowly south until it paused at the mouth of the estuary.

'Look at that. Look at the river just there. What does it remind you of?'

There was a hint of impatience in his voice. This, he seemed to be saying, is obvious. Suttle was trying to make sense of the shape of the river. The way the harbour nosed into the tidal stream. The long curl of a feature on the bank opposite. The narrowness of the gap between them.

Suttle asked about the bank opposite. What was he looking at?

'It's called Dawlish Warren. It's a protected bird site. Magic place.'

Suttle nodded. He was still no closer to an answer.

'You can't see it?' Symons couldn't keep the disappointment out of his voice.

'No.'

'Truly?'

'Yes.'

'It's a fanny. A woman's vagina. That was her insight, Tash's, a stroke of total brilliance. Just here, where the river gets tight, is where the barge is moored. That's where the action takes place. Within touching distance of the Warren. Just here. Just across the water where the sweet spot is. And here's another thing. *Touching distance*. Tash again. The perfect title. Why? Because we're talking every kind of distance. Geographical distance. Historical distance. The distance between two people.

And the way that passion, or the tide, or the history, can *bridge* that distance, even *abolish* it.'

Way back in the eighteenth century, he said, a group of Dutch seamen got themselves shipwrecked on the Warren. There was a big south-easterly blow and their ship ended up on the beach. The locals came over from Exmouth and slaughtered every last man.

'That'll be in the movie too. My idea this time, not Tash's.'

His finger had found the sweet spot again. Suttle was looking hard at the map. This time he got it.

'That's Regatta Court. That's where Kinsey lived.'

'Exactly. He thought it was really funny. We needed a development budget and Tash thought he might like the idea. He knew nothing about flux but he understood the rest of it.'

'You're telling me he gave you money?'

'Not me. Tash. She did the negotiations, got him sold on the idea. First off he wanted to see the kind of stuff I'd done already. I've got some work from way back but Tash said we could go one better and shoot a couple of scenes from the script and show him those.'

Suttle's eyes had gone back to the PC. He was beginning to understand.

'So that's what you did?'

'Yeah. Kinsey bought us a decent camera and gave Tash a couple of grand to make it happen and we did the rest.'

'You're talking about the stuff I just watched?'

'Yeah.'

'So who chose the sequences?'

'Tash did. She chooses everything.'

'And Kinsey?'

'He only saw a rough cut. I gave him a DVD and he watched it on his laptop.'

'And?'

'He loved it. Totally knocked out.'

'He told you personally?'

'Yeah.'

'When?'

'Last night, in the pub. He'd told Tash already but last night he made a big thing of it. He said the rest of the budget wouldn't be a problem. Not after watching what we'd done.'

'How much are we talking?'

'Forty-five grand. Quite a lot of that is for the hire of the barge.'

'Right.' Suttle nodded. 'Right.'

There was a long silence. Would someone about to field a cheque for forty-five thousand pounds toss their benefactor into oblivion? Suttle thought not.

'How well did you know Kinsey?' he asked. 'Be honest.'

'Not well. Not really. If you want the truth I got into his crew because of Tash.'

'I'm not with you.'

'Kinsey fancied her. He'd do anything for her. And that turned out to be a bit of a blessing.'

'For you?'

'For both of us.'

'Because of the movie?'

'Of course. And the rowing too. Yesterday was magic. That guy Andy Poole's taught me loads.'

'He thinks you're good.'

'Does he?' The grin was unfeigned. 'Did he *say* that?'

'Yeah. Not to me. Not directly. But yeah. So tell me – what did you make of Kinsey?'

Symons thought about the question. Finally he sat down again, leaning forward, his voice lowered, almost conspiratorial. A kid. Definitely.

'This is just between us two, right?' Suttle didn't answer. Symons went on regardless. 'I think he was lonely.'

'Why?'

'I don't know. I just got the feeling. He didn't seem to have any friends, any mates. Mates matter.'

'No girlfriends? No one special?'

'I don't think so.'

'Was there a wife once?'

'Dunno. I suppose there may have been.'

'Right.' Suttle nodded. 'So you're telling me the guy was pretty much alone?'

'A loner, sure.'

'And Tash?'

'Tash?'

Suttle recognised the flicker of alarm in Symons' eyes.

'She got close to him?'

'He fancied her. I told you.'

'That's not what I'm asking.'

'Listen, man. The woman's my partner. She's beautiful. Everyone fancies her. So what are you suggesting?'

'I'm suggesting nothing.' Suttle had noted the sudden flash of anger. 'I'm asking you whether she might know more about Kinsey than you do.'

'And not tell me, you mean?'

'Yes.'

Symons considered the proposition before rejecting it with a vigorous shake of his head.

'No way,' he said. 'No fucking way.'

Suttle held his gaze. At length he asked how Symons made his living.

'I do stuff for my dad.'

'What sort of stuff?'

'You've seen the van out there? I collect and deliver bits and pieces of furniture. He's got a couple of antique shops. He bids in the auctions and I pick the stuff up.'

'And that gives you enough to live on?'

'Yeah.'

Suttle nodded and scribbled himself a note. The earlier warmth had gone out of this conversation. Symons was visibly upset now. Suttle asked him where Tash would be tomorrow morning.

'Here,' Symons shrugged, 'I guess.'

Suttle took her mobile number and then got to his feet.

'There's a guy called Pendrick,' he said. 'He rows in Kinsey's crew. You'll know him.'

'Of course.'

'Any idea where he might be?'

'No.'

'He didn't mention anything last night? Plans he might have had for today?'

'No.' The smile had returned. 'But then he wouldn't.'

'Why's that?'

'The guy's another loner. Just like Jake.'

Suttle was back at Exmouth police station in time for the first of the *Constantine* squad meets. Nandy had returned from a busy afternoon in Torbay, and the house-to-house teams filled the rest of the office. As a courtesy, Houghton had also asked the duty uniformed Inspector to attend.

She kicked off with a brisk summary of progress to date. House-to-house teams had knocked on every door in Regatta Court. They'd scored a response from maybe two thirds of the apartments but failed to gather anything of evidential use. Only one resident had laid eyes on Kinsey's partying crew. She'd seen them streaming out of Regatta House around midnight. Hand on heart she couldn't be sure but she thought four or five people, one of whom was definitely a woman.

Detectives had also covered every property with line of sight on Kinsey's balcony. Again, nothing.

'What's the lighting like?' This from Nandy. One of the D/Cs fielded the question.

'Crap, sir. We're talking lights at knee level on the walkway by the dock. No way would they reach the fifth floor.'

'So no witnesses?' Nandy was looking at Houghton.

'None, I'm afraid.'

'And definitely no CCTV?'

'No.'

Houghton went on to describe the kind of ripples Kinsey had been making. No one seemed to like him. His reputation for arrogance had spread beyond Exmouth Quays. There was even a question mark about the crew he'd put together.

'Who says?' Nandy again.

'Me, sir.' Suttle told him about Lenahan and Symons. In his view Kinsey had bought their loyalty. These were guys who got on among themselves, and after yesterday's win they might still carry on rowing with someone else in the bow seat, but neither Lenahan nor Symons seemed over-distressed by Kinsey's passing.

'So what are you telling me?'

'Nothing, sir. Except no one seems surprised that the guy's dead.'

'You think someone killed him?'

'I think he may have had it coming.'

'And we can prove that?'

'Of course not. Not yet.'

'But you think we might?'

'I think it's possible, sir, yes.'

Suttle was getting uncomfortable. The last thing he wanted was a public pissing match with Nandy.

Houghton stepped in. The post-mortem, she reminded everyone, was scheduled for tomorrow morning. After that, things might be a great deal clearer. In the meantime, D/S Suttle would be pulling together the background intel.

Suttle nodded, glad of the reprieve. There was a pile of Kinsey's files on his desk, material seized from the apartment, and he'd be spending most of tomorrow trying to build a picture of the man's life.

Houghton wanted to know what they'd missed. She was still looking at Suttle.

'Pendrick,' he said. 'We still haven't nailed the guy.'

Houghton nodded. Detectives had returned to his flat throughout the day but failed to raise him. Messages left on his mobile had gone unanswered. She'd tasked two D/Cs to sit on his address throughout the evening. If necessary, they'd be relieved by another shift at midnight. SOC had already retrieved some shots of last night's celebration from Kinsey's camera, and a process of elimination had ID'd Pendrick. If the guy hadn't turned up by first thing tomorrow morning, she'd be circulating the mugshot and other details force-wide.

Houghton had printed a couple of photos. Suttle, reaching for one of them, found himself looking at a big guy in his mid-thirties. A brutal grade one darkened his shaved skull and there was something about the cast of his face that seemed vaguely familiar. He had a deep scar that tracked diagonally down his right cheek and he was wearing jeans and a blue sweat top that had seen better days. Unlike the rest of the crew, he wasn't punching the air. On the contrary, he seemed preoccupied, almost detached. A loner, he thought, remembering Symons' parting shot.

The meeting broke up. Nandy told Suttle to stay put. Already Suttle sensed what was to come. It was this man's job to match ever-thinning resources against the incessant demands on the Major Crime machine. MCIT inquiries were horribly expensive, as the headbangers at HQ were only too eager to point out. In any enquiry the only currency that mattered was evidence.

'We've got Kinsey's crew alibied. Am I right?'

'Yes, sir. With the exception of Pendrick.'

'And Scenes of Crime have found nothing material in the apartment?'

'Not so far.'

'We've no witnesses to what happened?'

'No.'

'And not much prospect of finding any?'

This was a question Suttle wasn't prepared to answer. He didn't go as far back as Nandy, nowhere near, but his years on the Major Crime Team in Pompey had taught him never to discount a surprise. Solid effort, meticulous investigation and a helping of luck could sometimes transform a faltering enquiry and something told him that *Constantine* was far from over.

Nandy rarely left a suspicion unvoiced.

'You don't think this man had an accident, do you?'

'No, sir.'

'And you don't think he topped himself?'

'I think it's unlikely.'

'Why?'

'Because he doesn't seem that kind of guy.'

'Who says?'

'Pretty much everyone.'

'I see.' Nandy nodded and turned away.

There was a long silence. Suttle thought the conversation was over. He asked whether the Det-Supt would be down in Exmouth tomorrow. Nandy ignored the question. He hadn't finished with Kinsey.

'You think these people knew him, this man? Really knew him? You think anyone knows anyone? You really think there aren't parts of us we keep hidden? You? Me? Every other poor sod?'

Suttle blinked. This was suddenly personal. He seemed to have touched a nerve in Nandy, stirred feelings much deeper than irritation at defending his precious budget.

Nandy hadn't finished. He said he'd lost count of the sus deaths he'd tried to stand up as murder. As a younger copper he'd taken far too much notice of people telling him that so-and-so would have been incapable of suicide. They were probably sincere, they probably meant it at the time, but the truth was that deep down we were all in the dark, all strangers to each other.

'You don't believe that?' There was something almost

plaintive in his voice. 'You don't think that's the way we really are?'

Suttle left the nick shortly afterwards. He'd phoned ahead, checking in with Lizzie, but had raised no answer. The road back to Colaton Raleigh took him down into the town centre. On an impulse he headed for the seafront. The rowing club lay at the far end of the long curve of yellow sand. He found a parking space on the promenade and got out.

The days were lengthening now and the sun was still high in the west. The tide had turned a couple of hours ago and water was pouring back into the mouth of the river. After a morning of low cloud and drizzly rain Suttle could scarcely credit the transformation. A sturdy little trawler was wallowing in through the deep-water channel, a cloud of seagulls in pursuit. More gulls wheeled and dived over the distant smudge of Dawlish Warren while a pair of cormorants arrowed seawards, barely feet above the churning tide.

Watching the cormorants, Suttle thought suddenly of Joe Faraday. His ex-boss had been a manic birder. On a number of occasions down by the water in Old Portsmouth he'd abandon a review of this job or that to bring some passing blur to Suttle's attention. Suttle, who knew absolutely nothing about birds, had always been touched by this passion for the natural order of things. Faraday, to his certain knowledge, had despaired of the chaos that passed for daily life, and from the world of birds he appeared to derive both comfort and solace. Nature, he'd once confided, represented sanity. You could rely on a mother to feed her chicks. You could set your watch by the arrival of birds of passage. Spot a skein of Brent geese lifting off for the long flight north, you knew it had to be April.

Suttle paused on the front, enjoying the sun on his face. Nandy, somewhat to his surprise, seemed to share a little of Faraday's view of the world. In Faraday's case, deep pessimism had hardened into despair – and it was that despair, in the end, that had taken him to his death. Nandy, on the evidence of six busy months, appeared to be far more robust, but after their last exchange, just minutes ago, Suttle was beginning to wonder. Was there something that came with higher command, some subtle alteration to your DNA, that took you to a very bad place? Had Nandy been serious about the stranger at the heart of every friend?

In truth, he didn't know, and just for a moment, standing in this puddle of sunshine, the wind in his hair, he knew he didn't much care. He liked this new job of his. There wasn't much of a social life as far as work was concerned because most of the guys lived a fair distance away, scattered across the hugeness of Devon. Some lived up near the north coast, an area they referred to as the Tundra. A commute like that didn't leave much room for a pint or two after work, and in any case most of his new colleagues had young families to think about, a gravitational tug about which Suttle knew a great deal.

He grinned to himself. Despite the grief he was occasionally getting from Lizzie, he loved going back to Chantry Cottage. He wasn't the least bit daunted by the ever-lengthening list of jobs he had to sort and rather liked the way they'd managed to turn camping into a way of life. Nocturnal scufflings from the mice, he told himself, brought you closer to nature. That had to be good for Grace, and good for all of them in the end, and if Lizzie occasionally lost her sense of humour then so be it. Faraday, he thought, would have definitely approved.

On the point of returning to the car, his eye was caught by wheel marks tracking down to the water's edge. Then he spotted a boat trailer, tucked up beyond the tideline. The trailer was tiny, way too small for the big sea boats he'd seen earlier in the club compound, and he peered out at the water, shading his eyes against the glare of the sun, not quite sure what he might find.

For a long moment he could see nothing but the dance of

the incoming tide. Then he caught a movement, a black speck, away to the east.

The speck was moving fast, buoyed by the tide. Within seconds he could make out the shape of a single rower. He was big, powerful. He was wearing a red singlet. Each stroke seemed to flow effortlessly into the next one, his long arms reaching forward, his legs driving hard, his hands tucking the oars into his body until the cycle started all over again and he leaned forward over his knees, his hands feeling for the grain of the water, driving the tiny scull closer and closer.

Suttle grinned to himself, suddenly recognising what Lizzie needed in her life, what would chase the demons away, what would put the sunshine back. She should be down here. She should have her three free rows and get stuck in. She'd never been frightened by exercise. Back in Pompey she'd been running two or three times a week. She loved the water too, and they'd often fantasised about getting a little dinghy and sailing across to the Isle of Wight.

Suttle fumbled for his mobile, hoping Lizzie would pick up. Good news was for sharing. The sculler had stopped now and was drifting down with the tide, his body sagging, his head on his chest. Then came Lizzie's voice on the phone. She sounded exhausted. And there was something else there. Anger.

'Thank Christ it's you,' she said. 'I've had enough.'

He found her curled in a ball in the darkness of the living room. He'd never seen her sucking her thumb before. Even Grace, safe in her playpen, was looking anxious.

Suttle squatted beside her. She'd been crying. He knew it. Another first.

'What's happened?'

'I don't know.' She clung to him. 'I just don't know.'

'Shit.' He held her close. 'Tell me. Just tell me.'

'There's nothing to tell. I'm just … Fuck …' Her hand felt

blindly for the tissues balled beside her. 'This is horrible ... I'm sorry ... I'm really sorry.'

'But what is it? Tell me. What's happened?'

She began to cry again, gulping for air, real pain, real misery. Suttle tried to get to his feet but she wouldn't let go. Grace couldn't take her eyes off her.

At last she released her grip. Her face was shiny with tears.

'I'm useless,' she whispered. 'Totally pathetic. Ignore me. Forget it. I'm sorry to get you back like this.'

'I was coming home anyway,' Suttle pointed out.

'I know but ...' She sniffed. 'This is the last bloody thing you need.'

Suttle struggled to his feet and she stared up at him then turned her head away. Grace was agitated now, shaking the wooden bars of her pen in bewilderment. Suttle lifted her up and gave her a cuddle. She struggled in his arms. She wanted to be with her mum.

Lizzie reached out, taking the baby.

'It's on the table,' she said.

Suttle found her mobile. It was still switched on. He read the message.

'Who's this from?'

'Gill.'

'Gill Reynolds?'

'Yes.'

'And she wants to come down?'

'She *is* coming down.'

'You said yes?'

'I did.'

'Shit.'

'Quite.'

Suttle absorbed the news. He'd never had any patience with Reynolds. Once you got past the obvious there was nothing there but self-obsession. As long as she'd just been a mate of Lizzie's, Suttle had bitten his tongue, but after what happened to Joe Faraday he'd consciously blanked the woman from his life.

'I'll cancel her,' he said. 'Leave it to me.'

'I've tried.'

'When?'

'This afternoon. I gave myself a talking-to. I knew you wouldn't want her down. It took me for ever to make the call but in the end I did it.'

'And?'

'It made no difference. You know what she's like. She never listens.' She took a deep breath and held Grace tight. 'Tomorrow morning. Around twelve.'

'I'll phone her again.'

'It's pointless. You could go one better though.'

'How?'

'By being here.'

Suttle thought about it, tallying the work he had to get through by lunchtime. Day two of *Constantine*. No chance.

'I can't, my love.'

'You could. If it was that important.'

'Of course it's important. You're important. You're both important. All this is important. But I can't just—' He broke off. 'Leave it to me. I'll phone her.'

Lizzie began to protest again, telling him she'd cope somehow, but Suttle wasn't listening. The weakness of the signal drove him onto the patio. It was a beautiful evening, the sun sinking in the west, the wind beginning to die. They'd discovered a troop of ducklings on the stream at the bottom of the garden only yesterday. Suttle could hear them pestering their mother.

'Gill?' Suttle could feel the patio slabs moving under his weight. 'Is that you?'

'Of course it is. Jimmy?' She sounded surprised.

'Yeah, me. Listen. Something's come up. Lizzie's not too good. Some kind of bug. She'd never tell you in a million years but I honestly think—'

73

Gill broke in. She had a habit of ignoring the end of other peoples' sentences.

'She sounded fine this afternoon. It won't be a problem. You know me. Iron constitution.'

'It's not you I'm worried about. It's Lizzie. She needs—'

'I know what she needs. I know that girl like a sister. I probably know her better than you do. I expect she needs a bit of TLC. I'm good with that. Just ask her.'

Suttle wasn't having it. It was flu. Definitely. Lizzie needed peace and quiet. She needed to be left alone. Please, Gill. Just this once.

There was a brief silence on the line. The mother duck had mounted the bank, an unsteady line of fluffy nothings behind her. Under any other circumstances this would have been a precious moment. He'd run for the camera. Grace. Lizzie. The ducklings. One for the family scrapbook. Then Gill was back. There was something new in her voice, a definite edge.

'I'll be there for lunch, Jimmy. You won't regret it.'

'I beg your pardon?'

'You heard what I said. You'll be around too?'

'No.'

'Then I'll stay for dinner. Don't worry. No pressure. I'll sort an Indian or something. Do they have takeaways in the country?' She laughed, then hung up.

Suttle was still staring at the phone. *You won't regret it?*

For a moment he thought about phoning back, upping the ante, going for broke, but then he heard a movement behind him and he turned to find Lizzie standing in the open doorway. She'd heard every word he'd said.

'See?' she said.

'Fucking woman.' Suttle risked a smile. 'We're doomed.'

They didn't talk until later. Suttle had bathed and changed Grace, leaving Lizzie to do her best with a packet of pasta and what was left in the vegetable basket. After he'd put his daughter down and blown on the mobile over her bed, he drove down to the village store and bought a bottle of Chianti. The wine turned out to be on special so he grabbed another before returning to Chantry Cottage.

Lizzie had made a definite effort with the pasta. She'd even found a candle to soften the overhead light in the gloom of the living room. Suttle uncorked the Chianti and poured two glasses, raising his own in a toast.

'To us.'

They touched glasses but then Lizzie put hers down.

'Something wrong?'

She smiled. For some reason she seemed to find the question genuinely funny.

'You want a list?' she said.

'Yeah. Since you ask.'

'No, you don't. And I'm sorry. I'm really, really sorry. I'm supposed to be better than this.'

'You're lovely. I love you.'

'Really?'

'Yeah, really. I know I'm not, you know ...'

'Here much?'

'Yeah.'

'It's not that. It's this. All of it.'

'What?'

'Everything.' She made a vague, circular motion with her hand. 'You, me, Grace, this horrible cottage, the country, the rain, the silence – it's driving me nuts, Jimmy. I just don't know who I am any more. Have you ever had that feeling? Not knowing what's happening to you? Not knowing if it's ever going to stop? I'm out of tune, my love. I'm not me any more. Do you know what I'm talking about? Has something like this ever happened to you?'

Suttle had to shake his head. Life had dealt him a number of evil hands. Twice he'd been hospitalised after making the wrong call in dodgy circumstances, once in the Job and once in his private life. That had hurt, sure, but he'd never suffered anything remotely like this.

'I'm sorry,' he said. 'I'm really, really sorry.'

'Sorry doesn't cut it. Not any longer. I've got to *do* something, Jimmy. I've got to take some decisions.'

'About?'

'Us.'

'Ah.' Suttle's head went back. He reached for his glass. For the first time he realised they were facing something really serious. Not once had he ever thought she might leave him.

'Is it me?' he said at last. 'Be honest.'

'Yes, in a way it is. Because this, all this, is you. You love it. I can see you love it. You love the country, the space, the fresh air. Even the fucking rain seems to turn you on. Me? I loathe it.'

'Then we'll move.'

'Where to?'

'Somewhere the roof doesn't leak. Somewhere with windows that fit. Somewhere mouse-proof.'

'In the country?'

Suttle didn't answer. Just looked at her. The silence stretched and stretched. She'd said her piece. The situation couldn't have been clearer.

'You want to live in a town,' he said. 'Or a city.'

'Yes, please.'

'Plymouth? Exeter?'

'I don't care. Pompey, if I have to.'

'That sounds like a threat.'

'You're right. That's where I am. Mrs Desperate. Dreaming of Copnor Bridge.' She smiled and reached for his hand across the table, throwing Suttle into confusion. He was lost now. Was she really packing her bags? Were they really headed for some shitty ground-floor flat in a gutty part of Guz?

He voiced the thought aloud. Cards on the table.

'Guz?' she said blankly.

'Plymouth. It's what the locals call the place. Tells you everything you need to know.'

'I see.' She was toying with her glass. 'How come the ground-floor flat?'

'Because it's all we could afford. I've been round this course before. Prices are astronomic down here.'

'Dearer than Pompey?'

'Big time.'

She nodded, then took a tiny sip of wine. Maybe she's not aware of all the implications, thought Suttle. Maybe this isn't quite as dire as I thought.

Wrong.

'I talked to Gill for quite a while this afternoon,' she said softly. 'We had a proper conversation for once.'

'And?'

'She's just moved into a new flat. Three bedrooms? In Southsea? Can you believe that? It turns out they gave her a rise. She's mad about the place. It's even got a bit of garden. She says it's lovely.'

Suttle's heart sank. The implications couldn't be clearer.

'You're telling me you'd move in with her?'

'Either that or my mum's, yes.'

'Both of you?'

'Obviously.'

Suttle stared at her, not quite believing his ears. Lizzie and Grace? Camping out with Gill fucking *Reynolds*?

'Cheers,' he said, reaching for his glass.

Lizzie waited for him to swallow a mouthful or two. Then she leaned forward across the table. She wanted him to be reasonable. She wanted him to understand.

'Think about it. My job's still open if I want it. I could go back to work, earn us a bit of money, give us some options.'

'And Grace?'

'My mum would look after her.'

'You've asked her?'

77

'No. But she would, I know she would.'

'So how long would this ...' Suttle shrugged '... go on for?'

'For as long as it takes. Until we had a decent stash.'

'That could be years.'

'Yeah. It could.'

'Living apart? Me down here? You back in Pompey?'

'Yeah. Unless you did what I'd do.'

'Go back to my old job?'

'Exactly.'

'I doubt they'd have me.'

'Of course they'd have you. You're the guy who put Mackenzie away. Local hero, you.'

'No.' Suttle shook his head. 'Going back never works, never.'

'How do you know? When you've never tried it?'

'Because I wouldn't. No way. You go on in life. You look forward.'

'So what does that make me?'

'Good question.'

Silence again. Upstairs, Suttle could hear Grace beginning to grumble. If you caught her early enough you could head off the tears and get her back to sleep. He was half out of his chair but Lizzie beat him to it.

'Leave it to me.'

Suttle listened to her footsteps on the stairs. All the earlier drama seemed to have gone. This was a different Lizzie. She must have been planning something like this for weeks, maybe months. He should have seen it coming. He should have headed it off.

He poured himself another glass of wine. By the time Lizzie was back at the table, his glass was empty again.

'Well?' she said.

Suttle began to talk. He told her about *Constantine*, about the lone dog walker from Exmouth Quays finding Kinsey's body sprawled on the promenade, about his involvement with the rowing club, and about the investigative pathways Suttle had to start exploring first thing tomorrow. Despite herself, Lizzie found herself engaged. At heart she was still a journalist. Stories like this had always fascinated her.

'So what do you think?' she asked.

'Honestly?'

'Honestly.'

'I think somebody killed him. I haven't a clue who and I might well be wrong, but that's not the point. Hunch isn't a word my bosses have much time for. They prefer evidence.'

'And?'

'There isn't any. Not yet.'

Lizzie reached for his hand again. In the early days he'd often let her into the world of the Job, sharing odd titbits from ongoing investigations, and she'd always loved him for it. It was an act of trust. It made her feel special. It made her feel loved. Lately all that had stopped. These days Jimmy very rarely talked about his work. Now this.

'So how do you –' she reached for her glass '– progress something like this?'

'By grafting. By looking. By building the intel picture. By establishing a timeline. By wondering about motive and opportunity. By getting inside this guy's head.'

'The killer's?'

'Kinsey's.'

'And then the killer?'

'Maybe …' he nodded '… if it pans out that way.'

'But it will, won't it? You're good at this. Paul thought you were the best.'

Lizzie was the only person Suttle knew who always called Winter by his Christian name. Winter had a famously soft spot for Lizzie. He'd once told Suttle she was the only journalist in the city with real bollocks. At the time Suttle hadn't known quite what to make of the comment but in time he recognised it as a shrewd judgement. Winter was right. This lovely wife of his rarely lost her nerve.

Now she wanted to know more about Kinsey. Suttle shook his head. He'd said enough.

'Then why bring all this up?'

'Because of the rowing. I've spent most of the day talking to people who are crazy about it.'

'And?'

'I think you should have a go.'

'*Me?*'

'Yeah. Why not? You need to get out, my love. You need to put this place behind you once in a while. I'm sure running helps but maybe it's not enough.'

'Running round here is crap. Grace obviously comes too. I do my best with the buggy but on these roads you take your life in your hands.'

'Lives. Plural.'

'Exactly.'

'OK.' Suttle nodded. 'So maybe I'm right. So maybe rowing's the answer.'

Lizzie wasn't at all sure. Suttle could see it in her face. She'd started this conversation with her bags practically packed. Now this husband of hers was talking about some rowing club.

'How would it work?'

Suttle explained about the trial offer, three free rows. Suttle would drive her down to Exmouth next Sunday, and if her maiden voyage worked out OK then she could return for the club sessions on Tuesday and Thursday night.

'But what about Grace?'

'I'd look after her.'

'You'd get back in time?'

'Of course I would.'

She nodded, doing her best to fight her excitement. She'd always relished a challenge.

'Does anyone know about this?'

'About what?'

'About your missus maybe joining up? Only the way I read it most of your suspects belong to the club.'

Suttle had the grace to laugh. In truth, he hadn't thought this thing through at all. Not properly.

'So what would you prefer?' he said. 'How would you want to play it?'

'I'd need to be me,' she said. 'Lizzie Hodson.'

'Not some copper's wife?'

'Exactly.'

'Fine.' He shrugged. 'In that case you'd drive yourself down on Sunday. Use the TomTom. There's no drama finding the place.'

'And you'd really stay behind? With Grace?'

'Of course.'

'Do the washing? Sort the cat out? Peel the spuds? Mend the fucking door? Not go mad?'

'No problem.'

'And you're telling me it's not a hard thing to do? Rowing?'

'I'm telling you you might like it. I'm telling you you might love it. And I'm telling you it's the least we can do.'

'To keep this thing afloat?'

'Exactly.'

Lizzie pondered the proposition, then emptied her glass and reached for the bottle. Her turn to propose a toast.

'Here's to Guz,' she said.

'Meaning?'

'We'll see.'

Two

Lizzie woke early on Monday morning, recognising a sound she dreaded. In the distance, coming down the lane outside the cottage, she could hear a squad of young marines from the nearby Commando Training Centre at Lympstone. They spent all night on Woodbury Common, doing God knows what, and then jogged down through the village to be picked up by trucks at first light. When she'd first got used to this early-morning wake-up call, she'd thought it mildly quaint. If Grace had woken early, they'd stand at the window and wave as the young lads sped by. But then she'd realised that the rhythm of all these boots could tell her what the weather was doing. And this morning, as the *splash-splash* of the approaching squad grew louder, she knew it was raining again.

She closed her eyes, willing herself back to sleep, telling herself that it was a passing shower, that she'd wake later to bright sunshine and maybe the prospect of a new chapter in this life of theirs. Sleep came more quickly than she expected, and she woke again an hour or so later, reaching for Jimmy's hand under the sheet, but he'd gone. Downstairs, the kettle and the teapot were still hot to her touch and she realised that the growl of the car that had woken her up was probably the Impreza. She checked the clock on the wall: 07.03. Even earlier than usual.

*

Suttle was at Exmouth nick by half seven. To his surprise, Carole Houghton was already at her desk, busy on the phone. Suttle sorted a couple of coffees from the adjoining kitchenette. By the time he got back, Houghton had finished her call.

'We found Pendrick,' she said. 'He turned up last night.'

'Where?'

'Back home at his place. He told us he never checks his phone. Not on Sundays.'

Pendrick, she said, had evidently gone to north Cornwall in search of some decent surf. He'd returned late afternoon and gone down to the rowing club to use one of their single sculls. You couldn't waste a sunset like last night's, he'd told the D/C.

'We get the feeling he likes exercise.' Houghton was reaching for a pad of jotted notes.

Suttle was back on the seafront at Exmouth, watching the lone sculler in the red singlet powering back on the flooding tide. This had to be Pendrick, he thought. Had to be.

'So what did he tell us?'

'Not a lot, to be frank. He confirmed all the other accounts. They won the race, came back, got pissed, went over to Kinsey's place. Kinsey, as we know, started throwing up off the balcony. Pendrick thought he'd gone out for a breath of air. He put the guy to bed and soon afterwards they all left in a taxi. Pendrick was the first to be dropped off.'

Pendrick, she said, lived alone in an upstairs flat in an area of Exmouth known as the Colonies. Saturday night the flat below was empty. One of his neighbours in the terrace had heard the taxi arriving but had gone to bed shortly afterwards. Pendrick had stayed up a while to check out the weather on his PC and watch the first half of a DVD. He'd been out of the house by eight the next morning to catch the tide at Widemouth Bay. The surf, he'd told the D/C, had been crap. He'd tried other beaches further north but had drawn a blank. Hence his visit to the rowing club.

Suttle wanted to know what the interviewing D/Cs had made of Pendrick.

'They thought he sounded pretty credible.'

'Was he surprised? About Kinsey?'

'Yes, apparently he was.'

'Upset?'

'The guys think not but we can't do him for that, can we?'

Suttle smiled. The coffee was horrible. He was trying to imagine this man, trying to get beyond the slumped figure in the red singlet. How did he present himself? What kind of place did he live in?

'Very tidy, very together. Andy says the guy reads a lot. Loads of music too, neat little sound system. Not too much furniture but loads of photos on the wall. Apparently the man's surfed everywhere: California, Oz, New Zealand, Hawaii, the lot. Been around a bit.'

Suttle nodded. Simon Maffett was one of the older D/Cs on the squad, an ex-marine who'd put in a couple of decent years on the force rugby fifteen until his knees gave out and his missus persuaded him to chuck it in. Andy could build a rapport as quickly as any detective Suttle had met. He also knew a thing or two about pushing the physical limits. Pendrick, Suttle suspected, would have recognised a fellow soul.

'What else did he say about Kinsey?'

'Not a lot. Like I say, Andy got the impression there was no love lost but he didn't press him.'

'And the rowing?'

'He loves it. Nearly as much as surfing.' Houghton paused, a rare smile on her face, and Suttle realised there was something she was holding back.

'Well?' he said. 'What else?'

'Pendrick? Doesn't the name mean anything to you?'

Suttle shook his head, remembering the prickle of recognition he'd felt when he'd seen the slightly scary face in the photo Houghton had circulated but failing to suss exactly why.

'Tell me.'

'It was last year. Summer. June 24 to be exact. I just looked it up on CIS. You remember the bloke who rowed the Atlantic and lost his wife en route? That was Pendrick.'

CIS was force-speak for the Crime Information System, a database that listed everyone who'd appeared on the Devon and Cornwall radar. Suttle had it now. The story had been all over the media. The couple had been rowing west to east. They'd made the Western Approaches after God knows how long at sea and Pendrick had woken up early one morning to find his wife missing. He'd alerted the Coastguard, and the rescue centre at Falmouth had coordinated an air search that had lasted a couple of days before being called off. At this point Pendrick could have made a landing in southern Ireland or been retrieved by any number of ships in the area, but he'd insisted on completing his voyage alone, ending up in Penzance Harbour, fighting for balance on the quayside as media crews battled for a word or two.

'He had hair then,' Suttle said. 'Lots of it. Hippy-looking guy. Never said much.'

'You're right. A couple of the uniforms at PZ took a statement, and there was a longer interview afterwards, CID this time.' Houghton scribbled a name and slipped it across the desk. Suttle stared at it. D/I Gina Hamilton. Another face from the past.

'You know her?'

'Yeah. Not well, but yeah.'

Hamilton, he said, had been part of a Devon and Cornwall intel operation a couple of years back. They had a bunch of local dealers plotted up and had successfully traced a supply source back to a Spanish fishing port called Cambados in Galicia. The cocaine, lots of it, was coming into the UK through Portsmouth, and Suttle, then a D/C, had been tasked to give her whatever assistance she needed when she drove east to coordinate the surveillance.

In the event Ms Hamilton been impressively well organised and the operation had ended with a meticulously planned hard arrest on Honiton bypass. The Drugs Squad had actioned a whole pile of warrants that same night, scooping up dealers across the entire force area. Hamilton herself had made a bit of an impact up in the social club at Fratton nick. Tall, blonde, nice leather jacket, bit of a looker. Even Faraday had been impressed.

'You know her?' Suttle asked.

'Of course.'

'Wouldn't have done her any harm, that job.'

'It didn't.'

'But?'

'But nothing.' Houghton nodded at the contact details. 'You might want a conversation. I gather she did the interview with Pendrick herself.'

Minutes later, Houghton was gone. She had a meet with Nandy at force HQ in Exeter, and then she was due at the Royal Devon and Exeter Hospital for the post-mortem on Kinsey. She'd be back, fingers crossed, in time for a bite of lunch. By which time, the future of *Constantine* might be a great deal clearer.

Suttle went through the morning's tasking for Houghton's squad of D/Cs. In truth, the guys were already beginning to run out of doors to knock on and Suttle knew that the preliminary findings from the PM would probably be decisive. Evidence of injury to Kinsey before the fall would bump up the enquiry to a full murder investigation. Anything else, especially with Nandy at the helm, might well be curtains.

Already Suttle had started the process of applying for the dead man's financial records, plus billing on his landline and mobile. It would be a day or two before the banks and the phone companies came through with anything solid and in the meantime Suttle needed to get a feel for exactly how this man had led his life. What did he do for a living? Where had his money come from? And who else might have shared his life in Regatta Court?

By late morning, with the help of a couple of phone calls, Suttle had the answers to most of these questions. Kinsey, it turned out, had been an engineer. For a while he'd worked for Boeing in Seattle. Afterwards, still living in the States, he'd run a one-man consultancy, Kittiwake, which specialised in wind-turbine technology. He'd come up with a new way of configuring the power train that converted blade movement to grid-ready electricity, and had sold the process to a major international corporation with operations across the globe. The proceeds of this deal appeared nowhere in the files at Suttle's disposal but a conversation with a contact in the Department for Business, Innovation and Skills put the figure at not less than $35 million. In three short years Kinsey had made himself a very rich man.

At this point, though, his success had been evidently soured by two developments. An industrial competitor, in the shape of a Swiss engineer called Henri Laffont, had threatened to sue Kinsey for patent infringement. Laffont claimed that Kinsey had ripped off key elements of his own wind-turbine design and owed him compensation that would have taken a huge bite out of the $35 million.

As far as Suttle could judge, this was an ongoing battle. Kinsey had refused Laffont's claims point blank and hired a firm of expensive commercial lawyers, Zurich-based, to put the Swiss engineer back in his box. The last email in the file was dated 8 February 2011, barely two months ago. Laffont, it seemed, was currently working on a contract in Shanghai. He was due to fly into London 'in early April' and was demanding a meet. He was tired of dealing through attorneys and suggested they could sort out a settlement, amicable or otherwise, face to face. Kinsey didn't seem to have replied to this suggestion but Suttle made a note to check on the seized PC. 'Amicable or otherwise' was an interesting phrase and he ringed it before putting the file aside.

Kinsey's other source of grief was his ex-wife. He'd met Sonya in Seattle. Her half-brother lived in Bristol. Suttle had found a phone number in one of Kinsey's files and given him a ring. Sonya, of course, needed to be made aware of Kinsey's death, but the brother-in-law, whose name was Bill, was more than happy to fill in a little of the background.

His half-sister, he said, had been making a decent living in the real estate business when she married Kinsey, but the crash of 2008–9 had wiped her out. At this point Kinsey had decided to return to the UK to look for new business opportunities. With some reluctance Sonya followed, but the marriage was a disaster. After less than a year, she'd maxed out her credit cards, emptied the joint bank account, left a pile of plastic on Kinsey's desk and flown back to Seattle. Since then she'd been fighting to extract every last cent from the divorce settlement. Even now, said Bill, she was still harassing Jay for money, and lately her demands had escalated. Only last week, to his certain knowledge, she'd been threatening to pay her ex-husband a personal visit.

Surprised by his candour, Suttle had asked Bill how things were between himself and his half-sister.

'You want the truth?' he'd said. 'Those two folks deserved each other. Anything for money. And I mean anything.'

'Do you see her at all, Sonya? Fly over for the occasional visit maybe?'

'Never.'

'And Kinsey?'

'I wouldn't spend a second with the guy. You've got an experience to share with him? A holiday, maybe? A trip to some nice Polynesian island? He's been there already, probably owns the place. You're proud of your new Prius? Want to show off about it a little? He tells you you've just made the dumbest purchase of your life. He knew everything about everything.

He just didn't need the other ten trillion people on the planet. This is a guy happiest in his own company. This stuff about the rowing is news to me. Those other guys must have had a lot of patience.'

The conversation had ended shortly afterwards. Reviewing his notes, Suttle knew he'd unearthed two fresh lines of enquiry, both of which needed serious attention. A multi-million-dollar settlement for patent infringement might offer ample motivation for a personal visit, while a vengeful ex-wife – under the right circumstances – could do worse than dump her ex-husband off his fifth-floor balcony.

He was still deciding how to develop each of these when Houghton returned. She eyed the spread of paperwork on Suttle's desk. He brought her up to speed. Two more potential suspects for the pot. Maybe.

'But what has he been doing since selling up?'

'Property development.'

'Where? How?'

'He's got a new company now, Kittiwake Oceanside. He seems to be catering to a particular demographic. These are couples in their sixties, made a bit of money – often in London – and they want to buy somewhere down here, nice view, private beach, total privacy, total peace of mind, full service, like-minded people, all that bollocks. Think retirement lite.'

Suttle had skimmed the Kittiwake files. Kinsey had been paying estate agents in Cornwall to scout for suitable sites. So far he'd identified three and was in ongoing contact with the relevant planning authorities. In every case his pitch was the same. As a successful businessman committed to developments of the highest standard, he was keen – in his phrase – to add value to outstanding locations. In this context, he defined value in terms of employment opportunities, net capital inflows and what he called 'the aesthetic and social gain from the provision of signature destinations'.

Kittiwake Oceanside, he said, would attract high net worth individuals to areas of Cornwall that were demonstrably struggling. These discreet, beautifully designed retirement communities would kick-start the local economy. From every point of view, he wrote, 'we're looking at the perfect win-win'.

Houghton was studying one of the brochures Suttle had extracted from the Kittiwake files. A sleek collection of apartment blocks towered above a line of sand dunes. There was lots of glass, lots of boasts about sustainability, and lots of hints that slouching in front of crap telly was strictly for losers. Couples playing tennis. A peleton of gym-honed retirees departing for a spin on their bikes. A woman in a bikini heading for the nearby surf. Kittiwake Oceanside, thought Suttle, was selling a kind of immortality. Settle here and your body will never let you down.

'I wonder what the locals think?' Houghton was equally unimpressed.

'Exactly. Maybe we should talk to the local journos and find out. People are getting pissed off with tosh like this. Views are for everyone. They shouldn't be something you have to reserve with a huge deposit.'

'Sweet. Where have you been these last few years?'

Suttle ignored the question. He sensed already that *Constantine* was dead in the water.

'So what happened at the PM?'

'Nothing. The guy died of impact injuries. Cranial contusions, severe spinal trauma and heart failure. Quick, if you're looking for a way out.'

'And you think he was?'

'There's no evidence to suggest otherwise.'

Suttle nodded. Post-mortems were never less than thorough. Scrapings from under the fingernails to indicate some kind of resistance. Special attention to the throat and larynx to determine possible strangulation. Try as he might to find evidence of prior assault, the pathologist had drawn a blank. Houghton was right: there was absolutely nothing to suggest that Kinsey hadn't been alone when he met his death.

'But why?' Suttle asked, 'Why would he have done it?'

Houghton shrugged. 'Not our call, Jimmy. People do what they do.'

'And Mr Nandy?'

'I haven't managed to talk to him yet. We've got a body in a field down near Bodmin. It hasn't got a head. I expect Mr Nandy thinks that's a bit of a clue.'

Gill Reynolds turned up just before lunch. Lizzie, deeply grateful that the sun had come out, met her on the patch of muddy gravel that served as parking for Chantry Cottage. She was driving a new-looking scarlet Megane convertible, a perfect match for her nails. Newsroom pay rates were clearly on the up.

She swung her long legs out of the car and leaned back to retrieve a bag of goodies. Lizzie had Grace beside her. When Gill knelt for a kiss Grace turned away and hid her face in Lizzie's jeans, plainly terrified by this sudden intrusion.

'Lunch?' Lizzie led Grace back towards the open kitchen door, determined to stay ahead of the game. Even when she was fit and well, doing a job she loved, Gill had always had a habit of swamping her.

The kitchen, for once, looked almost presentable. Lizzie had worked all morning to clean the place up. There was nothing she could do about the dripping tap and the state of the units, but she'd brightened the general shabbiness with the last of the daffodils from the garden and she had a pot of chilli con carne bubbling on the stove. Gill had a famous appetite, a tribute to her hours at the gym.

With the chilli went hunks of newly baked bread and a salad Lizzie had bought from the village store. Gill was in the garden, striding through the long grass, peering into a hedgerow, stooping to retrieve something from the reeds beside the stream. Frothy white blossom was beginning to appear on both fruit trees and she paused, gazing up, her face splashed with sunshine.

Seconds later, she was at the kitchen door.

'Fantastic,' she announced. 'So wild. So unspoiled. So fuck-ing *authentic*. Lucky girl. Lucky old you. You have to keep it exactly this way. Promise me you will.'

Lizzie smiled but said nothing. She was tempted to suggest that Gill stay a while, get a real taste of life in the country, see whether she could cope with the isolation and the damp and the mobile signal that seemed to come and go like the wind. Instead she perched Grace in her high chair and dished out the chilli.

Gill had already started on office gossip. It seemed there'd been a big turnover of staff recently, and most of the new people Lizzie had never heard of, but Gill – as ever – had identified a target or two and was currently shagging a married man in his thirties who worked on the sports desk. Three times a week they'd been meeting at the leisure centre for a midday game of squash. Lately they'd given up on the squash and gone straight back to Gill's new place.

'The guy goes at it like a madman,' she said. 'The squash used to knacker me but this is ridiculous.'

She paused to try and tease a spoonful of chilli into Grace's mouth. Sex was the closest Gill had got to ever having babies and she'd always been clueless about the dos and don'ts of motherhood. Grace spat the chilli out and started to cry.

Gill seemed oblivious. A couple of months back she'd been offered the kind of feature pieces that had always gone Lizzie's way and she'd leapt at the chance. Her speciality just now was celebrity interviews, and she was speculating on the chances of bedding a soap star Lizzie had never heard of when she remembered a call she had to make.

Lizzie was still trying to settle Grace. Gill poked at her Blackberry, not understanding why it wouldn't respond.

'You have to take it outside,' Lizzie said. 'Point it at the sun and hope for the best.'

'You're not serious.'

'I am.'

'What about the laptop? Have you got broadband?'

'Dial-up.'

'*Dial-up?* Christ. You'll be sending pigeons next.'

Lizzie offered her landline but Gill was already out of the door. Minutes later she was back. Pointing it at the sun had evidently worked. She'd also remembered there was someone else in the room, another life, so different to hers.

'So tell me,' she said. 'How's it going?'

Lizzie had been anticipating this question all morning. In truth she'd have liked nothing better than to get the whole thing off her chest but she was determined to hang on to what was left of her dignity.

'It's fine,' she said. 'Just different.'

'You hate it.'

'That's not what I said.'

'You don't have to. I can see it on your face. So let's start again. What's it *really* like?'

Lizzie was nonplussed. This was the last thing she'd expected. Gill Reynolds, it turned out, was infinitely more tuned-in than she'd ever remembered. No wonder they'd given her promotion.

'You want the truth? It's a nightmare.'

She talked about what she'd found when they'd first moved down. She described the state of the cottage, and the garden, and the life she seemed incapable of putting together when her husband was at work. She told Gill about Christmas, two long days of unrelieved gloom while Jimmy tried to coax a little heat from the fire. And then she brought the story up to date. She'd decided she was a lousy wife and – even worse – a hopeless mother. By giving in to Jimmy, by agreeing to go along with his rural fantasy, she'd probably inflicted untold damage on her daughter. Kids were smart. They sensed when things were going wrong. For her sake and for Grace's, before it was too late, she needed to take a few decisions.

'You'll *leave* him?'

'Not him, Gill. This. I'll leave this. We both will, me and Grace. It's beaten us. I've tried. Believe me I've tried. I've *really* tried. But every time I think I'm getting somewhere something else kicks off and I'm back where I started. Central heating? Windows that fit? Maybe a little car to get out in? Is that too much to ask?'

Gill was trying to think this thing through. Another novelty.

'Maybe you haven't tried hard enough,' she said at last.

'That's an insult.'

'No, it's not. Of course this is different. You must have expected that. No way is this Fratton or Southsea or wherever. It's the country, Lou. Different mindset. Different everything. Like I say, try harder. *Adapt.*'

'Christ …' Lizzie turned away. She had an overpowering urge to cry again. Then came an arm round her shoulders.

'I believe you, Lou. I really do. I'm just thinking about the alternative, that's all. Where will you go? What will you do?'

Lizzie was back in control of herself. She apologised for losing it and began to get to her feet.

'Don't.' Gill put out a restraining hand. 'Just answer my question. What will you *do*?'

Lizzie gazed at her for a long moment. The fact was she didn't know. On the phone yesterday she'd nearly asked Gill whether there was room for them at this new place of hers but in the end she'd drawn back. That wasn't something she'd shared with Jimmy last night but it hadn't seemed to matter because she'd assumed Gill's answer would be yes. Now she wasn't so sure.

'You're think of coming back?' Once again Gill was ahead of the game. 'Staying at my place?'

'It had crossed my mind, yes.'

'Forget it, Lou. It won't happen.'

'Why?'

'It just won't.'

'You don't want us?'

'Of course I want you. That's not the issue.'

'So what is? I don't understand.'

Gill studied her, then shook her head. No clues. No conferring.

'We'll go to my mum's then.' Lizzie was getting angry again. 'She'll definitely have us.'

'Not a great idea.'

'But why? Is it the job?'

'The job's fine. I'm sure the job's yours for the asking. It's just ...' She shrugged, picked at her chilli, then looked up again. 'Never go backwards, Lou. It never works.'

'That's what Jimmy said.'

'Then believe him. He's right. One way or another you have to make this work.' She paused. 'Is the seaside near here? Only I really fancy a walk on the beach.'

By mid-afternoon, Jimmy Suttle suspected it was all over. He'd tasked a handful of D/Cs to start exploring the new lines of enquiry – Henri Laffont and Kinsey's vengeful ex-wife – but Nandy was due any time and Suttle knew that Houghton would have told him about the post-mortem. These days, through no fault of his own, Nandy had become a juggler, forever trying to keep all the force's investigative balls in the air. As calls increased on precious Major Crime resources, there were balls he knew he'd have to put to one side, and while he'd never abandon an enquiry that showed genuine promise, he was bound by the iron demands of the Criminal Prosecution Service. No one had ever invented a form for a hunch, and if there was no evidence to suggest that Kinsey had died at someone else's hands, then Detective Superintendent Nandy would be moving swiftly on.

He arrived at the makeshift office within the hour. Suttle briefed him on the problems Kinsey had been facing in his business and personal life and tallied the actions he'd commissioned to find out more. Nandy nodded, unimpressed. No one, he said, got that rich without making enemies. That was one of the joys of capitalism, something you could rely on, but from where he was sitting there wasn't a particle of evidence that a pissed-off Swiss engineer or a homicidal ex-wife had chucked Kinsey into oblivion. The thing just didn't fly. While he was happy to have Suttle's D/Cs complete their preliminary enquiries in both instances, he was minded to redeploy the rest of the squad.

'Including me, sir?'

'No.' Nandy closed the door. 'Carole tells me you've been under some pressure lately.'

'Does she?' Suttle was astonished.

'Yeah. Not much gets by her, believe me. You should be grateful, son.' He paused. 'Everything OK at home?'

'Yeah …' Suttle ducked his head. 'More or less.'

'Good to hear it. From tomorrow onwards I want you to take over the *Constantine* file and prepare it for the Coroner. We're looking at a couple of weeks, max. That's the good news. The bad news is you're on your own. Happy with that?'

'Perfectly.'

'If you really need help D/I Houghton might release D/C Golding on a temporary basis but that's absolutely last resort. We understand each other?'

'Of course.'

'Good. Any questions? Anything you're not clear about?'

Suttle gave the question some thought, then nodded.

'Yes, sir. What happens if …?'

'If what?'

'If I end up believing there's grounds for further investigation?'

'Then you lift the phone –' he offered Suttle the ghost of a smile '– and we crank it all up again.'

It was gone six by the time Lizzie and Gill returned to the rowing club compound. They'd spent the afternoon on the beach at Exmouth, walking the couple of miles past the ochre jut of Orcombe Point and onwards to the distant wall of rock that marked the end of Sandy Bay. It was low tide and the sand was firm underfoot. Oystercatchers were feasting on the weed-strewn rocks at the water's edge and in the distance they could hear the *pock-pock* of live firing from the Royal Marines' range at Straight Point.

Gill's delight at what they'd stumbled on was unfeigned, and even Lizzie had to admit that this stretch of God's coastline was pretty special. Gill had insisted on carrying Grace, who was already getting too big for the chest sling, but she and Gill seemed to be friends at last, and Gill paused every now and again to show her something that had caught her eye. The beach was big and bare and flawless, gleaming as the sun began to sink, and when a couple of horses appeared, clattering awkwardly down the concrete slip from the caravan camp above, the picture was complete. They thundered past, splashing through the shallows, heading back towards Exmouth, and the noise and the movement drew shrieks of pleasure from Grace. Lizzie had remembered to pack a couple of spare bottles and some mashed-up swede in case she got hungry, but as they approached the rowing club she seemed content.

Gill's Megane was parked beyond the compound. Lizzie had told her all about Jimmy's suggestion that she join and Gill was adamant that she should, at the very least, give the thing a try. She was curious about this new departure in Lizzie's life and demanded a look at what lay in store. When they got to the compound, the doors to the clubhouse were open. Lizzie hung back, a little uncertain, but Gill wasn't having it.

'Come,' she said. 'We need to do this.'

Lizzie knew she was right. She negotiated the steps up to the clubhouse and pushed in through the door. The near-darkness took her by surprise. She could make out shapes on the rowing machines, three of them. Slowly, one by one, they came to a halt. They were all women.

Lizzie explained she'd come for a look, apologised for the interruption.

'Not at all. Are you interested?' The nearest woman had got off her machine and extended a hand. She said her name was Tessa. When Lizzie confirmed that she fancied having a go, Tessa grinned.

'No problem.'

'Now?'

'If you like. You don't need the anorak. Runners and jeans are fine. Nothing strenuous. Just the basics.'

Lizzie gave her jacket to Gill. This wasn't at all what she'd expected. She perched on the seat which slid up and down towards a tiny electronic screen. A handle was attached to a flywheel by a chain. The trick, said Tessa, was to use the muscles that really mattered to get the flywheel spinning.

She strapped Lizzie's feet into the footstretchers beneath the screen, asked her to take a pull or two and stepped back to watch. With a glance towards Gill, Lizzie did her bidding. She'd never been on a rowing machine in her life.

'You're bending your arms way too early.' This from Tessa. 'The real power comes from your legs. Push away and use your arms as levers. Only bend them at the end of the stroke. You'll be amazed at how much difference that makes.'

'Difference how?'

'Watch the readout. The figures never lie.'

The other two girls laughed. Too right, they seemed to be saying. Lizzie gave it another go, keeping her arms straight this time. Tessa was right. The numbers zipped forward.

'Much better. But you're holding the handle way too tight. It needs to be loose. Right. That's it. Now concentrate on getting the rhythm. It's a cycle. Your body leans forward, your hands go over your knees, you push back with the legs to take the stroke, you tuck the handle under your ribcage, then it's hands away quickly and you repeat the cycle all over again. Excellent. You're a natural. I didn't catch your name.'

'Lizzie.'

'I'm serious, Lizzie. This could be for you. Am I right, girls?'

There was a murmur of approval. Lizzie was still on the machine, still rowing, trying to get one of the numbers down. According to Tessa this calculated how long she'd take to cover 500 metres. Two minutes seventeen seconds, for a novice, appeared to be OK.

'More than OK. Now give it some welly. We're talking flat out. You've got a minute. After that we stop.'

Lizzie took it as a challenge. She increased her rate, driving hard against the footplate, trying to keep her back straight as she took the stroke, throwing her hands forward, keeping the movement going, chasing the numbers on the readout. By now she was fighting for breath, the lactic acid beginning to scald the muscles in her calves and thighs, the numbers dancing in front of her eyes. She could feel the sweat beneath her T-shirt, on her face. Two minutes ten. Two minutes seven. Two minutes six.

'Twenty seconds to go, Lizzie. Work for it. *Want* it.'

She shut her eyes, pushing ever harder. She was hurting now and the sheer effort lifted her bum from the seat at the start of every stroke. Then it was over and she slumped on the seat, sucking in the cold air, aware of the whine of the flywheel as it began to slow.

From somewhere above her came a noise she dimly recognised as applause. All the girls were clapping. Gill was clapping. Even Grace looked pleased. Lizzie grinned, trying to get to her feet. She hadn't felt so good, so complete, for months.

'Thank you, ladies,' she managed.

Tessa helped her up, said she'd done well, better than well, then her attention was caught by a movement in the doorway and Lizzie turned to see someone else silhouetted against the brightness of the sunshine outside. It was a man, tall, broad-shouldered, perfectly still. He was wearing shorts and a red singlet. He didn't have much hair.

'This is Tom.' Tessa laughed. 'Impress him, and you'll never look back.'

On the way home Suttle made a detour to Pendrick's flat. He was still in two minds about Nandy's real motivation in charging him with the preparation of a file for the Coroner. A task like this usually fell to a D/C, and something in Nandy's manner told him there was more to this decision that met the eye. Maybe Nandy wasn't convinced that *Constantine* had really hit the buffers. Maybe this was a clever move to keep the investigation at least semi-active. Either way, he didn't much care. Suttle had never had a problem working by himself. On the contrary, he rather enjoyed it.

Pendrick lived in the top half of a terraced house a couple of minutes' drive from the nick. A sign in the downstairs window read, *Dominic Widdows – Chiropractor. For appointments ring 01395 268078*. Suttle made a note of the name and number and rang Pendrick's bell. No reply. He rang again. Nothing. He stepped back into the road, gazing up at the top window. The curtains were pulled tight against the world outside.

Suttle drove home. Expecting to find evidence of Gill, he was surprised to find the parking area empty. He killed the engine and checked his watch. Nearly seven. He sat in the Impreza a moment, aware of the acids churning in his stomach. It's a beautiful evening, he told himself. They've gone for a walk.

The house was locked. He fumbled for his key, pushed at the door and stepped into the kitchen. Plates were piled in the sink and the remains of a chilli con carne had crusted in the saucepan. He wondered about a note but found nothing. There were still a couple of Stellas in the fridge. He fetched one out and snapped open the tinnie, trying to resist the obvious conclusion. Lizzie had spent the morning packing. Gill had arrived. Lunch would have been over in no time at all. Lizzie had strapped the baby in the back of Gill's car, stuffed her bags in the boot, and all three of them had fucked off back to Pompey. Job done. Game over. End of.

At this time in the evening a long low slant of sunshine added a rare warmth to the kitchen. Suttle inched his chair sideways, taking full advantage, reaching for the tinnie again. Was this what was left of his marriage? A sink full of washing-up and a spoonful or two of cold mince? He fought the hollowness inside, knowing that life banged up by himself would be a hard ask. He'd miss Lizzie like hell. He'd probably miss Grace even more. Family life, with all its imperfections, was what softened his working days. He was lucky enough to love what he did for a living, at least most of the time, but never for a second did he kid himself that it was enough.

Over the years he'd met countless cops who'd let the Job drive everything else out of their lives, and in every case they'd come to regret it. These were the guys suggesting a drink or two in the pub around the corner after work. These were the loners desperate for company and a listening ear. Suttle had always resisted these invitations, telling himself he'd never make the same mistake, but now – for the first time – he realised how easy it was to miss the obvious clues. He was a detective, for fuck's sake. So how come he'd let his marriage come to this?

He was contemplating the prospect of the other Stella when he heard a car slowing outside. Then came the crunch of wheels on gravel and a peal of laughter as a door opened. Moments later he was out in the sunshine. Lizzie hadn't laughed like that for weeks. Months. She was standing there with Grace in her arms. She had a huge grin on her face. Suttle put his arms round her, kissed them both. Relief had seldom tasted so sweet.

'And me?'

He kissed Gill too. She had a bottle of vodka in her hand. Bliss.

Gill had collected two bags of assorted Bangladeshi dishes from a takeaway in Exmouth. Suttle fired up the oven while Lizzie disappeared for a shower. The shower never got beyond lukewarm but on this occasion she didn't seem to care. By now Suttle was upstairs readying Grace for bed. Lizzie joined him, drying her hair with a towel.

'What happened?' he asked. 'Where did you go?'

Lizzie explained about the walk, and then the rowing club.

'They let you have a go?'

'They insisted. We're talking machines not the real thing but – hey – who cares?'

'It was good?'

'It was better than good.'

'Difficult?'

'Yeah. But good.'

She explained about the three girls in the Portakabin, the warmth of their welcome, her five-minute introduction to the mysteries of rowing and her dash for the line when Tessa cranked up the pace.

'The longest sixty seconds of my life,' she said.

Suttle was delighted. Was this Gill's doing?

'Yeah. I'd have wimped. She's been great, really supportive, really strong.'

Suttle was impressed. Maybe he'd got Gill Reynolds wrong. Maybe life had dealt her a wonderful hand these past few months and turned her into a human being. Either way, he wasn't complaining.

He found her downstairs, laying the table. He poured her a huge vodka and found some lemonade to go with it. The lemonade was flat but she never said a word. Another first.

By the time Lizzie came down, Suttle was dishing out the curry. Gill had brought a couple of bottles of wine too, and proposed a toast to life in the country before they started on the food. Barely hours ago, thought Suttle, his wife would have turned her head away, her glass untouched, but now Lizzie was the first to respond.

'*Salut*,' she said. 'And thanks.'

The evening slipped by in a warm fug of alcohol and laughter. They never left the kitchen. Suttle sorted the dodgy fuse in the plug that fed the one-bar electric fire, shut all the windows, left the oven door open and found a couple of candles for the rough wooden table. The soft throw of light danced on the walls, the perfect counterpoint to Lizzie's Muse CD, and Suttle allowed himself to get gently pissed. The girls at the rowing club, it seemed, were insisting that Lizzie return for a proper training session the following evening. Tuesday nights were club nights and boats would be on the beach from six onwards. When Gill suggested that Suttle drive her down there, he shook his head. This was Lizzie's gig, he insisted. He'd stay behind and play mum.

By half ten, with both bottles empty, Lizzie was knackered. She'd made up a bed for Gill in the spare room upstairs. She'd see them tomorrow. She gave Gill a hug and offered Suttle a lingering kiss. Then she was gone.

Suttle was suggesting a nightcap when he felt Gill's hand on his arm. She was very close. For a moment he thought she was coming on to him but then she ducked below the table, rummaged in her bag and emerged with a letter.

Suttle peered at it. Manila envelope. A single scribbled name. Suttle.

'What's this?' he mumbled.

Gill told him to open it. She had the impression it was important. Something in her voice told Suttle she wasn't as pissed as he was. Far from it.

'This is why you came down? To give me this?'

'Partly, yes.'

'So what is it?'

'I don't know. Like I say, open it.'

Suttle did what he was told. Moments later he was looking at a single sheet of paper. The message, poorly typed, was brisk: 'You'll know where to find Paul Winter,' it went. 'We need an address. leave a message on the number at the bottom and there won't be a problem.' Suttle reached for the candle, trying to read the handwritten number. Mobile. For sure.

Problem? He looked up.

Gill was shaking the envelope. A photo fell out. Then another. She took a quick look then slid them across to Suttle. He stared at them for a moment, side by side on the table. In one shot Lizzie was emerging from the village store with Grace in the buggy. In the other, presumably the same day, mother and child were walking away towards the road that led to Chantry Cottage. Same clothes. Same weather.

Suttle studied the photos a moment longer, his brain beginning to function at last. Paul Winter was the guy who'd taught Suttle everything he knew as a rookie detective on divisional CID. The guy who'd copped the lead role in a complex undercover operation to snare Mackenzie. The guy who'd resigned in earnest after Operation *Tumbril* had gone tits up and nearly got Winter killed. After that Winter had joined Pompey's top criminal. For real.

For years afterwards Mackenzie had laundered his drug millions and gone from strength to strength as a legit businessman. Paul Winter, as Bazza's key lieutenant, had been at the wheel for most of that ride, but a couple of episodes had opened his eyes and by last year he was ready to grass Mackenzie up. The result was Operation *Gehenna*, in which both Suttle and Gill Reynolds had played key roles.

This time Mackenzie had ended up the loser, shot dead by the ninjas from the Tactical Firearms Unit. Now Mackenzie's mates were obviously interested in settling a debt or two. And the guy they needed to find was Paul Winter.

'So where did this lot come from?'

'They came to the *News* in another envelope.'

'Addressed to you?'

'Yes.'

'Hand delivered?'

'By post. First class.'

'Postmark?'

'Pompey.'

'With my envelope inside?'

'Yeah.'

'Right.' Suttle was looking at the photos again. 'So why did it come to you in the first place?'

Gill wanted to read the note. Suttle passed it across.

'Because these people knew where to find me,' she said. 'My name's in the paper most days.' She looked up. 'So where's Winter?'

'I haven't a clue.'

'Really?'

'Really. And if I did I wouldn't be telling these numpties.'

'Even if they ...' Her eyes strayed to the photos again. Lizzie and Grace. These people knew where they lived. They knew where to find them. Scary.

'They wouldn't.' Suttle shook his head. 'They won't.'

'How do you know?'

'I don't. But I'll make sure it never happens.'

'That might be difficult.'

'You're right.'

Gill was watching him carefully.

'You really think Winter's more important than Lizzie and Grace?' she said at last.

'Of course he's not. But that's not the point.'

Winter, he explained, had done a deal with Hantspol in return for a significant cash settlement. With this, Suttle suspected he'd bought himself a new identity and moved abroad.

'Like where?'

'I haven't the faintest idea. If you were Winter, you wouldn't tell a soul.'

'You think he's alone?'

'Pass.'

Gill frowned, not quite believing him, then leaned forward. Suttle could smell cardamom on her breath.

'Mackenzie knew Winter had got it on with Misty Gallagher.'

'Is that right?'

'Yes. He told me himself when we were shagging. He said I was as good as her. I think he meant it as a compliment.'

'I'm sure he did.'

'So it stands to reason they might be still together, Winter and Misty.'

Suttle, far later than he should, realised she was fishing for details. Once a journalist always a fucking journalist. He told her again that he knew nothing. He liked Winter. He'd always liked Winter. He owed the man a lot. Winter's move to the Dark Side had disgusted him and he'd told Winter so, but their friendship had survived pretty much intact.

'And you're telling me you're not in touch?'

'I'm telling you the best favour I can do the guy is to stay well clear. What I don't know I can't pass on.'

Gill didn't want to believe him. He could see it in her face. Too bad.

'Have these guys been in contact with you?' Suttle was back with the photos. 'A name would be handy.'

'No. All I ever got was the envelope.'

'No phone calls? No pressure?'

'Nothing.'

Suttle didn't believe her. Mackenzie had always been able to call on muscle from the 6.57, a bunch of tooled-up football hooligans at the core of Pompey's away support. These guys were middle-aged now but no less handy. In any situation, no matter what kicked off, they always favoured direct action.

'They've been down here,' he said.

'Obviously.'

'So who told them where to find me? Who knew where we lived?'

There was a edge of accusation in his voice. Gill caught it at once.

'You think that was me? You think I'd sell my best mate down the river?'

'I'm asking, that's all.'

'Then the answer's no. Fuck knows how they found you. Maybe they looked in the phone book. Maybe they did a Google search. Maybe they've got sources in the Filth. There's nowhere to hide these days.'

'Really? You believe that?'

'Of course I do.'

'So how come they can't find Winter?'

It was the obvious question and she sat back, annoyed at falling into Suttle's little trap. *Filth*, thought Suttle, was an interesting word. This was fighting talk. This was what the 6.57 called the men in blue. Gill had definitely been mixing in bad company.

Suttle pushed his chair back and confected a yawn. He wanted to know whether Lizzie knew anything about the photographs.

'Of course not. They'd scare her to death.'

She stared at him. She was upset now. She'd started by bossing this conversation and somehow she seemed to have lost control.

'There's something you ought to know,' she said. 'Lizzie wants to move back to Pompey. And guess who told her she shouldn't?'

'You.'

'Yeah, me.'

'Because of these?' Suttle was looking at the photos again.

'Yeah, partly.'

'You knew they were in the envelope? You'd taken a look?'

'Fuck off. Mail turns up out of the blue. I find an envelope

107

with your name on. You don't have to be super-bright to know it's not going to be good news.'

'So you're telling me you guessed the rest?'

'Pretty much. Don't look surprised. It's what I do for a living.'

Suttle offered her a nod. Touché. He was about to offer an apology but Gill hadn't finished.

'If you want the truth, I came down because of you guys, because of Grace, the family thing, the whole shtick. Fuck knows how but you've got a great thing going. That was the way I read it in Pompey. That woman loves you, believe it or not. I'm not sure living in the country was a brilliant decision but that's something you have to sort out. Me? I'm just the messenger.'

She checked her watch and bent down for her bag again. Time for bed.

Jimmy reached across as she began to get to her feet. He put his hand on her arm, gave it a little squeeze. She hesitated, looking down at him, a new expression on her face, surprise salted with something else.

'I just want to say thank you,' he muttered.

'For the note? For the photos?'

'For what you did this afternoon.'

For a moment Gill was lost. Then she remembered.

'The rowing, you mean?' She bent and kissed him on the lips. 'You need to be careful, Jimmy Suttle. You might lose that woman one day.'

Three

Suttle was at his desk at Exmouth nick by eight next day. Already the bulk of *Constantine*'s D/Cs had been redeployed on other inquiries and a text from Houghton instructed Suttle to vacate their temporary office and return to MCIT's permanent base in Exeter. The message was plain. In the absence of hard evidence, *Constantine* was effectively over.

An admin assistant from up the corridor supplied Suttle with a couple of cardboard boxes. He filled them with the seized files from Kinsey's apartment and headed out to the car park. That morning, for once, he hadn't been woken by Grace. Both Lizzie and Gill had still been asleep when he'd left. With last night's photos tucked safely in his jacket pocket, *Constantine*'s demise gave him a little time to frame up some kind of plan.

Houghton's Major Crime Investigation Team worked out of a converted police house on the sprawling force HQ site at Middlemoor, on the edges of Exeter. Suttle's desk occupied a corner of a ground-floor office with views of the car park. The other three desks in the room belonged to squad D/Cs, all of whom had been with the MCIT far longer than Suttle. As well as the usual maps and whiteboards on the wall, tracking progress on current investigations, he'd arrived to find a World War Two poster (KEEP CALM AND CARRY ON), a photocopy of the Obama electoral chant ('Yes, we can') and a medal for the Exeter half-marathon draped over a framed copy of a Robert Frost poem, 'The Road Not Taken'.

Suttle was looking at it now. The office was empty.

> Two roads diverged in a wood, and I –
> I took the one less traveled by,
> And that has made all the difference.

Really? He dumped the file boxes on the floor and sank into his chair. Twice in the last twenty-four hours he'd had to face the consequences of his move west. First, his wife threatens to leave him. Next, her best friend arrives with evidence that he and his family are under surveillance. On both counts, Pompey's shadow was far longer than he'd ever imagined.

He got out the note and the photos. His only real lead was the mobile number. He was tempted to add it to the list going to the phone companies but knew that the intel techies would be the first to review the data that came back and he didn't fancy trying to explain how a Pompey address might fit into the vanishing phantom that was *Constantine*. In any case, it was odds on that the phone was pay as you go, registered to a hookey name and address. These people weren't stupid.

His phone began to ring. It was Luke Golding, the young D/C tasked with chasing up Henri Laffont and Kinsey's ex-wife. More bad news.

'I've nailed Kinsey's missus, Sarge. I talked to that guy in Bristol again, Bill. He gave me a couple of numbers in Seattle.'

Sonya, it turned out, had spent the weekend with a bunch of religious fundamentalists on a retreat in the Cascade Mountains. If Suttle fancied taking this thing any further, Golding had a list of witnesses who'd willingly attest to her presence. It seemed she'd discovered Christ big time. The Cascade Mountains, he added as an afterthought, were on the west coast of America so it seemed unlikely she'd find the time or opportunity to dispatch her ex-husband to his death.

'And Laffont?'

'We're still working on that but my money's on Shanghai. I managed to make contact with the woman who organises his diary, Chinese lady, very helpful. I don't think he ever made it to London.'

'Great.'

'Sorry, Sarge. You want me to stick at it? Only time might be a problem now.'

'Of course.'

The phone went dead, leaving Suttle gazing at the whiteboard. To date, *Constantine* didn't even merit a mention because inquiries had been coordinated out of Exmouth. He got to his feet and found a marker pen. The fact that both Sonya and Laffont were probably out of the frame was, he tried to tell himself, a definite plus. It meant that he could concentrate on the ripples that Kinsey had been making locally. The guys in the boat. Maybe other rowers at the club. Possibly someone from Exmouth Quays, or the wider community, who'd nurtured some kind of grudge. This was a guy who was serially offensive. He thrived on pissing people off. That, at the very least, Suttle knew he could prove.

He blocked off a square of the whiteboard and scrawled *Constantine* across the top. Then he returned to his desk and fired up his PC. It took him seconds to find D/I Gina Hamilton's details. She was working out of the Plymouth HQ at Crownhill. She answered on the second ring.

Suttle introduced himself, mentioned their previous meeting back in Pompey. For a moment there was silence. Suttle could hear her talking to someone else. Then she was on the line again.

'You had a beard,' she said. 'And an office on the third floor.'

'That was my boss. D/I Faraday. I was the one who took you for a drink.'

'The younger guy? Reddish hair?' She was laughing.

'That's me.'

'Gotcha. What can I do for you, young man?'

Suttle explained about Tom Pendrick. He understood Hamilton had interviewed him down in Penzance after the Atlantic crossing.

'That's right. I did.'

'You mind if I come and see you? Talk about him?'

'Of course not.' She paused. 'What's he done?'

'I don't know.' Suttle was looking at the whiteboard. 'Yet.'

It took more than an hour to drive to Plymouth. An accident near Ivybridge had brought traffic to a standstill and Suttle spent the time reviewing his options on the surveillance photos. The thought of a bunch of Pompey heavies sniffing around Lizzie first angered then alarmed him. Last night, with Gill, he'd tried to be cool about it, telling her he'd get the thing sorted, but in the cold light of day he knew that wouldn't be simple. The temptation was to call in a favour or two from CID mates still working in the city. He could think of a couple, in particular, who'd relish the chance to have a quiet conversation and stir these guys up. But that, he knew, wouldn't hack it.

Neither was he prepared to make it official by lodging the evidence with Det-Supt Gail Parsons. His ex-boss on the Pompey-based Major Crime Team would doubtless view the photos as yet another opportunity to advance her ACPO prospects. She'd take the issue to the top. She'd knock on the Chief's door and tell him it was a direct threat to the force's standing in the city. The moment these people were allowed to get away with a threat this crude was the moment Hantspol should call it a day and look for something else to do. A threat against one of us, she'd say, was a threat against us all.

In this, thought Suttle, she was probably right, but leaving a bunch of Pompey heavies to the likes of Parsons wouldn't work either. They played by different rules. They didn't care a fuck about ambitious detective superintendents banged up in a bubble of their own making. The Filth, in their view, were like the weather. A minor inconvenience.

So what to do? As the traffic at last began to inch forward he was no closer to cracking it, but minutes later, as the dual carriageway crested the last hill before the distant sprawl of Plymouth, he thought – quite suddenly – of Paul Winter. A situation like this, back in the day, would have been meat and drink to Suttle's one-time mentor. He'd have studied it from every angle, looking for advantage, scenting a weakness here, identifying an opportunity there, finally lifting the phone to arrange a meet. Somewhere quiet. Somewhere companionable. Some pub where he could open negotiations, bait traps, orchestrate an outcome that the enemy, far too late, would recognise as a total stitch-up. Suttle could imagine him now. Steady on, son, he'd say. You always have more time than you think.

Suttle caught the first of the gantry signs indicating the turn-off for Crownhill. He indicated left, slipped into the nearside lane, hoping to God that Winter had it right.

It was mid-morning before Gill Reynolds left Chantry Cottage. Three ibuprofen and a plate of scrambled eggs had softened the worst of her hangover, and by the time she and Lizzie said their goodbyes she was feeling mildly euphoric. Their little stroll yesterday afternoon, Gill announced, had been fantastic. The rowing was going to do Lizzie a power of good. She wanted – demanded – regular progress reports including Lizzie's take on the available crumpet. East Devon, to her surprise, was only three hours away. With the right incentive, she could be back any time.

Lizzie waved as she accelerated away down the lane. To her relief, Gill's brief visit had turned out to be a real pleasure. Better than that, it seemed to have lifted the depression that had threatened to swamp her little boat. Gill was right about the rowing. She needed exercise. She wanted new people in her life. After her initial misgivings, she was now relishing the chance to conquer something difficult and worthwhile. She took Grace back inside, gazing at the wreckage from last night's meal. All this, she told herself, could wait. They needed supplies, something for Jimmy to cook this evening while she was down at the rowing club. With the sun out again, she and Grace should make the most of it.

It was a fifteen-minute push to the village store. Lizzie bought bread, milk, fresh vegetables, bananas for Grace, and – as an afterthought – a bottle of Jimmy's favourite Rioja. On the way back she paused outside the store to talk to an elderly woman she recognised from her recent visit to the church. The woman was collecting for an Aids charity in Africa and Lizzie dropped a pound coin in her box.

Shortly before noon, Lizzie and Grace were back at Chantry Cottage. She let herself in, settled Grace in her playpen and returned to the chaos of the kitchen. Minutes later, clearing the table, she caught sight of something tucked beneath the breadboard. It was a Pompey programme, the last home game, Portsmouth vs Preston North End. She gazed at it, trying to work out where it had come from. Gill, to her certain knowledge, loathed football. Jimmy, she knew, had been at home last weekend. So what on earth was this little bit of Pompey doing in her kitchen?

The phone rang. It was Jimmy. He'd just arrived in Plymouth and he wanted her to know if she was OK.

Lizzie was still looking at the programme.

'I'm fine,' she said. 'Don't be late tonight, eh? I'm going rowing.'

Crownhill was the biggest of the force outposts in Plymouth. D/I Gina Hamilton occupied a first-floor office close to the lift. Something had changed since they'd last met and it took Suttle a moment or two to work out what.

'The hair,' he said. 'Am I right?'

Hamilton had got to her feet, extending a hand.

'I had it done last week. I was going for the full butch but it hasn't worked, has it?'

She was right. Back in Pompey, five years ago, her blonde hair had been shoulder length, maybe longer. Now, still blonde, it was savagely cropped, giving her face a younger look. Delicate features. Flawless complexion. Full lips. And hints of fatigue shadowing her pale blue eyes.

'Anything interesting?' Suttle nodded at the paperwork on her desk.

'Performance reviews.'

'What did you do wrong?'

'That's not as funny as you think. Do you want a list?'

'Yeah, if you're offering.' Suttle had yet to take a seat.

She looked at him a moment, amused. Suttle was trying to guess her age. Forty? Maybe a year or two younger?

'Tell me about Mr Pendrick,' she said. 'I got hold of the file after you phoned, just to remind myself. Interesting guy.'

Suttle told her about Kinsey's death, about the resources Nandy had piled into *Constantine*, about their fruitless attempts to turn a sus death into something they might one day take to court. In the end, he said, they seemed to have drawn one fat blank with absolutely nothing to show for hundreds of man-hours of investigative effort.

'Except Pendrick?'

'Yeah. Maybe.' Suttle sat down at last. 'So what did you make of him?'

Hamilton pondered the question. Back last year, she said, she'd been relief D/I down at the far end of Cornwall. The Coastguard had been in touch with force HQ as soon as Pendrick had alerted them to the mystery disappearance of his wife, and Hamilton had been nominated to sit on top of the job. A couple of uniforms had taken a statement after Pendrick made landfall in Penzance and Hamilton had invited him up to the nick a couple of days later to expand on one or two elements in his account.

'HQ were getting twitchy by then.' She laughed. 'The papers were starting to speculate about what might have happened and we needed to be sure we had the thing covered.'

Suttle wanted to know about Pendrick's account. How much detail had he offered?

'Not a lot, to be honest. The way he told it, the crossing had been pretty boring. Most of the time they just rowed, which you can believe, and the week before it happened they'd had some pretty shit weather. I got the impression the thing had been a bit of a let-down, a bit of a disappointment. And then, of course, the wife disappeared.'

She talked Suttle through the sequence of events. They'd had a little cubby at the front of the boat. Pendrick used to sleep from two in the morning until four. Then he'd take over from his wife. They'd worked it this way for pretty much all of the crossing. On this occasion, like always, he'd been ready to take over and let her get some kip but when he emerged from the cabin she'd gone.

'Just disappeared?'

'Yeah.'

'No huge waves during the night?'

'No. According to Pendrick it was flat calm.'

'No note? No reason she might have gone overboard?'

'Nothing.'

'Did she ever take a dip? Just slip over the side and paddle around?'

'I asked him that and the answer was yes. But they only swam when the other one was there too. And only when they had knotted ropes trailing in the water.'

'So not at night?'

'Never. He said she was really responsible that way. They both were. House rules.'

Suttle nodded. He remembered an article in one of the tabloids. They'd never gone as far as directly accusing the hippy rower of getting rid of his wife, but they had run a series of articles profiling other guys who'd tried to fake the death of a spouse or a partner.

'Did you believe him?'

'I had no grounds not to.'

'That wasn't my question.'

'I know.'

Suttle held her gaze, aware that she was enjoying this exchange. Anything to liven up another Tuesday morning, he thought. Any escape from the pile of performance reviews.

'What about third parties?' Suttle asked. 'Did they have some kind of shore-based thing? Someone who kept an eye on them? Someone they checked in with?'

Hamilton nodded. Back in Woods Hole in Massachusetts, where they'd begun the voyage, were a couple of friends who fielded regular reports. Calling them a control centre was a bit of a stretch but they'd sent stuff on to the US media and generally done their best. After a while the reports from mid-Atlantic had become sporadic and – to be frank – a bit thin.

'They were their words, not mine.'

'You talked to these guys?'

'Of course.'

'And?'

'They didn't seem to have any cause for concern. Until the wife disappeared.'

'And then?'

'It became a bit of a news story. For a day or two.'

Suttle nodded. He was thinking about the crossing, what it must have taken to make the initial commitment.

'Did you *like* Pendrick?'

'What sort of question is that?'

'Well? Did you?'

'I liked what he'd done, what they'd both done. Rowing the Atlantic? You had to give the guy a bit of respect.'

'Sure but ... you know ...' Suttle smiled. 'Did you get *through* to him?'

'No, I don't think I did. From where I was sitting the man was on another planet.'

'Because of his wife?'

'You couldn't tell. Did he miss her? Yes, I think he did. Was that the end of the story? No way.'

'There was other stuff?'

'There had to be. He wasn't difficult or uncooperative, don't get me wrong. He just didn't say a lot.'

'Meaning he had something to hide?'

'Meaning there were limits, places you didn't go. I can't remember meeting anyone so private.'

'Fuck-off private? Or private private?'

'Private private. We're not talking aggression. Far from it. I had the impression he'd be a good guy to have a drink with.'

'Because?'

'Because, deep down, he probably had lots to say. And most of it would be worth listening to.'

Suttle smiled. Nicely phrased, he thought.

'What about other evidence? Did SOC bosh the boat?'

'Of course.'

'And?'

'Nothing material. They found traces of blood on a runner beneath one of the seats but it turned out to be mackerel. Our man was home safe.'

'What was the gap between his wife disappearing and Pendrick making it back?'

Hamilton frowned, doing the calculations.

'Over a week. He was single-handed. That boat must have weighed a ton.'

'So he had plenty of time to give the thing a proper seeing-to?'

'Of course.'

'When he could have been picked up? Gone for early doors?'

'Yeah.'

'Did you think that was dodgy at all? Carrying on the way he did?'

'Not really. I put it to him that it was a strange thing to do, rowing single-handed when most people would have been in bits about what had happened, but he just shook his head. The word he used was tribute.'

'Tribute?'

'To his dead wife. To Kate. Finishing was the least he owed her. It's in the transcript. I remember him saying exactly that.'

Suttle scribbled himself a note. *Finishing was the least I owed her.* It was an arresting phrase.

'What about passive evidence?'

'She had a camera which she apparently took with her when she went over the side.'

'Stills? Video?'

'Both.'

'And you're saying it disappeared?'

'Yeah.'

Suttle bent to his pad. Made another note. Then his head came up again.

'Did she keep a diary? Some kind of journal?'

'Yeah. Plus an audio account.'

'You seized them?'

'Of course.'

'And?'

'Evidentially it took us nowhere. I got the impression she was quite a literal-minded woman. From time to time the wild life would do it for her – the birds, dolphins, a couple of whales – and sunsets and sunrises always got a mention, but most of the stuff was pretty dull. Distance covered. Weather details. How much water they were making every day. Worries about the food stocks. Housekeeping really. One thing was interesting, though.'

'What?'

'I remember thinking the deeper they got into this thing, the less she wrote. It was the same with the audio. You could sense it in her voice. There was a weariness there. You could hear it.'

'She was probably knackered.'

'Sure. Of course she was. But there was something else. It was as if she couldn't be bothered any more.'

'Right.' Another note. 'And what about Pendrick? Was he keeping any kind of diary?'

'He said he wasn't.'

'Did you believe him?'

'No.'

'Why not?'

'Because he was so thoughtful, so *deep*. Pendrick was exactly the kind of guy to write stuff down. But no way would you ever get to read it.'

'Because he was hiding something?'

'Because he was so private.'

'What about the state of the relationship? What impression did you get about that?'

'They'd been married for a while. Five, six years, something like that.'

'Kids?'

'No.'

'But they were tight? Made it work?'

'I imagine so. You're going to be spending a lot of time together. Why do something like that with someone you don't much like?'

Suttle said he didn't know. Relationships were complicated enough on dry land. Just imagine what a couple of months alone at sea would do to most marriages.

Hamilton said nothing. Just shot him a look. Suttle asked her about the couple's life insurance.

'They'd both taken out policies. They were raising money for some charity and the people in charge insisted on proper cover. That was interesting.'

'How come?'

'The insurance thing was a bit of an issue for a couple of the media guys. One of the reporters did a bit of digging and discovered that Pendrick stood to gain half a million dollars from his wife's death. Of course it wasn't as simple as that. The insurance company wanted proof of death and it was months before they accepted the claim, but when I put it to Pendrick he just shrugged, said he wasn't interested, told me the money had never crossed his mind.'

'Did you check with the insurance people? Later?'

'Yeah. We had a wash-up at the back end of last year.'

'Performance review?'

'Very funny.' She had the grace to laugh. 'I put a call through and after the usual dramas they confirmed they'd paid out.'

'To Pendrick?'

'To the charity. It turned out that's what Pendrick and his wife had wanted all along. That was their decision. That's what they'd stipulated. And I'm guessing that's why Pendrick was never bothered about the money.'

'OK.' Suttle was impressed. 'So which charity are we talking about?'

'I knew you'd ask.' She opened a drawer and produced a file. Lovely hands, Suttle thought. No rings. Hamilton looked up, one finger anchored in the file. 'It's called Phra Mae Khongka. She's a Thai water goddess. I gather it's something to do with the tsunami.'

'How come?'

'You want the truth?'

'Please.'

'I haven't a clue.'

Lizzie got Gill on her mobile shortly after lunch. She was speeding through the New Forest with the top down and Muse full blast on the audio. She'd borrowed the CD from Lizzie and would bring it back next time round.

Lizzie wanted to know whether she'd had anything to do

with a football programme that had appeared on the kitchen table.

'A what?'

'A football programme. Portsmouth versus Preston. Last weekend.'

Lizzie heard the music level dip. Then Gill was back on the phone.

'Nothing to do with me,' she said. She wanted to know how come it had got there.

'Good question.' Lizzie was watching Dexter stalking something in the long grass.

She rang off as the signal began to fade and went back into the kitchen. The programme was still on the table. When she'd found it she'd done nothing but stare at the front cover. Blue shirts in front of a sea of faces. A white blur might have been a football. Now she went through the programme page by page. She found the phone number at the end, a line of carefully transcribed figures beneath an advert for a demolition company. The number was underlined and there was a question mark at the end. She studied the number a moment and wondered what would happen if she phoned it. Then something else claimed her attention.

The last time she'd checked the dodgy window in the living room, it had been loosely secured. There was no way it would ever keep anyone out but this way it at least minimised the draught. Now, though, it was completely unlatched. Someone had been at it. She knew they had. There was no other explanation. Someone had reached in, opened the window and climbed inside.

She peered hard at the windowsill, then at the carpet beneath. Sure enough, among all the ingrained crud, she could see tiny fragments of gravel and dirt. She turned away from the window, feeling a sudden chill despite the warmth of the sun. Grace was in her playpen, taking wet bites at her stuffed rabbit. Lizzie stared at her for a long moment then summoned the courage to venture upstairs. Both bedrooms were empty. She came down again, her pulse back under control, wondering what to do. Should she phone Jimmy? Or should she wait until this evening?

She glanced at her watch and decided not to bother him. Mercifully, the bolts on both the front and back doors still worked. With a bit of ingenuity, she might be able to re-fasten the window. Whoever had left the calling card was probably miles away by now. Her eyes strayed to the programme again and despite everything she found herself wondering what on earth lay behind its sudden appearance in this tomb of a house. Pompey, she thought. Never lets you down.

Suttle had decided to nail the photos as soon as he got back to Middlemoor. Apart from the Admin Manager and a lone D/C, the MCIT offices were empty. Suttle closed his door and extracted the mystery number from his wallet. Using his own mobile, he keyed in the digits.

The number rang and rang. Finally, a voice. Gruff Pompey accent. No surprise there.

'My name's Suttle. You want to talk to me.'

'That's right. We do.'

'When? Where?'

'How about this afternoon?'

'You have to be joking. I'm in fucking Exeter.'

'So are we, mush.' The voice was laughing. 'Bet your life we are.'

Suttle was thinking fast. They've been back to the village, he told himself. He'd talked to Lizzie a couple of hours ago. She'd seemed perfectly OK.

'Listen.' He bent to the phone again. 'If anyone lays a finger on my family, they'll regret it. Are we cool with that? Are you listening?'

'I'm listening.'

'So leave it out, yeah?'

The guy was still there. Suttle could hear him. Heavy breather. Probably fat. Probably enormous. Finally he came back on the phone.

'Pub called the Angel. Opposite Central Station. You know it?'

'Yeah.'

'Three o'clock. If you're not there by quarter past, all bets are off.'

'What's that supposed to mean?'

'You don't want to know, mush.'

The line went dead. Suttle slipped the phone back in his pocket and checked his watch. 14.27. Getting into the city centre and finding somewhere to park would take at least twenty minutes, probably longer. And no way was he going into this without back-up.

In the next office D/C Luke Golding was on the phone. He'd been with Major Crimes less than a month. Suttle barely knew the lad.

He stood over him, tapping his watch. Get off the phone. Like now.

'Sarge?' Golding looked startled.

'There's a meet we have to get to.' Suttle was already heading for the door. 'That's me and you, son.'

In the car Suttle left the details vague. When Golding asked which bit of *Constantine* this linked to, Suttle said it was impossible to say. Call it a fishing expedition. Call it any fucking thing. Just do what I say, right?

Golding nodded. He was small and slight but Suttle had listened to a couple of the other guys on the squad and knew the boy could handle himself. In uniform, still a probationer, he'd evidently faced down a bunch of pissed marine recruits in an Exmouth pub. That very definitely took bottle. Good sign.

The traffic, mercifully, was light. Suttle was in the city centre by five to three. There was even a parking space outside the

Central Station. He killed the engine and sat in silence for a moment. The Angel was directly across the road. He'd never been in the pub in his life but a big plate-glass window offered a view inside. It was dark, impossible to see further than the tables beside the window.

'So what now, Sarge?' Golding had to be back for a meet by four fifteen.

'You watch my back, OK? I'll be sitting at one of those tables you can see across the road there in the pub. There'll be someone with me. If anything kicks off I want you to call for the cavalry. You happy with that?'

'No sweat.' He could see the lad warming to the task. Maybe he enjoyed physical violence. Maybe he was a stranger to the strokes the 6.57 could pull.

Suttle got out of the Impreza and crossed the road. The pub was near-empty, a couple of derelicts at the bar, a younger man with a copy of the *Independent* curled on the sofa beside the brick fireplace. None of them looked remotely Pompey. Suttle asked for a small shandy and took it to the table beside the window. He could see Golding across the road. He was studying his mobile.

Moments later the door opened. Two guys, one fat, one black. Suttle recognised neither of them. The fat guy muttered something Suttle didn't catch to his mate and dispatched him to the bar before wedging himself into the chair across the table from Suttle. His tiny shaved skull seemed to wobble on the folds of fat at the back of his neck. Baggy jeans and a black leather jacket over a black woollen polo neck.

'So who's the kid in the Impreza?'

'A mate of mine.'

'He knows about this?'

'He knows I'm meeting someone heavy.'

'Too fucking right. Does he know why?'

'No.'

'Straight up?'

'Yeah. There'd be no point telling him. Pompey's a mystery to these people.'

'You're right, mush. Wrong fucking league, eh? Wrong fucking end of the country. What's it like then? Life in the sticks?'

Suttle didn't answer. He hadn't any interest in conversation. He was simply here to deliver a message.

The black guy was back with the drinks. Two pints of Stella and a packet of cheese and onion. Suttle was looking at the fat guy.

'You've got a name?' he asked.

'Of course I've got a fucking name.'

'What is it?'

'None of your business. If it helps you can call me Jonno.'

'OK, Jonno, so why don't you say your piece? What exactly do you want from me?'

'You know what we want.'

'All I know is you've been sniffing around my missus. Nice pix, by the way.'

Jonno had caught sight of the crisps. He was staring at the black guy.

'I said salt and vinegar, didn't I? Can't you fucking read?'

'They've run out.'

'*Run out?*' His eyes revolved. 'Fucking carrot crunchers.' He opened the packet and emptied the crisps across the table. 'Help yourself, mush. Lunch on us, eh?' He gave the crisps a poke. The back of his right hand carried an eagle tat. On his left, a name framed in an elaborate scroll. Even upside down Suttle had no difficulty deciphering it.

'He lives down this way.' Suttle nodded at the tat. 'Not many people know that.'

'Who?'

'David James.'

'Know him, do you?'

'I've met him a couple of times, yeah. He's big on the charity front. Nice bloke.'

David James had been a legend at Fratton Park, a command-ing goalie with a huge Afro and a string of England caps.

Jonno was impressed.

'You talk to him at all?'

'Of course.'

'Fuck me,' he said. 'You're starting to sound half human.'

He pushed the crisps towards Suttle. He wanted be out of this khazi of a city and back on the road east as soon as pos-sible. So why didn't Suttle do himself a favour and help him out?

'How?'

'You know how. That cunt Winter was totally out of order. You think we can let something like that go? In case you don't remember, Mr Filth, your guys shot the Man dead. That's life, mush. That's what happens. Some tosser pulls the trigger and Bazza Mac's history. You'll be glad to know we don't have a problem with that. The arsehole with the shooter's doing a job. But what we don't put up with is a fucking two-timing lowlife grass like Winter. Without him, the arsehole with the shooter would never have been anywhere near Bazza Mac. And so our Mr Winter's on a slapping. Happy to oblige.'

'I don't doubt it.'

'You shouldn't, mush. We're quality when it comes to slap-pings.'

'Great. So what do you want from me?'

'An address. Nothing more, nothing less. Give us an address and we're out of your face. Never trouble you again.'

'I haven't got an address. I haven't got a clue where he is.'

'Think again, mush. It happens we know how you cunts operate. Witness protection? New ID? Plastic surgery? Set the fat cunt up in some fucking bungalow on the other side of the globe? Make sure he blends in with the wildlife? Dunsnitching? Dungrassing? We know all that. And so do you.' He picked at a crisp. 'So where is he?'

'I just told you. I don't know.'

'OK.' Jonno nodded. 'And if you did know?'

'I still wouldn't tell you.'

'Really?' The expression on his face could have been a smile. 'So how do we know you're not lying?'

'You don't. You have to believe me.'

'But what's the point, mush?'

'There isn't one. Our gang's bigger than yours. Which is why you're best off forgetting all about Winter.'

'That ain't going to happen, mush. And you know it. You know something else? Young Karl here, the genius who doesn't know a salt and vinegar crisp from the hole in his arse, thinks you're probably wearing a wire. You mind if he checks?'

'Go ahead. Help yourself.'

The black guy took his cue. He swallowed a mouthful of Stella and then gestured Suttle to his feet. Suttle stood up. A single nudge with his knee was enough to upset all three glasses, sending a tidal wave of cold lager across the table.

'Fuck me.' Jonno, outraged, was looking at a lapful of soggy crisps. He tried to push away from the edge of the table. More lager.

Suttle was aware of Golding racing across the road, body-checking through a line of cyclists. Then he was in through the door. Suttle told him to cool it.

'Little accident, son.' He shot Golding a grin. 'I think my new friends are leaving.'

As promised, Suttle was back at Chantry Cottage by half five. It was a thirty-minute drive to Exmouth, absolute max, and he knew Lizzie wanted to be on the beach by six. He reversed the Impreza and left the driver's door open.

Lizzie emerged from the back door. She was wearing shorts and a T-shirt with a trackie top draped over her shoulders. She'd just fed Grace, she said, and there was plenty of food in case Suttle fancied getting some supper together. She'd no idea when she'd be back but imagined it wouldn't be late.

Suttle was still standing by the Impreza. There was an edge in Lizzie's voice he didn't much like.

'Everything all right?'

'No.'

'What's happened?'

'There's a message on the answering machine. I don't know what's going on but maybe you ought to check it out.'

Suttle watched her drive away without a backward glance. He ducked into the kitchen. The phone had been readied in the living room. Grace gave him a little wave and rattled the bars of her playpen.

Suttle recognised the voice at once. The message couldn't have been simpler. 'Top mistake, mush. Next time, eh? Looking forward to it.' Suttle hit the replay button. He and Golding had left the two guys in the pub. Mercifully, Golding hadn't had time to call for help, deciding that his D/S could do with a bit of physical support. For this Suttle had been genuinely grateful but he'd spent most of the journey back to Middlemoor fending the lad off. Yes, these guys were very definitely the enemy. No, he couldn't reveal more at this stage. And, by the way, would he mind keeping radio silence for the time being?

'Radio silence' hadn't cut much ice with Golding. He was both curious and alarmed. Curious because he had a nose for serious trouble, and alarmed because he didn't begin to understand why Suttle wasn't pushing all the panic buttons. The young D/C had seen enough to suss that the two heavies in the Angel had fuck all to do with *Constantine*. Bosses existed to take care of situations like these and D/I Houghton, in Golding's eyes, was one of the best. Getting out of the Impreza back at Middlemoor, he nodded up towards Houghton's office window.

'Just tell her, Sarge. Whatever it is, she'll understand.'

'Sure.'

'I'm serious.'

'Yeah, thanks …'

Golding had shrugged, leaving him to it, but now – hours later – Suttle suspected he was right. In the pub he'd definitely overstepped the mark. The sudden gust of Pompey, like the stale breath of a party you'd prefer to forget, had irritated him. The cartoon threats hadn't helped. And when those numpties had played him like he was an extra in some Al Pacino movie, wanting to pat him down, he'd truly had enough. You didn't put up with stuff like that, not if you had an ounce of self-respect. Hence the spilled lager and the soggy crisps and the fat guy shouting to the barman to bring him a fucking cloth.

Suttle replayed the message again, sitting in the armchair, Grace in his lap. If he took Golding's advice and went to Houghton she'd have no choice but to refer the whole matter back to Hantspol. Hantspol meant Gail Parsons and the new Head of CID who'd replaced Willard. He trusted neither of these people not to cook up some clever plan to flush Winter out. Someone at the top of the force would probably have a lead on his whereabouts and one way or another this info would find its way to the 6.57. They'd jump on the next plane, give Winter a thorough battering, maybe even kill him. At Hantspol HQ there'd be a quiet flurry of nods and winks – Winter nailed, justice finally done – and up in his new office in the West Mids force ACC Willard would doubtless raise a glass when Parsons phoned with the news. Did Suttle really want that? Did he want to spend the rest of his life knowing that he'd sent a man he liked and still admired to his death? He thought not.

He nuzzled Grace and gave her a cuddle. Then, for the first time, he saw the football programme, propped against the bars of the playpen. He picked it up, clocked the date, and leafed through until he found the number at the back. Now he understood why Lizzie had been so iffy. They must have slipped it through the letter box, leaving her to puzzle out the implications. First a Pompey stranger at the door. Then the voice on the answering machine.

He got to his feet and carried Grace to the window. These people, he knew, were serious. They had reach. They had limitless patience. Winter, in their view, had killed Mackenzie. And, one way or another, they were going to settle the debt.

He thought of Parsons again. Maybe – after all – he should lift the phone, tell her exactly what had happened, then leave it for his old employers to sort out. That way he might get these animals off his back. But deep down he knew a call like that would solve nothing. There has to be a better way, he told himself. Has to be.

Lizzie saw the boats the moment she hit the seafront. There were two of them, still on their trailers, down by the water's edge. Among the gaggle of rowers rigging the oars were the women she'd met in the Portakabin. Spotting a parking place, she pulled in.

It was Tessa who saw her first. Lizzie waved back. A concrete slip offered access to the beach. She was unaware that anyone was behind her.

'Come back for more?'

She spun round, recognising the big guy she'd briefly met yesterday. Shaved head. Three-day stubble. And an intriguing scar down the side of his face.

'Tom?' she said, uncertain.

'Yeah. Tom Pendrick.'

He fell into step beside her. He was wearing shorts and a scruffy top he must have used for painting. He was tall, way over six feet, and his sheer bulk made her feel almost comically small. Stepping onto the beach, she might have been back at school.

Tessa was organising crews. Lizzie's arrival was a godsend. With one seat unfilled in the second boat, she'd slot in perfectly.

'But I've never done this,' Lizzie pointed out.

'No problem.' Tessa was already rigging the second boat. 'Tom?'

The big man did the honours. With the help of Tessa and a couple of others, he slipped the quad off the trailer and into the water. The tide had just turned and was beginning to push back into the estuary. Another rower held the nose of the quad into the current while Pendrick helped Lizzie into the bow seat. Adjusting the footstretchers to the length of her legs, Pendrick told her to push back in the seat. Lizzie watched him tightening the pegs that secured the footstretchers.

'Try now,' he said.

'Try what?'

'Try moving the seat. Here ...'

The oars had been stowed across Lizzie's midriff. Pendrick pushed them out through the gates until Lizzie was in the rowing position.

'OK. Now come forward. Keep the blades out of the water. Just get a feel for the weight and the movement. That's good. That's fine. Thumbs on the ends of the handles. No pressure, eh? Just treat them like a friend.'

Lizzie took a couple of practice strokes. Pendrick would be rowing in front of her. The rest of the crew, all women, were still on the beach, watching.

'How does it feel?' Pendrick again.

'Fine.'

It was true. The seat moved sweetly beneath her bum. The oars, to her surprise, were nicely balanced. She couldn't wait to get going.

Pendrick was still squatting beside her, briefing her on this detail and that. She couldn't take her eyes off his hands. Worker's hands. Big. Calloused. Dirt under the nicely shaped fingernails. He tested the tension on her foot straps, then made an adjustment to a bungee that secured the life jackets on the bulkhead behind her.

'Anyone ask you whether you can swim?'

'No.'

'Well?'

'I can swim fine.'

'Good. If anything happens, stay with the boat. The guy to listen to is the cox. She's in charge. OK?'

He got to his feet and threw a look at Tessa. He didn't seem to smile much.

Tessa, it turned out, would be cox. She told Pendrick to get in the boat. For such a big man he moved with surprising grace. Tessa steadied the quad as he stepped in and settled his weight on the number two seat. The rest of the crew joined them.

'Just do what I do, OK?' Pendrick again.

Lizzie nodded. The woman holding the boat gave the bow a push. Lizzie could feel a shiver of current beneath them as the quad slipped free from the beach. It was an extraordinary sensation and she wanted to cherish it, this first taste of the real thing, but she was concentrating too hard on Pendrick.

'Take a stroke,' he said. 'Just the right-hand oar. Help me pull us round.'

She did her best. Her blade skidded across the surface of the water. She felt hopelessly awkward. She panicked and tried again. This time her blade clashed with Pendrick's. Horrible sound. Deeply embarrassing.

'No problem. We've all done it. Just take it really easy, yeah?'

He reached forward, took another long slow stroke. Lizzie did the same. This time it worked. They were out now in the current, clear water between the boat and the beach, landmarks up on the promenade slipping by. She couldn't believe it.

'Even pressure.' Pendrick's head was half turned.

'What's that?'

'Both oars.'

Lizzie did what she was told. Another stroke. Another little triumph.

'Easy up. Sort yourselves out.' Tessa this time.

Everyone stopped rowing. The boat drifted on. Tessa wanted to know whether Lizzie was OK, whether Tom was taking care of her. One of the other girls laughed. Lizzie said she was fine. The crew numbered off from the bow, Lizzie first.

'I'm fine,' she repeated.

'Two.'

'Three.'

'Stroke.'

'Come forward to row.' Tessa again. 'Ready to row. Row.'

At the other end of the boat Lizzie had no idea what was happening. All she could do was follow the big man in front of her, do her best to mirror his every move and try not to screw things up. Most of the time it worked, stroke after stroke, fierce concentration, trying to store Pendrick's muttered asides in her teeming brain, reaching forward to take the catch, keeping her arms straight as she pushed back against the footplate, remembering not to bury the whole blade in the water as she pulled hard before the extraction. By the time they'd made it down to the dock, she was wiped out. Not physically but mentally.

Tessa had called for another stop. Pendrick turned in his seat. Lizzie was staring up at the biggest of the apartment blocks on the waterfront. It had to be at least six storeys.

'What's that place?' she asked.

'Regatta Court.'

'It's gross.'

'You think so?'

'I do. And the colour. Who ever let that happen?'

'Fuck knows.'

The big man was shaking his head. And when he turned to her again, he at last had a smile on his face.

An hour or so later, back on dry land, he walked her to the Impreza.

'You were good,' he said. 'I mean it.'

Lizzie was touched. She wanted to thank him. She wanted to thank them all. She'd arrived with zero expectations, pre-occupied with not making a fool of herself. She sensed it might be tricky and she hadn't been wrong, but there was something about these people that gave her immense confidence. They'd made room for her. They'd expected her to measure up. And that's exactly what she'd done. No drama. No girly hysterics. Just the calm sweep of water at the end of each new stroke and the comforting tug as the boat surged forward.

Pendrick wanted to know whether she'd enjoyed it.

'It was brilliant,' she said.

'You mean that?'

'Yeah, I do.'

'You'll come again?'

'Definitely.'

'Thursday?'

'For sure.'

They were at the car by now and she was looking for her keys. Pendrick was gazing out at the water. Another crew was pushing hard against the tide.

'Got far to go?'

'Colaton Raleigh.'

'Country girl?' He seemed surprised.

'Far from it.'

She'd found the keys at last. She thanked him again, then paused.

'You mind me asking a question?' she said.

'Of course not.'

'This guy who was found dead the other day. The one on the TV news. The guy the girls were talking about in the boat.'

'Kinsey?'

'Yeah.' Lizzie bent to re-tie her shoe lace. 'You knew him?'

'Sort of.'

'So ...' Lizzie glanced up. 'What do you think happened?'

Suttle was at the stove when Lizzie got back. There was a pile of sliced potatoes ready for the frying pan and he'd opened a tin of baked beans to go with the sausages. Grace had been bathed and might fancy a story. So far, Lizzie hadn't said a word.

'So how was it?' he asked at last.

'Great,' she said. 'Fantastic. They're all talking about Kinsey. Fascinating.'

'Really?'

'Yeah. Don't worry. No one knows I'm married to a cop.'

'Thank fuck for that.'

'So how's it going? This Kinsey thing?'

Suttle studied her a moment, then turned back to the stove.

'Later,' he said. 'Why don't you sort Grace out first?'

She was back downstairs within minutes. Grace was already asleep. She'd showered and changed and now she had something else on her mind.

'That message on the answering machine,' she said. 'What was that about?'

Suttle explained. Lizzie had always had a soft spot for Winter. 'You're telling me they want his address?'

'I'm telling you they want to hurt the man. Maybe worse than that.'

'You mean *kill* him?'

'These things can get out of control. It's best if they never catch up with him.'

'Shit.' Lizzie told him about finding the Pompey programme on the kitchen table.

Suttle stared at her.

'On the where?'

'There.' Lizzie pointed at the table. 'I was out for maybe an hour. Maybe less. When I came back, there it was. They must have got in through the window next door.'

Suttle gave up on the potatoes. His briefcase was still in the car. When he returned he had the photographs. Lizzie was horrified.

'Where did you get these?'

'Gill brought them down.' He explained about the envelope

that had landed on her desk at work. It would have come from mates of Mackenzie, he said. And Gill had been chosen to play postman.

'Why?'

'Because they know you two are mates.'

'How?'

'Because Gill had been shagging Mackenzie and probably told him.'

'Christ.'

Lizzie sat down. She understood now why Gill was less than keen to have her and Grace around the new flat. The last thing she needed in her life was a bunch of middle-aged heavies from the 6.57.

'So what do we do?' She was looking at the photos again. 'These people frighten me. They shouldn't but they do.'

Suttle had already decided to spare her the details of this afternoon's meet in the Angel. Now he told her that he had the thing under control.

'I don't believe you.' She looked up. 'Have you told someone? Reported it?'

'Yeah.'

'Who? Who have you told?'

'Someone in Pompey.'

'Police? Someone in the Job?'

'No.'

'Why not?'

'Because I don't trust them.'

'Don't *trust* them? Christ, Jimmy, this is our daughter we're talking about, our house, everything we have. The police are supposed to look after us, protect us. Isn't that the way it works or have I got this thing wrong?'

Suttle did his best to explain. It was about Winter, he said, not them.

'You think he's more important? More important than us? Than Grace?'

'That's not the point.'

'It's not? Jesus, you're supposed to be my husband. My daughter's father. What is this?'

Suttle held his ground. He'd thought the thing through. Tomorrow he'd be going to Pompey. By Thursday he'd have everything sorted.

'How can I know that? How can I be sure?'

'You have to trust me.'

'Sure, but ... fuck, Jimmy, these people are creepy. Worse than that they want to hurt us.'

'No.' Suttle was emphatic. 'That won't happen.'

'You say.'

'I say.'

She looked at him for a long moment.

'I could phone the police myself,' she said at last.

'You could. Of course you could. Then it would be your fault.'

'My fault what?'

'Your fault when they get to Winter.'

'You really think that would happen?'

'I think it might. And that's enough.'

Lizzie had slumped in the chair. The fight had gone out of her. She felt physically smaller. Suttle went back to the stove, started cooking again.

After a while Lizzie stirred. 'What would the police do?'

'I've no idea. We're thin on the ground just now. Plotting up the house would be a no-no. What with the cuts and everything, there just aren't the bodies any more. If we're lucky we might get some kind of alarm.'

'Like old people? Wear it round our necks?'

'Yeah.'

'Call for help after they've burned the house down?'

'Yeah.'

'OK.' She shrugged. 'You win. Just make sure Grace stays in one piece, yeah?'

Suttle served the meal. The sauté potatoes were fried to a crisp and the sausages in the oven had dried out. So much for the meal of his dreams.

Lizzie mentioned Kinsey again. She'd been chatting to a guy at the club. He'd sorted her out in the boat, been really helpful.

Suttle speared a sausage, dipped it in a puddle of mustard.

'He's got a name, this guy?'

'Tom. Tom Pendrick.'

Suttle nodded. The mustard had done nothing for the sausage.

'So what did you make of him?' he said after a while. 'This Pendrick?'

'I liked him. He was solid. He was kind too. Rowing isn't as easy as it looks.'

'I'm sure.' Suttle's face was a mask. 'So what did this guy have to say about Kinsey?'

'You're fishing.'

'I am.'

'He said he was rich. He said he wanted to be a winner. And he said something else too.'

'What?'

'He said guys like that are driven. They never lift their heads up, never look around, never see the obvious in front of their noses. In Kinsey's case that might have been fatal.'

'He *said* that last bit?'

'No.' She pushed her plate away. 'I just did.'

Four

Suttle drove to Portsmouth the following afternoon, telling Houghton on the phone that he had a couple of domestic difficulties to resolve. Houghton, as far as he could gauge, was unsurprised.

'Take care,' she said. 'If you want a couple of days, book it as leave.'

The road east was clotted with late-spring traffic and it was early evening on the M27 before Suttle was stealing a glance at the familiar sprawl of Pompey in the thickening light. He took the exit at the foot of the motorway and drove through the suburbs of Cosham before taking the road up to the top of Portsdown Hill. There was a car park here with a view over the entire city. He'd used it a thousand times, often with Winter when they were working together on divisional CID, and it was ideal if you wanted to steal a little time for a coffee or a think.

Suttle killed the engine and settled back. Marie was Mackenzie's widow, a classy High School girl whom Bazza had kidnapped and made rich. Opinions differed on exactly how keen Marie had been to join the world of the young Bazza Mac, but Winter, who was in a position to know, had always insisted that she'd made the running. She was wild as well as beautiful, and she'd seen something deeply promising in her new beau. Life with Bazza, as it turned out, had been everything he'd promised – unpredictable, never risk-free, always fun – and when he'd died at the hands of the Tactical Firearms Unit, she'd been beyond consolation.

Suttle had seen photos of Marie following her husband's coffin into the cathedral. She'd maintained a dignified silence in the face of ceaseless media attention, and at the funeral, a step or two behind the pall-bearers from the 6.57, she'd graced the occasion with poise and elegance. In a brief tribute to her dead husband she'd talked about his loyalty and warmth. He'd been the rock at the very centre of countless lives, she said, and his absence left a void that would never be filled. She'd spoken without notes, her eyes moving from face to face in the packed congregation, and she'd ended by calling for one of her grandsons to read a poem he'd penned only the previous night. The poem was moving in its simplicity and stirred a low rumble of applause that had ended by engulfing the entire cathedral. If anyone would understand the importance of family life, Suttle thought, then it had to be Marie.

She answered his call within seconds. They'd already been in touch on the phone the previous day and she was prepared to meet. Now she named a restaurant in Southsea. She'd be there in half an hour.

Suttle knew Sopranos well. He and Lizzie had used it regularly before they'd left the city and the food was never less than excellent. He arrived a couple of minutes early and found himself a table in the corner. He'd bought a copy of the *News* from the Co-op down the street and he flicked through to the back to check on the football news. The Preston game had ended in a 1–1 draw. Pompey, it seemed, had been lucky to steal a point.

'Hi.'

He looked up to find Marie standing beside the table. She was wearing a white knee-length dress that definitely hadn't come from a chain store and the tan suggested a recent holiday. Suttle got to his feet. A handshake would have been too formal, a kiss way too familiar. He pulled out the other chair and gestured for her to sit down.

She told him she hadn't come to eat. When he suggested a drink she asked for a spritzer. Suttle went to the bar and ordered himself a San Miguel. The owner, whom he knew, raised an eyebrow at the sight of Marie.

'Known her long?' She was smiling.

'Not that long.'

'Business or pleasure?'

'Both.'

'So how's life in Devon?'

'Fraught.'

He returned to the table with the drinks. Marie looked up at him. The last thing Suttle wanted was silence.

'Been somewhere nice?' he enquired.

'Madeira. Big mistake.'

'No good?'

'The weather was lovely. But you need to be over seventy to have a conversation.'

'You went by yourself?'

'No.' Marie glanced at her watch. 'So what's this about?'

Suttle saw no point in glossing over what had happened. A bunch of Pompey guys were giving him a hard time. They wanted to lay hands on Paul Winter and thought Suttle had the key to his door. All this he could cope with but he drew the line at pressure on his wife and daughter. They'd staked out his house. They'd photographed Lizzie and Grace. The threat was explicit. We know where you live. We know who you love. He needed this kind of stuff to stop.

'What's any of this got to do with me?'

'These people were mates of your husband. They think Winter needs a seeing-to.'

'Maybe they're right.'

'Maybe they are, but that's not the point. Number one I

haven't a clue where Winter is. Number two I wouldn't tell them if I did.'

'Do they know that?'

'Yes.'

'You told them?'

'I did.'

'And?'

'They weren't pleased.'

For the first time Suttle detected a flicker of approval. Was she applauding the heavies who'd driven down to Devon? Or was there something in Suttle's defiance that had won her respect? In truth he didn't know but sensed there was no point in taking his foot off the throttle.

'I could take this to the police,' he said.

'You are the police.'

'I know. But I could make it official, make life hard for these guys. That's not something I want to do.'

'Why not? I thought that's what you people were for?'

'It's not as simple as that.'

'It never is.' She leaned forward, toying with her drink. 'You know what I liked about Winter? Apart from the fact that he made me laugh? I liked his mind. I liked his deviousness. He did us a lot of favours, that man. I'd be the first to admit it. Which makes what he did all the more unforgivable. We took him in. We treated him as one of the family. And then he betrayed us.'

Suttle nodded. He wasn't here for a moral debate. If you were looking for devious, serious devious, Paul Winter was world class. All Suttle wanted to do was to get these monkeys off his back.

Marie hadn't finished. Winter, she said, had often talked about Suttle. This was the young kid he'd turned into a detective of real quality. More to the point, Jimmy Suttle had remained one of the few ex-colleagues prepared to give Winter the time of day.

'Is that true?' she asked.

'Yeah. More or less. I'd no time for what he'd done and I told him so, but yeah, we stayed friends.'

'He told me you once saved his life.'

'I did what I could. He was a sick man.'

'He appreciated that.'

'I'm sure he did.'

'And he appreciated the way you stuck with him.'

'That was different. I had a job to do. There was always a reason we got together.'

'On his part?'

'On mine.'

'I see.' She was watching him carefully. 'So does that make my husband's death your fault?'

'Yes. We never set out to kill him ... but yes. It's my job to put people like your husband away and that's exactly what we did.'

'We?'

'The team.'

'Including Winter?'

'Obviously. It wouldn't have happened without him. I've no idea how much you know about all this, Mrs Mackenzie, but your husband exposed Winter to situations that seriously upset him.'

'Are you telling me that came as some kind of surprise? That's what he signed up for.'

'Really? Murder? In cold blood? Not just the target but the target's girlfriend? Someone this guy had known for a couple of days? Someone who never deserved to be killed?'

Marie blinked. *She knows nothing of this*, Suttle thought. Absolutely fuck all.

'This is nonsense,' she said. She didn't sound convinced.

Suttle shook his head. The day before he'd ghosted himself into another life, Winter had shared a story or two that explained his decision to grass Mackenzie up. One of them had to do with a contract killing in the shell of a hotel near Malaga.

Winter had been the sole witness when the gunman stepped into a half-built bar and blew two people away. Minutes later he was still picking tiny gobbets of brain off his best suit. The memory had haunted him ever since and the nightmare had worsened as the prospect of a European Arrest Warrant drew steadily closer. The last thing Winter wanted was the rest of his life in a Spanish prison cell.

'Are you going to tell me more?' Marie was reaching for her drink.

'No.'

'Why not?'

'I promised him I wouldn't.'

'Do you always keep your word?'

'I try.'

'That's admirable.' She offered Suttle a cold smile. 'Tell me something else then.'

'What?'

'This friendship with Winter. Do you think he deserved you?'

'That's a silly fucking question.'

'Is it? Is it really? I trusted that man. I trusted him with our lives. And you know what? He screwed us.'

Suttle fought the waves of scalding anger that threatened to engulf him. For reasons he'd never understood, he also regarded Winter as family.

'I'm sorry.' He ducked his head. 'I'm not here to lose my rag.'

'Whatever. I just want you to know how I might feel about it.'

'It?'

'Winter. He killed my husband.'

'Got him killed.'

'Sure. And from where I'm sitting that's hard to forgive.'

A silence settled on the conversation. Then Marie pushed her glass away and stood up.

'It's been a revelation,' she said. 'And I mean that.'

Suttle didn't know what to do with himself afterwards. It was still early, barely half past seven. He'd set up this conversation in the hope that he might be able to sweet-talk Marie into calling off Bazza's attack dogs, but blood and battle ties were thick in this city and he was beginning to suspect that the guys he'd met down in Exeter were way beyond listening to the likes of Bazza's widow. Even if she put the word out, tried to call them to heel, Suttle doubted they'd listen. Winter was a grass. Winter had fucked Bazza over. Winter deserved everything that was coming to him.

Suttle left the restaurant and walked the half-mile to the Royal Trafalgar Hotel. Barely a year ago this had been the jewel in Bazza's crown. A fourth AA rosette was living proof that he could cut it as a legitimate businessman, and he'd relished the evenings when he hosted discreet dinners for the city's movers and shakers, paving the way for his bid to become one of the city's two MPs. It was Winter who'd sussed that the general election would trigger Mackenzie's downfall, and so it had proved. With his commercial empire in free fall, Bazza had staked everything on a final throw of the dice. His campaign for Portsmouth North had burned money he didn't have, and by the time he died, taken out by the Tactical Firearms Unit in a shop called Pompey Reptiles, he was effectively bankrupt.

The Royal Trafalgar had gone to a rival businessman, a heavyset Pole from nearby Southampton, which made him a Scummer. Suttle paused at the door and then stepped inside. The bar lay beyond reception. This was where the 6.57 would gather for a drink on football nights, reliving old campaigns over a couple of Stellas, and Suttle half-hoped that a face or two would still be around. Maybe he should talk to these people in person, get them to recognise that Winter was history. Maybe Marie had been the wrong place to start.

The bar was empty. Suttle ordered a Guinness, sensing at once that the hotel was on the skids. One look at the clientele in the adjacent restaurant told him that Dobreslaw, the Pole, had taken the whole operation downmarket. Coach-loads of pensioners from up north were tucking into mountains of chicken nuggets. There wasn't a soul under sixty-five, and when a guy in a shiny tux arrived to announce a bingo session afterwards, Suttle knew that this was the last place that any 6.57 would show up. The Pole had bought the hotel for a song and carefully destroyed Bazza's hard-won reputation as a hotelier of serious quality. Revenge, in the ongoing war between the two cities, couldn't have been sweeter.

Depressed, Suttle swallowed the Guinness and crossed the road to the seafront. No closer to fending off his new friends, he knew there was no way he was going to tackle the long drive home until he'd settled down. Maybe a walk by the sea. Maybe another pint or two. Anything to shake himself free of the troubling suspicion that life was beginning to gang up on him.

Lizzie spent the evening alone with Grace. After putting her daughter to bed, she drifted around the kitchen wondering what to make for supper. She'd no idea when Jimmy might be back and had half-expected a call by now. In the end she settled for making a salad with boiled eggs and new potatoes. By gone nine, when he still hadn't appeared, she loaded a plate on a tray and ate a glum supper in front of a repeat of *Shameless*. At ten came the news. By now she was seriously worried. What if he'd had some kind of accident on the way home? Far more likely, what if his attempts to head off the threat to their little family had gone horribly wrong? She was on the point of putting a call through to A & E in Pompey when the phone rang. It was Jimmy. She knew at once he'd been drinking.

'Where are you?'

'Southsea.'

'*Still?*'

'Yeah.'

'Why?'

'It's complicated. I just wanted ...' He tailed off.

'Wanted what? What did you want?'

'It's hard, my love. It's just hard.'

'What's just hard? For fuck's sake, Jimmy. I'm sitting here waiting for you. We both are. So when are you back?'

'Tomorrow.'

'*Tomorrow?*'

Lizzie was staring at the dodgy window. It was open again. Her clever wedge must have dropped out. *Great*.

Suttle was trying to apologise. He'd talked to someone he thought might help. Afterwards he'd had a bit of a think, trying to work out exactly what to do. This thing's really tricky, he kept saying. It's not as simple as you might expect.

Lizzie had ceased to be interested. A cold hard anger had iced what was left of her patience. She was alone in the middle of nowhere with an infant daughter and a bunch of lunatics trying to barge into her life. The very least she wanted was her husband back home to take care of them both. Yet here he was, 130 miles away, pissed as a rat.

'So what's going to happen?' she asked.

There was a long silence. In the background Lizzie thought she caught the parp of a ship's siren. Then Suttle was back on the line.

'Fuck knows,' he said. And rang off.

Suttle walked and walked, wondering whether he should drive home. The third pub had been a mistake, and he'd known it, but after the fourth pint he hadn't much cared, a feeling of release that had taken him by surprise. The temptation now was to get back on the phone, bell a couple of his ex-colleagues, seek a little advice. That way, he told himself, he'd at least have something to show for his evening in Pompey, but the moment he tried to imagine these conversations the more he realised the idea was a non-starter. These guys would suss at once that he was shit-faced. He'd left this city with a decent reputation. Why put all that at risk?

The cheapest Southsea B & Bs were in Granada Road. By now it was raining. The first three doors he knocked on didn't answer. The fourth was opened by an Asian guy in a grease-stained Pompey shirt. Yes, he had a room upstairs. Forty-five quid cash. In advance.

Suttle peeled off the notes, too knackered to barter. The room was horrible: pink bedspread, cracked handbasin, no shade on the overhead bulb, mauve carpet, everything stinking of cigarettes. Suttle lay on his back, staring up. There were damp patches on the ceiling and canned laughter from the TV in the next room. Forget the TV and the fags, he told himself, and he might easily have been at home. The dripping tap. The draught through the window stirring the thin strip of curtain. The overpowering evidence that someone didn't care, that someone should have tried harder. The thought sobered him. Lizzie deserved better than this. He reached for his mobile and keyed her number. It rang and rang before going onto divert. He stared at it, perplexed, then tried again. Still no answer. Only on his third attempt did Lizzie answer.

'Are you coming home?' Her voice was cold.

'I've hurt you,' he said.

'You're right. So when are you coming home?'

'Tomorrow,' he said. 'I'll be up first thing. Should be back by—'

He broke off, staring at the phone. She'd hung up. He shut his eyes. For a minute or two he tried to think of nothing. When he opened them again, the damp patches, the canned laughter and the sour reek of a million cigarettes were still there. Rolling over, he hammered on the thin partition wall.

'Shut the fuck up,' he yelled.

Nothing happened. He beat on the wall again. Nothing. Finally he rolled off the bed and went out into the corridor. The door to the adjoining room was unlocked. He pushed it open. The room was empty. He bent to the TV and ripped the plug out of the socket in the skirting board.

Back in his own room, he sat on the bed, his elbows on his knees. Ten to midnight. At length he reached for the mobile again. He'd stored Gina Hamilton's number only yesterday. She answered on the second ring.

'Who is this?'

'Jimmy. Jimmy Suttle.'

'What do you want?'

Her voice wasn't as hostile as he might have expected. He even sensed a a hint of warmth when she asked what he was up to.

'Fuck knows,' he said.

'Where are you?'

'Pompey. This is a room you will not believe.'

'What room?'

Suttle tried to explain but gave up. When he tried to pretend a renewed interest in Tom Pendrick she saw through it at once.

'What are you after?' she said.

Suttle stared at the rain dripping down the window pane. Good question.

'A meet. A drink,' he said at last. 'I need someone to talk to. You call it.'

'You're serious?'

'Yeah.' He'd shut his eyes again. 'I think I am.'

Lizzie lay in bed. Grace's cot was beside her. Lizzie had moved it in as a precaution. If anything happened, she told herself, better that they faced it together.

The last couple of hours the wind had got up. She pulled the duvet closer, buried herself in its warmth, tried not to listen to the noises outside in the garden, but every creak, every sigh, every rustle in the long grass beyond the patio sparked another image. Someone watching. Someone waiting. Someone stealing ever closer to the gaping window downstairs.

Once she switched on the light and risked a look at her watch. 03.17. In a couple of hours a pale grey light would wash through the thin curtains. After that, God willing, she might sleep. In the meantime she had to fight this sense of welling panic, this certainty that things could only get worse, and to do that she had to concentrate on something amusing, something positive, a single image that might keep the busy darkness at bay.

She tried and tried, raiding her memories from Gill's visit. The ducklings in the stream at the bottom of the garden. The horses on the beach the afternoon they'd walked to Straight Point. The expression on Grace's tiny face when her mum had staggered to her feet after the first session on the rowing machine. For a moment or two this worked. But then the images faded and the darkness crowded back in and she flailed around in her mind's eye, looking for some place to hide.

Then, quite suddenly, she had it. She was afloat again, taking her first strokes towards the dock, listening to the big man with the huge hands. He'd told her she could do it. And he'd been right.

Five

Suttle was on the road early next morning. By five to nine he was mopping up the last of a hangover with an all-day breakfast in a café off the Bridport bypass. The rain had cleared overnight and the hills in west Dorset were a vivid green in the fitful sunshine. He stood in the car park, enjoying the taste of the wind, waiting for Lizzie to pick up. After some thought he'd decided to pretend last night never happened. When she finally answered, he could hear banging in the background.

'What's going on?'

'I've got a guy in from down the road. He's fixing the window.'

'Right ...' Suttle wondered who was paying but decided not to ask. 'You OK?'

'We're fine.'

'Grace?'

'She's teething again. Don't forget about tonight.'

'What?' Suttle was fumbling for his car keys.

'I'm rowing. You need to be back by half five. You think you can manage that?'

Suttle's office was still empty when he made it to Exeter. The Office Manager, a resourceful divorcee called Leslie, brought him coffee and a couple of stale biscuits. Luke Golding, she said, was about to be redeployed by Mr Nandy but the lad was still upstairs. She knew he wanted a word.

Suttle nodded. He was looking at the list of messages on his desk. Leslie had already arranged them in order of priority. The first one asked him to bell the CSI at Scenes of Crime.

Mark was en route to an aggravated burglary in Totnes. Suttle heard the *tick-tock* of his indicator as he pulled in to take the call.

'Kinsey's PC,' he said. 'Christ knows how but we got bumped up the queue. They haven't done full analysis yet but they've taken a good look.'

Suttle was impressed. The techies were as hard-pressed as everyone else in the force and the wait for hard disk analysis often stretched to weeks, sometimes months. Nandy's doing, he thought. Has to be.

Mark told him to get a pen. He'd spent a couple of hours with the key data yesterday afternoon and sorted what he thought might be useful.

'The guy's a businessman, right?'

'Right.'

'Building resort hotels?'

'Retirement communities. Top-end stuff. High six figures for a nice view and fancy CCTV.'

'Gotcha.' For once in his life Mark was laughing. 'There's a whole load of emails about a site at a place called Trezillion. It's hard to get the context without more info but I get the feeling this thing's still on the drawing board. He's forever nailing the planning guys to the wall. Telling these people what to do and when. Real fucking arsewipe.'

Suttle reached for a pen. Mark's language always enriched a conversation. Scene of Crimes guys were a special breed but Mark was a one-off. Mr Gloom one minute. Mr Yippee the next. Definitely bipolar.

'Where's Trezillion?'

'Cornwall. North coast. Lovely little bay with nothing but a public lavatory and a bit of car park. Used to be a top bogging spot for gays down from Newquay. You should give it a go before Kinsey gets his hands on it.'

'He's dead, Mark.'

'Fuck me, so he is. Surprise or what?' Another growl of laughter. 'I'll ping you the meat of this stuff. See what you make of it.'

'Anything else?'

'Yeah. We've got a single blonde hair from the floor beside Kinsey's bed. Proves nothing except he might have got lucky.'

Suttle scribbled himself a note. The Viking, he thought. Definitely worth a return visit.

'Is that it?'

'No.' Mark confirmed that Kinsey hadn't belonged to Facebook or any of the other social sites. Neither did he appear to have any close mates worth an email or two. There was, however, one chink in his armour.

'What's that?'

'The guy was a huge video gamer. Played most nights.'

'Really?'

'Yeah. I don't know how much you know about all this gaming shit but there's a service called Steam. It's a deal you sign up to. You buy games through the site and they organise everything else for you, keep your games in the cloud, help you find friends in multiplayer, keep a record of how you're doing, sort out the social side.'

'Social side?'

'Yeah. Most of these games you can either play solo against the computer or with other people. The guys you're playing with have weird screen names. Think cyber handles.'

'Who was Kinsey? What did he call himself?'

'Jalf Rezi. As in you know what.' Mark invited Suttle to picture Kinsey bent over the rail of his balcony, barfing mouthfuls of chicken jalfrezi into the night.

Suttle needed to get back to the video games.

'Kinsey was part of a team? Is that what you're telling me?'

'Yeah. Definitely. Some nights he must have played alone. Other nights he logged into a server and went out with his mates.'

'What kind of games are we talking about?'

'I can only give you names, I'm afraid. Most of this shit's way over my head.'

He tallied some of the games in Kinsey's Steam library: Grand Theft Auto IV, Arma 2, Need for Speed, Shift, Assassin's Creed Brotherhood, Battlefield 2, Civilisation IV, Half Life 2, Left 4 Dead, Left 4 Dead 2, Counterstrike, God of War, Team Fortress 2, Wings of Prey.

Suttle was scribbling fast. He wanted to know what these games were like.

'Haven't a clue. I'll email you the guy's Steam profile. You might need someone younger to make sense of it. These guys live under stones during the day, which is why they've all got such shit complexions. Good luck, eh? And tell him to get a life.'

Kinsey's Steam profile arrived by email within minutes. Suttle could make little sense of it. Luke Golding, mercifully, was still at his desk. Suttle drew up a chair while the young D/C explained that Henri Laffont, the Swiss engineer, had definitely spent the weekend in Shanghai. Another name off the suspect list.

'Sorry, Sarge.'

'No problem. How much do you know about video games?'

'Why?'

'Just answer the question.'

'Quite a lot.'

'OK ...'

Suttle consulted the Steam profile and read out the list of games. Golding wanted to know what this had to do with Kinsey.

'They were on his computer.'

'Really? He was a *gamer*?'

'Yeah. Surprised?'

'Very.'

Suttle wanted to know what you could read into a guy by his choice of favourite games.

'Lots. Show me.'

Suttle gave him the Steam profile. Golding studied Kinsey's list of games, which included the hours Kinsey had logged on each. His head came up.

'Well, he certainly liked his shooters.'

'What do you mean?'

'Kinsey was big on two games, right? Counterstrike and Team Fortress 2. Look, he played 400 hours on Counterstrike. That's serious addiction. Plus nearly 200 on TF2. OK. They're both shooter games but the likeness ends there. TF2 is basically one big party. The action could come straight out of *Looney Tunes*. It's also way more player-friendly than CS, especially when it comes to respawning.'

'Respawning?'

'That's when you're returned to the game after you die. On most games you wait a couple of seconds and then bang, you're back in the game. Not with Counterstrike. When you get killed playing CS, that's it for the rest of the round. You're dead. End of.'

CS, he said, was pure. It had no fancy bells and whistles, no back story, no million-dollar cut scenes, just a very simple premise: beat the other team. To do that, in Golding's view, you had to be fucking ace.

'Plus it's multiplayer only, Sarge. Which means you're always playing against real humans so practising against the computer is out of the question.'

'So you have to play with other people? Is that what you're telling me?'

'Yeah.'

'And the other game? Team Fortress 2?'

'Completely different. TF2 is way too anarchic for someone as hard core as Kinsey. It's a bit tongue-in-cheek.'

'So why would he play it so often?'

'Good question.' Golding's gaze had returned to the Steam page. 'This must have to do with the company he's been keeping.'

The notion of company was intriguing. So far, according to dozens of accounts, Kinsey was the near-perfect definition of a loner. On the face of it, all the guys in Saturday's winning quad had been his buddies, but the closer you questioned them the more obvious it became that Kinsey had bought their friendship, or perhaps just their company. So how come he'd spent most nights banged up in cyberspace with a bunch of gamers? Were relationships simpler this way? No messy stuff like having to talk face to face, or having to cope with the million tiny aggravations that came with having real mates?

Golding was still engrossed in the printouts from Kinsey's Steam page.

'I need to have a proper look at this.'

'Why?'

'Because you're going to ask me whether he had a special friend. And the way Steam works, the answer is yes.'

'So who is he?'

'This guy.'

Suttle followed his pointing finger. Somehow he'd missed the name on the bottom left of the page. He reached for a pen and ringed it carefully. ShattAr. Then he looked up.

'So this guy has to be a mate of Kinsey's? Is that what we're saying?'

'Yeah.'

'So how do we find out his real name?'

Suttle's question hung in the air. What he dreaded was having to go to one of the companies that controlled the servers.

Most of them were in the States and in his experience even a routine enquiry could take months to process.

Golding, it turned out, had another idea.

'We join the games, Sarge. We play Counterstrike and TF2. And we pretend to be Jalf Rezi.'

'We? I think not. You mean you.'

'Sure.' He was grinning. 'My pleasure.'

Suttle phoned Nandy from his own office. He caught the Det-Supt emerging from a meeting. A million detectives, he said, had been looking for a head to fit the body at the Bodmin scene of crime and so far they'd got nowhere. He'd like to chalk this up to a superior breed of criminal but his instincts told him it was pure luck. Nandy hated factors like luck. Luck, in his view, had no role to play in a properly run investigation.

'You're going to give me a name?'

'Sorry, sir?'

'For Kinsey?'

'I'm afraid not. Not yet.'

Suttle briefly explained about Kinsey's passion for video games. He needed D/C Golding's help just a little while longer. He'd have asked D/I Houghton for the go-ahead but she wasn't picking up.

'She's gone to Brittany,' Nandy said. 'She's looking for the head.'

'Did she mention Kinsey's bank statements and those phone billings before she went?'

'Yes. It'll be a couple of days yet. Are you sure you need them? The banks are charging us the earth.'

Suttle confirmed he'd need the records for the Coroner's file. Nandy wanted to know how long he'd be hanging on to Golding.

'Couple of days, sir. Max.'

There was a long silence. Suttle was wondering about the

ethics of a police officer impersonating someone else online. Then Nandy was back on the phone.

'Two days it is, son. Consider yourself lucky.'

Lizzie picked up a copy of the *Exmouth Journal* at lunchtime. She'd wheeled Grace down to the village store and only caught the headline on her way out. She stopped beside the rack of newspapers. The story occupied the entire front page. Beneath the headline – MURDER SQUAD PROBE MARINA DEATH – was a colour photo of a bunch of guys in a pub. She recognised the biggest at once, Tom Pendrick. Kinsey, according to the paper, was the little guy centre stage.

Lizzie bought the paper and took it home. The handyman she'd found had finished with the window, hammering the metal frame back into line and reseating the hinges. It was a snug fit now and Lizzie told herself it would resist all intruders. The residue of last night had stayed with her, but she saw no point in letting it spoil the sunshine. The last forty-eight hours had taught her a great deal about her marriage, but the lessons she knew she must draw were still unclear. For the time being, boxed in, she'd simply have to bide her time.

Kinsey's death had spilled onto page 2 of the paper. A reporter looking for another angle had put a call through to the secretary of the rowing club. She'd confirmed that everyone was deeply shocked by what had happened and were discussing what the club might organise in the way of a tribute. Jake Kinsey, she said, had been more than generous in his support for local rowing.

Lizzie went back to the front page, wondering how she'd be dealing with a story like this if she was back in the newsroom. She knew for a fact that the police were treating Kinsey's death as suspicious and all the chatter she'd overheard in the boat and on the beach suggested that the club's benefactor had been far from popular. One of the girls had called him The

Passenger. Another had said he was creepy. Tonight, maybe, she'd find out more.

Suttle was contemplating a sandwich when he took the call from Exmouth Quays. As the last man standing in *Constantine*'s abandoned stockade, all inquiries to the central control room were being routed to him.

Suttle bent to the phone and introduced himself. It was a woman's voice. He didn't understand why she was shouting.

'That Kinsey man,' she bellowed. 'He'd no right. Absolutely no right.'

'No right to do what?'

'To act the way he did. This is enslavement pure and simple. He simply didn't care. No man should be allowed to do that.' She paused. 'Did you get my letter about Prince William?'

'I'm afraid I didn't.'

'His life is under threat. I have the documents, the proof. You should come and see them.' Another pause. 'Are you a monarchist, by any chance?'

'No.'

'Neither am I. Do come round. Number 31.'

'Where?'

'Regatta Court. The name's Peggy Brims. My mother was half-French.'

The phone went dead. Suttle did a reverse number search to check the address. Peggy Brims, 31 Regatta Court. He turned to his PC. A couple of keystrokes took him into the Operational Information System. He needed a couple of checks before he could decide whether to turn this woman's call into an action.

He waited for a moment or two then keyed in her name and postcode. It turned out she had an entire file of her own. It stretched back more than eighteen months, call after call alerting the forces of law and order to a long list of imminent threats. She'd been worried sick about gunrunning in Cuba, about the activities of a gangster called Marc Puyrol in Marseilles, about a bunch of goths in Whitby who were trying to set fire to a hotel on the harbourside.

In every case these pleas for action had been dismissed as crank calls. This woman had form as well as money. She spent most of her waking life dreaming up fictions to keep the police on their toes. But then Suttle's eye was caught by another entry. Back last summer she'd reported a local woman speeding out to sea on a borrowed jet ski. It was Peggy Brims' settled view that this woman had been rendezvousing with one of the huge oil tankers anchored out in Lyme Bay. She'd doubtless returned with thousands of pounds' worth of cocaine or heroin or something equally noxious, determined to corrupt and subvert the nation's youth.

In her choice of language and the sheer force of her indignation, there was absolutely nothing to distinguish this call from any of the others. Except that she'd been right. HMCR had been running an intel operation in the bay for months. And a couple of weeks later, partly thanks to her contribution, arrests had been made. There were difficulties producing her as a witness in court because of her looniness, but the fact remained that she kept her eyes open and had – for once – lifted the phone in genuine anger.

Suttle binned the idea of a sandwich and drove down to Exmouth Quays. Number 31 was on the third floor, served by the same lift as Kinsey's flat. Peggy Brims came to the door the moment Suttle knocked. She was a big woman, nudging sixty, beautifully dressed. She walked with the aid of a stick and was followed everywhere by a small brown dog. The dog's name was Pétain.

'As in Maréchal, young man. How much do you know about French history?'

'Very little.'

'Petain? The hero of Verdun? The saviour of *la belle France*? Went to seed later but a great, great man. Do you drink vermouth by any chance?'

She led him through to the sitting room at the front of the apartment. This was a miniature version of Kinsey's view, smaller but no less impressive. Suttle was watching a yellow kayak crabbing across the tide when he felt a glass in his hand. Dry Martini with a single green olive.

'*Salut*. What shall I call you?'

Suttle had already shown her his warrant card. She wasn't interested in surnames.

'I shall call you André,' she announced. 'We must raise a glass to those imps in the City. Did I mention the Libor rate? I'm deeply, *deeply* concerned.'

Suttle hadn't the faintest what she was talking about. The Martini must have been 90 per cent gin. He wanted to know about Kinsey.

Peggy had settled on a long crescent of sofa. Suttle had last seen furniture like this in a National Trust property he'd visited with Lizzie before the baby arrived. There were pictures on the wall, the frames equally ornate, that oozed money and taste. Dark landscapes in oil. Maritime etchings with a naval flavour that took him back to Pompey. He was beginning to wonder whether she entertained coach parties at the weekend when she reached across and tapped him lightly on the arm. She couldn't get this horrible man out of her mind.

'Kinsey?'

'Of course. He was thoroughly unpleasant, I'm afraid. No class. Absolutely no breeding. Which, of course, is why he did it.'

'Did what?'

'Had those little girls round.'

'I'm not with you.'

'The girls. The oriental girls. The girls in the lift. They belonged on my mantlepiece, some of them. Truly exquisite. A couple, one in particular, I even talked to.'

'Where?'

'In the lift. A pretty, pretty little thing. I was worried about cholera then. They used to call it the flux. I expect you know that.'

The word flux brought Suttle's head up. Milo Symons had used exactly the same term when he was talking about his film. *Flux*, he'd said. Tasha's idea.

'You discussed cholera with the girl in the lift?'

'I did. I think she was alarmed. I *hope* she was alarmed. She didn't say much. One has a duty in this life. Bad news should be shared. Don't you agree, André?'

She emptied her glass and held it out. Suttle refilled it from the cocktail shaker on the sideboard. A line of nicely mounted black and white photos featured a couple in their early twenties. Peggy was watching him in the huge mirror that dominated the wall opposite.

'My ma and pa, André. Pa served in the Diplomatic Corps before the war. A handsome man, my father. Knew nothing of the flux.'

Suttle wanted to be sure about Kinsey. 'These girls were definitely going up to his flat?'

'Of course.'

'How do you know?'

'I accompanied them. Just to make sure they came to no harm.'

'No harm how?'

'En route, André.' Her face darkened. 'Highwaymen.'

'In the lift?'

'Everywhere. *Partout*. Of course they never tell you in the brochure, and there's another thing.'

'What?'

'That man Kinsey. He had twelve fingers, you know. Ten for himself, and two for special pies.'

'I don't understand.'

'What don't you understand? The fingers?'

'The pies.'

'Ah, my poor André, *mon pauvre*. *Viens*. Come ...' She

struggled off the sofa, gathered up the dog in her spare arm and led Suttle through to a bedroom. The window was framed with heavily ruched curtains and offered a view of the dockside and the waterfront beyond. Immediately below was the stretch of promenade where Kinsey had met his death.

'There ...' A quivering finger indicated something in the distance.

'Where?'

'There. Beyond those hideous flats. That's where they're going to build the next one. They call it Pier Head. And you know who wanted to put his snout in that ghastly trough?'

'Kinsey?'

'Of course. My André ... so quick off the mark.' She patted his arm, delighted at this meeting of minds, then led him back to the sitting room.

'I need to be sure about these girls,' Suttle said. 'Would you recognise them again?'

'Of course.'

'If I brought photographs?'

'A great pleasure, André. You'll take care on the way out? After dark is worse, of course, but daylight can be equally unnerving. You understand my drift?'

Suttle was still on his feet. The interview was evidently over.

'Of course,' he said 'because of the highwaymen.'

'Wrong, my dear André,' she was beaming now. 'Because of the *flux*.'

Mark was still at Totnes when Suttle phoned him. Suttle wanted to know about Kinsey's seized iPhone.

'Did you go through all the pictures?'

'No. There were hundreds,' said the CSI.

'Where's the phone now?'

'Back in the office. I've bagged it for analysis. Mr Nandy's definitely got the inside track with the techies. Shouldn't be more than a couple of days.'

'I need it faster than that.'

'Do it yourself, then. Ask for Lola. She's got the magic key.'

Suttle drove across to Scenes of Crime at Heavitree Road to take a look at the iPhone. Lola wasn't prepared to release it. If Suttle was going to go through Kinsey's pictures there had to be someone else on hand to testify he hadn't inserted any new material. Otherwise there might be evidential problems down the line in court.

Suttle shrugged. More and more these days detectives had to put up with this kind of procedural nonsense but he understood the logic and knew he had no choice.

'Splash of milk, please,' he said. 'No sugar.'

He settled down to await her return before boredom drove him to scroll through Kinsey's address book. He had a print-out of this already but needed to remind himself about Molly Doyle, the rowing club secretary. A single blonde hair had the makings of a serious interview. He scribbled down her number as his coffee arrived. Lola, it turned out, was a busy girl. Time to browse Kinsey's gallery.

The first sequence of shots were trophy views from Kinsey's penthouse. April had sparked a series of sensational sunsets and Kinsey had taken full advantage. Next came photos snapped from an accompanying launch on what Suttle assumed was a training row. He recognised the elfin figure of Lenahan in the cox's seat and the towering bulk of Pendrick rowing behind the stroke. Milo Symons was in the number two seat with Kinsey himself in bow. These were very telling. Only Kinsey ever stole a glance towards the camera. And only Kinsey's blades were ever out of sync with the rest of the crew. Stick insect, Suttle thought. Another of Tasha Donovan's little phrases.

'What exactly are we looking for?' Lola was on the meter. She had another ten minutes, absolute max.

'We'll know it when we see it.' Suttle was looking at a matchless crescent of sand softened on the landward side by a line of dunes. An offshore wind had sculpted the incoming tide into surf to die for, and the blueness of the water was dotted with tiny black figures waiting for the perfect wave.

Suttle scrolled on. There were more shots, the same cove photographed from every conceivable angle.

'Where's that?' He offered Lola the phone.

'Haven't a clue. Are those the ones you're after?'

Suttle shook his head. This must be Trezillion, he thought, the jewel in Kittiwake Oceanside's crown. He scrolled on, finding more shots, a different location this time. Finally, at the back end of last year, came the proof that his afternoon visit to Exmouth Quays had scored a modest result. The date – 24.12.2010 – was the only clue Suttle needed. Jake Kinsey, in his big fuck-off apartment, had bought himself an early Christmas prezzie.

'That's gross. That's horrible.' Lola turned away. 'You'd have to pay someone to do that.'

Lizzie was changed and ready half an hour before Suttle got home. She offered a cold cheek for a kiss, reminded him about a bowl of puréed bananas she'd left in the fridge for Grace and asked him to keep an eye open for the cat.

'Has he gone?' Suttle sounded hopeful.

'I doubt it.' Lizzie got in the car and adjusted the seat. 'One other thing. There's a bill needs settling for the window. It's on the table. I said you'd drop a cheque off tonight. A Mr Willoughby. He's just up the road. Sweetest man.'

She pulled the door shut, backed into the lane and floored the acclerator. In the rear-view mirror she could see Suttle watching her. He didn't wave.

At Exmouth once again a couple of quads were already on the beach. Thursdays, she knew already, was a big night for the juniors, and Tessa was doing her best to organise them. The club captain was due down any minute and wanted to have a word with everyone about Kinsey. Coverage in the local paper had made the club front-page news and in his view, according to Tessa, there had to be ways of turning all this publicity to ERC's advantage.

Lizzie parked, aware at once of Pendrick crossing the road. She got out and gave him a wave. He fell into step beside her.

'Back for more?'

'Of course.'

'Ever thought about the double?'

'I wouldn't know what a double is.'

'Come with me. I'll show you.'

They walked back to the compound. The club's double scull was half the length of the big quads and looked, to Lizzie's eye, a serious challenge.

'I'm a novice,' she said. 'The quad gives me somewhere to hide.'

'You don't need it. Just trust me. We're talking a 1.8 tide tonight. It's low water at half six. No wind to speak of. We couldn't capsize this baby if we tried.'

We? She looked up at him, already half persuaded, wanting the chance to prove she could do it. This guy's probably been rowing for ever, she told herself. And if he thinks I can hack it who is little me to spoil the party?

'OK.' She grinned and dropped a little curtsy. 'As long as you're sure.'

By the time they'd rigged the double and dragged it across the road towards the slipway, a sizeable group of rowers had gathered on the beach. The club captain was an older man, tall, visibly weathered by life. He was already in full flow, talking about what Kinsey had brought to the club, and as she and Pendrick paused to listen, Lizzie became aware of a younger guy with a video camera circling the group. His long black hair was gathered into a ponytail with a twist of yellow ribbon and he panned the camera to catch a listening face or two before returning to the captain.

By now the shape of the club's tribute to Kinsey was clear. Weather permitting, the club would be launching all its boats on Sunday. On an ebbing tide they'd row in line abreast towards the dock. Abeam of Regatta House they'd pause and hold formation before releasing a wreath of interwoven flowers. The specially designed wreath had been guaranteed to float. As it drifted down-tide, the club's boats would form an escort. Molly Doyle, said the club captain, had contacts in the local press. With luck a TV crew might even turn up. The resulting pictures, if they got it right, would do the club no end of good. The flowers, he added, included red camellias. These he understood to be Kinsey's favourite.

There was a mutter of approval. Several of the younger girls were comforting each other. One of the older boys eyed them in disbelief.

'Let's go.' Pendrick jerked his head towards the water.

They tugged the double scull down the beach beyond the quads. Pendrick untied it from the trailer and began to talk Lizzie through the next stage in the operation. Lizzie, still watching the crowd of rowers on the beach, wasn't listening.

'That's a nice thing to do,' she said. 'The wreath should work beautifully.'

Pendrick, steadying the double, shot her a look.

'It's bullshit,' he said.

'Why? How?'

'Kinsey was clueless about flowers. He wouldn't have known a red camellia from a hole in the road.'

'But what about the juniors? Those girlies?'

'They didn't know the first thing about him, probably never met the guy. It's showtime. Cameras. Grief. These days, unless you shed a tear it isn't real.' He frowned, then nodded at the double. 'Are we going to do this thing or what?'

Despite the fact she was teething, it took Suttle less than half an hour to get Grace settled. Before he'd got to the end of her favourite story she was asleep. Suttle returned downstairs. Lizzie had left a pile of vegetables for his attention but he

ignored them in favour of a Stella from the fridge. He opened
the tinnie and reached for a glass. The bill for the window
refurb was lying on the kitchen table – ninety-five pounds.

He went next door and inspected the window before settling
in the Ikea rocker beside the ancient telly. By the time he'd left
the office, Suttle had secured Carole Houghton's permission
to explore Kinsey's affection for video games. He'd explained
Golding's suspicions that Kinsey had developed an online
relationship. In the young D/C's view there might be a special
person in Kinsey's cyber life who would repay a little attention.
Maybe, in the vast spaces of the Internet, Kinsey had let slip a
confidence or two. Maybe.

Houghton had accepted the logic and checked out the RIPA
situation with Nandy. Under the Regulation of Investigative
Powers Act, *Constantine* might need a warrant if Golding
was to pose as Kinsey. Nandy loved the idea. A warrant, he
said, would be no problem. The more proactive *Constantine*
became, the better he liked it.

The warrant had been signed off before close of play.
Tonight Golding would be settling at his own PC, monitoring
both Counterstrike and Team Fortress 2, jumping in as Jalf
Rezi and hoping that ShattAr showed up. He'd promised Suttle
a call if he struck lucky but was gloomy about his chances
of surviving the killing fields of Counterstrike. He'd log on to
different servers for a bit of discreet practice but it was years
since he'd played the game and he knew how tough it could be.

Suttle swallowed a mouthful or two of Stella, trying to imagine Kinsey at his PC up in the emptiness of his trophy apartment. Tired or drunk, according to Luke, he'd probably take a
gentler ride with Team Fortress 2. That way he could rely on
being respawned, an endless process of reincarnation, keeping
himself from the jaws of death. On screen it had doubtless
worked. In real life, alas, it hadn't.

The brutality of this contrast between the make-believe of
cyberspace and the lethal suck of gravity was, Suttle sensed,

one of the keys to *Constantine*. The more he thought about it, the more he suspected that video games must have offered Kinsey the perfect surrogate for real friendship. Any attachments he formed on the Internet were risk-free. He could expose as much or as little of himself as he chose. And every time he logged on there was the prospect of another hour or so in the company of like-minded loners, busy zapping the next shadow lurking at the edge of the screen.

This was fine as far as it went, an intriguing line of enquiry that might yield a name and even a confidence or two. But what was he to make of SOC's blonde hair retrieved from Kinsey's bedroom? And of Peggy Brims' impassioned belief that Kinsey's interest in real estate extended further than a clutch of picturesque waterside sites in north Cornwall?

The latter had taken Suttle to the East Devon District Council website. These people were the planning authority for Exmouth, and a couple of minutes' research had revealed an application to develop Pier Head, adjacent to Exmouth Quays.

Peggy Brims, once again, had her thumb on the pulse of local life. The architectural drawings showed a towering apartment block that would dwarf everything else in the area. The application was the work of Devon-based property developers. Accompanying the drawings was the usual tosh about gateway locations, iconic structures and local employment opportunities, and Suttle's suspicions that the sheer size of this proposed monster would have sparked local opposition turned out to be spot on. A call to the *Exmouth Journal* confirmed a flood of objections. Many of the locals, said the news editor, were outraged.

But did Kinsey really want to help himself to a slice of the action? Or might his interest be limited to the spec purchase of an apartment or two, something way up at the top of the building, an asset he could flog on when prices started to rise again? Suttle had tried to raise some kind of answer from the developers, leaving a message on their switchboard, but so far no one had returned his call.

He finished the Stella and stole upstairs to check on Grace. She was curled in her cot, a corner of the sheet bunched in her tiny hand, oblivious to the world. Back in the living room Suttle tried to map out the coming days. The key to every live enquiry was the Policy Book. *Constantine*'s had been in the hands of Carole Houghton. She'd now handed it over to Suttle and already he'd drawn on its contents to better understand *Constantine*'s brief history. Houghton, as he expected, had been characteristically thorough, recording and explaining every investigative decision she'd taken. Suttle's next task was to add a sheaf of statements, especially from the winning crew, who'd been the last people to see Kinsey alive.

Andy Poole's statement was already in the file, as was the account *Constantine*'s D/Cs had taken from Tom Pendrick the night he'd come back from north Cornwall. But both Eamonn Lenahan and Milo Symons would need a revisit for statementing, and Natasha Donovan – Milo's partner – had yet to be interviewed at all. These calls would now fall to Suttle and he made a mental note to start with Tash Donovan. The word flux kept coming back to him. His years in CID had taught Suttle to discount the likelihood of coincidence. How come both Tash and Peggy Brims had been so interested in 'flux'?

Suttle was thinking about the single blonde hair and wondering when to make another call on Molly Doyle when his landline rang. It was Luke Golding.

'How's it going?'

'It isn't, Sarge. I got Scenes of Crime to rip Kinsey's Steam password from his hard drive and logged on as Jalf.'

'And?'

'I got zapped within seconds. Total fucking disaster.'

'Counterstrike?'

'Too right. I waited until the game ended and respawned. Survived for a whole minute this time then crashed and burned again. Horrible.'

By now, he said, his performance had begun to attract

attention. He wasn't on headphones for obvious reasons but he'd got a couple of messages. One of the players had asked whether he was pissed. Another, interestingly, thought that Kinsey might have been subbed by his brother. Or more likely his granny. Either way, there was a general consensus that Kinsey had stepped out of his former persona and become someone else. Which was, of course, exactly right.

'Anything else?'

'Yeah. There was a third message. This was definitely kinder.'

'What did it say?'

'It wanted to know what the problem was. You want to guess the sender?'

'ShattAr.'

'Spot on.'

'So what did you say?'

'Nothing. But that's not the point, Sarge. This one used Kinsey's real name. He called me Jake. The guy's in touch. He's out there. He exists.'

Suttle thought about the implications. At last Kinsey might have found someone he could confide in.

'So how do we progress this?' he said at last. 'What do we do next?'

'I log on again. Tonight. Tomorrow. Whenever. Wait for the guy to reappear.'

'But you're still pretending to be Kinsey, right?'

'Right.'

'So how do you handle him? What do you say?'

'Number one, I'm still going to be crap at Counterstrike. So the guy's going to start wondering if I really am Kinsey. So maybe I should go on headphones and have a conversation.'

'Saying what?'

'I could tell him Jake's had a bit of an accident. I could tell him I'm standing in. That way I could maybe get a steer on who this guy is.'

Suttle smiled. A bit of an accident, he thought. He bent to the phone again.

'And you think that might work?'

'It might. It's possible. But there's another way. Maybe better.'

'Like what?'

'Like I log on again as Jalf and wait for him to appear. Then I send him a message asking him to be a Facebook friend.'

'What if he's a Facebook friend of Kinsey's already?'

'He can't be. You told me Kinsey wasn't on Facebook.'

'You're right. He wasn't. Brain-dead, me. So what do we do about that?'

'I get myself a Facebook page.'

'As Kinsey?'

'Of course. Then send this guy a friend request and add a message about Counterstrike so he knows who I am. Fingers crossed, he friends me.'

Suttle nodded in approval. Once ShattAr got in touch, his Facebook profile might give them everything they'd need to have a proper conversation.

'You really think he'll do it?'

'I've no idea, Sarge. Worth a try though, eh?'

The line went dead. Outside, after a decent sunset, the light was beginning to die. Suttle got up and went to the window, peering into the gathering darkness. Lately he'd made an effort to tally the jobs that badly needed doing around the property but knew that lists were no substitute for the real thing. He checked his watch, wondering how Lizzie was getting on. Nearly half eight. Late.

Lizzie's outing with Pendrick was a disaster. Rowing in the double turned out to be a circus act after the comforting embrace of the quad. The slightest wobble, a single mistake with either blade, seemed to threaten a capsize. By the time she and Pendrick got down to the dock, she was ready to give up.

Pendrick was rowing in the bow seat, checking their progress over his shoulder, feeding her instructions as they picked their way through the buoys and moorings. Heavy on green. Go red. Equal pressure. Lizzie tried to process all these commands, turning them into strong tugs on the right-hand oar or the left, but her brain had turned to mush.

In the end Pendrick beached them on the long curve of Dawlish Warren and helped Lizzie get out.

'Useless,' she said. 'Totally fucking hopeless.'

He told her not to be dramatic. Rowing the double after a single outing in the quad was a tough call.

'So why are we doing it?'

'Because I thought you could hack it.'

'Wrong. I can't.'

'You can. You just have to relax. Listen to me.'

With infinite patience he pointed out what she was doing wrong. She had to ride the double like a horse. She had to feel the river through her bum. She had to think of the double as a musical instrument, amplifying the suck and nudge of the tide.

'Listen to your body,' he said, 'and you won't go wrong.'

Lizzie began to laugh. This sounded wildly karmic. She'd tried yoga once and been just as challenged.

A smile ghosted over Pendrick's face. Maybe he'd got the wrong metaphor, he said. Maybe she should start thinking about the *grain* of the river, how to feel it, how to make it a friend.

'That's even worse. We're talking water, not wood.'

'Same difference. It's a living thing. And so are you. Fight it, like just now, and the river will always win. Make it your friend –' the sudden grin took her by surprise '– and anything can happen.'

They tried again. This time, Lizzie was worse. Sheer concentration made her nervous. Nervous, she began to wobble. Wobbling finally brought them to a halt. By now they were back beside the stretch of beach that led to the compound.

At slack tide the water was like a mirror. Downstream, Lizzie could see a couple of quads heading seawards. For a moment she envied them but then she felt the gentlest tap on her shoulder. It was Pendrick.

'Drink?' he suggested.

They went to a pub on the seafront. To Lizzie, it was the sanest decision they'd made all evening. There were benches and tables on the big apron of forecourt and Pendrick disappeared inside to the bar. Lizzie gazed out at the beginnings of a decent sunset. For mid-April, it was still warm.

'Cheers. Here's to your lovely bum.'

Pendrick was back with the drinks. He slid into the bench across the table. The same subtle grace, she thought. The same instinctive sense of balance that had just steadied the bloody double.

'Thanks for putting up with me.' She lifted her glass.

Pendrick shrugged. The double was history. They'd have another go when she was ready. Meantime he'd just remembered what date it was.

'You know what I was doing this time last year?'

'Surprise me.'

'Rowing.'

'I said surprise me.'

'We were a week out from Cape Cod. It was an evening like this. I remember it like yesterday.'

Lizzie was staring at him.

'Cape Cod's in Massachusetts,' she said.

'You're right.'

'You're telling me you were on the Atlantic? For a whole week? *Rowing?*'

'Yeah. And the next week and the week after and ...' his hand closed around the pint of Guinness '... for ever really.'

Lizzie had abandoned her drink. Something in this man's face had been nagging at her since she'd first met him and now she realised what it was. The hair, she thought. He had hair then.

'You're the guy who rowed the Atlantic,' she said.

'Yeah.'

'And lost his wife.'

'Yeah.'

'It was all over the papers.'

'Yeah.'

'Shit.'

'Yeah.' He lifted his glass. 'Happy anniversary, eh?'

Lizzie didn't know where to take this conversation next. As a working journalist she'd have had no problems. There were ways you could get people to open up. But this was different. She felt she'd begun to know this man a little. She'd shared something precious with him. She might have fucked up just now in the double but she'd fallen in love with rowing and that she owed to Pendrick.

'You want to talk about it?' she said at last.

'You want to listen?'

'Of course.' Lizzie fought an urge to reach for his hand. 'Tell me.'

He gazed at her then looked away. For a moment Lizzie thought she'd blown it – too hasty, too blatant – but then he was back with her. He wanted to start somewhere else. He wanted to start in Thailand.

He and his wife, he said, had spent the best part of three years bumming round the world with a couple of surfboards and not much else. They'd spent time in California, in Oz, in New Zealand. He was an electrician by trade, and Kate had nursing qualifications, and whenever the money ran out they'd work for a couple of months then hit the beaches again.

'Is that when you got your scar?' Lizzie had been dying to ask.

'Yeah. I got dumped on a reef down near Melbourne. Place called Suicide Beach. Split my face open from here to here ...'

His finger tracked down from the corner of his eye. 'Thank Christ Kate was there. She stopped most of the bleeding and got me to a hospital. My own bloody fault.'

'It didn't put you off?'

'Never. Surfing's a drug. You can't get enough.'

'Sounds great.'

'It was. Kate and I? We had nothing in the world except the ocean. It's amazing how rich that can make you feel.'

'I'm sure. Did Kate think that way as well?'

'Most of the time.' He nodded. 'Yeah.'

After New Zealand, he said, they took a flight to Bangkok, bought an old camper van from a Scouser heading home and drove south.

'You know Thailand at all?'

'No.'

'The best bits are down by the Malay border. We ended up in a village just inland from the beach, place called Ao Lok. We spent the whole summer there, Mr and Mrs Idle, just surfing, swimming, making friends with the locals, totally lovely people. It was a brilliant time.'

After a while, he said, they'd become part of the village. They were renting a hut from someone who'd gone off to work in Phuket. Pendrick would do the odd wiring job for various neighbours while Kate would help out with the kids when they got sick. In return, families would give them food and invite them along for the party when a daughter was getting married or a long-lost cousin flew in from Europe or the States.

'It was like we belonged.' He was smiling. 'It was a nice feeling.'

'And Kate?'

'She was cool with it. In fact she loved it. I think it gave her something we'd never had before. We both came from broken homes. The last thing these people were was broken.'

Ao Lok, he said, was as perfect as perfect can be.

'Like how? Tell me.'

'You could hear the surf at night through the trees. We lived on fruit and bread and fish and rice. Like I say, we were in the water most days. Kate used to look after this little boy, Niran, and she taught him to swim. Once he'd got his confidence, I'd paddle him out on the surf board. He loved it. Fantastic little kid. Always grinning. Happiness on legs. We wanted to kidnap him. Tuck him in the back of the camper and drive away. But what would be the point? Where in the world would ever be more perfect than Ao Lok?'

Lizzie mistook this as a question. She was trying to offer something similar in her own life but failed completely. Pendrick hadn't finished.

'You know something really strange?' he said. 'For years we'd always been moving on. It becomes a kind of habit, maybe stronger than that, maybe a kind of addiction. You're convinced there's always something better round the next corner, and so you look and you look and then you find somewhere like Ao Lok and you realise you've found it. It's the end of the line. It's where you belong. It's where you want to stay. Maybe for ever. Except we couldn't. Because it became impossible.'

'How come?'

'You really want to know?'

'Daft question.'

Pendrick got up to fetch another Guinness. Then he was back.

'Boxing Day.' He wiped his mouth. 'We're up and about and Kate's taken Niran down to the beach. I've told them I'll be along later. We've sold the camper and I'm trying to sort an old moped we've just bought. Next thing I know, there's this roaring noise, a bit like thunder. It gets louder and louder then there are people running up from the beach through the trees. They're yelling about a huge wave coming. I run down towards the beach and get there in time to see this wave breaking way out in the bay. They're right. It's vast. Kate's down there too. The water is being sucked out to sea ahead of the wave and she's running after Niran. By the time she catches him, the wave's on top of them both. That's the last I saw of the kid. No one ever found him.'

'And Kate?'

'She survived. Sort of.'

Afterwards, he said, he and Kate went to America. They'd made friends a while back with a couple from California, surfers like themselves. Kate was really close to the woman – nice girl, half Sri-Lankan. They picked up casual jobs for a while, then got green cards, which made it all legit. They were still spending time by the ocean, he said, but it was never the same.

'That was five years ago.' He was studying his hands. 'Time's supposed to be the healer, isn't it? Time's supposed to make the difference. No chance. Kate had lost it. She became someone else.'

Lizzie nodded. This, at last, sounded familiar. She was getting to know a lot about strangers in her life.

'Difficult,' she said simply.

'It was, believe me. And it was especially hard because I couldn't see an end to it. There was no way Kate could make peace with what had happened because there was no peace to make. Ao Lok and Niran and all the rest of it had taken us to a place we could never get back to. And once that happens, believe me, you're fucked.'

Lizzie reached for his hand. It seemed the simplest thing in the world.

'So what did you do?' she said.

'In the end, you mean?'

'Yes.'

'I figured we had to do something big, something amazing. Double or quits time. The ocean again. Another crap decision.'

They'd saved like crazy for a couple of years and moved east to Cape Cod. Backers had paid for the boat and the provisions and everything else they needed, and they'd made contact with one of the charities that had sprung up after the tsunami.

They'd put together a support team in a town called Woods Hole and spent a week or two rowing up and down the coast to get the feel of the boat.

'And then?'

'We went for it. April's supposed to be kind, and to be fair the weather wasn't that bad, but what nobody ever tells you about is the rowing, the routine, the sheer fucking monotony of going on and on, day after day, just on and on. If you're not careful, if you're not strong, something like that can break your heart.'

'And did it?'

'You're talking about me?'

'Yes.'

'No.' He shook his head. 'I more or less survived.'

'But Kate?'

'Definitely.'

'It broke her heart?'

'Yes.'

He looked up. His eyes were glassy. He gave Lizzie's hand a squeeze and then withdrew his own.

'We had a couple of storms on the way over.' He reached for his drink. 'In that kind of sea there's no way you can keep rowing so you get into this shithole of a cabin, the pair of you, and try and make sure the hatch is watertight, and just ride the storm out. This kind of stuff can go on for days. The cabin's tiny, just room for the two of you. Kate had done her best to cheer the place up. She'd put photos everywhere, places we'd been, friends we were missing, but it's dark most of the time because you're trying to preserve the batteries, and the boat's all over the place and you start to recognise the pattern of the waves, the intervals before they hit you, and you realise after a while that you're just helpless, a sitting target, tense as fuck, waiting for the big one.'

'And did it come?'

'Yeah. Middle of the night. Turned us over. Total capsize.

Kate was crying. She wanted out. She'd had enough. In the end the boat bobbed up again, righted itself, but she cried for hours, really quietly, no big drama. There was nothing I could do, nothing I could say. She'd gone. It was hopeless.'

Lizzie wanted to know if this was when she disappeared. Pendrick shook his head. That happened weeks later. By the next day, he said, the storm had blown itself out. They did their best to get everything back together again, to lash stuff down, to figure out what was missing and what wasn't, but the truth was that the fight had gone out of them.

'You lose heart,' he said. 'Because you keep realising there's something else you've lost, something else you can't put your hand on. It's a bit like being burgled. This stuff's personal. It hurts.'

The worst, he said, was a stone that Kate had kept from the beach at Ao Lok. She'd hung onto it from the day Niran had disappeared, and now it too had gone.

'We looked for it everywhere. We emptied the cabin, shook everything out, looked under the thwarts, tore the boat apart, but it had gone. That did it for her. After that, I knew she'd had enough.'

'Meaning?'

'She wanted to end it all. Slip overboard. Go where Niran had gone.'

'And that's what happened?'

'Yes.'

'Did you talk about it? Before?'

'No.'

'Why not?'

'Good question.' His glass was empty again. Lizzie wondered whether to buy him another Guinness but knew this wasn't the moment. Her hand was back in his.

'You know something about the sea?' He nodded out beyond the promenade.

'Tell me.'

'It puts you to the test. Take on a voyage like we did, day after day, and if there's the slightest weakness in the relationship, the sea will find you out. You set off on a high. You think you're immortal. You think you'll conquer the world. And then it turns out you're wrong.'

'So what happened?'

'We got found out.'

'Because of Niran?'

'Because of me.'

'You blame yourself?'

'Yes.'

'Why?'

'Because I should have been bigger, stronger, more attentive, more loving, more understanding, more ...' He shrugged. 'What the fuck do I know?'

'You know everything. Because you were there. And from where I'm sitting I doubt there's anything else you could have done. We're talking serious depression, right? Depression's a horrible thing. It eats you away inside. You try really hard to get on top of it, you think you've got it nailed, and then you wake up next day and it's *still* there. That's Kate ... no?'

'Yes.' He was studying her. 'So how come you know all this?'

Lizzie held his gaze. Then she lifted his hand to her lips and kissed it.

'Don't ask,' she muttered.

It was dark by the time Suttle decided to make the call. He'd put together a rudimentary stew and boiled a panful of rice. Twice he'd tried to call Lizzie but both times her mobile was on divert. There was no more Stella in the fridge and he couldn't find the remains of Gill Reynolds' Stolly.

'Gina? Jimmy.'

'Hi.' She sounded far away. Non-committal.

'I was just wondering about a meet.'

'Is that right?'

'Yeah. We're still on?'

'I'm not sure.' She paused. 'Do you always call this time of night? Only I might have difficulty getting my head round that.'

'Round what?'

'Becoming your answering service.'

'That's not the way it is.'

'Oh yeah? Tell me more.'

'Like I said last night, I just need to talk.'

'About Pendrick?'

'About me.'

'Why?'

'That's what I want to talk about.'

Another silence, longer this time.

'Tell me something, Jimmy. Are you married?'

'Yes.'

'Kids?'

'A daughter. Grace. She's asleep upstairs.'

'And do you love her?'

'Yes. Very much.'

'I meant your wife.'

It was Suttle's turn to hesitate. The silence stretched and stretched.

'That's a no then,' he said at last.

'No to what?'

'No to a meet. No to a conversation. I just thought ... you know ... sometimes you meet someone and you think there's something there and you need someone to share stuff with and you lift the phone and ... whatever.'

'That someone would be me?'

'Yes.'

'And you think I felt the same? When we met?'

'Yes.'

'Why?'

'Because we're still talking. Because you haven't told me to fuck off.'

'You think I'd do that?'

'I do, yes.'

'Good, because you're right.'

'You're telling me to fuck off?'

'No, Jimmy, I'm not. I'm telling you to sort out exactly what you're after in that lovely head of yours and then pay me the compliment of a decent conversation ...' she paused '... at a reasonable hour.'

'Like tomorrow?'

'Like when you start to make some kind of sense. I'm in bed, by the way. If that's important.'

The phone went dead. Suttle could hear Grace beginning to stir. Within seconds she was crying. Suttle brought her down and settled in the rocker again, trying to calm her.

It was gone eleven when Lizzie finally returned. She stood in the open doorway, framed against the chaos of the kitchen. Both the stew and the rice were cold.

Suttle asked her about the rowing.

'Fabulous evening.' Lizzie was grinning. 'The best.'

Six

D/I Carole Houghton was back from Brittany. She'd been enchanted by Saint-Malo but despite some promising intel she still hadn't found the head.

'So how's *Constantine*?'

Suttle brought her up to date. The Coroner's file was coming along nicely but he thought it a shame not to explore a new lead or two.

'Like?'

Suttle explained about the possibility that Kinsey might have had a gaming buddy.

'Where would that take us?'

'I've no idea, boss, until I bottom it out.'

'And you can do that?'

'Yes.'

It was a bold claim and he'd no idea whether Luke Golding could deliver, but *Constantine* was no longer a mission for the faint-hearted. With everything else falling apart around him, Suttle had decided to pile all his chips on a single square. Shit or bust wasn't a phrase he'd ever had much time for, but just now he told himself he didn't have an option. One way or another, something good had to come out of this new life of his.

'Then there's a couple of other developments.'

He told her about the Scenes of Crime find in Kinsey's

bedroom, the single blonde hair, and about Peggy Brims keeping watch on the lift. Houghton was even less impressed.

'He was a rich man, Jimmy. There's nothing wrong with buying a sex life if he needed it that badly. What's in it for us?'

'Here, boss.'

Suttle handed her the photos retrieved from Kinsey's iPhone. A very beautiful Thai girl was sprawled on Kinsey's bed doing something inventive with an empty bottle of Krug. The little wave with her spare hand was far from convincing.

'You're telling me she did it? She killed him?' Houghton was having a bad day. First the still-missing head. Now her newest D/S trying to turn a probable suicide into something wildly implausible.

'Not her, boss. Not the girl.'

'Who, then?'

'I've no idea. It's just part of the picture.'

'And you think the Coroner will be interested in this?'

'Probably not. But maybe we should.'

'Why?'

'Because Kinsey simply wasn't the kind of guy to top himself.'

'Says who?'

'Me. And pretty much everyone who knew him.'

'Have you talked to Mr Nandy about this?'

'Yeah.'

'And?'

'He doesn't agree. He thinks people are unknowable.'

'Maybe he's got a point.'

'Sure. And maybe he needs to save on the budget.'

There was a long silence. Suttle wondered whether he'd gone too far. Houghton was studying the photo again.

'She's not blonde.' She looked up. 'So maybe you ought to find someone else who is.'

*

Molly Doyle, it turned out, worked as a solicitor at a partnership in Exmouth town centre. In answer to Suttle's phone call, the Viking had freed up half an hour at lunchtime and was happy to help him in whatever way she could.

Suttle found her in an office at the top of the building. She was wearing a black suit, smartly cut. Her nails were carefully varnished and she'd applied a little make-up to hide the shadows beneath her eyes. The only concession to the woman Suttle had met on Sunday morning was a playful pair of black plastic earrings.

'You've heard about the little ceremony we're having for Kinsey?' She told him about the wreath and the escort of boats from the club. The weather forecast, she said, wasn't brilliant, but fingers crossed they'd be able to launch.

She fetched Suttle a coffee from the machine down the corridor. When she got back she wanted to know how he was getting on.

'Fine,' Suttle said.

'You've established what happened?'

'No, not entirely.'

He began to describe the steps they'd taken to understand the kind of life Kinsey had been leading. An obvious source was his iPhone.

'I know about all this. I used to be a criminal lawyer. We're talking intel, yes?' There was a hint of impatience in her voice. She was a busy woman.

Suttle asked about the emails Kinsey had been sending her. Seven in the past month alone, including Saturday night's invite to the party in his apartment.

'Seven?'

'You're surprised?'

'I am. I never kept count. I never answered them either. But you'd know that, wouldn't you?'

Suttle didn't respond. Scenes of Crime had sent him hard copy of all the texts Kinsey had sent her.

'"Loved the way you handled Andy on the beach tonight. When do we get to have another drink?"' he read. '"Bought a couple of pheasants this morning. My place or yours?"' Suttle looked up. 'Are you married, Mrs Doyle?'

'Why do you ask?'

'Because it might be germane.'

'Germane?' She rolled the word round her tongue. She seemed amused. 'You think all this has something to do with his death? You think my husband might have nipped along on Saturday night and chucked him off his balcony?'

Suttle held her gaze.

'Where was your husband on Saturday night?'

'In Hong Kong. He's a pilot with Cathay Pacific.'

'And you?'

'I was at home. With the kids.'

'Have you had any kind of relationship with Kinsey?'

'No.'

'But you *did* have a drink with him?' Suttle gestured at the texts.

'Yes. That was ages ago when we were sorting out the money for the boat he bought us. Kinsey insisted we did it over a drink. His idea, not mine.'

'And?'

'We got it nailed. I had an orange and soda –' her smile was cold '– if that's germane.'

'You've never been in his apartment?'

'Never. He was keen to get me up there but I always said no. If you want the truth, I think he was mad about tall women. Kinsey was a titch. Bedding people like me would make him feel better about himself.'

'So how did you fend him off?'

'I told him I had a punchy husband. And I told him I hated heights. In case you're wondering, neither's true.'

Suttle scribbled himself a note. Molly was watching him carefully.

'My husband and I are going through a trial separation,' she said. 'I'm telling you now because you're bound to find out one way or another but it makes no difference as far as Kinsey's concerned. Of course he pushed his luck. He was that kind of man. But the answer, I'm afraid, was always no.'

'Afraid?'

'If I was that desperate, there are nicer men around than Kinsey.'

'But you're not that desperate?'

'No.'

'So there's no one who might look at texts like these and draw the wrong conclusion?'

'No, Mr Suttle.' The smile again, even chillier. 'Only you.'

Lizzie spent the morning trying to put her thoughts down on paper. What began as a letter to Gill Reynolds quickly became a confessional Q & A to try and fix her bearings in what felt like a gathering storm. Was she still angry with Jimmy? Yes. Did she blame him for everything that had happened to her head since the move west from Pompey? Yes. Was she still determined to make some kind of change to this half-life of theirs? Again, yes. And had the rowing – Jimmy's idea – made any kind of difference?

At this point her faith in the brisk succession of affirmatives began to waver. Twenty-four hours ago, after a night of feeling more alone, more vulnerable, than she could ever have imagined, she'd been ready once again to scoop up Grace and leave. Now, after last night, she hadn't the first idea how she felt. Meeting a giant of a guy who'd lost his wife to the sea was the last thing she'd ever expected. Among the swamp of emotions he seemed to have unleashed – surprise, curiosity, plus a deep, deep sympathy – was something else. Excitement.

At every level, if she had it right, this man seemed to care about her. More importantly he seemed to understand exactly what she was feeling. After the pub he'd taken her to his place.

He lived in an upstairs flat at the back of Exmouth. He'd made her coffee and asked her to sort out a CD for the audio, and agreed that Neil Young could definitely turn a shit day into something altogether more mellow.

For the rest of the evening they'd sat on the sofa and he'd asked about her – who she really was, what she really wanted – and after a while she'd seen no point messing with the truth. She was living with a really sweet guy who was turning out to be different to the man she'd married. He had a job he loved. He adored the countryside. He was crazy about his daughter. But it hadn't occurred to him for a second that his wife was going nuts.

Until now, she said, that hadn't really mattered. Until now, she'd been able to cope. Just. But stuff was happening that she didn't want to talk about and she'd realised, maybe late in the day, that she was living with a stranger.

Pendrick had said very little. The lamp on the bookcase behind the sofa threw his face into deep shadow, hiding the scar, and it was hard to gauge exactly what he was making of this story of hers. When she finally stopped talking, feeling the first twinges of guilt, he drew her towards him and said he'd like to help. When she asked how, he said he didn't know. The most precious relationships, in his view, were based on conversation, on sharing, on those precious moments when a phrase or a memory or even an opinion proved you weren't entirely alone. Laughter mattered, he said. And so did the preparedness to take a risk or two.

'Like rowing the Atlantic?' she'd asked.

'No,' he'd said. 'Like this.'

She'd left shortly afterwards, kissed him in the darkness of the hall downstairs, thanked him for his patience. He'd walked her to the door, told her to take care on the drive home, given her his mobile number in case she wanted to talk more.

'There's more?' She'd been looking at him from the street.

And she'd loved the grin on his face. *He feels it too*, she'd told herself, driving home.

It was early afternoon before Suttle heard back from the Pier Head property developers. The voice on the phone introduced himself as one of the prime movers in the project and enquired as to the exact nature of Suttle's interest. Suttle explained about Kinsey and asked whether he'd had any kind of stake in the development.

'None at all, I'm afraid. It's way too early for anyone to be buying off-plan. I'm afraid Mr Kinsey isn't on our radar.'

Disappointed, Suttle thanked him for his time and struck the Pier Head development off the fast dwindling list of possible lines of enquiry. So far, he'd resisted the temptation to trawl through the local escort agencies in search of Thai lovelies, preferring to wait for sight of Kinsey's financial records. These days, unless they were married and had secrets to keep, most punters paid with their credit cards. On the point of trying Natasha Donovan again, Suttle looked up to find Luke Golding at his door.

'Sorry, Sarge. I got waylaid this morning. Houghton's fault.'

'Has she found the head yet?'

'No.'

Golding took a seat. Last night, he said, he'd stayed up until two in the morning in the hope that ShattAr might appear.

'And?'

'He did. 01.49. I sent him a message through Steam. Asked him for a link to his Facebook profile. Told him I was setting up an account of my own.'

'Did you get a reply?'

'No. But that means nothing.'

'So what do we do?'

'We wait, Sarge. And I get better at playing bastard Counter-strike.'

*

Minutes later Suttle phoned Natasha Donovan. According to her partner, Milo Symons, she should be back from a couple of days with friends in Bristol. When she picked up, Suttle had the impression she'd been asleep. Yes, she'd be happy to see him. Yes, she was at home. But just now, as soon as she'd got her shit together, she'd be out in the open air, trying to establish contact again.

'With who?'

'Come and see.'

'But how do I find you?'

'It's easy. You can't miss me.'

Intrigued, Suttle made a couple of calls to chase Kinsey's financial records then headed for the coast again. The lane to Tusker Farm was caked with mud from the big fat tractor ahead. The air smelled sweetly of dung. He turned in through the open gate and parked the Impreza beside the mobile home. A woman he assumed was Donovan was standing in the middle of the meadow. She was wearing something white and floaty. Her back was arched and her head was up and her splayed fingers were reaching for the sky. The fall of purple hair rippled in the wind from the valley below, and as Suttle drew closer her head came down and she folded her hands across her chest as she sank to her knees.

He paused beside her. Her feet were bare, dirtied with soil, and she wore a thin silver chain looped around one ankle.

'Natasha Donovan?'

For a moment she didn't move. A second later she opened her eyes and looked up at the proffered warrant card.

'Mr Policeman?' London accent. Appraising smile.

She led him to the mobile home. A newish black Toyota sports coupé was parked where the Transit van had been. Milo, she said, was away for the day. Come in.

Inside, the place had been warmed by the sunshine and the musky scent of incense hung in the stale air. Donovan filled the kettle. She was nearly as tall as her partner and she moved with an artful vagueness that, to Suttle, smacked of long practice. He wanted to ask her about the routine out in the field but she was already in full flow.

'You'll want to know about my journey,' she said. 'It begins with desire and it ends with embodiment. You start with simple movement. Then it gets more complex. The important thing is to *connect*. The body is a springboard. Once you understand that, anything is possible. You connect with nature. You connect with the clouds, the trees, the buttercups, the river, the wind. And most important of all you connect with yourself. It's circular, you see.'

'What is?'

'The journey.'

She threw him a look over her shoulder and reached for a couple of mugs. Her nails were the colour of her hair. She wanted to know whether Suttle was spiritual or not.

'I've never thought about it.'

His answer sparked a small, private smile. She decanted hot water into two mugs. She had loads of stuff on non-stylised body movement if he was interested.

Suttle shook his head. He was grateful for her time. As he'd explained on the phone, he was here to talk about Kinsey.

'Jake? He was lost. He could have gone so far if he'd only listened.'

'To who?'

'Me. Jake lived on the fault line between madness and something worse. You like that phrase? Fault line? That's Milo. Sometimes that man can be so fucking *deep*, you know what I mean?'

Suttle didn't. He was looking at the contents of the mug she'd just given him. Hot water.

'Do I get anything in this?'

'No. Hot water's a cleanser. It has properties you won't believe. I drink it neat. The hotter the better.'

Suttle put the mug to one side. Donovan had settled on the

sofa, her long legs folded beneath her. According to Eamonn Lenahan, this woman had really taken Kinsey's fancy and Suttle could believe it. She was probably the wrong side of forty but you'd never guess.

Suttle wanted her to tell him about Saturday. Had she gone to watch the race?

'No. I was doing a workshop with a friend. Movement and dance for the over-sixties. I hooked up with the guys later. Milo had texted me the result. Can you believe that? My lovely boys? *Winning?*'

By the time she got to the pub, she said, the crew were on their third bottle of champagne. She never touched alcohol herself.

'So what were you drinking?'

'Water.'

'And Kinsey?'

'The man was out of his head. And very happy.'

'Was that unusual?'

'Yeah.' She smiled. 'On both counts.'

They'd stayed in the pub for maybe another half an hour before deciding on a takeaway. The best Indian in Exmouth didn't do deliveries so she'd volunteered to drive into town and get the food. Kinsey, she said, had made a list. In the end the curry had been a big disappointment. Not that anyone was in the mood to complain.

'So how long were you in the apartment?'

'Not that long. Jake was ill, poor lamb. And the guys were knackered.'

'How did you get home?'

'By car. I was the only one sober so I drove. It's a little sports car – you probably saw it – just room for Milo and me. I called a taxi for the others.'

'What time did you get back?'

'I don't know. Past midnight but not that late.'

'And then?'

'We crashed. Milo was asleep in the car. Never marry an athlete.'

'You're married? You and Milo?'

'No.' The smile again. 'Marriage is a killer. Look at Jake.'

The phrase hung between them. *Marriage is a killer.*

'What exactly do you mean?' Suttle asked.

'I mean that marriage gets in the way. It stops life in its tracks. It makes you lazy. You stop trying.'

'Is that what happened to Kinsey?'

'Big time.' She nodded. 'Big time.'

'He talked to you about it?'

'Of course he did. It was hard to stop him sometimes. I don't know what he and that woman had to begin with, but marriage killed it. Stone dead.'

'That woman?'

'Sonya. He'd show me photos. She was really attractive. Great eyes. He couldn't understand how she'd changed. He couldn't understand what she'd *become*.'

'And you sympathised?'

'Not at all. I told him it was his own fault. Poor Jake never looked hard enough, never listened. He lived in a bubble, that man. He needed to get out more. He needed to *connect*.'

'You helped him that way?'

'Of course. We did sessions together, up in his apartment. It's all about vitality. It's all about awareness, about tapping into your hidden energy. I'd write simple movement scores, and when the weather was OK we'd go out on the balcony so we could reach for the river, for the beach, for the wind. Jake always found it hard to relax. He'd never close his eyes. I remember that.'

Suttle was trying to imagine Kinsey out on the balcony, showcasing this woman to the world at large, an image totally in keeping with everything else he knew about the man.

'Was he good at this stuff?'

'He was crap at it. Like I say, he could never relax. It was always the next thing and the next thing with Jake. I'd tell him to stop, to mark time, to slip his life into neutral and park it for a while. That way he'd be able to give himself to something bigger, something vaguer, something he didn't necessarily understand, but I think that was beyond him.'

'You charged for these sessions?'

'Of course.'

'How much?'

'A hundred pounds a go.'

'That's a lot.'

'You're right. I normally charge forty. That was his price, not mine.'

'And how often would this happen?'

'It depended. Sometimes twice a week, sometimes more often. Other times he'd be away on business so we might just meet for a Friday-night session.'

'And this went on for how long?'

'More than a year.'

'And he got better at it? He started to relax?'

'Never.'

'So why did he carry on?'

'Because he fancied me. It was obvious. He wanted to shag the arse off me, and the only way he could do that was by getting me up to that apartment of his. A hundred quid for an hour of dance and movement? A girl could do a lot worse.'

'But was that enough for him? Dance and movement?'

'Of course not. Sometimes I shagged him as well.'

'For more money?'

'Yes.' She yawned.

'How much?'

'Five hundred quid a pop. He was crap in bed too. Five minutes, tops.'

'That's a hundred quid a minute.'

'Yeah. I tried the oils and everything. I even brought candles sometimes, but he wasn't interested. Sex was something he needed. It had to be got out of the way. Then he felt better and he could move on to the next thing.'

'Which was?'

'Work. Always work. He was into property development. He tried to explain it to me one time, tried to get me interested, but I'm useless at all that stuff. Told him not to bother.'

Suttle looked up from his notes. He'd rarely stumbled on someone so recklessly candid. *Constantine*, at last, was beginning to pick up speed.

'Did Milo know about this?'

'Of course he did.'

'He didn't mind?'

'He thought it was funny.'

'*Funny?*'

'Yeah. He knew Jake like we all did, and if you want the truth I think he felt sorry for the man. What you have to understand about Milo is that the guy's a bunny, a child. What we have is brilliant. We fuck like angels. He knows that, and he knows I know it, and it makes him feel very good about everything. So when I come home and tell him about Kinsey, how hopeless the guy is, how rich he's making us, it just makes everything even better.'

'No jealousy?'

'None.'

'And Kinsey? Did it stop with dance and movement and the odd shag?'

For the first time Suttle caught a tiny hint of wariness in her face. She wanted to know exactly what he meant.

'I get the impression Kinsey wanted to own everything,' he said.

'Including me?'

'That's my question.'

'By taking me away from Milo? By moving me into his apartment? Some kind of trophy fuck?'

'Yes.'

'But why would I do that? When I've got Milo?'

'I've no idea. I'm just asking.'

She nodded. Then her head went down and she picked at a nail.

'You're right,' she said at last. 'But he knew there'd never be a way.'

'And Milo?'

'He knew too. Which is why he never even asked the question.'

She got to her feet. Her mug was empty. She needed more hot water. Suttle didn't move. He wanted to know about the film Kinsey was funding.

'That was for Milo.'

'I know. But it was you who got the money out of Kinsey.'

'That's true. He'd give me anything.'

'A two grand down payment and forty-five to come? Have I got that right?'

'Yeah. Jake was minted, though. That sort of money was nothing to him.'

'How do you know?'

'He told me. It was a little boast. He thought it might impress me.'

'And did it?'

'Never. A day with Milo is better than a lifetime with a man like that. He'd want to bang you up. He'd want to own you. I don't want to be owned. I want to be set free.'

'And Milo does that?'

'All the time. And you know something else? He's not even aware of how good he is. There's not an ounce of malice in that man. He's truly beautiful.'

She talked about the film they'd wanted to make and how excited Milo had been at the concept they'd both shaped. The spirit of the river. The ancient ghosts of long-dead Dutchmen haunting the Warren. And a love affair untainted by either time or circumstance.

'We shot a trial sequence. Milo called it a taster.'

'I've seen it. He showed me.'

'Us getting it on?'

'Yes.'

'What did you think?'

'Very impressive. Did Kinsey see it?'

'Yes. It was his idea. He'd read the script and when he asked for a taster we left the choice to him.'

'What did he say when he saw it?'

'He thought it was great. That's why he agreed to fund the rest of the movie. Did Milo tell you about that?'

'Yeah.'

'And the training stuff we're doing for the club?'

'No.'

'Come.'

She poured herself more hot water and led Suttle to Milo's PC. A couple of keystrokes took her into an editing programme. Suttle found himself looking at a bunch of people on a beach, mainly youngsters. They were listening to an older man in a grey tracksuit.

'This was stuff Milo shot yesterday. He's putting together a little movie for the club to help with fund-raising. That was the deal when Jake paid for the camera. You want to see Jake in the flesh?'

Suttle was staring at the screen. At the back of the group was a huge guy in a scruffy blue top. Beside him, dwarfed, was Lizzie. They seemed to be swapping glances. They seemed to be sharing a joke. He remembered the photo Houghton had been preparing to circulate, the mugshot she'd ripped from Kinsey's camera in the pub. On the PC this same face was partially obscured. He had to be sure.

'Who's that?' He touched the screen.

'The big guy?'

'Yeah.'

'His name's Pendrick. Awesome man. Everything Jake wasn't.'

Already she was running backwards through a blur of sequences. Finally she found what she was after.

Suttle bent to the PC. Another view of the same beach hung on the screen. A new-looking sea boat waited at the water's edge. Kinsey's crew were taking their seats, one by one. Suttle recognised the little guy steadying the bow as Lenahan. Big Andy Poole was already in the stroke seat. Pendrick was behind him. Then two other figures stepped into the frame. One of them was Donovan. The other, much smaller, had to be Kinsey.

He was first to the boat. He bent to adjust Donovan's seat, then helped her in. His body language spoke volumes. He was bossy, the authority figure, almost proprietorial. This was his boat, his crew, his woman. Once Donovan was safely seated, he clambered into the bow seat and threw an order over his shoulder at Lenahan, who was knee-deep in the water, holding the boat against the current. Lenahan stowed the rope among a press of life jackets, gave the bow a nudge and stepped into the cox's seat as Donovan and Kinsey eased the quad into the incoming tide. The quad paused a moment, then all four sets of blades were out and the boat was moving quickly upstream.

Kinsey rowed the way he seemed to do everything else. He was choppy, impatient, over-hasty, and as the camera panned the quad into the blaze of sunshine the blackness of the silhouette was unforgiving. Three sets of blades were in perfect harmony. Kinsey, the little guy in the bow, was always half a beat too early.

'Stick insect,' Suttle muttered.

'Too right. Even I'm better than he was.'

Suttle asked her to go back to yesterday's sequence. Donovan shot him a look.

'You won't find Kinsey there,' she said.

'I know. Just do it, please.'

They were on the beach again. The older guy in the tracksuit was walking back towards the slipway. As the camera panned left across the mill of young rowers, Suttle found himself watching his wife and Pendrick easing a two-seat rowing skiff into the water. The shot tightened as Lizzie made herself comfortable. She was laughing now as she leaned forward to tighten something that seemed to hold the blade in the gate. Then Pendrick knelt beside her in the shallows, talking her through some detail or other, and the camera settled on Lizzie's face as she tried to follow him. Suttle hadn't seen this expression for years. There was an eagerness, a hunger for what was coming next, and when the camera eased out again as Pendrick stepped into the bow seat Suttle caught the moment when she reached back to steady him.

'Who's that?' he asked.

'Pendrick. I just told you.'

'I meant the woman.'

'Fuck knows. I asked Milo that this morning. Apparently she's new, just moved into the area, lots of potential. The girls say she responds well to coaching, really quick on the uptake. Definitely does it for Pendrick too. Just look at the guy.'

The skiff was on the move now, silhouetted against the sun, exactly the same effect Milo had conjured for Kinsey's quad. The sheer bulk of Pendrick had wiped Lizzie from the shot and only her flailing oars were evidence that there was anybody else in the boat. The skiff was wobbling badly. The oars came to a halt. Then a cloud hid the sun and detail returned to the shot. Pendrick was leaning forward, his hand on Lizzie's shoulder, his mouth inches from her ear.

Suttle had seen enough. He'd wanted to ask Donovan about the word flux and whether or not she knew Peggy Brims, the woman who lived in the apartment beneath Kinsey, but he no longer saw the point. He gathered up his notes and told Donovan she'd have to attend the police station to read and sign a formal statement. He'd do his best to have it ready by midday tomorrow but clerical staff were under enormous pressure and he couldn't guarantee it.

Donovan was still looking at Milo's shots from yesterday. On the way out, Suttle paused by the door.

'You dye your hair that colour, right?'

'Of course.' She looked up at him, surprised.

'So what colour was it before?'

'Blonde.'

Pendrick phoned Lizzie in mid-afternoon. He'd just finished a rewiring job at a house in Woodbury and wondered whether she fancied a coffee.

'I'm at home,' she pointed out. 'With an infant daughter and no car.'

'You want me to drop round? No pressure.'

Lizzie thought about it for a split second.

'No.'

'Sure?'

'Yes.'

She could hear the disappointment in his voice but knew she had no choice.

'Don't go,' she said quickly. 'Talk to me.'

'About?'

'You could start with last night.'

'Last night was great. You know it was great. Except for the bloody rowing.'

'Bugger the rowing. That was my fault. I meant the rest of it.'

'The rest of it was what it was.'

'Meaning?'

'I'd love to see you again. Talk some more. Get one or two things straight.'

Lizzie giggled. She felt about twelve.

'Nice idea,' she said. 'Let's work on that.'

'How about tomorrow? There's a quad going up to Topsham.

One of the girls wants to be subbed on the way back. It's five miles. Could you cope with that?'

'No problem.' She was laughing now. 'The mood I'm in I could cope with anything.'

Suttle took his interview notes back to the MCIT offices at Middlemoor. D/I Carole Houghton, to his intense relief, was at her desk upstairs. The missing head had finally turned up in a Bodmin wood a couple of hundred metres from the rest of the body, a discovery that had done nothing for her respect for intel.

'This better be good,' she warned as Suttle eased himself into her spare chair.

He took her briefly through the bones of the interview. Tash Donovan had freely admitted having regular sex with Jake Kinsey. She claimed that her partner was cool with this arrangement but Symons hadn't mentioned it in interview. On the contrary, towards the end of their conversation he'd become visibly irritated at Suttle's suggestion that Kinsey might have had some kind of relationship with Tash.

'But he didn't, Jimmy. That's not how it happened. The way you're telling it they danced round together and did lots of hippy stuff and had sex from time to time. He was paying her for it. That's not a relationship. That's business.'

'Not to Symons. Not if you're crazy about the woman. Not if she's older than you and pretty much controls every aspect of your life. The way I see it, the guy's hugely vulnerable. We could nick Donovan for child abuse.'

Houghton laughed. But she still wasn't convinced.

'There's no way she'd have told you all that stuff if he didn't know too. She's putting it on the record before you get there first. That makes her clever, not guilty.'

'Wrong, boss.' Suttle wasn't having it. 'She wants me to believe that she and Symons have a great sex life. I'm in no position to know for sure, but I'll give her the benefit of the doubt. Let's say they get it on loads. Let's accept it's great for both of them. Let's even agree that Symons knows about the deal with Kinsey and is happy to rent out his partner for five hundred quid a pop.'

'It's her decision, Jimmy, not his.' The expression on Houghton's face might have been a smile.

'Sure. Fine. OK. But we're missing something, aren't we?'

'What?'

'Symons is a bloke. He knows about blokes. He knows how territorial they can get. More to the point, he knows Kinsey. And when it comes to territory, he knows that Kinsey has to be top dog. There isn't a lamp post he won't piss on. Including Tash Donovan.'

'That's unnecessary.'

'My apologies. But you see the logic? You see where this thing leads? Symons knows Kinsey can't help himself as far as Donovan's concerned. He knows the guy probably wants every bit of her, for keeps. They win their race. All the guys get pissed in the pub. They go back to Kinsey's apartment. Donovan's the only one still standing. After Kinsey's gone off to bed they all go home. Donovan and Symons are in their little car together. They have a monster row. Maybe Kinsey's said something out of turn. Maybe he's come on to Donovan in the apartment. Whatever. By the time they're back home, or tucked up in some little lay-by, it's got really nasty. Symons has had enough. He's going to sort this guy out. Bosh. Back he goes.'

'How does he get in?'

'She'll have a key. Bound to.'

'So she's part of this? She drives him back? Lends a hand? Gets rid of the guy who's keeping them afloat?'

'I've no idea, boss. All I know is that they're alibiing each other but they've got fuck all corroboration. Plus Symons isn't comfortable with what his partner's up to. All it takes is a night on the piss. That and a decent opportunity. From where I'm sitting, Symons had both.'

Houghton nodded. It was true that booze played a huge part in most murders.

'What about this film of his? Why would he want to kiss all that goodbye?'

'Because there was something else in his life that was even more important.'

'Donovan?'

'Of course. These people are off the planet most of the time, Symons especially. I'm not saying for a moment that his movie wasn't important. It was huge. But you know why? Because of her input. Because she made the running – the idea to begin with, getting the development money out of Kinsey, starring in their little movie trailer so Kinsey could perve over it, all of that was her. She's the driver, boss. She's in charge of this relationship. Without her, Symons would be nowhere. Fuck the movie. When Symons feels under threat, Donovan is what really matters.'

Houghton was silent. Suttle knew she sensed the logic in the case he was trying to make but he knew too that she was under the same cosh as Nandy. In every investigation you think court from the off. So where was the incontestable evidence to pin either of these people to Kinsey's death? First call in any murder lay with the Crown Prosecution Service. And so far, as Houghton pointed out, the CPS wouldn't waste a second on this horse shit.

'It's supposition, Jimmy. It's a nice little fairy tale. It's neat. It sounds more than plausible. But it's still supposition.'

'It's early days, boss. We're not through yet.'

'You mean *you're* not through yet.'

'Exactly. Help would be nice but I'm not complaining.'

'Remind me how long you've got on the Coroner's file.'

'Another week. Give or take.'

'And will that be enough?'

'Sure,' Suttle forced a grin. 'You're spoiling me.'

*

He phoned Gina Hamilton when he got back downstairs. The office was still empty. He could tell at once that she'd been expecting his call.

'How about an early drink?' he said.

'How about supper?'

'Where?'

'My place if you don't mind pasta.'

'I love pasta.'

She gave him a postcode and a street number. He'd never been to Modbury in his life.

'What time?'

'You say.'

Suttle checked his watch. 17.12. He still had a number of calls to make and the rush-hour traffic on the A38 could be brutal.

'Seven o'clock?'

'Perfect. If you're late don't even bother knocking.'

She rang off, leaving Suttle gazing at the phone. He knew he should be calling Lizzie. He knew, at the very least, he should give himself some kind of cover. A couple of late interviews. A squad meet he couldn't afford to miss. But then he was back in front of Symons' PC, watching Lizzie and Pendrick hauling the skiff away from the beach, and he knew he couldn't be bothered. A moment later the office door opened and he found himself looking at the Office Manager. Leslie had taken a call earlier. It was personal for Jimmy and it sounded urgent.

'She wouldn't leave a name but she wants you to bell her,' she laid a number on Suttle's desk. 'It's a Portsmouth number. I checked.'

Pendrick called again as Lizzie was trying to wrestle Grace upstairs for a bath. Thinking it was Jimmy, she hesitated a moment then decided to ignore it, but when it rang a second time she returned downstairs.

Pendrick apologised for phoning so late. He hoped it wasn't a problem.

'It's not. Did you phone just now?'

'Yes. Tomorrow's off. We've got a big front coming in and there's no way we'll be going to Topsham.'

'Oh ...' Lizzie tried to mask her disappointment. 'Never mind.'

'I had another idea.'

'Does it involve rowing?'

'Sadly not.'

'Thank Christ for that.'

Pendrick laughed. He was planning a trip to the north coast. Wondered if she'd like to come along.

'The north coast of where?'

'Cornwall. Just a place I think you might like.'

'Is Grace invited?'

'No.'

'At least you're honest.' It was her turn to laugh.

There was a moment of silence. Lizzie could hear a car approaching up the lane. She very much wanted it not to be Jimmy. The car went past.

'What time?' she said. 'And where?'

Suttle made the call from a lay-by on the A38. As he expected, the number belonged to Marie Mackenzie.

'I've made some inquiries,' she said. 'I don't know why I bothered but there it is.'

'And?'

'It turns out there's very little I can do. Your friend Winter has made some serious enemies. These people aren't as stupid as you might think.'

'I never thought for a moment they were.'

'Then this won't come as a surprise.'

'What?'

He listened intently for the best part of a minute, doing his best to shield the phone from the thunder of the passing traffic. Finally, at her prompting, he reached for a pen. In the absence of anything else, he wrote the number on the back of his hand. Pompey again.

'And you really think they'll leave Lizzie and Grace alone?'

'Yes. As long as you make the call.'

'I have your word on that?'

'It's not my word you need. It's theirs. Make the call. That's my advice. Everything else is down to you.'

Modbury was a small town cupped by rolling green hills south of the A38. Gina Hamilton's house lay in a small estate of newbuilds. Suttle had looked at similar developments in Exeter last year when he was searching for somewhere they could live and knew he'd die in a house like this. Tiny windows. Tiny rooms. And a scrap of threadbare turf instead of a garden.

Hamilton's Golf was parked outside, the tailgate open. The front door to the house was open as well and she stepped into the sunshine as Suttle approached.

'I just got back myself,' she said. 'Give me a hand?'

Suttle helped her carry shopping and a couple of tins of paint into the kitchen. She'd been to Sainsbury and B&Q on the way home. Lots of stuff for the freezer and four bottles of Australian Chardonnay. Suttle gave her a bottle of red he'd picked up on the way over. The galley kitchen was spotless. A wine rack beside the fridge badly needed restocking and there was a National Trust calendar on the wall above a bowl of fruit. April featured a drift of purple crocuses at Lacock Abbey.

'What are the green ticks?' Suttle was still looking at the calendar.

'I go running. The green ticks make me feel virtuous. Anything else you want to know about my social life?'

Suttle looked harder. Not much seemed to have happened over the last fortnight.

'You find the Job knackers you?'

'Yeah. But for the wrong reasons.'

She shot him a look but wouldn't take the conversation further. She nodded at the vegetable basket beneath the work surface and asked him to sort out an onion and some garlic. Tomato paste in the fridge. Olive oil in the cupboard. She also fancied something to drink.

Suttle was looking at the remaining bottles of wine. The red he'd bought had been on offer, a South African Merlot that Lizzie adored.

'You've got a corkscrew?'

'Silly question. Drawer on the left.'

They sat down to eat half an hour or so later. The lounge diner extended the full depth of the house: magnolia walls, a big plasma TV and a line of stuffed animals carefully arranged on the Ikea sofa. This house, Suttle thought, might have belonged to Kinsey. No clutter. None of the chaos of normal life. No photos of family or friends. Just somewhere to crash after yet another day among the performance reviews.

Suttle poured more wine and asked how long she'd been in Modbury.

'Just over a year. John and I went our separate ways and this was all I could afford. We used to have a place in Tavistock. It was sweet.'

'John?'

'My husband. He was a D/C on the drugs squad. The best. The very best. And that's not just my opinion.'

She'd met him, she said, on the operation that had taken her to Pompey five years ago. He'd been driving the intel and she'd fancied him from the off. He was an older man, a grizzly bear of a guy, rock solid. The drugs operation had won her a commendation from the Chief, plus lots of media exposure, and she and John had got married within months.

'That job was a real result,' she said. 'One of those moments when you think you're immortal.'

Suttle nodded, telling her he'd been through something similar himself back in Pompey. He explained about the u/c operation to pot Bazza Mackenzie and all the plaudits that had followed. This guy had dicked them around for years and it was sweet to have finally nailed him.

'Literally?'

'Yeah. It got heavy at the end and the ninjas had to take him out. Incredible evening. He ended up in a shop full of snakes he happened to own. He was about to do something evil to the key informant and we had no choice. Bam-bam. You're right. After that you feel you can do anything.'

'And afterwards?'

'Afterwards I came down here.'

'Good move?'

'The best.'

'You mean that?'

'I do, yeah. But it's not just about me, is it?'

There was a silence. Then Hamilton asked him whether he wanted to talk about it. Suttle told her about finding the cottage, about moving the family down, about living with a woman who couldn't wait to take her life in another direction.

'Why?'

'Because living in the country drives her nuts.'

'You still love her?'

'I do, yes.'

'Then sort it out.'

'I can't. I try and I can't. It just doesn't work.'

'Why not?'

'Because she's become someone different, a different person. Because everything's different. Have you ever had kids?'

'No.'

'They don't help. We've got a daughter. She's lovely. I adore her. But she doesn't help.'

'That's harsh.'

'But it's true, believe me. If there's something wrong in a

relationship, if something's not working, a child makes everything worse.'

Hamilton nodded and reached for the bottle. Her third glass. When she offered Suttle a refill, he shook his head. He wanted to know more about Hamilton's marriage.

'That didn't work either.'

'Why not?'

'Because I couldn't let go of the Job. I'm good. I know I'm good. I'm ambitious too. It's not going to end with D/I, not if I have anything to do with it, but these days that kind of pressure eats you up. You have to watch your back all the time. You have to make the right friends in the right places, walk the walk, talk the talk, make sure there's nothing in your in-tray that's going to come back and bite you in the arse. At the end of every day you're wasted. And since you've asked, there's another problem too.'

'What's that?'

'I'm two people. At work I'm Ms Efficient. Ms Gimme. Ms Sort It. But you know something? It's all pretend. I do pretend brilliantly. Pretend decisive. Pretend organised. Pretend savvy. People look at me and think wow, that woman's got it cracked. But you want to know the truth?' She touched her chest. 'In here it's all mush. I haven't got a clue what's going on. It's horrible. Just horrible. Some days I think I'm going mad.'

'And John? Your husband?'

'He saw right through it. He understood. He tried to make me get a grip, do something about myself, take the Job less seriously, but I never could. He'd got the Job totally sussed. He knew exactly what he was good at and he knew exactly where to draw the line. I don't do lines. Which is why the marriage turned to rat shit. John gave up in the end and I don't blame him. You're right. You become strangers to each other. And after that you're dead in the water.'

In the end, she said, John applied for a job in another force.

She knew that it had been for her sake more than his and the gesture had touched her deeply.

'Where's he gone?'

'Dorset. He works out of Bournemouth. They're lucky to have him.'

'You're divorced?'

'Yes.'

'But you still talk?'

'Yes. Occasionally.'

'And that's OK?'

'It's weird. It's like we were never married in the first place. You know my theory? We've all got a default setting and no matter what you do it'll always reset.'

'So what's yours?'

'Don't go there.'

She went into the kitchen to fetch another bottle of wine. Suttle was looking at the stuffed animals on the sofa. The biggest, the elephant, was pink.

Hamilton had appeared at the kitchen door.

'Red or white?'

'You choose. I'm driving.'

'Yeah?' She lingered a moment, then disappeared again. Suttle heard the pop of the cork. When she came back, Suttle asked her about the running.

'You really want to know?'

'Yeah.'

'That was another drama. There's a bunch of local joggers here and I joined up. They go out a couple of nights a week, decent distances, nice enough people I thought at first, but then some of the guys turned out to be pretty gross. We'd go to the pub afterwards and they'd find out you were living alone and after that they just wanted to get into your knickers. It wasn't anything personal. They were all happily married, or that's what they'd tell you, but then they'd come on to me like it was some kind of favour. It was so blatant. They assumed I

212

couldn't wait to get fucked. Like I say. Totally gross.'

In the end, she said, she'd abandoned the group outings and started running by herself. She had a handful of favourite circuits and lately she'd been wondering about getting a dog for company when winter came and the nights drew in. Either way she felt the exercise was keeping her half sane but there were moments when she doubted even that.

'It's really hard to explain. Some nights when I go out I take me with me. Then other nights I'm running with a total stranger. Does that make sense? Is that *normal*?'

Suttle laughed. Mercifully, he always excused himself serious exercise. He asked to use the loo. She directed him upstairs. Afterwards, drying his hands, Suttle could hear the clatter of plates in the kitchen. Her bedroom lay across the tiny landing at the top of the stairs. The door was open and he could see a pair of running shoes abandoned on the carpet. He stepped inside. The bed was turned down. A Tiffany-style lamp on the bedside table cast a soft light across the whiteness of the sheet. There were more stuffed animals on the duvet, partly covered by a powder-blue towelling gown. Over the bed, hanging on the wall, a framed poster of Amy Winehouse.

Back downstairs, Suttle found himself looking at a plate of blueberries. His hunger had gone but he accepted a spoonful of cream.

'You're big on Amy Winehouse?'

Hamilton was pouring herself another glass of wine. Nearly a bottle so far, thought Suttle.

'You've been in my bedroom.' It was a statement, not a question.

'Yes.'

'Why?'

'I'm curious.'

'About what?'

'About you. About this ...' He gestured around.

She nodded, sipped the wine.

'Are we talking intel here? Or something else?'

'You tell me.'

'You think your luck's in? You fancy a quickie before you go?'

Suttle didn't answer. She was drunk now, something that probably happened night after night, and he sensed her neediness. He very definitely didn't want to hurt her but he understood all too clearly where this might lead.

He reached out and took her hand.

'I'm glad I came,' he said.

'Why?'

'Because I needed to talk.'

'Great. Happy to oblige.' She held his gaze for a long moment, then nodded down at the number scrawled on the back of his hand. 'That's a Portsmouth code. You want to tell me more?'

Suttle shook his head. He had to go. The meal had been great. Maybe they could meet again, his shout next time.

She looked at him, saying nothing, then her eyes went to the bottle and she lifted an enquiring eyebrow.

'No,' he said. 'But thanks for the offer.'

She accompanied him to the front door. He was reaching for the latch when he felt her hand on his arm

'There's something I meant to tell you,' she said, 'about Pendrick.'

'What's that?'

'It turns out he kept half of the insurance settlement. That's three hundred grand.'

'How do you know?'

'I checked on the charity's website.' She offered him a weary smile. 'That's what detectives do, isn't it? You get that for free, by the way.'

Suttle nodded, then opened the door. 'I'll be in touch, yeah?'

'Yeah?'

They both stepped out into the night air. Suttle held her for a moment. She was shivering in the cold. He kissed her briefly, thanked her again for the pasta and headed for the garden gate. The car door unlocked, he turned to wave goodbye but she'd gone.

Suttle was pushing 90 mph on the outside lane of the A38 when, too late, he saw the police car tucked into a lay-by. The road was empty. He throttled back and hoped to God they hadn't tracked him with the radar gun. The patrol car had already pulled out and was accelerating hard. Then came the flashing blue light and Suttle knew they were going to give him a tug.

He was in the slow lane now, still decelerating, trying to play the good citizen. On his side of the carriageway he was the only vehicle for at least half a mile. He had to be the target. Had to be.

The patrol car was beside him now, the pale face in the passenger seat checking him out. He signalled Suttle to pull over. The next lay-by was a couple of hundred metres ahead. At a steady 40 mph, Suttle was trying to work out exactly how many glasses of wine he'd had. Two? Three? Getting pulled for speeding was one thing. Failing the breathalyser would land him with a driving ban, a disciplinary charge and possible suspension. Without a licence, the Job and life in general would become a nightmare. Not good.

The patrol car followed him into the lay-by. Both officers got out and approached the Impreza. The guy in the passenger seat squatted beside Suttle's door. The wind had got up and rain pebbled on his hi-vis jacket.

'Do you have your licence, sir? May I see it?'

Suttle produced his licence. The patrol officer scanned it quickly and handed it back. He was in his mid-forties. He looked unforgiving.

'Where have you come from, sir?'

'Modbury.'

'And you're going to ...?'

'Home. Colaton Raleigh.'

'Are you aware that you were exceeding the speed limit just now?'

'Yeah.'

The patrol officer nodded. He'd caught the sour taint of alcohol on Suttle's breath. Then his eyes strayed to the dashboard where Suttle had left a pass for the MCIT car park at Middlemoor.

'In the Job, are you, sir?'

'Yeah.'

'CID?'

'Yeah.'

'Have you been drinking by any chance, sir?'

'Yeah.'

'Well, well ...' The beginnings of a smile ghosted across the big face. Uniforms liked nothing better than nailing pissed detectives.

'Out of the car if you please, sir.'

Suttle did what he was told. The officer read him the caution and warned him that he faced arrest if he failed a breathalyser test. The rain was heavier now and Suttle was soaking in seconds but he didn't much care. One way or another, the next minute or so might decide the fate of his entire career.

The officer had returned to the patrol car to fetch the breathalyser. Suttle waited in the rain, wondering whether he should – after all – have stayed at Gina Hamilton's place. Then he put the thought out of his mind. What will be will be. Fuck it.

The officer returned with the breathalyser. Suttle blew into the tube. The PC watched the figures on the readout climb and climb. His mate had joined him by now. Their backs were turned and Suttle caught a mumbled exchange before the officer was back in his face. The reading was just short of the figure that would haul him back to the nick for a blood test and a great deal of paperwork.

'Who's a lucky boy then?' He didn't bother to hide his disappointment. 'Would you step this way, sir?'

Suttle sat in the patrol car while the PC wrote up his details for the speeding offence. Ninety-two mph would probably earn him a three-point deduction and a biggish fine. The deduction was no problem, and though the fine was a pain in the arse it was nothing compared to what might have happened.

Swamped with relief, Suttle closed his eyes and let his head sink back against the restraint. When the officer asked him whether he had anything to say with regard to his excess speed, he said he wanted to get home. The officer turned and shot him a look.

'Little woman waiting up is she, sir?'

Suttle held his gaze and then shut his eyes again.

'I doubt it,' he said.

He was wrong. Lizzie was downstairs nursing a glass of red wine. Dexter was curled on her lap, ignoring the remains of a fish pie beside the chair.

She looked up as Suttle came in from the kitchen. His hair was plastered against the whiteness of his skull and the rain had darkened his suit.

Lizzie studied him a moment. The cat didn't stir.

'Should I ask where you've been?' she said.

'Sure. Why not?'

Suttle told her about his drive out to Modbury. A D/I called Gina Hamilton lived there.

'Alone?'

'Yes.'

'Business or pleasure?'

'Bit of both.'

'Nice evening?'

'Not bad. I got stopped on the way back.'

He told her about the traffic car and the breathalyser.

'And?'

'I passed.'

'Not too pissed then? To come home?'

Suttle knew exactly what lay behind the remarks and ignored them. Lizzie, in the parlance, was after the full account. What was this woman like? How come they'd met at her house? Why hadn't he phoned her earlier? What was so important it couldn't be done in office hours?

Suttle fetched a towel from upstairs. He'd never lied to Lizzie, and now wasn't the time to start. He dried his hair as best he could and hung his jacket over the back of the kitchen door.

'What do you fancy tomorrow?' he said. 'I thought we might go into Exeter. There's a festival thing on.'

'I'm sorry, I can't.'

'Why not?'

Lizzie explained about a call she'd taken from one of the girls at the rowing club. After the wreath tribute on Sunday the crews were returning to the compound for a naming ceremony. The newest boat was to be called the *Jake Kinsey* after the guy who'd so generously signed the cheque. With luck, the media might use it as a photo opportunity.

'Tomorrow's Saturday,' Suttle pointed out.

'I know. We have to sort the compound out. Make it look half decent. A bunch of us are meeting at ten. I couldn't say no.'

'And that takes all day?'

'I've no idea. Judging by the state of the place, it might well do.'

Suttle studied her for a moment, loosening his tie.

'And Sunday?'

'We've got the tribute thing. I have to go, Jimmy. There's no way I can't.'

'OK.' Suttle shrugged. 'Whatever ...'

He turned away, trying to mask his anger, but she knew him too well to be fooled.

'It was your idea, Jimmy.'

'What?'

'The rowing club.'

'You're right. So it's me and Grace then. All weekend.'

'I'm afraid so.' She still hadn't moved. 'Welcome to my little world.'

Seven

Lizzie was out of the cottage by nine o'clock. Suttle was still in bed with Grace, celebrating last night's escape with a lie-in. In truth, he'd no idea where Lizzie was really going but supposed the compound clean-up was at least semi-plausible. Whatever happened, he was certain that Pendrick would be around. Time and again he tried to fight off the image of his wife and one of Kinsey's star rowers on the beach. He'd seen the grin on Lizzie's face. He knew exactly what it meant.

She'd been that way with him once, playful and reckless, happy to surrender to something new and faintly exotic in her life. Suttle was a cop. She'd never fucked a cop before. More to the point, she really fancied him. That's what had taken them to bed the first time and all the times after that, and when he'd recognised there was something really substantial there, something important, the knowledge had been all the sweeter because the laughter and the often brilliant sex had never stopped. Even pregnancy and motherhood hadn't diminished her appetite for that raw enjoyment of each other, and it was only after the move west that married life had begun to seize up. They'd almost stopped talking. They'd definitely stopped laughing. And even the prospect of sex had become strangely awkward, something best avoided in case it sparked a row.

Suttle waited until the burble of the Impreza had disappeared down the lane. The temptation was to have a prowl around the bedroom in case Lizzie had left her mobile. Maybe she'd added Pendrick to her contacts file. Maybe they'd been texting each other. Maybe the other contents of her bag might yield a clue or two. He eyed the scatter of clothes she'd left beneath the window, wondering whether he really wanted to treat his own bedroom as some kind of crime scene, then decided against it. Grace, he knew, would be hungry. Thank God for someone else in his life.

Downstairs, he strapped Grace into her high chair in front of the TV while he went into the kitchen. Lizzie had forgotten to get the puréed banana out of the fridge so he put a saucepan of water on the stove to warm it up. Next door he could hear Grace kicking her legs in time to Horrid Henry. Even with the crap reception, the TV seemed to have become a permanent guest in the house, masking the never-ending drips that penetrated the silence.

Suttle went out onto the patio and put a call through to the Pompey number Marie had given him. The rain had cleared overnight and there was a clarity and brightness to the sunshine that lifted his spirits.

The number answered at once. Pompey accent again but a different voice.

'I know you,' Suttle said.

'You do, son. You do.'

'Dave Fallon.'

'The same.'

Dave Fallon was an ex-6.57 who now ran one of Pompey's biggest cab companies. He'd always been a special favourite of Mackenzie's, a trusted lieutenant in the legendary Millwall rucks in the late 80s and a tactician of genius when it came to laying siege to some of the tastier away firms. Fallon affected a gruff Pompey swagger that led people to dismiss him as a mush, but Suttle had never been fooled. Mackenzie, he knew, had rated Fallon as one of the city's top businessmen.

'We need to meet, son,' Fallon said.

'Why?'

'There's no way I'm going into this on the phone. It has to be Monday night. You decide where.'

Suttle gave the proposition some thought. He didn't want to go back to Pompey again. Not yet.

'How about halfway?' he said. 'I'm in Devon.'

'Wherever, mush. Your call. Have a think and bell me back, yeah?'

The phone went dead. Suttle checked on Grace then stepped back into the sunshine. Gina Hamilton was slower to pick up.

'You,' she said.

'Me,' Suttle agreed.

'Get home OK?'

'No.'

When he told her about the patrol car she laughed.

'Your own fault,' she said. 'You should have stayed.'

She'd decided to turn the memory of last night into a joke, Suttle thought. Better that than more angst.

'I need a favour,' he said.

'Another one?'

'I'm serious.'

'So was I.'

'Your husband ...'

'John?'

'Yeah. You told me he was in Bournemouth. If I asked nicely, would he mind my back on Monday night?'

'I've no idea.' She was laughing again. 'I'll give you his number and you can ask him yourself. Send him my best, eh?'

It was still early when Lizzie got to the rowing club. Tessa was already there with a couple of the other girls and they'd wheeled out the heavy boats prior to attacking the tangle of weeds that threatened to engulf the corners of the compound. A young guy Lizzie had never met was trying to coax some life out of a strimmer while a bunch of juniors lounged on the wooden steps of the Portakabin, enjoying the sunshine.

Over the next hour or so more rowers turned up to lend a hand to sort out the Portakabin, and by late morning the job was done. Tessa took Lizzie to one side. She'd broached an idea to the club captain about tomorrow's tribute on the water and he'd given it the thumbs up.

With the exception of the newest quad, the Kinsey boat, the club's entire fleet would be holding station off the dock. Upstream, meanwhile, the new quad would be waiting with Kinsey's crew aboard. The moment the wreath hit the water they'd scull downstream at racing speed, carving a path through the fleet. Kinsey had been forty-one when he died. Once the quad passed the wreath, they'd put in another forty-one strokes before drifting to a halt and waiting for the rest of the fleet to catch them up. This little piece of maritime theatre, in Tessa's view, would provide a focus for the cameras, the press, and however many spectators chose to turn up.

'Great.' Lizzie was wondering what this had to do with her.

'It's a question of the crew. Kinsey's obviously no longer with us and Tom Pendrick's decided he doesn't want to do it.'

'Why?'

'I've no idea. Ask him.'

Tash Donovan, she said, had agreed to stand in for Pendrick, which left one empty seat at bow.

'So who have you got?'

'You.'

'*Me?*'

'Yeah. Clive and I agreed that we needed the newest recruit in bow. Clive thinks it's symbolic, a vote of faith in the future. It's a nice line for the press too.' Clive Knightly was the club captain.

'But I'm a novice,' Lizzie pointed out.

'That's exactly the point.'

'Racing speed? Are you serious?'

'You'll pick it up. Clive's impressed already. We all are.'

'Did you see me in the double the other night?'

'We did. We think you had other things on your mind.'

'Like?'

Tessa shot her a look. 'You think we're blind?'

Lizzie felt herself blushing. This was juvenile, she told herself. She began to protest again, telling Tessa the whole thing was out of the question, that she'd never hack something like that in front of other people, the whole club for God's sake, but Tessa was adamant. The Kinsey crew would be on the water at least an hour before the ceremony. Racing starts were a piece of cake. All Lizzie needed was practice.

'You should be flattered,' she added. 'This is as big as it gets in Exmouth.'

Pendrick turned up minutes later. He was driving a yellow VW van and bumped it onto the pavement on the seafront. Lizzie checked her watch. On the phone they'd agreed midday. It was two minutes past.

Pendrick leaned across and opened the passenger door. He was wearing jeans and a bleached-out T-shirt with a skull on the front.

'You look like a biker,' she said. 'Where are we going?'

'Cornwall.' He was looking down the cut towards the club compound. 'Mystery tour.'

On the way out of Exmouth the weekend traffic was heavy. Lizzie had sneaked a look at the back of the van. Among the clutter of wetsuits and surfboards was a full-size blow-up air-bed and a couple of sleeping bags.

'You kip in here?'

'When I have to, yeah.'

'Cosy?'

'Always.'

She told him about the addition to tomorrow's ceremony. When she asked why he wouldn't be rowing himself he just shook his head.

'What does that mean?'

'It means I've got better things to do. This tribute thing's a joke. Everyone hated the guy. All he had was money. Does that justify all this bollocks?'

'But it's not about him. Not the way I've been told. The club needs the publicity.'

'Why?'

'To bring in new members. To bring in money. Isn't that what it's all about? Profile? Presence?'

'Sure. You're right.' He glanced across, gave her hand a squeeze. 'Maybe I'll help with the safety boat. Just in case you go overboard.'

'Is that in the script?'

'Christ knows.' He glanced at his watch. 'What time do you need to be back?'

Suttle took Grace on a tour of the village, mainly because she was beginning to drive him nuts. She was fretful and upset and whatever he did, however he tried to comfort her, nothing seemed to work. She'd stagger round the sitting room, banging into the furniture, yelling for her mummy, totally inconsolable, and in the end he strapped her in the buggy and set off down the road. Within a minute or so, probably exhausted, she'd fallen asleep.

A tour of Colaton Raleigh was a novelty for Suttle. He crossed the main road down by the store and kept walking. A line of cheerless bungalows led to the church. Beyond the church the road petered out. He lifted the buggy and carried it across a cattle grid. A path led towards the river. The meadows, dotted with cows, were boggy underfoot after the rain and the river itself was the colour of peat. He'd remembered to bring the remains of a stale loaf and he stood on the riverbank, wondering whether or not to wake Grace up. There were ducklings on the river, in line astern behind their mum, and he knew Grace would adore them, but in the end he opted for the rare moment of peace. On the way home, after a brief expedition to the village play-park, she was howling again.

The cottage, after the brightness of the sunshine, felt damp and airless. Suttle opened the windows and put the TV back on. He'd no idea whether Grace had any interest in rugby league but he thought it was worth a try. To his relief, it seemed to do the trick. She sat on his lap, peering at the screen, following the players with her tiny finger. After a while he settled her on the floor in front of the TV and went into the kitchen to sort her out something for lunch. He found a jar of mashed apricots in the fridge and cut up another banana to go with it. Grace gobbled up the fruit with evident relish, losing interest in the rugby.

'You want to come outside? In the sunshine? Help Daddy sort the garden?'

She seemed to nod. Suttle carried the playpen outside and filled it with a small army of cuddly toys. The sight of Grace nursing a stuffed giraffe stirred memories of last night, and he found himself wondering whether Gina Hamilton had ended up preferring the company of stuffed animals to the complications of a proper relationship. Maybe that's what lies in wait for us all, he thought. At least the animals never betray you.

Trezillion turned out to be a perfect cove nestling between two headlands west of Padstow. The tide was out and the blueness of the water stretched unbroken to the far horizon. Gulls were prowling among the hummocks of seaweed on the beach and a lone cormorant was patrolling the creamy froth at the water's edge. It was a magical place, Lizzie thought. No wonder Pendrick had always treasured it.

Out of the wind, among the stands of marram grass on the dunes, it was warm enough to sit in the sunshine. They'd detoured through the outskirts of Camelford and Pendrick had shown her the council house where he'd grown up. Kate, he said, had come off the same estate. They'd gone to school together, learned how to get drunk together, and later – both mad about the rave culture – they'd hitchhiked up-country for festival after festival.

By now they'd both become hard-core surfers, and when the winds were right and a big Atlantic depression brought the heavy ocean swells rolling in, there was no better place to be than Trezillion. It wasn't to everyone's taste. A heavy break on the far side of the cove was tricky to get right and the shape of the bottom at certain states of the tide didn't leave much room for beginners, but the sheer intimacy of the place made it one of Cornwall's best-kept secrets.

'Which I guess is what turned the little bastard on.'

A brown envelope lay between them on the blanket he'd brought from the van. Lizzie had been intrigued by its contents since she'd spotted it on the dashboard. Pendrick extracted a glossy-looking brochure and handed it across. They'd bought tins of Guinness and a cooked chicken from a Spar store on the Camelford estate. Lizzie licked the grease from her fingers and picked the brochure up.

'Right here.' Pendrick gestured at the photo on the front of the brochure. 'That's where he wanted to build. That's the view you'd get. Exactly here.'

Lizzie checked the photo against the real thing. He was right. For £899K you could buy this view for the rest of your life.

'And it's going to happen?'

'No one knows. Kinsey was the driving force, but he's got a partner up north somewhere, and these days it's all about property development. If the sums stack up, if there's a profit to be had, my guess is he'll make it happen.'

'But it's protected, surely. National Trust? RSPB? All that?'

'Big deal. Money talks round here. Cornwall's on the bones of its arse. It's fine if you're minted like Kinsey was. He's pitching to people like himself, people with London property, zillions in the bank, not a clue what to do with it. Kinsey made it easy for them. You get the view. You get peace of mind, 24/7 security, high-end catering, like-minded neighbours, the whole deal. He sells this dog wank to the local planners, promises them a couple of memorial benches or a playground or whatever they want, and the rest is conversation. Thank you, Mr Kinsey. We're grateful, Mr Kinsey. Just sign here, Mr Kinsey, and bung us a few quid to keep the punters happy.'

'Punters?'

'Us.'

Lizzie looked away, surprised by the venom in Pendrick's voice. He really feels it, she told herself. And why not? He grew up here. He fell in love here. He's carried this view to the other side of the planet and he still treasures it. Except it appears to be doomed, tucked into a developer's swag bag and sold to a bunch of rich cardigans for silly money.

She took another pull at the Guinness, leaning against Pendrick, letting her head fall against his shoulder. She felt him stiffen, then relax again.

'So what do you do about it?' she asked.

'You fight it whatever way you can. Not just me, dozens of other guys, hundreds of them. But you know what? We don't have a prayer, none of us, because the whole fucking thing is a game and whoever dreams up the rules gets to win. This country's fucked, Lizzie. You heard it here first.'

'So what do you do about it?' she asked again. Second time round it seemed an even saner question.

He didn't answer. Instead he picked up the brochure and began to leaf through. His fingers left grease marks over the architect's impression of life at Trezillion Oceanside. Finally, he tossed it aside. He was gazing out to sea.

'Do you ever dream of sailing away?' he said.

'Yes. Since you ask.'

'I'm serious.'

'I'm sure you are.' She reached up for him, kissed the stubble on his cheek. 'So how would you do it?'

'I'd buy a yacht. Something that would get me anywhere. I

did the nav stuff for the crossing with Kate. I'd need hands-on experience but that wouldn't be a problem.' He was looking down at her. 'How does that sound?'

Lizzie was stroking his arm.

'It sounds great,' she said. 'What would you do for money?'

'I've got money.'

'Enough?'

'Yeah. Money wouldn't be a problem.' He was lying full length now, his head propped on one arm. 'So what do you think?'

'I think it's brilliant. I think you should do it. Unless ...'

'Unless what?'

'Unless you want to buy one of these.' She nodded at the brochure.

He gazed at her blankly. 'Why would I do that?'

'It's a joke, Tom. Of course you wouldn't do that.'

He looked at her a moment longer, still uncertain, then forced a laugh before popping another tinnie. He took a couple of swallows and then wiped his mouth with the back of his hand.

'How about you?'

'How about me what?'

'Would you fancy it?'

'I'm married. I've got a little girl. I think I mentioned her.'

'She could come too.'

'That's kind.'

'I mean it.'

'Yeah? Do you? Do you really?'

She put her tinnie down and cupped his face in her hands. There was something new in his eyes and it took her a moment or two to realise what it was. Alarm.

'Does this bother you?' Her fingers followed the crease of the scar down his face. 'Because it shouldn't. You want to know a secret? I've got a scar too. Down here. Way down below my belly.'

'How come?'

'It happened when I was a kid. I was climbing some railings with a friend and slipped and got caught by the spike. My mum always said it could have been worse, but the older I got the uglier it made me feel.'

He smiled at her. She kissed him on the lips.

'You're a beautiful man, do you know that?'

'No.' He shook his head.

'Yes. Believe me. You are. Take it from me, people like you are rare. How does that work? You're rare because you take a risk or two. You're rare because you stick to what you believe in. And you're rare because you dare to care.'

She broke off, embarrassed. Rare, dare, care. She hadn't meant it to come out that way. Garbage like that belonged in a Hallmark card.

'You haven't answered my question,' he said.

'I know.'

'So how would you feel about it? Hopping aboard and sailing away?'

They were nose to nose now, the wind fluting through the marram grass.

'I don't know you,' she said.

'You do.'

'No.' She moistened a finger and traced the shape of his lips. 'But maybe we could remedy that.'

'Sure.' He didn't sound at all certain. 'And then?'

'Then we'd be closer. Then we'd get to know each other. Properly.'

He nodded, said nothing. He seemed to have lost focus. He was gazing out to sea again. He wanted to talk about the places they could go, the beaches he could show her, the people she could meet. Simple people. Real people. People who'd never let you down.

'Are we talking Thailand?' she said softly.

'Yeah. And a thousand other places. Think about it, Lizzie. Please.'

The conversation appeared to be over. They lay in silence for a while. The stiffening wind was blowing sand in Lizzie's face. She thought about seizing the initiative, about taking him by the hand and going back to the van and making a space in the back for the airbed. It might work. It might even be wildly successful. But something told her that this was the last thing he wanted and she didn't understand why.

'Do you find me attractive?' she asked after a while. 'Be honest.'

'I love you.'

'That's a big word.'

'I know. I mean it.'

'But how do you know?'

'I just do. It's something you feel. Don't ask me how. It's just there. It's happened. It's real. It exists. It just feels ...' he shrugged '... right.'

Lizzie said nothing. This was a conversation that was fast getting out of control. She closed her eyes. Could you really fall in love that quickly? And if you could, should you ever admit it?

She felt a movement beside her and became aware of his face looming over hers. He was smiling.

'The answer's yes,' he said softly. 'Of course I find you attractive.'

'Do you fancy me?'

'Yes.'

'That's good.' She nodded. 'Good.'

Another silence, longer this time. Pendrick lay back again, his huge hands clasped behind his head, his eyes closed. She wanted to kiss him properly, to unpick a little of the mystery that was complicating something that should have been so simple, but she couldn't bring herself to do it. It wasn't meant to be this way. She'd wanted them to make love, to share each other physically, to get to a place beyond the rights and wrongs of stony-hearted developers and the wickedness of the Western world, but deep down she realised it wasn't going to work. For all his talk of falling in love, something was holding him back.

At length she picked the brochure up and flicked through it again, aware that he was watching her. She looked up at him.

'Where did you get this?'

'Kinsey's apartment.' He seemed to be smiling at the memory. 'If you want the truth, I nicked it.'

It was gone six before John Hamilton phoned back. Suttle had left a message on his mobile asking him to call. Suttle was still introducing himself when Hamilton interrupted.

'I know who you are,' he said.

'How?'

'I got a call from Gina. She seems to think you're all right. Does that come as a surprise?'

'Yes, definitely.'

'Should I know more?'

'There isn't more to know.'

'Ah …' Suttle thought he caught the softest of chuckles. 'Then I think I understand.'

Suttle briefly described the meet he was setting up for Monday night. Bournemouth seemed a good location, but he didn't know the town and he needed a steer on an appropriate rendezvous.

'Is that all you need?'

'No. I want someone to watch my back. Put me down as paranoid but in this kind of company I need to have a back-stop.'

'Sure. That's understood.'

Hamilton said he had a flat in Westbourne. There was a Café Rouge up the road at the end of a crescent of shops. Suttle could get directions from Google or his satnav. The parking was fine across the road and the cafe might do nicely. He'd be happy to ride shotgun.

'That's good of you.'

'Not at all. Blame my crazy wife.'

'You're still married?'

'Yes.' The chuckle again, but louder. 'She told you otherwise?'

Lizzie was back in Exmouth by half six. She and Pendrick had shared the journey back in a companionable silence. He'd reached for her hand from time to time, a form of physical solace that made Lizzie begin to suspect that Pendrick – in some dimly understood way – was damaged goods. When he stopped on the seafront and let her out beside her car, he wanted to know when he'd see her again.

'Tomorrow,' she said brightly. 'I'm the girlie in bow making a fool of herself.'

She drove home, increasingly perplexed. In many respects it had been a lovely afternoon. In others, though it shamed her to admit it to herself, it had been deeply disappointing. On the way up to the north coast she'd rather assumed they'd get it on. She was curious to know whether they'd work together, and to be blunt there was only one way of finding out. Yet it hadn't happened, and the more she thought about it the more she realised that it probably never would.

There was a wariness in Pendrick that seemed to stand guard against the encroachments of the outside world. You stepped towards him and extended a hand only to watch him back off. To begin with she'd blamed herself for being too eager, too pushy, but then she found herself wondering why he and his wife had never had kids. Did they ever screw? Or had the marriage been based on something else?

In truth she didn't know, and as she turned the Impreza onto the parking area beside Chantry Cottage she found herself confronting another surprise. Driving up the lane, she'd assumed that the curl of blue smoke had come from the adjoining farm.

Now she was watching her husband circling a sizeable bonfire with his daughter in his arms.

She got out of the car. Suttle met her on the patio. He smelled of woodsmoke. He told her he'd had a great day. Even Grace was beaming. Together, they toured the garden. Suttle, it turned out, had parked Grace in her playpen in the sunshine and taken a scythe to the long grass. He'd hacked away at the dead vegetation along the wall that led down to the brook and raked a small mountain of twigs and assorted leaves into a monster bonfire. A lot of the stuff was still wet, he said, hence the lack of a proper flame, but if the weather held over the coming week he'd have another go.

Lizzie was surprised and impressed. With her eyes half closed the garden resembled a savage grade two. Far more importantly, her ever-distracted husband had at last made a start on the chaos of their domestic life. She lifted Grace from Suttle's arms and gave her a hug. Suttle wanted to know how the clear-up at the club had gone.

'Fine,' she said. 'But it took for ever.'

Later, after Lizzie had put Grace to bed, Suttle made supper and explained about Monday night. Lizzie, who knew Dave Fallon by reputation from her days on the Pompey *News*, warned Suttle to be careful. He said he'd already taken care of it.

'How?'

'The D/I I saw last night? She's got an estranged husband who lives in Bournemouth. He's agreed to keep an eye on me.'

'That's nice of him.'

'Gina's doing. Not mine.'

'She vouched for you?'

'Absolutely.'

'So what's in it for her?'

The moment she said it Lizzie knew she'd kicked open a door she should have left well alone.

Suttle was standing by the cooker, stirring a pan of fried rice.

'How about you?' he said softly.

'How about me what?'

'How about you and all your new buddies?'

'You mean the rowing club?'

'Sure. Unless it's gone beyond that.'

'Beyond what? I haven't a clue what you're talking about.'

'You haven't? A couple of nights ago you're back at eleven. What's going on with these people? Do they row in the dark?'

'We had a drink.'

'Who had a drink?'

'A bunch of us. They're very social. That's nice. Bit of a novelty, if you want the truth.'

'And today? Out at nine? Back at six? That's a lot of sweeping-up.'

'It was a shit heap. I told you.'

'Sure.'

'You don't believe me?'

'No.'

'You think I'm lying?'

'I think you're hiding something.'

'Same thing, isn't it?'

'Yeah.' He nodded. 'It is.'

'Great. You want the truth? Then here it is.' Lizzie stepped towards him. A vivid blush of colour pinked her face. He could feel her anger. 'Just for the record I object to this cop routine. I'm your wife, not some bloody suspect. I'm sure you're great in interview but marriage is a different gig. Have I been fucking some he-man rower ? No. Have I been tempted? As it happens, yes. Why? Because I can't stand living the way we live.'

Suttle nodded. He'd given up on the fried rice.

'So where did you go this afternoon?'

'I'm not answering that question.'

'But you did go somewhere?'

'Yes.'

'Great.' He turned back to the pan and gave the rice a savage poke. 'Thanks for fucking nothing.'

'You spent last night with a woman who just happens to live alone.' Lizzie was in his face now. 'You came home at God knows what time. Good was she? Worth it?'

'She's nuts, if you really want to know. Totally out of her tree.'

'Perfect.'

'What does that mean?'

'It means you could fuck the arse off her and walk away. No commitment on your part. No comeback. A totally risk-free screw. Like I say, perfect.'

'And you think that's what I did?'

'I don't know. Because you won't tell me. And even if you told me, even if we had a conversation, I'm not sure I'd believe you.'

'You wouldn't?'

'No. Not now. Not here. Not the way we are.'

'Great. Then that's it, yeah?'

'That's what?'

'Everything. You. Me. Grace. This khazi of a house you hate so much. Let's just bin it, shall we? The lot.'

'Call it a day?'

'Sure. If that's what you want.'

She stared at him for a long moment. She was shaking inside. She'd never imagined a scene like this. Never.

'I'm sorry.' She reached for the car keys. 'I'll go.'

She drove fast, keeping to the country lanes, swamped by her anger, fighting to concentrate on the next bend and the bend after that. Among the trees on top of the common, she nearly killed a fox. She had time to register the piercing redness of its eyes in the darkness as it turned to face her headlights. Instinctively, she stamped on the brakes and swung the wheel to the right, heading for woodland at the side of the road. The car shuddered and began to slide sideways. Finally it stopped. Lizzie closed her eyes. She was shaking again. Then she opened the door and threw up.

Exmouth was fifteen minutes away. She knew that Pendrick lived in a web of streets near the river and the station. She drove up and down, looking for his van, trying to fix his front door in her mind. There'd been some kind of card in the window of the flat downstairs. A tatty knocker and peeling paint on the door itself.

Finally, she found it. She parked across the road and switched the engine off. The light was on in the upstairs flat and the curtains were pulled back. She stared up at it for a long moment, trying to steady her pulse, trying to regain control of herself. She'd never snapped like that in her entire life, and the knowledge of where it might lead alarmed her deeply. She'd never been frightened of making decisions. On the contrary, especially at work, she'd won a reputation for being on top and ballsy in the trickiest situations.

This, though, was different. She'd pushed married life to the very edge of the cliff and she wasn't at all sure what she wanted to happen next. She needed to talk this thing through. She needed a listening ear, someone who'd understand, someone who wouldn't take advantage. Pendrick, she knew, would give her that kind of space, that kind of attention. If necessary, she could stay over. Whether she slept in his bed or not didn't matter. She wanted to be close to somebody. She wanted to be touched, to be held, to be told she wasn't some ditzy slapper cheating on her husband. Chantry Cottage had never been a great idea. She wanted out.

She rinsed her mouth with water from the bottle Jimmy kept in the glovebox. Then, reaching for the door handle, she paused. There was movement in the upstairs window. Someone was standing there, staring down at the street, a black silhouette against the light inside. It was a woman. She turned her head and must have said something because she was joined by another figure, bigger, broader. It was Pendrick. For a moment or two he and the woman were both immobile, watching her, then Pendrick reached out for the curtains and the tableau was gone.

Lizzie stared up at the window, trying to make sense of this image. Then her gaze lowered to Pendrick's van at the kerbside. Parked in front, neatly wedged into a tiny space, was a small black sports car.

Suttle was asleep when Lizzie slipped into bed beside him. She touched his face, told him she loved him, told him she was sorry, promised it would never happen again. Suttle stirred, grunted something she didn't catch, then rolled over. When dawn broke, hours later, she was still lying there, staring up at the damp patches on the ceiling, the tears cold on her cheeks.

Eight

It was Suttle's idea to drive the whole family to Exmouth for the Kinsey tribute. Lizzie, exhausted, was tempted to phone Tessa and cancel, but Suttle insisted she see the thing through. The way he read it, they were offering her a leading role in this morning's ceremony. If the rowing was doing her good, if she enjoyed it, the last thing she should do was let them down.

Lizzie knew she had no choice but to agree. Last night, to her immense relief, appeared to be history. Suttle was cheerful, positive and starving hungry. Making bonfires, he told her, was hard-core exercise. He made porridge for them all and patiently monitored Grace's attempts to spoon-feed herself in her high chair.

They were on the road by half nine. Suttle dropped Lizzie on the seafront, a discreet distance from the club compound, and drove on towards Exmouth Quays. The porridge hadn't quite filled the hole. He and the *Constantine* team had used the Docks Café earlier in the week and now he decided to share an egg and bacon butty with his infant daughter.

The café was packed. With Grace in his arms he was about to step back into the street when he caught a wave from a table in the corner. It was Carole Houghton. She was with her partner, a tall handsome woman called Jules. He went over, did the introductions. Grace gave them both a precautionary look and then nestled on her father's lap as he took the spare seat.

Houghton insisted on buying their egg and bacon butty. Suttle had mentioned the Kinsey tribute on Friday and she had thought it only proper to make an appearance. A full week had gone by since the investigation kicked off and, in the absence of a result, this was the least she could do on behalf of what remained of the *Constantine* squad.

'Does Grace like brown sauce?' Houghton was already on her feet, en route to the counter.

'Loves it.'

Suttle turned to her companion. Jules, he knew, was a lawyer, and he'd always suspected that Houghton shared one or two details of the more interesting jobs with her. He was right.

'Carole tells me you're the last man standing.'

'On *Constantine*?'

'Yes.'

'That's true. Short straw, me.'

'Coroner's file?'

'You've got it.'

'And it stops there?' She smiled. 'I think not.'

Houghton was still at the counter. Suttle was looking at Jules. He wanted to know more.

'Carole really rates you,' she said. 'I shouldn't be telling you but it's true. She thinks you're shrewd. And more to the point she thinks you're honest.'

'That's nice to hear. What does honest mean?'

'It means you're hard on yourself. It means you don't take short cuts. And I guess that means life isn't always easy.'

'Too right.' Suttle was thinking of last night. 'What else did she say?'

'She said that this investigation of yours, whatever it's called, is still in the balance. That you shouldn't give up.'

Suttle blinked. Houghton, he knew, was a class operator. Was this why she'd volunteered to fetch the butty? So her partner could deliver a discreet message? He voiced the thought as Houghton returned.

'Of course.' Jules was clearing a space on the table. 'You read her well, young man.'

Lizzie met Tash Donovan at the club compound. Tessa did the introductions and said that Tash would be rowing in the number two seat ahead of Lizzie in bow. The rest of the crew, including Tash's partner Milo, were already on the beach helping to rig the boats. God speed, Tessa said, and when it comes to the row-past be sure to give it some welly.

Lizzie and Tash crossed the seafront road and headed down the slipway towards the beach. The tide was falling fast, flooding out of the estuary, and a ledge of high cloud had thinned the sunshine.

Lizzie wanted to know how long Tash had been rowing. She loved the colour of her hair.

'Couple of years. I'm first reserve with this lot.' She nodded at the nearest quad. 'Four of them are bloody good. Kinsey was deadweight.'

'That's what everyone says.'

'It's true. The poor lamb had his strengths but rowing wasn't one of them.'

They joined the rest of the crew at the water's edge. Tash did the introductions. Lizzie recognised Milo from the Thursday session. This was the guy with the camera, she thought. Andy Poole offered her a crushing handshake and a wide grin. Lenahan, the cox, asked whether she was cool with rowing bow.

'I need to be out of the way,' Lizzie said. 'Bow sounds fine to me.'

'A little bird told me that you and racing starts are strangers.'

'Your little bird's right.'

'We can fix that. Leave it to me. No problem.'

He was as good as his word. He supervised the launch, and the quad nosed out into the current. There was still plenty of water over the offshore sandbank and they crabbed away from the beach towards the nose of a distant promontory.

Lenahan was calling the stroke rate, warming the crew up, and Lizzie could feel the power in the boat. Despite her exhaustion, she realised she was beginning to enjoy this. Then came a small dot powering out of the harbour. The dot grew rapidly bigger and Lenahan gave the speeding safety boat a wave as it circled the quad. There were two men aboard. The portly guy at the wheel Lizzie had never seen before. The other one was all too familiar. Pendrick.

Suttle and Grace found a space near the edge of the dock for the tribute ceremony. Houghton had taken Jules for a stroll round Regatta House. Under the circumstances, she thought her partner deserved a proper look at the crime scene. They'd rejoin Suttle later.

The last of the sunshine had gone by now and it was appreciably colder. Suttle bent to the buggy, tucking Grace in. Earlier he'd watched Lizzie's boat out in the far distance, stopping and starting, time after time. Now the other quads from the club were pulling hard against the tide, forming a protective square around a couple of smaller skiffs, slowly closing on the dancing water off the dock. All the rowers were wearing club colours, red and white, and as the boats approached, each crew in perfect time, a murmur of approval went through the watching spectators.

By now a decent crowd had gathered and a second TV crew had joined the BBC South West team who had earlier been prowling around Regatta Court. Suttle had watched the reporter on the phone before doing his piece to camera. He'd stationed himself on the stretch of promenade immediately below Kinsey's apartment, trying to flatten his thinning hair in the rising wind. Suttle was too far away to catch what he was saying, but the cameraman's dramatic tilt upwards towards Kinsey's balcony was all too eloquent. *The dead man fell from here, and still nobody knows why.*

'Mummy!'

Grace had seen her first. She was waving her little arms in excitement. Suttle turned to find himself looking at the Kinsey boat as it passed through the rest of the fleet on its way upriver. Lizzie was at the front and Suttle felt a jolt of admiration at the way she seemed to have mastered the business. He supposed that rowing was difficult. Lizzie had told him so. And yet there she was, perfectly in tune with this strange music, her blades dipping in and out with the rest of the crew, her back straight as she pulled on the oars, her body moving sweetly forward to take the next stroke.

'Which one?'

'At the front there. The small one.'

Houghton had appeared behind them. She pointed Lizzie out to Jules, who stepped forward and cupped her hands.

'Go Lizzie!'

Someone else in the crowd took up the chant. Then another. Then a third. Even Grace was having a squeal. Lizzie had caught the chant. Suttle saw the tiny nod of her head, an acknowledgement. Suttle cupped his own hands.

'Go! Go Lizzie! GO!' he roared.

She recognised his voice. A grin this time, spreading and spreading. Suttle turned to Houghton.

'She's not bad, eh? For a probationer?'

Lenahan had elected to make the turn about 500 metres upstream from the dock. His cue to start would be an orange distress maroon fired from the quad dropping the wreath. Molly Doyle had cleared this through the Coastguard at Brixham late last night and they'd assured her they'd resist the temptation to launch the lifeboat or a chopper.

'Red, please.'

Lenahan had got to the turn point. The crew hauled on their right-hand blades, pivoting the quad around a buoy.

'Next stroke, easy up.'

The crew stopped rowing. Lizzie could feel the tide beneath her, lifting the hull and carrying it downstream. Lenahan was waiting for the maroon.

'Come on,' he muttered. 'Jesus, what's the matter with those eejits?'

Lizzie wanted to glance over her shoulder and watch the maroon go off, but she knew she'd get bollocked. Eyes in the boat. Always eyes in the boat.

'Whole crew come forward to row.' Lenahan had his gaze locked on the dock.

The whole crew came forward, blades in the water, ready for the racing start. The first time she'd tried it, half an hour ago, Lizzie had nearly totalled Tash's oars. Her second attempt had been better and after that she'd started to get the feel of what was required. She was still playing catch-up, though, and just hoped that no one watching had binos.

'Ready to row?' Lizzie caught the muffled bang of the maroon. 'ROW!'

Andy Poole was leader of this tiny orchestra. Rigid in his seat, he took a swift choppy stroke. Then another. Then a third. The quad surged forward. After five strokes, in a blur of scarlet, the crew went to half slide, a foot of movement under their bums, the strokes longer, more power in the water. Another five strokes and they settled into racing speed, thirty-two strokes a minute, every oarsman intent on pouring maximum effort into the churning blades.

To her immense relief, Lizzie was still in one piece. She hadn't caught a crab, she hadn't got in Tash's way, and while she knew she was a minim off the beat she quickly settled down. By now the quad was, in Lenahan's phrase, at battle speed. With the looming orange presence of Regatta House fast approaching, Lizzie concentrated on giving it everything. *Lean forward*, she told herself. *Take the catch. Push back hard with legs. Arms straight. Accelerate the blade through the water. Feel it in the thighs. Go for the burn. Big tug at the end.* Then hands away quickly and do it all over again.

Off to her right she could hear cheering and applause from the dock. She pictured Jimmy and Grace. She hoped they were watching her. She hoped they weren't laughing. Then, much closer, came the other club boats, the rowers keeping station with tiny movements of their blades, and a brief snatched glimpse of Kinsey's wreath bobbing gently in the middle of the formation.

'Forty-one big ones. GO!'

They'd passed the wreath. Lenahan was driving them on. This could have been a race, easily. Tash had already warned her about what to expect. Flat out, she'd said, it's the lungs that seize up first. Keep sucking in the air. Keep pushing hard on the footstretcher. Above all, watch the timing. Catch, extract. Catch, extract. Get it right. Exactly right. Keep on the beat.

'Twenty to go. Own the water, people. Make it yours.'

Lizzie was starting to struggle. Then she remembered her first outing on the rowing machine, how she'd kept the pressure up until the very end, chasing the numbers on the readout, ignoring all the distress calls her body was putting out.

'Five of your best. Your very best.'

Lizzie's eyes were shut. She was rowing on empty. She squeezed every last ounce of effort into those final strokes. Then, quite suddenly, it was all over.

'Easy up, guys. Angels, all of you.'

She barely heard Lenahan. She let go of her oars and reached forward to pat Tash on the back. The boat was still moving at speed. The water caught her blades, smashing both against her midriff and sweeping her overboard. It happened so quickly Lizzie hadn't a clue what had happened. All she knew was that she was underwater, being dragged along by the boat.

She struggled, starting to panic. One of her feet was still trapped in the footstretcher. She must have over-tightened the strap. She shut her eyes a moment, fighting the temptation to take a breath, trying to get her head out of the water. It was hopeless. Her body was twisted and she no longer had the energy or the strength to break free. By now her lungs were bursting. They must have seen me, she kept telling herself. A couple of hundred people can't all be blind.

Desperate for air, she opened her mouth. The water was ice cold. She could feel it in her chest. She began to cough, to choke. More water. Then she sensed hands beneath her arms and her head at last broke the surface, and seconds before she passed out she caught the looming face of Pendrick, treading water beside her, the white hull of the safety boat inches from his back.

'You'll be fine,' she heard him say. 'I've got you.'

A chopper flew her to A & E in Exeter. Wrapped in a space blanket with another blanket on top, she'd managed to stop the shakes. The accompanying paramedic told her it was the shock as well as the water temperature. She supposed that was a comfort but she wasn't sure.

In A & E they put her in a giant suit that looked like a duvet with arms. She lay in a cubicle trying not to relive those final few strokes before she'd gone overboard. It had to be her own fault, had to be, but she simply couldn't work out why. One moment she'd been telling Tash what a star she was. The next she'd been fighting for her life.

Jimmy and Grace turned up minutes later. They squeezed into the tiny cubicle. Jimmy gave her a hug and then found a chair and sat by the bed while Lizzie clung to Grace. Jimmy's boss seemed to have come too. She'd found some change for the machine in the waiting room and returned with teas and coffees, keeping a discreet distance while Jimmy described the scene on the dock.

Most people, including him, had been unaware of the incident. All they'd seen was the safety boat racing to the still-moving quad, and then a big guy going overboard to fish someone out of the water. Only a nearby birdwatcher in the crowd on the quay had the full story. He'd watched the whole episode through his binos. It's the girl in the front, he told Suttle. She seems to have come a cropper.

'That was me,' Lizzie said. 'What a wuss.'

Suttle told her to forget it. Stuff happens. Thank Christ someone had been on hand to fish her out.

'Who was it?' he asked.

'Pendrick.' She found his hand and gave it a squeeze. 'Who else?'

Lizzie was released a couple of hours later. The consultant took Suttle aside and told him not to hesitate to seek help if there were any after-effects.

'Your wife's been through serious trauma,' he warned. 'This can mess with people's idea of themselves in all kinds of ways.'

Suttle was intrigued by the phrase. He'd have liked to find out more but one glance at the consultant's face told him this wasn't the place or the time. Lizzie's GP, he said, should be the first port of call. After, of course, a little home-grown TLC.

'No problem.' Suttle thanked him and returned to the cubicle. To his delight, Lizzie wanted to go home.

'Say it again –' he bent to kiss her '– then I'll believe it.'

That evening, for the first time in months, they felt good with each other. Houghton had offered Suttle a couple of days off to help Lizzie get over her little accident but Lizzie herself wouldn't hear of it. She was embarrassed, and grateful to the small army of folk who'd fished her out, emptied her lungs, strapped her into the chopper and flown her away. Now she'd be grateful for a little time on her own with just the baby for company and the knowledge that Suttle would be back before nightfall.

'That could be a problem.' He was thinking about tomorrow's meet in Bournemouth. 'I'll cancel.'

'Don't.' She put her hand on his arm. 'I'm a strong girl. Stronger than you think. Stick with the arrangements, but nothing silly, eh?'

'You're sure?'

'I'm sure. And you know something else?' She beckoned him closer, kissed him on the lips and nodded towards the stairs. 'I owe you.'

Nine

Suttle was in his office at Middlemoor by eight o'clock next morning. Lizzie had insisted he leave early to beat the rush-hour traffic and had dismissed his offer to return at midday to sort her out a bit of lunch. She had a long list of apologetic phone calls to make. Mea culpa. My fault. Sitting beside the bed, Suttle had wondered whether the list of calls included Pendrick. Given the fact that he'd saved his wife's life, he fancied the answer was liable to be yes. Lizzie was watching him carefully. In certain moods, like now, Jimmy Suttle was an open book.

'Don't worry,' she'd said. 'That man's the reason I'm still here.'

'How does that work?'

'It's complicated.' She'd kissed him. 'One day, if you're good, I might tell you.'

Now, Suttle took a call from D/I Houghton. She had good news and bad. Preferably face to face.

Suttle went upstairs. Houghton had found a traffic cone from somewhere to keep her office door open when she was in the mood for callers. Now she asked Suttle to close it.

He took a seat in front of her desk. A large Manila envelope had his name on it.

'I had Traffic on first thing,' she said. 'About Friday night.'

Suttle owned up at once. He'd been going way too fast. He'd

249

had a couple of drinks. Next time he'd suss these Traffic numpties way earlier.

'That's not what bothers me.'

'It's not?'

'No. I understand you'd just been to Modbury.'

'That's right.'

'D/I Hamilton lives in Modbury.'

'Right again, boss. We had dinner together. I needed to sort
some stuff out.'

'*Constantine* stuff?'

'Partly.'

'Private stuff?'

'Yes.'

She nodded. The more Suttle saw of her, the more he liked
her. It was rare to find someone so astute, so direct, so switched
on, who applied that intelligence to the people around her.
Suttle had never been quite clear about the phrase grown-up
but fancied that it pretty much covered Carole Houghton.

'D/I Hamilton is neediness on legs,' she said. 'You ought to
be aware of that.'

'I am, boss. Believe me.'

'She has a talent for wrecking other people's marriages.
It may not be her fault but it happens nonetheless. She's an
attractive woman. She can talk a good war. But beware, Jimmy.
This job's tough enough as it is.'

'Crime wise?' Suttle was intrigued.

'No.' Houghton was reaching for the envelope. 'Some days I
think the bad guys are the least of our problems. Do we understand each other?'

'We do, boss.'

Suttle took the envelope downstairs. It had come from the force
intel department and contained Kinsey's financial records.
Grateful, once again, to have the office to himself Suttle sorted
the information into separate piles on a neighbouring desk

and began to go through it. Expecting a complicated web of accounts, he was surprised by its simplicity. On the business side, Kinsey had operated two accounts, one for Kittiwake and one for Kittiwake Oceanside. When it came to his personal life, he drew on a single account in his own name.

By mid-morning, after an initial trawl through all three piles, Suttle had enough information to map the shape of Kinsey's growing business empire. Over the past few months the Kittiwake account had been largely dormant. All Kinsey's energies had been spent on the development of a series of sites across north Cornwall. Most of these, as far as Suttle could judge, were no more than a wish list of locations that might, one day, host Kittiwake Oceanside gated retirement communities. Cheques drawn on the Oceanside business account had gone to a range of planning and landscape consultants, all of whom had featured in the business files Suttle had analysed earlier. Only one of the sites, Trezillion, showed any signs of happening, and this was reflected in payments to a Leeds-based firm of solicitors. A couple of these tied in with credit card payments to Flybe for return tickets to Leeds Bradford Airport.

Suttle had hung on to Kinsey's business correspondence in the belief that it might feature in the file he was preparing for the Coroner. Cheque by cheque, he tied the payments to the paperwork. Planning permission for Trezillion was clearly a huge obstacle to the project going forward, but phrases in a couple of the letters to his legal adviser hinted that this problem might be far from insoluble. Hence, Suttle assumed, the £4.5K Kinsey had been prepared to blow on the design and printing of glossy brochures.

He was about to start on the personal bank records when his eye was caught by another large cheque. On 21 January 2011 Kinsey had paid £13,000 to a Mr Waheed Akhtar. The name alone was totally out of keeping with the rest of Kinsey's disbursements. There was no matching invoice in his business records, and no correspondence that Suttle could find. Was this an Asian businessman Kinsey had tapped up for advice? Was he taking the Kittiwake concept abroad? Would elderly couples with a taste for year-round sunshine be spending their twilight years in Oceanside Dubai?

Suttle thought it was worth a note. He scribbled the details on his pad and reached for the pile of personal bank account statements. Most of this stuff was mundane – direct debits on power, water and council tax, card payments for anything from petrol to booze, plus a recent cheque for £607 to the Exeter Porsche dealer for a service. On top of that came regular expenditure that had to be connected to the rowing club. Repairs to the new quad after a collision with an estuary buoy. Hotel and ferry bills for a winter training camp on Lake Garda. Three-figure payments to Andy Poole for 'miscellaneous services'.

Month by month, Suttle went backwards, looking for anomalies that might flag something interesting, but after a full year and a half he'd found nothing. Kinsey seemed to have lived his life exactly in step with everything the intel had already established. He kept himself to himself, didn't go out much, and spent more than was probably wise on his precious rowing.

Only after he'd finished his initial trawl, making himself another mug of coffee in the squad kitchenette, did Suttle realise what he was missing. Where were the payments to the escort agency for his regular Thai girlies? And how come there was no trace of the money he'd spent on Tash Donovan?

Suttle took the coffee back to his desk. His task this time was to revisit all the personal stuff – bank accounts, credit card billings – and look for cash withdrawals. Within the hour he was satisfied that these couldn't possibly have paid for Kinsey's sex life. In terms of ready money, he appeared to live on surprisingly little. A hundred and ten pounds a week was his average spend. How many girlies could you buy for that?

A knock at the door brought Luke Golding into the office. The young D/C had some good news.

'TF2, Sarge. I cracked it.'

Suttle had almost forgotten about Team Fortress 2. Golding, it turned out, had spent most of the last couple of days on the Internet. It happened to be his weekend off and he'd hooked up with ShattAr on three separate occasions. During the third game he'd saved the guy's life, not just once but on four separate occasions, and this had been enough to finally coax a reply from his earlier message. He'd wanted a link to ShattAr's Facebook profile. And he'd finally got it.

'His real name's Zameer Akhtar, Sarge. And as far as I can judge, he lives in Leeds.'

'Zameer what?'

'Akhtar.' Golding wrote it down for Suttle's benefit.

'You've PNC'd him?'

'Yeah. The guy just picked up a twelve months suspended for possession.'

Suttle raised an eyebrow. He'd been expecting a sleek Pakistani businessman, not a lowlife druggie.

'Have you talked to the locals?'

'Yeah, I got through to their intel set-up in Wakefield. They're busy as fuck just now but the woman promised to come back before close of play. I gave her your name and number, Sarge. Happy days, eh?'

Suttle was looking at the pile of bank statements. Kinsey had business connections in Leeds. He made regular visits on Flybe. The recurrence of the name Akhtar had to be more than coincidence. Were these two people brothers or was there some other family connection?

He glanced up. He wanted to know how Golding was getting on with the Exeter escort agencies.

'That was the other thing, Sarge. I think I've nailed the girl in the photo we ripped from Kinsey's phone. She works for an outfit called Twosomes. They operate out of a grungy little room over a Chinese takeaway in Heavitree. Real shit hole.'

'They ID'd the photo?'

'Of course not. But there was a mug shot on a wallboard. I swear it was the same woman.' He paused and shot Suttle a grin. 'Maybe you should take a look.'

By lunchtime Lizzie was nearing the end of her list of thank you phone calls. Tessa had been more than understanding. The girls, she said, were thinking of buying Lizzie a safety belt for use in the boat, while Clive, the Club Captain, was definitely going to nominate her for the Cock-Up of the Year Award. Molly Doyle had successfully kept the details of the incident from the local press and was anticipating great coverage for the tribute ceremony and the row-through. The Kinsey crew, meanwhile, had been so impressed by Lizzie's capacity to hold her breath underwater that she was in some danger of becoming a regular sub.

'Sub? Submarine? Get it?' Andy Poole roared with laughter, wished her well and hung up.

Lizzie's last call went to Tash Donovan. When she admitted she still wanted to row, Donovan told her she must have balls of steel.

'You're coming out again? After something like *that*?'

'Of course I am. If anyone'll have me.'

'You're famous, girl. We talk of nothing else. Invites to row? Shall I make a list?'

Touched by the gentle piss-takes, Lizzie sat down and wrote a semi-formal letter to Molly Doyle. She wanted the club to know that she was sorry for letting everyone down and grateful for all the calls and support she'd received since. She would definitely be keeping her foot straps looser from now on and looked forward to the next outing. Hopefully, she added, she might even make it back in one piece. She signed herself Lizzie Hodson in keeping with the pact she'd made with Jimmy.

Sitting at the kitchen table, rereading the letter, she glimpsed a wraith-like presence behind the careful prose. It was like writing to someone about a bereavement. Her old gloomy self seemed to have passed away. All you need, she thought, is a half a minute or so underneath a moving boat with a lungful of seawater sloshing around inside you. Near-death experiences cure anything.

She glanced through the door into the living room. Grace was asleep on a pair of cushions in her playpen. Every day the shafts of sunlight edged down the back wall as the sun rose higher in the sky. At last the house was beginning to dry out. Soon, with a helping hand or two, Chantry Cottage might even feel like a proper home.

The knock at the kitchen window made her jump. For a moment she had no idea who it was, then her blood froze. Pendrick was wearing a pair of blue overalls and a black beanie. He seemed to be tapping his watch. There was no way she could ignore him but her instinct was to pretend he wasn't there, to somehow turn the clock back to this time last week when she'd never heard of the guy. Then she got to her feet, telling herself that this was the man who'd probably saved her life. The very least she owed him was a thank you.

She opened the kitchen door, standing aside as he stepped past her. He looked around the way a buyer might, noting this detail and that, not bothering to hide his curiosity. Lizzie was fighting hard to keep the smile on her face.

'Grace?' Pendrick was peering into the living room.

'Yeah. Don't wake her up, whatever you do.'

'She's lovely.'

Lizzie didn't know what he meant, didn't know what he was doing here. Trespass wasn't a word she would ever use lightly but this felt very close.

'How did you know where we live?'

'You told me Colaton Raleigh. I asked down in the village. Lovely young mum? Sweet little girl? Can't be that much competition round here.'

Lizzie was filling the kettle. Half an hour, she told herself. Tops.

'Tea?'

'Coffee if you've got it.'

He'd disappeared behind the living-room door. Lizzie found him crouching in a corner, examining one of the sockets that was fast parting company with the skirting board. She'd mentioned the state of the place when they'd been up in north Cornwall. Bad move.

Pendrick had moved on to the radiator under the window-sill. The bowl to catch the drips from the leak was half full. He gave it a poke and grunted something Lizzie didn't catch.

'Sugar?' she said brightly. 'I can't remember.'

'Two.' He didn't look round. 'The socket'll take no time at all. The radiator's trickier. I'll have to drain the system.'

'Who said you need to?'

'You'll have a flood otherwise.'

'That's not what I meant.'

'I know.' He was on his feet again, looking down at her. 'We need to talk about Saturday night. Am I right?'

'No. I need to thank you for what you did on Sunday morning. I should have phoned. I should have thanked you. I can't tell you how grateful I am. Without you, I might have drowned.'

'Who says?'

'The people at the hospital. The medics.'

This news put a smile on Pendrick's face. He took a seat at the kitchen table, reached for one of Grace's toys, a squashy rubber ball, and began to play with it. He looked strangely relaxed. This might have been his own home.

'Right time, right place.' He shrugged. 'If only ... eh?'

'If only what?' Lizzie was mystified again.

'If only I'd been able to do the same for Kate.'

'But I thought you said she wanted to go overboard. That it was her decision.'

'Yeah. But it didn't make it any easier, did it?'

'For her?'

'For me.' He was crushing the ball now. It had disappeared beneath the whiteness of his huge knuckles. 'You know Tash, right?'

'Yes. I met her yesterday.'

'That was her at my place on Saturday night, in case you were wondering.'

'Fine.' It was Lizzie's turn to shrug. 'And why not?'

'You don't care? You don't want to know more?'

'No.'

'OK. So why did you come round?'

'Because I was upset about something. Because I wanted to talk.'

'Fine. Go ahead.'

'There's no point. It's resolved. It's finished. It's over.'

Pendrick released the ball and watched it roll slowly towards the edge of the table. He seemed to have lost interest in the socket and the radiator.

'Tash and me are friends. Just friends. She comes round sometimes when Milo's driving her crazy. We talk. That's pretty much it.'

'I believe you. You're good at that. You must have lots of practice.'

'Good at what?'

'Listening.'

'Is that what this is about?' He gestured loosely at the space between them. 'Only I had a different impression.'

'I expect that was my fault. I always dive into things. It used to get me into all kinds of trouble.'

'I'm not surprised.' He caught the ball as it fell from the table and gave it another squeeze. 'You wanted me to fuck you on Saturday, didn't you?'

'I wanted us to make love. There might be a difference.'

'And were you disappointed when we didn't? Was that why you got so upset?'

Lizzie gazed at him. There were some men who needed to

put their smell on everything they touched, and Pendrick, she was beginning to realise, might just be one of them. Territorial was too feeble a word. She shuddered to think what might be more appropriate.

She got up to turn off the electric kettle. As she passed Pendrick he reached out for her.

'Don't,' she said. 'Please don't.'

'Why not?'

'Because ...' she couldn't find the words '... stuff's happened.'

'You're right. And I meant everything I said.'

'About what?'

'About this khazi of a country. About arseholes like Kinsey. About getting hold of a yacht and doing something sane for once. You were up for that. I could see it in your face. You thought we could do it. Maybe you thought we *should* do it. Am I right?'

Lizzie didn't answer. She wanted this man out of her house, out of her life. The last thing she needed was a rerun of Saturday afternoon.

She poured hot water into two mugs and added a tea bag apiece.

'I haven't got coffee,' she said. 'I'm sorry.'

'Fuck the coffee. Tell me about Saturday. Tell me you meant it.'

She felt the first stirrings of impatience. She was being as civil as she could. She put the mugs on the table and sat down again. Then she reached for both his hands, removing the ball and dropping it on the floor.

'You saved my life,' she said quietly. 'Twice. I don't know how many times I have to say thank you but I mean it. I really do.'

Pendrick stared at her. He was confused as well as angry.

'And that's it?'

'I'm afraid so. I haven't a clue what it is between you and

Tash, and if you want the truth I'm not interested. All I know is that this – the house, my marriage, even poor little Grace – took me to a very bad place. You helped me with that. You helped in ways you'll never ever suspect. For that, I thank you. And I thank you. And I thank you again.' She bent and kissed his hand. 'Does that make any sense?'

'None at all. I know you, Lizzie. I know what you want. I know what's real to you. I know what really *matters*. I've been around a bit, believe me. And I *know*.'

To this Lizzie had no answer. They were heading up a cul-de-sac that held nothing but darkness. The last twenty-four hours, she thought she'd left all that behind. She wanted him gone.

'I'm due at a clinic in half an hour,' she said. 'Grace is due a check.'

'No, you're not. You're just trying to make it easy for me. I love that about you. Just the way I love everything else.' He gave her hand a little squeeze and then picked up the mug.

Lizzie stared at him. She was fast running out of options. There was a hint of madness in this man. Go for broke, she told herself. Double or quits.

'She stayed the night, didn't she?'

'Tash?' A smile ghosted across his face. 'No way. If you want the truth, she came round to try and get me to row.'

'On Sunday morning?'

'Yeah. She thought we all ought to be together.'

'Because of Kinsey?'

'Yes. That seemed to be important for her.'

'You instead of me?'

'Yes. It was nothing personal. She'd never even met you.'

'And you?'

'I told her I couldn't do it. Why? Because I couldn't stand the guy. I also told her I was glad he'd gone. She had a problem with that. She thought I was totally out of order.' He reached for her hand. 'Are we friends now?'

259

It was an impossible question to answer. Lizzie just shook her head and turned away.

'Leave me alone, please. Let go of my hand.'

'No problem. My pleasure.' He nodded next door. 'You want me to sort that stuff out or not?'

'No, thank you.'

'Fine.' He drained the mug and got to his feet. 'Next time, eh?'

The Golden Dragon lay at the end of a terrace of shops in Heavitree, a scruffy red-brick suburb to the east of Exeter. Suttle found a parking spot in a lay-by across the road. When he asked at the counter for the Twosomes agency, the woman simply pointed upstairs.

Access was via an exterior staircase at the back of the property. The window in the door at the top had been boarded up after some kind of break-in, and there were fresh-looking chisel marks around the Yale lock.

A youngish guy opened the door. He was pale and thin. His patched jeans hung off his bony frame and his trainers had definitely seen better days. As far as Suttle could judge, he was eastern European.

'Who are you?' Poor English, heavily accented.

Suttle flashed his warrant card. He'd appreciate a word or two. It needn't take long.

The guy spent a long time examining the card. Then he asked Suttle to come inside. The room must once have been a kitchen. A jar of instant coffee and an electric kettle stood on the work surface beside a pile of newspapers. Suttle recognised a shot of Cracow on the front page of the top paper. There were scabs of ageing dog shit on the floor and a powerful smell of drains.

Suttle pushed the door shut behind him.

'I'm investigating a suspicious death,' he said.

'Where?'

'Exmouth. I need your help. We need to trace this woman.'

He laid the shot from Kinsey's phone on the work surface. Golding had been right. It exactly matched the photo pinned to the wall board. The guy peered at the proffered shot, then glanced up. He was looking alarmed.

'You say she's dead, this woman?'

'No. I'm saying we need to talk to her. Is that possible?'

'No.' He shook his head.

'Why not?'

'She doesn't speak English. She's not here. She's gone away.'

'Where?'

'Abroad. I don't know.'

Lies, Suttle thought.

'You're responsible for this woman? You take the bookings?'

'Yes. Me and my partner.'

'Who's your partner?'

'Mr Wattana. He's away too.'

'You keep records?'

'I don't understand.'

'When people pay?'

'Ah …' He looked thoughtful. 'Does that matter?'

'It might.'

Suttle bent forward, closing the distance between them. He needed to get this man onside. He wanted to offer him a word of advice.

'You need to make a choice here, my friend. Either you let me see your payment records or the whole thing gets much more complicated. The VAT inspector? The tax people?' He sniffed, looking round. 'Health and safety?'

The guy shook his head. He wanted to say no. He wanted Suttle out of his face. Suttle was looking at a filing cabinet wedged into an alcove beside the boiler. Judging by the state of the paintwork, it might have come out of a skip.

'In there, maybe? You want to give me a hand here?'

With some reluctance, the guy followed Suttle across to the

cabinet. It was locked. Suttle stepped back while the guy found the key. The middle drawer was packed with files. The guy looked up.

'You want the same girl?' he asked.

'Yeah. The punter's name was Kinsey.'

He shook his head. He'd never heard of anyone called Kinsey.

'Little guy? Middle-aged? Drove a Porsche? Big top-floor apartment down in Exmouth? Place called Regatta Court?'

Mention of Regatta Court sparked a nod of recognition. Maybe Kinsey used a false name, Suttle thought.

The guy was riffling through the files. At last he found what he was looking for. He took it out and held it close against his skinny chest.

'And after this?'

'I go.'

'And not come back?'

Suttle smiled. His turn to lie.

'Never.'

'OK.'

The guy handed over the file. Suttle opened it and found himself looking at a sheaf of A4 sheets. Each held a scribbled note or two – date, time, name of the attending escort – and stapled to each was a credit-card slip. These were the old sort, letter-box-shaped, bearing the imprint of the card. Suttle lifted out the first one and gazed at the name of the cardholder. Mrs Sonya Jacobson. Kinsey's ex-wife.

The guy wanted the file back. When Suttle said he was taking it away, the guy tried to protest. Then he was struck by another thought.

'Mr Jacobson?' he asked. 'He's dead?'

Lizzie was panicking. The only call she could think of making was to Gill Reynolds. Mercifully, she picked up.

'You've got a moment?'

'Yeah. If you're quick.'

'Later maybe?'

'Later's worse.'

Lizzie closed her eyes. She was in big trouble with someone at the rowing club. The details weren't important but she'd done something stupid, really stupid, and now the man wouldn't leave her alone.

'How stupid?'

'You don't want to know.'

'What kind of answer is that? Just tell me.'

Lizzie did her best. By the time she got to Trezillion, Gill was laughing.

'You're right,' she said. 'You've got to be barking. That husband of yours can be a dickhead sometimes but he's not that bad.' She paused. 'So what's this guy like?'

'He's OK. At least I thought he was OK. Now I'm not so sure.'

'Why?'

'Because he's all over me. Because he won't listen. Because he won't take no for an answer.'

'And are you surprised? After you came on to him like that?'

'I suppose not. But it gets worse.'

'*Worse?*'

'Yeah. Yesterday he saved my life. Major production. Chopper, paramedics, the lot.'

'Shit. Are you OK?'

'I'm fine. No, that's a lie. If you want the truth, I'm terrified.'

Lizzie explained about Pendrick and his wife rowing across the Atlantic, about the morning he woke up and found himself alone. It took a moment for Gill to place the story. Then she had it.

'Big hippy guy? Hair down round his shoulders? Bit of a looker?'

'That's him. He's cut most of his hair off but the rest is pretty much the same.'

'Fuck. I'm with you now. No wonder.'

'No wonder what?'

'No wonder you went to wherever it was.'

'Trezillion.'

'Yeah. Maybe you should have fucked him and got it over with. Most men lose interest after that.'

'Not this one. Not the way I read him.'

'What about Jimmy?'

'Jimmy's being sweet. Jimmy's noticed who I am at last.'

'Sure ... but does he *know*?'

'About what?'

'Yer man.'

'Yes, I think he does. Not the detail. Not Trezillion. He's a detective, Gill. He does this stuff for a living.'

'And if he found out about Trezillion? What then?'

Lizzie didn't answer for a moment. This was the question she'd been dreading. This was the reason she'd made the call in the first place. She needed clarity. She needed to understand exactly where she'd got to in this hideous story.

'I don't know,' she said at last. 'It's been rough these last few days, really horrible. Jimmy was brilliant yesterday, really cool with everything. He sorted me out after the accident. We even got it on last night. I don't want to lose that, Gill. I really don't.'

'And this other guy? Pendrick?'

'That's what terrifies me.'

'Why?'

'Because I'm beginning to wonder about him. And because he won't let go.'

Suttle phoned Carole Houghton from the car. He was still parked across the road from the Golden Dragon.

'Boss? We need to bottom out a credit card. Or it could be a debit card. Have you got a pen?'

Houghton, it turned out, was preparing performance reviews.

In other circumstances Suttle might have been amused. He gave her the details on the slip.

'And the name?'

'Sonya Jacobson.'

'Who's she?'

'Kinsey's ex-wife.'

'Should I be excited?'

'Definitely.'

Suttle's second call went to Eamonn Lenahan In these situations, especially with someone like Lenahan, Christian names often worked best.

'Eamonn? Jimmy Suttle.'

Lenahan remembered the name at once. He was doing a shift as a locum registrar in A & E at the Royal Devon and Exeter. Trade had been brisk all morning but he'd just seized a chance to put his feet up in the staffroom. Tea and biscuits. God's answer to terminal stress.

Suttle laughed. Just the mischief in the man's voice took him back to the hour or so they'd spent in his rented cottage in Lympstone. Interesting guy. Definitely a one-off.

'Something on that mind of yours?' he said. 'Because now would be a good time to talk. Ask for me at A & E. Doors will open, my friend. I'll save you a biscuit.'

Suttle turned the invitation down. The staff might recognise him from yesterday's drama and the last thing he wanted just now was the likes of Lenahan making the connection between him and Lizzie.

'I'm stuffed, mate,' he said. 'But tell me one thing.'

'What's that?'

'The takeaway you all had on the Saturday night, up in Kinsey's place. Where did it come from?'

'Fuck knows. Ask Tash.'

'I've tried.' Suttle was lying. 'She won't pick up.'

'Bell Pendrick then. I think he uses the same place.'

Suttle scribbled down a number, then checked his watch.

Aside from Andy Poole, Pendrick was the one person he'd yet to see.

'What time does he finish work?'

'He doesn't. He's off today. Number 94, Woodville Road. Fella in the flat down below cracks bones for a living. Charming guy. Give him my best if he opens the door. Canes the arse off us mere practitioners.'

Suttle was in Exmouth by half two. He'd called at Woodville Road days ago, but this time a yellow VW van was parked outside number 94. Suttle resisted the temptation to raise the chiropractor in the ground-floor flat and pressed Pendrick's bell. Moments later came heavy footsteps down the stairs and Suttle found himself looking at the figure he'd last seen on Milo Symons' PC screen. The same bulk. The same shaven head. The same scar. The same hint of amusement in the deep-set eyes.

He stooped to inspect Suttle's warrant card. He was wearing shorts and a thin singlet. The singlet was dark with sweat. He didn't appear to be surprised to find a detective at his door.

'You want to come in?'

'Please.'

Pendrick led the way upstairs. The living room was under-furnished but restful. Suttle liked the Moroccan throws on the sofa and the bookcases brimming with paperbacks. A set of weights lay on a folded towel on the polished floorboards. Miles Davis played softly on the sound system. It didn't need much imagination on Suttle's part to put a woman in here, someone maybe a bit stressed, a bit vulnerable. Someone in need of TLC and a listening ear.

Pendrick had departed to the bathroom. Suttle heard splashing. Minutes later Pendrick was back in a dressing gown, towelling his face dry, trailing the scent of shower gel. He wanted to know what Suttle was after.

'I read the account you gave to our guys back last week. You mind if we go over one or two points?'

'Sure. No problem.'

'Let's talk about Kinsey.'

'Must we?' The expression on his face might have been a smile, but Suttle wasn't sure. There was anger in this man. He could feel it.

'Why do you say that?'

'No reason. I didn't much like the guy but you probably know that already.'

'Something happened between you? Something personal?'

'Kinsey didn't do personal. The guy was a robot. If you want the truth, I felt sorry for him.'

'You knew him well?'

'Not at all. That was never on offer.'

'So how did you hook up in the first place?'

'He bought the boat. Then he bunged Andy Poole to fill it with decent rowers. Andy took advice from people round the club. I was one of the chosen ones.'

'Chosen' was laced with contempt. Suttle began to wonder whether anything put a real smile on this man's face.

'And the rest of the crew?'

'They were good rowers. Andy was the best. He had pedigree. But the rest of us weren't bad either.'

'That wasn't what I meant. I'm asking whether they all felt the way you felt.'

'About Kinsey?'

'Yeah.'

'I dunno. We never talked about him really. He sat up in bow and tried to boss us around, but no one took much notice. He should have learned to row properly. That might have helped.'

'What about Milo Symons?'

'What about him?'

'Did he get on with Kinsey?'

'That guy would get on with anyone. He's a nice man, Milo, but he's a child, a puppy dog. Kinsey would give him a pat from time to time, toss him a bone, and the guy would roll over. Quite sweet if you like that kind of thing.'

'And what about his partner? Tash?'

Pendrick gave Suttle a look. Amusement again? Or something more complex? Suttle couldn't decide.

'Tash is a law unto herself,' Pendrick said softly.

'Meaning?'

'Meaning Kinsey fancied the arse off her. Tash knew that. And made him look a complete dick.'

'How?'

'By filling his head with all the hippy crap. By going round there and trying to turn him into a human being.'

'Round where?'

'Round to his apartment. She does this stuff for a living. Touchy-feely. Astral therapy. Getting in touch with your inner self. That could have been ugly in Kinsey's case.'

'She told you all this?'

'Tash tells me everything. Tash tells everyone everything. That woman knows no shame.'

Suttle nodded, remembering how candid she'd been about servicing Kinsey's needs. Five minutes max. A hundred quid a minute.

'You think she had a relationship with Kinsey?'

'That wouldn't have been possible. There was nothing to have a relationship with. Did she teach him to get in tune with himself? Did she shag the man if the price was right? Quite possibly.'

'But you'd know though, wouldn't you? If she tells everyone?'

'I would, yeah.'

'So did she?'

'Of course she did.'

'And was she shagging anyone else?'

'Like who?'

'Like you?'

The suggestion appeared to amuse him.

'Are you serious?' he started to laugh. 'Me and Tash?'

Suttle let the silence thicken. Pendrick gave his face another wipe with the towel.

'Tell me about Milo,' Suttle said at last.

'I just did. Mr Puppy Dog.'

'His partner's Tash, am I right?'

'Yeah.'

'And she's shagging Kinsey and maybe one or two others and not bothering to keep it a secret, yes?'

'It's possible.'

'So how does that make him feel?'

The silence was much longer this time. There was a logic in these questions and Pendrick knew it.

'You're looking for motivation, right?'

'I'm asking a question.'

'Because you think someone *killed* Kinsey? Went up there and chucked him off his balcony?'

Suttle didn't answer. Pendrick held his gaze.

'Kinsey was an arsehole,' he said softly. 'Arseholes sometimes self-destruct. Fuck knows why, but they do. Maybe it's God paying debts. Maybe it's in the stars. Maybe Tash gave him the shag of his dreams and he decided to quit when he was ahead. Who cares? All I know is the guy's gone. And good fucking riddance.'

'The shag of his dreams? For winning, you mean?'

'Whatever.'

'But that night? Saturday night? After you'd all gone?'

'I've no idea.'

'You think she might have driven back to Exmouth Quays?'

'How would I know?'

'But she had a key to his apartment? Is that what you're telling me?'

This time Pendrick didn't answer. At length he checked his watch. Time was moving on. He had a couple of calls to make.

Suttle thanked him for his time. He might come back. He might ask Pendrick to attend the local nick for a more formal interview. In the meantime he had one last question.

'The takeaway Tash went to on Saturday night. Which one was it?'

Pendrick was picking at a loose thread in the towel. He looked up.

'The Taj,' he said. 'In Rolle Street.'

Rolle Street was a couple of minutes' drive from Pendrick's place. The Taj Mahal lay between a hairdressing salon and an estate agency. The door was locked. Suttle got the phone number from the menu in the window. When he rang the number he could hear a phone ringing inside. Then came a recorded message. The Taj could take reservations but take-away orders had to be collected in person.

Suttle tried again. This time the phone triggered a stir of movement from somewhere upstairs. Then came the clatter of feet on the stairs and a voice in Suttle's ear.

'What do you want? Who is it?'

'Police. Can you open the door please?'

The guy had obviously been asleep. He was middle-aged, portly. He was wearing loose cotton trousers and an Exeter FC football top. He rubbed his eyes, asked Suttle to come in.

'You own this place?'

'I do, yes.'

'What's your name?'

'Ratul.'

Suttle gave him Saturday's date. He wanted to know whether Ratul could lay his hands on the card receipts from takeaway orders.

'Upstairs,' he said. 'They're upstairs. You've got a name for the order?'

'Either Kinsey or Donovan.'

'Wait please.'

He disappeared up the stairs. Suttle could hear movement overhead. A drawer opened and closed. He picked up a menu, realising how hungry he was. Then Ratul was back.

'Here,' he said. 'It was a lady. I remember.'

He gave Suttle a copy of the order. It was in Tash Donovan's name. In all, the food for Saturday's little celebration had come to £67.49. The debit-card slip was stapled to the order. This time there was no name, just the last four digits of the number on the card.

Suttle had memorised the last four digits of the slips he'd seized from the escort agency: 2865. He checked the numbers: 2865. Ms Sonya Jacobson.

Suttle had time to grab a sandwich from an Exmouth café before he drove back to Middlemoor. He was certain now that *Constantine* should be revived, and that knowledge made him feel very good indeed. Everyone had put Kinsey's death in the wrong box. In the absence of any evidence to the contrary, it had been quicker and cheaper to assume suicide and consign the file to the Coroner's office. Only Suttle had taken the harder path. And now it turned out that he'd been right.

Carole Houghton was still in her office. In less than an hour Suttle needed to leave for Bournemouth.

'This has to be quick, boss.'

She already knew about the card receipt from the Exeter escort agency. Now he told her about the matching slip from the Taj.

'Same account, boss. Has to be.'

'So what are we saying?'

'We're saying that Tash Donovan was charging the earth for all kinds of stuff with Kinsey, including regular sex. That we can prove because she told me. We're also saying that Donovan persuaded Kinsey to bung Milo a couple of grand to help with his movie with more to follow.'

'How much?'

'Another forty-five grand.'

'Why would he do that?'

'To keep Symons sweet.'

'You can prove that too?'

'No.'

'But you're telling me we can evidence all these other payments?'

'Not so far. The two grand he paid Symons must have come out of the Jacobson account. The forty-five was on a promise. I'm guessing that the rest, the money he was paying Donovan, came out of the Jacobson account too. Donovan would have wanted cash. Kinsey must have had ATM drawing rights.'

'But what's he doing with his wife's account?'

'Ex-wife's. So far I don't know. But my guess is that it was some kind of private stash. Maybe he needed to hide money from the Revenue.'

'Sure. Or his ex-wife.'

Suttle nodded. Either way, they needed to access the Jacobson account.

'Donovan may still have the card, boss. And she's obviously got the PIN number.'

'The card wasn't retrieved by Scenes of Crime?'

'No. I checked just now.'

'And you're sure the Jacobson account doesn't figure in his business records?'

'Absolutely. And if he operated it through the Internet, there's no way you'd ever know it even existed.'

'His PC hard disk?'

'That's a possibility. I'll feed the account number through. See if they can raise anything.'

'Did he have a laptop?'

'Not that we've found.'

'Unusual.'

'That's what I thought.'

Houghton pushed the performance review files to one side

and reached for a pad. Suttle watched her making a neat list of bullet points. Then she looked up.

'Saturday night,' she said. 'Walk me through it.'

Suttle left for Bournemouth at half four, phoning Lizzie as he headed for his car. After the dramas of the past week, it was good to hear the lift in her voice.

'You'll be back when?'

'Tennish. I'll phone.'

'Be careful, yeah?'

'Always.'

'I love you. Remember that.'

Suttle grinned to himself. Traffic out of the city was already heavy but he edged into the outside lane as soon as he hit the Honiton road, maintaining a steady 70 mph as he headed east. Houghton had wanted him to hang on and talk to Nandy, but Suttle had pleaded a personal crisis at home. He'd be back first thing tomorrow. If she needed to make contact in the meantime she could always bell him.

As he left her office, she'd been on the phone to Nandy. The Det-Supt was driving the Bodmin job at breakneck speed but Suttle knew there was no way he'd ignore the weight of evidence he'd unearthed. Pausing at the door of Houghton's office, he'd looked back at her. Still on the phone, she'd smiled at him and raised a thumb. *Constantine* was obviously back from the dead. Brilliant.

Lizzie was feeding Grace when she got the call from Pendrick. She glanced at it and put the phone to one side. When he tried again, she didn't even pick it up. Then, moments later, came the beep that indicated a text waiting. With a tiny shiver of apprehension, she retrieved the phone. It was Pendrick again: 'If you don't pick up, I'll drive out to yr place. Yr call. XXX'.

She looked at the row of kisses, angry now. He answered as soon as she keyed recall.

'We need to talk,' he said.

'I can't.'

'We have to.'

'No way.'

'Is your husband there?'

'No. But he's back any minute.'

'We could meet in a pub. Invent an excuse. Bring the baby. Whatever.'

'You're out of your mind. There's nothing to talk about.'

'Wrong. There's everything to talk about.'

'Like what?'

'Like you and me.' He paused. 'And other stuff.'

'What other stuff?'

'Stuff about Tash. I've had the Old Bill round.'

'When?'

'This afternoon. These guys aren't stupid. I'm in a bad place. I mean it. I need your help. Is that too much to ask?'

The phone went dead. Lizzie didn't move for a moment or two. Then she stole into the hall, double-bolted the front door and returned to the kitchen.. She bolted the door from the kitchen out into the garden too, then looked at Grace. The biggest of the carving knives was in the drawer under the sink. She took it out, wrapped it in a tea towel and laid it carefully on the table. Then she reached for the cooling spoon of mashed potato.

'Open wide,' she said.

Suttle was on the outskirts of Bournemouth a couple of minutes before eight. With the help of his satnav he threaded his way through a tangle of streets and found a parking spot round the corner from the main parade of shops. He'd no idea what John Hamilton looked like but was alarmed to note the yellow no-parking line across the road from the Café Rouge. Traffic was still thick, clotted with buses. *This guy's supposed to be good*, he told himself. One way or another he'd have the rendezvous plotted up.

Suttle stepped into the café. Dave Fallon had already arrived. He was sitting at a table towards the back, with another man beside him. Suttle hadn't seen Fallon for a while, not face to face, and the intervening years had done nothing for his dress sense. The same tired leather jacket with the fraying cuffs. The same baggy jeans. The same curry flecks on his once-white shirt. Fallon had put on weight and it showed.

'This is Carlos.' He nodded at the other man. 'We're in business together. Right, Carlos?'

The other man said nothing. Younger than Fallon, he was tall and lean. He had steady eyes and the kind of tan you'd pay a lot of money to acquire. Beautiful suit, thought Suttle.

Fallon didn't want to waste Suttle's time. Carlos, he said, was in the delivery game. His mission in life was to please people who wanted wrong things put right. In this case they were dealing with a German art dealer who'd lost his daughter, a girl called Renata, to some scumbag thug in a botched contract killing near Malaga.

'With me so far, mush?' Fallon was looking at Suttle.

'Go on.'

'This German guy's got money. Quite a lot of money. In fact he's fucking minted. Losing his daughter like that has really upset him, and way down the line he wants to do something about it.'

'He's offering a reward?'

'Yeah. And a big one. Hundred K.'

'Euros?'

'Pounds.'

'Great. And Carlos?'

'Carlos is on the case. He's also fucking plugged in, believe me. Nothing moves along that bit of coast without Carlos being in the know. Good guys, bad guys, local Filth, even the fucking Russians – he's across them all. Right, *amigo*?'

Fallon gave Carlos a dig in the arm. Carlos was doing his best to ignore him. Suttle felt a tiny prickle of sympathy.

Fallon hadn't finished. All this had happened a while back. The contract killer was an animal from London called Tommy Peters. Bazza Mac had hired him to kill a lieutenant called Brett West who'd stepped out of line. Peters had done the job on Westie but had killed his new girlfriend as well for good measure. It was, said Fallon, a witness thing, just tidying up loose ends, and Peters had been good enough not to charge Baz for the extra body. The girlfriend's name was Renata. Hence the £100K from her dad.

'So this guy's after Peters? Is that right?'

'Yeah. But there's a problem.'

'What's that?'

'Peters is dead. Bowel cancer. Which leaves your mate Winter. He was there too. And as far as we can make out, he ain't got bowel cancer. Not yet anyway.'

Suttle nodded. He knew this story by heart. It was the reason Winter had finally decided to turn police informant, grass Mackenzie up and buy himself a new life abroad. Better that than a guy with a European Arrest Warrant at his door.

'So Carlos wants to find Winter? Is that it?'

'Yeah. Me too. We're in this together, me and Carlos. The minute we deliver Winter, you're looking at one happy man.'

A waiter approached. Suttle ordered a coffee. He thought he knew what was coming next but Fallon surprised him. *Never underestimate this man*, he reminded himself. You don't get to own half the cabs in Pompey by accident.

'That nice Marie you've been talking to? She gave us a look-see at Bazza's records. Turns out your Mr Winter made a couple of trips before all that election bollocks. Baz thought it was on business. From where I'm sitting, Baz was wrong.'

'So what do you want from me?'

'You were part of all this, yeah? The way I hear it, you were the guy pulling Winter's strings. So it stands to reason you know where he went.'

'But you know already.'

'Sure. But how about you tell us too?'

This, Suttle knew, was crunch time. From here on in he had to be very careful indeed. In truth, he was fairly certain where Winter had ended up, but the last thing he intended to do was share that hunch.

'He went to Poland and Montenegro,' he said slowly.

'Dead right, mush.' Fallon swapped glances with his friend. Carlos had produced an elegant notepad, leather-bound, and was making notes. 'And where else?'

Suttle studied him for a moment and then laughed. 'There's something we haven't discussed,' he said.

'Like what?'

'Like what do I get out of this?'

'You want money?' Fallon was looking outraged.

'Of course I don't want money. The deal was simple. I help you as best I can and you call the dogs off.'

'Jonno? The fat bastard that came down with the black cunt?'

'Yeah.'

'Dogs my arse.' It was Fallon's turn to laugh. 'That's a bit harsh, ain't it? On the fucking dogs?'

'You know what I mean. I help you. I tell you what I know. And you leave us alone. Not just now. Not just tomorrow. For ever.'

'Sweet. So where else did he go? Your grassing arsehole mate?'

'You haven't answered the question.'

'That's because you haven't told us nothing.'

'Fine.' Suttle stood up. 'There's a spare coffee coming if you're interested.'

It was the Spaniard who reached over. 'Please, my friend. Sit down.'

Suttle didn't move. He looked at Carlos. Then he looked at Fallon. A woman a couple of tables away had started to take an interest. Boots, jeans and a tight grey T-shirt.

Fallon muttered something that might have been an apology. Suttle resumed his seat.

'Carlos? I have your word?'

'Of course.' He extended a hand. Suttle shook it.

'The Ukraine,' Suttle said. 'Winter went to the Ukraine.'

Fallon's head came up. He couldn't mask his surprise.

'That's a big fucking place. We went there once. Away game. Europa Cup. Got stuffed 3–1. Horrible night.'

'Really?'

'Yeah. That's abroad. That's real abroad.'

'You're right. And it's not in the EU. Not yet.'

This, Suttle knew, mattered a great deal. Only EU countries recognised the European Arrest Warrant. Extradition treaties existed with a lot of other states but extradition was often a pain in the arse.

Fallon wanted to know where in the Ukraine.

'I know he bought a train ticket to Kiev. Beyond that I can't help you.'

'How? How do you know?'

'Because he kept dicking us around. In the end we had to have a sort-out. The trip to Kiev was nothing to do with our operation. Neither, as far as I know, did it have anything to do with Mackenzie. So there you go. The Ukraine. Kiev.'

'And that's it?'

'I'm afraid so.'

Fallon shot another look at Carlos. Then he turned back to Suttle.

'He also went to Montenegro, right?'

'Right.'

'Carlos here has been to Montenegro, talked to some people, a Russian bloke in particular, ex-cop, turned out to be a big mate of Winter's.'

'And?'

'Winter went to Croatia after. Took a taxi first. Then a coach. Carlos found the taxi driver too. Apparently your mate

278

Winter was asking about a place called ...' He frowned, checking with Carlos.

'Porec. Winter wanted to know about Porec.'

'There. Porec.' Fallon turned back to Suttle. 'Ring any bells?'

'Never heard of it.'

'You're kidding me.'

'I'm not, Dave. I've told you what I know. The Ukraine is definitely a runner.'

'Says you.'

'Says me.'

Fallon was giving him the hard stare. Suttle didn't flinch. Finally, it was Carlos' hand on his arm.

'Thank you,' he said softly. 'Thank you for coming.'

Outside the café Suttle checked as best he could for any signs of the surveillance he'd been expecting. Either these guys are as good as Gina Hamilton had promised, he thought, or I've been stiffed. Back in the Impreza, he was picking his way towards Poole and the road home when his phone began to trill. He pulled in, checking caller ID. John Hamilton.

'OK? Are we off the clock now?'

'Fine. Of course you are. And thanks, I owe you.' Suttle paused. 'Where were you, by the way?'

'I was in the pub across the road.'

'How does that work?'

'It doesn't. I was back-up in case anything kicked off.' He chuckled. 'Did you notice the woman a couple of tables away? Bit of a looker?'

'Boots? Grey T-shirt? Don't tell me.'

'Yeah. Class operator. Good on obs too.'

Suttle was back in Chantry Cottage by a quarter to ten. Lizzie was halfway through a bottle of red. She fetched Suttle's dinner from the oven and turned the TV off. She wanted to know what had happened.

It had taken a while for Suttle to tease the real meat out of the encounter in the Café Rouge. Now he saw no point keeping his conclusions to himself. Lizzie was part of this. Christ, if it came to more nonsense from the likes of fat Jonno, she'd be the one in the firing line.

'Dave Fallon's hooked up with a bounty hunter, a Spanish guy. I'm not sure I believe the figures but you're probably looking at the thick end of a hundred grand.'

'To do what?'

'To find Winter, stick him in the boot and take him back to Malaga. The Spanish police would take care of everything else and Fallon and his mate would cash the cheque.'

He explained about the killing of Brett West and the German girl who'd also died. Lizzie was horrified.

'Paul did that?'

'He was there. He could have stopped it. He didn't.'

'And the money?'

'It comes from the dead girl's father. Christ knows what it buys him. Peace of mind sounds nice but it can't be that simple.'

'So what did they want from you?'

'A steer on where Winter might have gone. I told them the Ukraine.'

'Was that wise?'

'It was a lie. I looked at the map this morning. The Ukraine's next to Poland. It's the best I could do.'

'And did they believe you?'

'Not for a moment.'

He told her about Carlos' enquiries in Montenegro. He seemed to have tracked Winter to Croatia. Worse still, he'd got the name of a specific town.

'What's it called?'

'Porec.'

'And you think he's there? Paul?'

'I've no idea. But Croatia makes perfect sense. It's bang next door to Montenegro. It's handy for flight connections. It's full of bloody tourists in the summer. And it's not in the EU. In his situation you could have done a lot worse.'

'So what do you think?'

'I think I did my best.'

'I meant about us?'

'I think they'll leave us alone.'

'You *think* they'll leave us alone?'

'I'm pretty certain. No guarantees but ...' he shrugged '... I'd be amazed if they turned up again.'

'Why's that?'

'You really want to know? Because I think they're a couple of days away from finding the old bugger. And you know what? That makes me fucking upset.'

Ten

Carole Houghton phoned at half past six next morning. Suttle was already up, trying to calm Grace after a fractious night.

'I would have called last night,' Houghton said, 'but I thought I'd leave you in peace.'

'That's kind. What's happened?'

The phone wedged in his ear, he was still cradling Grace. Mr Nandy, Houghton explained, had found a couple of D/Cs who would be joining *Constantine* by lunchtime. She was expecting a response on the Jacobson debit card before noon, and both guys would be deployed on checking ATM withdrawals. In the meantime, Mr Nandy was insisting that Suttle and Luke Golding get up to Leeds and interview Zameer Akhtar. If there was any chink in Kinsey's armour, any hint that he might – after all – have had a mate or two, then this might be the guy.

'When?'

'When what?'

'When do you want us up there?'

'This morning. You're both booked on Flybe. There's a flight at ten past nine. You should be at the airport by eight. That's why I'm phoning so early.'

Suttle met Luke Golding at Exeter Airport. Lines of beige-clad oldies were queueing for a holiday flight to Madeira. Suttle asked Golding to sort a couple of coffees and retired to a quiet corner to make a call. Thanks to Grace he'd spent the whole night awake, obsessing about Winter.

'Lizzie? I've been thinking about Paul. Somehow or other I need to make contact but I'm fucked if I know how.'

'It's not your job, my love. Not your responsibility.'

'He's a mate. Of course it's my responsibility.'

'It isn't. Believe me for once. Just relax, eh?'

Suttle was staring at the phone, bemused by Lizzie's response. What did she know here? What was she hiding? He was about to ask her when he felt a nudge on his arm. Golding had turned up with the coffees. Unless they joined the security queue now, they'd miss the flight.

Suttle bent to the phone again.

'Later, yeah? I'll call you from Leeds.'

The flight landed at 10.15. West Yorks had sent an intel civvy to pick them up. Sue was an older woman, broad Yorkshire, with three grown-up kids and a husband serving out his time on Traffic.

'It seems yer man were a bit of a handful.' She'd given the intel file to Suttle. 'Didn't like being arrested at all.'

Zameer Akhtar, Sue said, had been a sus small-time dealer, working out of premises in an area called Harehills. He'd been pulled a year or so back and got off with a caution. Then, less than a month ago, he was arrested again and this time he was taken to court.

'I blame Harehills myself. It's right kooky. Our Gary's got a mate who once lived there. Listen to Gary and you'd think it were hard not to end up dealing. Third World is what he calls it. Rubbish and all sorts everywhere. Kids, boy racers, you name it. Know what I'm saying?'

Suttle nodded. He wanted to know whether Akhtar had any family.

'Three sisters and his mum. His mum's an alcoholic. White

Lightning, the way yer man tells it. There used to be a dad too, but he's disappeared.'

'You've got a name for the father?'

'Yeah. Waheed.'

She drove them to police headquarters at Millgarth in the city centre. A uniformed inspector had arranged for them to use one of the interview rooms.

Suttle wanted to know about Akhtar. Was he being picked up or what?

'Voluntary attendance, love. If he doesn't show, he's on a nicking.'

At the police station she organised coffees and took them down to the interview room. To Suttle's surprise, Akhtar was already there. He was thin and pale with a mass of jet-black curls. According to the intel file he was twenty-three but he looked much younger. His jeans had been patched at least once, and the Iron Maiden motif on his freshly laundered T-shirt was beginning to wear off.

He got up the moment Suttle and Golding stepped in. Contrary to what the intel officer had said, the last thing this kid appeared to want was trouble. He'd been offered a solicitor but he wasn't being interviewed under caution, nor was he being investigated for any offence, so he'd decided to do without one.

Suttle did the introductions and thanked him in advance for his time. The next bit, he knew, was going to be tricky.

'We understand you knew a man called Kinsey.'

Akhtar looked blank.

'Jalf Rezi,' Golding said.

'You mean Jake?'

'Yes.'

'Yeah, I do. We just became Facebook friends. I'm waiting for a link to his page.' He had a soft voice, broad Yorkshire accent.

'That was us, I'm afraid.'

'What was us?'

'The Facebook message.'

'From Jake? The friending request? *You* sent that?'

'We did.'

Suttle explained what had happened at Regatta Court. They'd retrieved evidence that Akhtar and Kinsey might have been buddies through the video games they played. If that was the case then they needed to talk about Kinsey.

If anything, Akhtar was more confused.

'You're telling me he's dead?'

'I'm afraid so.'

'How?'

'Like I say, he fell.'

'Sure. But why are you here? Why are you talking to me?'

Suttle didn't answer. Akhtar was still trying to work out the implications of the friending request. He was looking at Golding. Then something seemed to dawn on him.

'So you were playing as Jake? As Jalf?'

'Yes.'

'Counterstrike?'

'Yes.'

'You were right crap. You know that?'

Golding shrugged and looked at his hands. Suttle laughed. A smile even crossed Akhtar's face.

'You were right rubbish,' he said. 'I should have sussed you.'

Suttle wanted to know when he'd first come across Jalf Rezi.

'Last year. I were playing Counterstrike for the first time and he wiped me out. I nearly didn't go back after that, but then I thought why not and I went on again. This time I was OK. Better than OK. After that I played a lot. Then he were sending me the odd message, telling me how much better I was getting, you know what I mean? So I texted back and asked him what other games he played. Turned out he was big on Left 4 Dead. That did it for me. You know it? Awesome game. The best.'

He looked from one face to the other. 'Is this OK, like? Is this what you want?'

Suttle gestured for him to carry on. Golding was making notes.

'Left 4 Dead drops you in the middle of this horrible place. It's a bit like where I live. There's just ruins and wreckage and all kinds of other shit and bad people everywhere. There's the Hunter, the Smoker, the Boomer, the Tank ...' He frowned, checking off the characters on his fingers.

'The Witch?' This from Golding.

'Yeah. Right. The Witch. You've played it too?'

'Years ago.'

'Right. So you know you have to get to the safe house? Get inside and like close the door? I was nearly there. I was outside the safe house and I was half blind because a Boomer had puked on me and the other three guys in the game were bleeding out really fast. You know like you watch their health bars? They were gone. End of.'

'Was Jalf one of them?' Golding again.

'Yeah. That's the whole point. I got into the safe house and I knew the other guys were fucked. The nearest one, right outside the safe house, was Jalf. I needn't have done it. I could have just let him die. I was safe in there. But Jalf comes on to me on the headphones, yells for help, really lays it on heavy. And me? I'm trying not to listen but then I think that makes me kinda mean. On the other side of the door I can hear the Boomer just waiting for me to come out so I blew him away with a couple of shotgun rounds through the door and then went out there again and killed a Hunter, and then another one, and then a Smoker, and it ended with me and Jalf back in the safe house. I needn't have done it, I needn't, but I did.' He was still looking at Golding. 'You understand that? You understand what I did?'

'Yeah, I do. Top move.'

'That's what Jalf said. That's when he asked me where I lived.'

Leeds, as it happened, had become a regular part of Kinsey's business life. A big law firm in the city centre handled contracts for something called Kittiwake and next time Kinsey was up for a meeting he invited Akhtar for lunch.

'We met at the Mint. You know the Mint at all? It's a big hotel down by the canal. It were right posh. Fourteen quid for fish 'n' chips. I had the works. It were lovely.'

Suttle was a spectator by now. Akhtar was addressing himself exclusively to Golding. Jalf, he said, wasn't at all what he expected. He thought he'd be meeting someone rough like himself. Instead he found himself sitting with a businessman at one of the city's top hotels.

'What do you think Kinsey made of you?'

'I think he thought I were all right. I told him a bit about myself, where I lived, my family, all that. My dad especially. He were very good about my dad.'

His father, he explained, had been badly injured on a building site back home. He came from a village in Mirpur and after a while in hospital he'd decided he didn't want to live in Pakistan any more and managed to make his way to England.

'Took him two years, that did. It must have been right hard the way he talked about it.'

Waheed settled in the big Mirpuri community in Leeds and took up with a local girl. Four kids came along. Akhtar was the eldest. By the time he was a teenager his mum was out of it on cheap cider and his dad had become a depressive.

'All he wanted to do was go back. He missed his real home. He missed his brothers and sisters. All he'd do was cry.'

'You told Jalf all this?'

'Yeah. We were playing Team Fortress 2 a lot by then, that's a favourite of mine. And Jake were good about my dad. Kind. *Really* kind.'

Listening, Suttle had the impression Akhtar had never come

across much kindness in his young life. With both his parents effectively off the plot, it had fallen to him to look after his sisters. No wonder he'd turned to drug dealing.

'So what did he do? Jalf?'

'He gave my dad some money. A shitload of money, if you really want to know. Enough to get him back to Mirpur and set him up.'

'You knew Kinsey well by now?'

'I knew him OK. We never went to the Mint again but he'd always buy me something to eat.'

Suttle was leaning back in his chair. Thirteen grand, he thought, Not a bad thank you for getting Jake Kinsey into the Left 4 Dead safe house.

'What did Jake tell you about himself?'

'Not a lot. Not really. Except rowing. Boat stuff. He were really keen on that. He had photos.'

'Did he talk about the guys he rowed with at all?'

'Yeah.' Akhtar nodded.

'What did he say?'

'He said they were good guys. He liked them.'

'All of them?'

Akhtar paused. He was looking at Golding again. The young D/C gestured for him to go on.

'He had a problem, did Jalf, if you really want to know. You could see it in his face. I thought he was, like, gay to begin with, but that weren't it.'

'So what was the problem?'

'I think it were to do with a woman and one of the guys in his boat. I don't know. He never gave me names or anything.'

'But what was the problem?'

'I dunno.'

'You do, Zameer, you do.' Golding bent forward. 'Just tell us.'

'But it sounds daft.'

'Tell us.'

'OK.' He shrugged. 'He thought one of the guys were going to kick off.'

'How?'

Akhtar shook his head, refusing to go any further.

Suttle and Golding exchanged glances. Then Golding leaned forward again.

'Are we talking health bars?' he said softly. 'Are we talking bleeding out?'

Akhtar nodded.

'Fucking right,' he whispered. 'And it were true, yeah?'

Suttle and Golding were back in Exeter by half four. Suttle rang Houghton from the airport. She asked him about Akhtar.

'Total result, boss. We need to talk.'

'Indeed. I've got Mr Nandy with me. As soon as you like, Jimmy.'

Nandy was waiting in Houghton's office. He was on his feet by the window, a mobile pressed to each ear. The Bodmin job was coming to the boil. As, it seemed, was *Constantine*.

Nandy finished both conversations. Houghton returned with a tray of coffees and an assortment of snacks.

'You've eaten?' Suttle shook his head. 'I thought not.'

Nandy had fetched another chair from the office next door. Suttle was already halfway through a packet of crisps. He summarised Akhtar's account. Nandy didn't bother to hide his disappointment.

'No names?'

'I'm afraid not.'

'Nothing in the way of hints? The look of the guy? How old he was?'

'No, sir.'

'Nothing about the woman involved?'

'No.'

'Then where does this take us?'

'Surely it establishes that Kinsey was worried.' It was

Houghton. She was frowning. 'And that could be significant, no?'

'Yeah, of course it could. Call me greedy but I'd have liked a little more.'

'There is no more, sir.' Suttle this time. 'The way I read it, the lad Akhtar was the closest Kinsey got to a mate. This was an arm's-length relationship. Most of it happened on the Internet. As it happens, they got to meet. Kinsey was grateful about all this safe-house game shit and Akhtar seems to have taken his fancy. Here was someone with a problem. He'd done Kinsey a favour. Kinsey did him one back.'

'Thirteen thousand pounds? For pressing a couple of buttons on a games console? You call that a *favour*?'

'Kinsey was showing off. He had money. He was a can-do guy. He liked solving problems. Maybe he felt sorry for the boy. Maybe there are bits of Kinsey we'll never know about.'

Houghton interrupted again. She thought Suttle had a point. One of the things about Kinsey's intel profile that had been bothering her was just how locked-down the guy appeared to have been. No one, she said, could be that alone, that cut-off, that solitary. And here was the proof.

'But he told the lad nothing. Except he was worried.' Nandy still wasn't convinced.

'Exactly. Because Kinsey always pulled back. So far and no further. Am I right, Jimmy?'

Suttle nodded. On the flight back he'd been picturing Kinsey up in the vastness of his apartment, bent over his PC, the lone figure blasting the likes of the Boomer and the Witch into oblivion. Video gaming had always been a cartoon world as far as Suttle was concerned but after an hour with Golding and Zameer Akhtar he'd begun to change his mind. Left 4 Dead had taken Kinsey into the no-man's-land between fantasy and friendship. And the rapport with Akhtar was the direct result. That kind of relationship wouldn't have been enough for most people but it suited Kinsey very nicely indeed. No real obligations. Nothing you couldn't settle with a couple of lunches and a cheque.

Nandy agreed to let the issue ride. Akhtar's account was a pointer, he said, an indicator. Nothing more. He told Houghton to brief Suttle about the ATMs. This, it appeared, was proper evidence.

Houghton was amused. The data on the Jacobson debit card had arrived earlier than expected. She ducked her head to a list of figures on a pad. In all the account held £107,638.34. There was a pattern of regular withdrawals going back more than a year, sums that would appear to pay for Donovan's supply of assorted services.

'Great.' Suttle had finished the crisps. 'Perfect.'

'Wait, Jimmy. It gets better. Kinsey's death should have stopped the withdrawals, am I right?'

'Yeah.'

'Then look at this.'

She passed across a list of the latest movements on the Jacobson account. At 23.45 on 9 April £200 had been withdrawn from an ATM in Exmouth. The following day another £200, this time from an ATM in Yeovil.

Suttle looked up. Moments like this, a sudden breakthrough that transformed suspicion into incontestable fact, were all too rare in complex investigations.

'Donovan's still got the card, boss. We were right.'

Nandy wanted to know how he could be so certain.

'Because she was in Yeovil on Sunday. It was her mum's birthday. Symons told me. It's in the notes.'

Suttle returned to the list. There were four more withdrawals: two of them local, one of them in Plymouth, the other in Bude.

Houghton wanted the list back. She scanned it quickly, then looked up. Excitement showed in her eyes. They glittered behind the rimless glasses. Suttle loved her in these moods.

'Symons' father runs an antiques business in Topsham. Right?'

'Right.'

'I sent a couple of guys round after lunch. That Transit Symons uses for pick-ups from auctions? He was down in Plymouth on the 15th. Up in Bude the next day. Bingo. Perfect match.'

'Do these ATMs have cameras?'

'That's what Mr Nandy asked. We're still checking. Most do, some don't.'

Suttle was doing the sums. Since Kinsey's death Donovan and Symons appeared to have helped themselves to £1200.

Suttle looked up, grinning. 'It's a stone-bonker, boss.'

'A stone what?'

'Stone-bonker. Pompey phrase. It means we've cracked it.'

Houghton was scribbling herself a note. One of Nandy's mobiles was ringing again. He spared it a glance then turned it off.

'OK,' he said. 'So we can probably prove theft. What about the rest of it?'

'You mean Kinsey?'

'Yes.'

Suttle nodded. Fair question.

'The way I see it, sir, is this. The guys win their race. They all come back to Exmouth and get hammered. Kinsey retires to bed and they all leave. Donovan and Symons are driving back alone. They stop at an ATM in Exmouth. There may be CCTV as well as an internal camera. We also need to check whether they got a receipt.'

'Why?'

'Because then they'd know how much was in the account. A hundred and seven grand? That sounds like motive to me.' Suttle paused. 'We should also be talking about Milo Symons. Donovan says he knew all about her and Kinsey occasionally shagging and didn't much care about it, but I've talked to the lad and I don't think that's true. I think he cared a lot. I think it upset him. Maybe other people in the crew knew about it too. And that would have upset him more. Either way, you're now looking at two reasons why he might want Kinsey out of his life. Number one, Tash. Number two, the money. This is a guy with big ambitions. He wants to make a movie. Movies are expensive. A hundred and seven K? Perfect.'

'So they drive back to the apartment?'

'Yeah. Tash has a key.'

'How come?'

'Kinsey gave it to her. Part of his fantasy, as far as I can gather. The walk-in shag.'

'And then what?'

'I've no idea. There are two of them. They're both rowers, both fit. Kinsey's probably still pissed. He's not a big guy. Between them, they could bundle him out of the bedroom and chuck him off the balcony. Piece of piss.'

There was a silence. Even Nandy appeared to be impressed. He was about to say something but Suttle hadn't finished.

'One other thing. Apparently Kinsey had a laptop. Symons mentioned it in his account. It doesn't appear on the Scenes of Crime log.'

'Meaning?'

'It got nicked. And that has to be down to Donovan and Symons. It's easy to carry. It's got value. You could wipe the hard disk and sell it on. We're dealing with thieves, remember.'

'As well as killers?'

'Yeah.' Suttle nodded. 'The way I see it, definitely.'

Carole Houghton called a *Constantine* squad meet for six o'clock. She spent ten minutes behind a closed door with Nandy to agree a strategy for the next twenty-four hours before the Det-Supt left once again for Bodmin. He met Suttle on the stairs. By the weekend, he muttered, he was in some danger of closing not just one job but two. He paused for a moment, looking Suttle in the eye. Then he offered a rare smile and gave him a pat on the shoulder.

'Good work, son.'

The *Constantine* squad now numbered three D/Cs plus Suttle and Houghton. In the light of the latest developments, Nandy had decided to keep the investigation paper-based and not bother with a transfer to the HOLMES suite. There'd be plenty of time to reorganise the file ahead of formal submission to the Crown Prosecution Service. Assuming, of course, that *Constantine* drew a cough from Donovan and Symons.

Houghton wanted thoughts on this issue. The more they could put on the table in the interview suite, the likelier they were to score a confession. So where should they look next?

Among the D/Cs there was a consensus for an early-doors arrest tomorrow morning. Bosh the mobile home and both vehicles. Nail the debit card and any ATM receipts they might have kept. Have a good look for the laptop. Keep Donovan and Symons apart – separate police stations, separate interviewing teams – and sweat their accounts until one or both of them broke.

Suttle wasn't so sure. Delay the arrest twenty-four hours, and he'd have a chance to talk to Eamonn Lenahan again.

'Why would you need to do that?' This from Houghton.

'Because he's the brightest guy in the boat. He listens. He watches. If anyone knew about Donovan and Kinsey it would have to be him.'

'How about tonight?'

'That's possible. I'd have to ring him.'

'How about Lizzie?'

'She'll be cool about it.'

'Are you sure?'

'Yeah.'

There was a brief silence. A couple of the D/Cs exchanged glances. Then Houghton nodded at the door.

'You want to bell him now? Then we can frame up the arrest strategy and sort the interviewing teams.'

Suttle made the call from his office. Lenahan, it turned out, had just come back from another shift at A & E. He was eye-balling the beginnings of a stir-fry and had plenty for two.

Suttle smiled. He wanted a chat, not a meal. Lenahan wouldn't budge.

'This is non-negotiable, my friend. Either we break bread together or you might find I'm busy. Give me half an hour. And bring something to drink.'

The line went dead. Suttle put his head round Houghton's door and promised to bell her later. Only when he was in the Impreza, wondering about an off-licence, did he remember to give Lizzie a call.

She was on the point of preparing supper. Suttle told her not to bother. Something had come up.

'Something that involves a meal?'

'Yes.'

'And a lonely policewoman?'

'Do me a favour.'

He was relieved to hear her laughing. He said he'd be back later, no real idea when but it shouldn't be late.

'No problem.'

'Are you sure?'

'Yeah. Another wild night in with my knitting? Bring it on.'

Suttle arrived in Lympstone with time to spare. He parked beside the railway halt and walked down to the Londis in the village centre. He'd already decided to end the day with a modest celebration and bought two bottles of Côtes-du-Rhône, one for Lenahan and one for afterwards once he'd got home.

Lenahan was alone once again in the tiny cottage. His lodger, he said, was doing Christian things at some night shelter in Exeter and wouldn't be back until God knows when. The kitchen formed part of the living space downstairs and Suttle caught the rich tang of ginger the moment he stepped in. When Lenahan broached the wine and offered him a glass, Suttle shook his head.

'You've got tea?'

'Has to be green, I'm afraid. Goes with the meal.'

'Whatever.'

Lenahan returned to his wok.

'We nearly had another body on Sunday. Did you hear about that? A fancy little tribute to our dead leader and this slip of a girl goes overboard. Another minute or so and we'd all be talking to the Coroner. Jesus, am I glad I listened when they taught us all those resus drills.'

Suttle expressed polite interest. One day, when *Constantine* was history, he'd come back and buy this man a serious drink. For the time being, he wanted to find out more about Donovan.

'Tash?' Lenahan was giving his rice a poke. 'That girl's a force of nature. Truly. I mean it. Astral Tash. Forty-plus years old and still at it.'

'At what?'

'Everything. With pretty much anyone. You know the story with Tash? Pendrick tells it best. It's Christmas Day. Pendrick's having a quiet one because he's that kind of guy and there comes a knock at the door and he looks out of the window like you do and there's Santa Claus outside, red coat, hat with a bobble on, funny beard. He thinks it's a piss-take to begin with but Santa's not going away so in the end he does the seasonal thing and opens the door. It's not Santa at all. It's Tash. She's spent half the day with Angel Dust and she's bored to death, and when she opens that red coat of hers it's pretty plain what kind of present she's got in mind.'

'Angel Dust?'

'Young Milo. That's what she calls him when the drink takes her.'

'She's drunk? Christmas night? On the doorstep?'

'Pissed as a rat. Pendrick gets her in, sits her down, gets her a mince pie or whatever treat he's giving himself, but she's not having it. Are we getting the picture here? Pendrick's under the cosh. And what's worse, he can't get rid of her. Took him hours to hose her down. And even then she was still giving him lists of what turned her on.'

'He was complaining? Pendrick?'

'Big time. He thought it was gross, and I think I would too. You could arrest a woman like that for something. Rape's too polite a word.'

'So she went? In the end.' Suttle was trying to picture the scene.

'Yeah. He managed to find a taxi. He stuffed her in the back with a note for Angel Dust. Return to Sender. Happy fucking Christmas.' Lenahan threw garlic and ginger in the wok and gave it a stir. 'So there you go. Astral Tash and Angel Dust. What else do you guys want to know?'

They sat down to eat minutes later. Out of deference to Lenahan's cooking skills, Suttle had changed the subject. The stir fry – prawns with Chinese lettuce – was excellent. His eye, once again, was taken by the scatter of photos on the wall. Some village in sub-Saharan Africa, every shot ablaze with the overwhelming brightness of the sunshine.

Lenahan caught his interest. Winter by the river in Lympstone had been arctic, he said. On Christmas Day, while Pendrick had been fighting Tash off, he'd been trying to get the ice off his crappy old Mondeo in case the call came from the hospital.

'You miss Africa?'

'Yeah, I do. Mid-morning you're talking forty in the shade. By lunchtime it's fifty. You type with tissue under your wrists to protect the circuits in the laptop from your own sweat. Wherever you go, you end up walking in zigzags just to stay in the shade. It takes for ever to get anywhere.'

'You speak the language?'

'No. A couple of words maybe, the odd phrase, but no. And that's a huge barrier. You know why? Because in my trade the backstory is 90 per cent of the diagnosis. A guy turns up at your door and he looks half dead. He probably *is* half dead. But if you don't know what's been going on in this guy's head, if you don't know what he's been up to, the pair of you are probably stuffed.'

Suttle nodded. He said it was exactly the same in his line of work.

'You're kidding.'

'I'm not.'

'I thought it was all forensics these days? DNA? CCTV? Some other fucking acronym? You're telling me you have to *listen* to people?'

'Exactly. And it's often what they don't say that really matters.'

'Right. Good. Excellent.' Lenahan took a long swallow of wine. 'So try me. Any question. Whatever you like.'

'OK. Let's go back to Tash.'

'Anything, my friend. Your call.'

'Was she shagging Kinsey?'

'Of course she was.'

'And did anyone else know? Apart from you?'

'We all did. She made no secret of it. And neither did Kinsey.'

'So what did that do for Symons?'

'Not a lot, the way I read the boy. She's older than him, of course. Maybe that's why he hated the word motherfucker.'

'Who called him that?'

'Kinsey. When he wanted to wind the poor eejit up.'

'You're kidding me.'

'Never. Kinsey never got his head around conversation, simple stuff like talking to people and not giving them a thousand reasons to punch your lights out. It didn't stop with Tash, either. He was a walking boast, that man. We all knew he was rich because he kept telling us, and we all knew you could buy girlies for a price if Tash wasn't enough, but it took Kinsey to treat us to the full à la carte. He was partial to Thai girls. He'd go on about them like it was some kind of meal he'd just had. What they did for him. How he liked them best.

Garlic and ginger and a sprinkle or two of soy sauce. Are you getting the picture?'

Suttle nodded. When Lenahan offered seconds he shook his head. He had enough. He was nearly through. Nearly.

'So when do you go back?' he said.

'To the Sudan? The sooner the better. You know something, my friend? I've spent the last six months trying to find trouble in paradise but it's hopeless. There's no civil war, no bodies by the side of the road, no dodgy situations to talk yourself out of, no so-called drinking water that will probably fry your guts. Everything works, or sort of works, so where's the challenge? Where's the *fun*?'

Trouble in paradise, Suttle thought. Didn't Kinsey's death qualify as trouble in paradise?

'That depends on your definition of paradise. Kinsey had it all, didn't he? Money? View? Girlies? Astral Tash? Us? Jesus, we even won him a cup. But it wasn't enough. Because it's never enough. Kinsey should have taken himself off to Africa. He should have seen the half-open eyes of the starving. That might have done him some good.' He reached for his glass again and then paused, struck by another thought. 'You're asking me for a diagnosis? Is that it? You want a hand here? From your tame little medic? The wild Irish guy from out yonder? You want a steer on what happened?'

'Go for it.'

'Kinsey ended up dead because he had too much. The poor wee guy choked to death on all that stuff. Me? I'd chuck the whole lot off the balcony. The bling. The money. The goodies. The extras. The Thai girlies. The Porsche. All that dinner-party shit. Everything. The lot. I'm with yer man.'

'Yer man?' Suttle was lost.

'Pendrick. He's like me, don't you see that? The guy's been around a bit. He's seen too much.' He tapped his head. 'Think too hard about what we've become and you end up fucking *ruined*.'

Lizzie was wondering about giving Jimmy a ring when she caught the sound of footsteps outside. Puzzled to know why she hadn't heard the Impreza, she got to her feet and went through to the kitchen. It was dark outside. She checked her watch. Nearly half nine. She switched on the light. She sensed a movement beyond the door that led to the patio. Then she heard a noise, a hard metallic noise, a snip. She froze, knowing now that there was somebody out there. She hadn't heard the Impreza because there was no Impreza. Someone else, God help me.

She edged slowly around the table. The door was unbolted. She'd been expecting Jimmy any time. Then a shape emerged from the darkness, someone big, someone clad in black. Black jacket, black T-shirt, black jeans, black everything. The whiteness of a face pressed itself against the glass panel in the door. A hand lifted wearily in salute. Pendrick.

He let himself in. He'd been drinking heavily. She could smell it. He reached for the support of the table, unsteady on his feet. Then he sank into a chair. He wanted to talk to her. He needed to explain one or two things. She wasn't to take offence. She wasn't to be frightened. He'd do her no harm. He'd never do her any harm. He'd treasure her for ever. And that was a promise.

'Where have you been?'

'The pub. Up the road.' He nodded vaguely towards the garden. 'The Otter? I left the van there.'

She stared at him. His eyes seemed to have lost focus. There was a terrible emptiness in his face. He seemed unaware of where he was, of how he'd got here, of what was supposed to happen next.

'Get out of my house,' she said softly. 'Please.'

He lifted an eyebrow. He hadn't heard a word of what she'd said. She repeated it, much louder, letting her anger show. Go. Leave. Now.

He stared at her for a long moment then shook his head.

'I can't,' he said. 'It's just not possible.'

'I'll phone the police.'

'Yeah. Sure.'

'I will. I'll do it now.'

'Whatever.'

She reached for the table, but his big hand had already closed over the mobile. He gazed up at her, trying to remember how to smile.

'I love you,' he whispered. 'I really, really do.'

Lizzie held his gaze a moment longer. When he tried to reach for her she avoided his outstretched arm and darted into the living room. The telephone was on the table beside the fireplace. When she lifted the receiver, she could hear nothing.

'I've done the line.' Pendrick was still at the table. 'Come back and talk to me.'

Lizzie was eyeing the stairs, but the last thing she wanted was Pendrick following her up to a bedroom. Grace was up there too. She couldn't leave the house without her.

She returned to the kitchen. A pair of wire cutters lay beside her mobile. Pendrick nodded at the other chair.

'Please. For me.'

She asked him again to leave. She promised not to breathe a word to anyone that he'd been here and frightened her shitless. She promised to keep it a secret.

'Just us?'

'Yes.'

'I like that. Why don't you sit down?'

The cutlery drawer was directly behind Pendrick. Even if she could grab a knife she knew it would be hopeless. He was far too strong.

With great reluctance she sat down. Pendrick asked for a drink.

'We haven't got any.'

'No?'

He got to his feet, his eyes never leaving her face. There were three Stellas in the fridge. He helped himself and returned to the table. He popped the tag and offered her the can. She shook her head.

'Here's to Kate,' he said.

He tipped the can and took a long swallow. Stella dripped down his chin.

'You remember Niran? The little Thai kid? The one who disappeared? Kate used to see him. Years afterwards, he kept turning up. He was the wind that opened the door. We'd get back home and he'd have put the lights on. We'd go fishing and he was the tug on the end of the line. He was everywhere that kid. And he was here too.'

'When?'

'Just now.' He nodded towards the window. 'He was the cloud in front of the moon. You should have seen it. I should have got you out there. He was beautiful, that child. Still is.'

'Please leave.'

'No.'

'You said you loved me.'

'I do. You know I do.'

'Then go. It's for the best, believe me.'

'For you?'

'For us.'

'You mean that?'

'I do, yes. If you want the truth, I loved being with you. I loved going to Cornwall that day. Trezillion. The dunes. The picnic. I meant everything I said. But it's like your cloud. Your Niran. It's gone.'

'You're wrong. He's still alive.'

'No, he's not. He's dead.'

'But he's here. He's around us. And we've got a second chance. Both of us. That's what we said, isn't it? At Trezillion?'

Lizzie didn't answer. Pendrick, she knew, was talking to himself. Some of her anger had gone. What he'd done tonight was inexcusable. She'd never forgive him. She'd never let it happen again. But way down inside, somewhere deeply private, she was beginning to feel sorry for this big man with the lostness in his eyes.

She got to her feet. He looked at her, suddenly alarmed.

'What are you doing?'

'I'm going upstairs to get my daughter,' she said. 'Then I'm going to put her in the buggy and we're going to take you back to your van. It's in the pub car park, right?' He nodded. 'Is the mattress still in the back? The sleeping bag?'

'Bags.' He was trying to smile again. 'Plural.'

'Whatever. Stay there. Don't move.'

She began to edge round him but he extended a leg, barring the way.

'I want to sleep here,' he said. 'With you.'

'That's not possible. Not now. Not ever.'

'Then when?'

'I just said. Never.'

He was staring up at her, wet-eyed, trying to coax some sense from the conversation.

'I just want you to hold me,' he muttered. 'Nothing else.'

She began to shake her head, to tell him he had to get a grip, to tell him to accept that whatever they had was over, but then came the burble of the Impreza coming down the lane and the glare of Jimmy's headlights reflected in the hedge beyond the patio. The car swung onto the gravel and Lizzie heard a brief snatch of Adele before Jimmy cut the engine. Then his footsteps quickened and his shadow darkened the window and he was pushing on the kitchen door.

For a second he stood there, holding a bottle of red wine, not understanding. It was Pendrick who spoke first. He'd seen this man only yesterday.

'Police?' He looked bewildered. It must be some conjuring trick. His gaze went to Lizzie. 'How the fuck did you manage that?'

'He's my husband. His name's Jimmy.'

'Hi, Jimmy.'

Suttle studied the outstretched hand.

'What are you doing here?' he said.

Pendrick didn't answer. He was looking at Lizzie.

'In your heart you know I love you. Isn't that right?'

Lizzie shook her head. Suttle hadn't moved.

'He's pissed,' she said quietly.

'Yeah, I can see. So what the fuck's going on?'

Pendrick stirred. He drained the Stella and crushed the can. His eyes had never left Lizzie.

'Tell him. Lizzie. Just tell him.'

'There's nothing to tell.'

'No?'

'No. There never was and there never will be.'

'Really?' A smile had warmed the big face. 'You don't remember? You don't remember Trezillion? All that?' His hand sank to his midriff and then crabbed down still further. 'Is it the scar? Is it that? Don't be ashamed, my love. I've seen worse.'

At last he got to his feet and slipped the wire cutters into his pocket. He offered Lizzie a dip of the head, a courtly little bow, then headed for the door. Suttle stood his ground.

'What is this?'

'Ask your wife.'

'I'm asking you.'

'Then I can't tell you. Either you see it or you don't. That's the thing about life, yeah?'

He gently pushed Suttle aside and stepped into the darkness. Suttle hesitated a moment, then followed. When Lizzie tried to get between them, he told her to go inside.

'Leave it, Jimmy.'

'Fuck off.'

He spun Pendrick round. Suttle's first blow caught him full on the mouth, the second put him on on the ground. Suttle began to kick him, driving the point of his toe into the big man's ribs. Pendrick offered no resistance, just soaked the punishment up. Finally, breathless, Suttle stood over him.

'If you set foot in my house again,' he said, 'I'll kill you. Right? You understand that? You hear what I'm saying? Do this again and you're a dead man.'

Pendrick peered up at him. His mouth was bleeding and he was nursing his bruised ribs.

'Too late, my friend.' He spat a tooth into the long grass and struggled to his feet. Moments later he'd disappeared into the darkness.

In the kitchen Lizzie was pale with shock. Suttle eased her into a chair, stood over her. She was shivering, her hands wrapped round herself. She wanted to know whether Pendrick had gone.

'Yeah, he has. You want to tell me what this is about?'

'Don't do the interview thing. Please.'

'OK.' He turned to the sink, trying to control his temper. Cold water from the tap eased his bruised knuckles. 'Just pretend I'm a bit confused. Trezillion? Scar? This is a guy that loves you, right?'

'So he says.'

'And you?'

'I've been stupid.'

'How stupid?'

'Crazy stupid. Stupid like you wouldn't believe.'

'Try me.' Suttle took a seat at the table.

Lizzie said nothing. She'd never felt smaller in her life.

'You want a Stella?' she said.

'You think that might help?'

'Yeah, I do.' She offered him a weary smile and tried to reach for him across the table. He shook his head and withdrew his hand.

She explained about meeting Pendrick, about how helpful he'd been with the rowing, how attractive he'd seemed, and how supportive.

'With the rowing, you mean?'

'With everything. I was in a bad place, Jimmy. And he seemed to understand.'

'Yeah, I bet he did. But you happen to be my wife.'

'He didn't know that.'

'Maybe not. But you did.'

'I was Lizzie Hodson. That's who you wanted me to be.'

'Makes no difference. I trusted you. I thought I knew you.'

'Then you'd have known how unhappy I was. How this house ...' She tailed off. They'd been this way too often. There was nothing left to say.

'You went to this place Trezillion?'

'Yes. He drove me there.'

'When?'

'On Saturday. I lied to you, Jimmy. We'd sorted the club compound by lunchtime. Then we drove out.'

'You and Pendrick.'

'Yeah.'

'And?'

'It was lovely.'

'What was lovely?'

'The cove. The dunes. Being there with him. Everything.'

'So what happened?'

'Nothing. Except we talked.'

'He didn't try and come on to you?'

'Not at all. He was very sweet.'

'You sound disappointed.'

'I was.'

'You mean that? You were fucking *disappointed*?'

'I told you. I was crazy. Out of my tree. I didn't know what I was doing.'

'But you'd have ...?'

'Yeah. I would. Definitely.'

Suttle nodded, said nothing. Then he half-turned at the table and stared out into the darkness. *I've hurt him*, Lizzie told herself. *I've really hurt him.*

'The scar?'

'We were comparing accidents. His was a surfing thing. Mine you know about. It was just conversation.'

'Nothing more?'

'No.'

'I have your word on that?'

'Absolutely.'

'But you would have done if you'd had the chance?'

'Yes.'

She reached for him again. She wanted to tell him that fucking wouldn't have mattered. That the truly unforgivable thing was going all that way in the first place. A conversation that intimate, that natural, was the worst possible kind of betrayal. She wondered about trying to put this into words but knew it would only hurt him more. No relationship, she thought, could survive that kind of honesty.

'I love you,' she said. 'It's important you know that.'

Suttle nodded. His face was a mask. She heard the click of the fridge door opening. He popped a can of Stella and tipped it to his lips.

Lizzie told him about the landline. Suttle listened without comment. More Stella.

'Is that why he had the wire cutters?' he asked at last.

'Yeah.' She felt cold again. She began to shiver. 'That man's so damaged, Jimmy. And I never realised.'

Eleven

Tash Donovan and Milo Symons were arrested at dawn. Uniforms took them to separate police stations in Exeter and Torbay. They were booked in by the respective Custody Sergeants and provided with legal representation. Tash Donovan chose a solicitor she'd met at festival last summer. Milo Symons was happy with the duty brief.

Scenes of Crime, meanwhile, went into the mobile home at Tusker Farm. Within the hour they'd unearthed the Jacobson debit card, the associated ATM slips, a decent cache of cannabis resin and just under a thousand pounds in cash. The latter had been stuffed into a Co-op plastic bag and hidden under the mattress, a hidey-hole the CSI thought quaintly retro. By close of play the previous evening, Donovan and Symons had got the credit balance in the Jacobson account down to a shade over £93K.

Houghton chaired a meet of the *Constantine* inner circle at eight. The PACE clock would give the interview teams twenty-four hours before she'd have to apply to a uniformed super-intendent for a twelve-hour extension. Under the circumstances she thought that wouldn't be necessary. The Scenes of Crime team had failed to locate Kinsey's laptop but they'd discovered two keys in the glovebox of Donovan's car. The team had the keys seized from Kinsey's flat and – subject to trying the new set in the apartment door – they were confident they had a match.

Houghton had asked Suttle to oversee and coordinate the two interviews. He'd already briefed the Tactical Interview Advisers working with each of the teams and agreed a strategy. Open account first, rapidly followed by the challenge phase. In Suttle's view there was no way either Donovan or Symons could survive the coming hours in the interview suite. They had both the motivation and the opportunity to return to the flat and consign Kinsey to oblivion. It was, he quietly confirmed to Houghton, a definite stone-bonker.

The eight o'clock meet was brief. At the end the interview teams departed to their respective police stations. Solicitors were due at the custody centres at nine o'clock. Disclosure and client meetings would occupy the next hour or so. By lunchtime, with a fair wind, *Constantine* might be close to a result.

Suttle was about to leave when Houghton called him back.

'You look tired, Jimmy.'

Suttle shot her a look, then nodded.

'Rough night, boss,' he muttered, heading for the door.

Both interview teams called a break at midday. Suttle had judged Symons the likelier to break first and had chosen to spend the morning at the Heavitree nick in Exeter. He was able to monitor proceedings via a video link from an adjoining room in the interview suite and had watched Symons explaining the events of Saturday night. His account exactly mirrored the story he'd told Suttle the first time they'd met in the mobile home: they'd won their race, they'd all had a drink or two, they'd walked across to Kinsey's apartment for a takeaway curry, and then they'd gone home. Only next day, when the detective guy arrived at Tusker Farm, did he realise anything had happened to Kinsey.

The two D/Cs on the interview team, both experienced, pressed him on a couple of points of detail and then tabled the evidence seized from Tusker Farm. Watching Symons on the video link, Suttle had the impression this moment came as no surprise. Symons admitted at once that they'd been to the ATM in Exmouth. Tash, he explained, needed the money to buy her mum a birthday present. She still had the card from collecting the takeaway and she definitely meant to pay Kinsey back when she next saw him. One of the D/Cs asked whether they'd got a receipt with the money and Symons said yes.

'How much money was in the account?'

'A lot.'

'How much?'

'Over a hundred thousand pounds.'

'Did that surprise you?'

'Of course it did. We knew Kinsey was minted but that's a huge amount of money to keep in an account like that.'

'Was your partner surprised?'

'Yes. She thought it was crazy too.'

'And did you intend to make more withdrawals?'

'Of course not. I just told you. We thought Kinsey was still alive. We knew we'd have to give the £200 back.'

'That's a lot of money for a birthday present.'

'That's what I thought, but Tash is like that. Always over the top. You get used to it in the end.'

The interview continued. The news that Kinsey was dead, admitted Symons, had changed everything. He'd phoned Tash in Yeovil and told her. She still had the card.

'Did she tell you she was going to make another withdrawal?'

'No.'

'When you found out, were you surprised?'

'Not really.' A tiny hesitation.

'Why's that?'

'Because Tash just gets an idea and goes for it. I was worried, to be honest. I thought there was no way we wouldn't get found out.'

'You were right.'

'Yeah.'

'And Tash?'

'She didn't see it that way. She said the guy's dead so we might as well help ourselves. She also said that Kinsey had kept the account secret so no one would know about it.'

'Why secret?'

'I don't really know. To hide the money, I suppose.'

'To hide the money from who?'

'I don't know. The taxman? I don't know.'

By now, he said, they had £400. A couple of days went by and nothing happened so they made another withdrawal and then another. In the end, he said, it became a kind of routine. Like the money was their own.

'But it wasn't, Mr Symons.'

'I know.'

'It belonged to Kinsey, to his estate. We call that theft.'

'Sure.'

'But you just carried on.'

'We did.'

The interviewing D/C wanted to know how long these withdrawals would have gone on. Rosie Tremayne was a woman in her thirties, one of Houghton's stars, and Suttle admired the cool rapport she so quickly established with Symons. It had been Houghton's idea to put her alongside the man in the belief he responded well to older women, and in every respect it had worked. He told her they'd have kept hammering the ATMs until the account was empty.

'And what would you have done with the money?'

'There's a project I'm trying to get off the ground, a film. Kinsey had helped me already, so in a way I was telling myself it wasn't really theft, just something he might have done in any case.'

'But you didn't know that, did you?'

'No. He'd promised me £45,000 but not that much, not a hundred grand.'

'So it was still theft? Is that what you're saying?'

'Yes. We stole the money. That's what we did.'

It was at this point that Suttle felt the first prickles of apprehension. Milo Symons was playing these questions with the straightest of bats. He wasn't evasive. He wasn't attempting to justify himself. He didn't seem to be hiding anything. On the contrary, there was a naivety – even an innocence – in his willingness to cooperate. From *Constantine*'s point of view, this would be a quick win when it came to a theft conviction. But would this man really have killed someone?

During the coffee break Suttle phoned the Tactical Interview Adviser supervising the other interview. His name was Frank Miller and – like Suttle – was an incomer from another force. After an uneasy start, Devon and Cornwall had definitely grown on him. Not least because major crime investigations exposed him to suspects like Tash Donovan.

'She's nuts, mate. Totally barking. We could have sold tickets for this morning.'

Like Symons, her description of the Saturday night in Exmouth Quays hadn't departed one jot from her initial witness statement. One of the two interviewing D/Cs was Luke Golding. The TIA had told him to press her on the relationship with Kinsey, and when he'd done so she'd happily complied, offering detailed descriptions of the movement sessions they'd shared up in his apartment. Once she'd even got to her feet in the interview room to demonstrate a particular cycle of gesture therapy and it was only her solicitor, in the end, who'd managed to get her to sit down again.

'What about the rest of it?'

'The sex, you mean? We got lots of that too. She had this guy for breakfast, but he was paying good money so he must have got something out of it. Five hundred quid for a quickie? Maybe they were both barking.'

'You think she liked him?'

'I don't think liking came into it. The woman's an actress. She can play a part. Bottom line, Kinsey was a punter. End of.'

Confronted with the evidence from the ATMs, Donovan

– like Symons – had admitted everything. Yes, she'd lifted an initial 200 quid from his account that Saturday night. Yes, she meant to give the money back. And yes, once she knew that Kinsey was dead, she'd seen no point letting all that money go to waste.

'She said that? She used that phrase?'

'Yeah. It was like she had some right to it. The dosh was hers. It was written in the stars. It was the earth giving her a little prezzie. Total bollocks, of course, but quite amusing. You have to hand it to this woman. Second house starts any time now. If you're looking for something a bit different, you should pop across.'

Suttle declined the invitation. He wanted to know how Donovan had been so sure they'd never get caught.

'To be honest, mate, I'm not sure that ever really occurred to her. At one point she told us that Kinsey was always boasting about his money, and how clever he was, making all this moolah. He told her about his ex-wife too, and how he'd managed to dream up some clever scheme to hide loads of dosh from the old dragon. Donovan said he called her the Gobbler. I think she assumed the Jacobson account was part of all that. I guess it was empty when the wife walked out and Kinsey filled it up again and kept it going.'

'She was specific about that? Donovan?'

'Not in so many words, but that was the drift. Like I say, Donovan lives on another planet. I don't think it's ever dawned on her that some of the stuff she does might have consequences. It's all hippy shit, I know, but it seems to work for her.'

'You think she's worried?'

'Not in the least.'

'You think she killed Kinsey?'

'I'm starting to wonder.'

The interviews recommenced at 12.45. This, Suttle knew, was the moment of truth. It fell to Rosie Tremayne, in Exeter, to suggest that Symons' misdemeanours might not have stopped at theft.

'In your statement to D/S Suttle you denied that your partner, Tash, had any kind of relationship with Kinsey.'

'I said he fancied her. Like everyone fancies her.'

'But you also said it ended there.'

'Yeah. That's true.'

'But it isn't, is it? Because your partner, Tash, has told us she had regular sex with Kinsey.'

'For money.'

'Yes. But it happened, didn't it? So it didn't – as you put it – end there?'

'That's shagging. That's all it is. For money.'

'But you knew.'

'Yeah. Me and Tash don't have secrets. The shag money was for the film fund. The one I told you about.'

'Sure. I believe you. But the fact is your partner was having sex with another man.'

'He was crap at it. Why would that worry me?'

'Because it might not end there.'

'What?'

'Because Kinsey might want more of Tash than you thought. The man had money, lots of money. Tash is a professional actress. Just lately, as we understand it, she hasn't done much. She's still attractive. She might still dream about making the big time. Kinsey could help that happen, couldn't he? With all his money? All the support he could give her? And all those doors he could open?'

Symons was staring at her. He was visibly upset. Rosie had touched a nerve. Suttle was tempted to applaud. At last, he thought.

'I don't have to listen to this, do I?' Symons was looking at his solicitor.

'Mr Symons?' Tremayne was waiting for an answer. 'Milo?'

Symons, angry now, abandoned his solicitor and turned back to Tremayne.

'You think Tash lied to me? Is that what you think? You're telling me she had something else going on with him?'

'I'm asking you a question. I'm suggesting that might have been a possibility.'

'Then the answer's no. No way. We're like that, me and Tash, always have been.' He interlinked his forefingers and tugged them hard. 'You know what I mean? Tash would never do that to me, never.'

'Why not?'

'Because she wouldn't.'

'But why?'

'Because she knows what it would do to me. How I'd feel about it.'

'And how would you feel about it?'

'I'd feel shit about it. I'd hate it.'

'So what might you do ...' Rosie gestured at the space between them, which had been warmed by this sudden burst of temper '... if you got really angry?'

Symons stared at her. It was beginning to dawn on him where these questions might be going.

'What do you mean?' he said.

'I'm asking you whether you have a temper. The answer appears to be yes. I'm also asking you whether Tash was – is – important to you.'

'Of course she's important. She means everything to me, Tash.'

'So what would you do to keep her? If you thought she might be tempted to go off with someone else?'

'But she wouldn't. Not Tash.'

'But she might, Milo. Or you might *think* she might.'

'Never. I never thought that. Never.'

'I don't believe you. Look at it from our point of view. Tash means everything to you. You've just admitted it. You know

315

she has sex with this man Kinsey. You know that Kinsey has the kind of money that might make a big difference to her career. You also know he's mad about her. Are you really telling me you were never – ever – worried she might leave you?'

'For him, you mean?' He laughed. 'You're mad. This is crazy.' He looked at his solicitor again. 'Tell her to stop.'

The solicitor gestured him closer. Suttle wished he could lip-read. Maybe he's telling his client to relax, he thought. Or maybe he's starting to see it Tremayne's way.

'My client needs to be clear about the precise allegation you're trying to make,' he said.

'Our allegation is this, Milo. That you were drunk on that Saturday night. This we know from your own account. That you had and have a passionate relationship with your partner, Tash. This too we know. That something probably happened that Saturday night, some remark, something inappropriate between Tash and Kinsey that later sparked a row between you both. Are you with me?'

Symons nodded. He looked transfixed. She might have been telling him a story, Suttle thought, about someone else.

'Go on,' he said.

'That you went back to the apartment that night, back to Exmouth Quays, either with Tash or without. That you got into the flat with Tash's key. And that you killed Kinsey.'

'*Killed* him?'

'Yes.'

'But why? How?'

'Why, I think we've dealt with. How has, at this point, to be supposition. In the end he fell from his own balcony. Perhaps you'd like to tell us exactly what happened before that moment?'

Symons began to shake his head. Disbelief had given way to something else. Fear.

'You really think I killed him? Kinsey? Jake? You think *I* did that?'

'Yes.'

'Why? Why would I have done it?'

'I think we've covered that. You were jealous. And you knew he had money.'

'How?'

'Because you'd seen the slip from the ATM. One hundred and seven thousand pounds, Milo. Think about it.'

'So I killed him? You really believe that?'

'Yes.'

From this point on, the interview went nowhere. The two D/Cs came at Symons from every point of the compass. They pointed out how heavily all the circumstantial evidence weighed against him. They thought it entirely reasonable that he would want to remove the threat of Kinsey from his private life. They agreed that one hundred thousand pounds would ease a lot of problems about funding Symons' precious film. Rosie Tremayne even hinted that the idea might have been Tash Donovan's in the first place, in which case Symons would earn himself a much lighter sentence by testifying against her.

The latter suggestion sparked another outburst from Symons. Tash had never said anything of the sort. And even if she had, there was no way he'd grass her up. To think otherwise was totally vile. This whole thing, he kept saying, is sick. He'd never hit anyone in his life, let alone killed anyone. After stopping at the ATM in Exmouth, he and Tash had gone home. Theft? Yeah. Murder? No way.

Mid-afternoon, Houghton called a meet in a borrowed office at Torbay. Donovan and Symons had been escorted back to their respective cells to ready themselves for the next round of questioning. In the meantime Houghton had to assess where *Constantine* might go next.

Suttle had driven over from Exeter with Rosie Tremayne. He was still convinced there was a way to go with Symons.

'We haven't bottomed him out yet,' he said. 'The guy's more

of a firework than I thought. Press the right buttons and we might still be in business.'

Houghton wanted Tremayne's opinion. She said she was doing her best but deep down thought Symons was telling the truth.

'How does that work?'

'He gave us everything on the ATMs. He coughed the lot. Frankly, I think murder's a bit out of his league. He wouldn't have the bottle for starters. Plus he comes over as quite a gentle guy.'

'He was pissed,' Suttle said. 'And that can change everything.'

Houghton turned to Frank Miller. She wanted the TIA's take on Tash Donovan. How had she reacted to the suggestion that she'd been complicit in Kinsey's death?

'She laughed. I think she was genuinely amused. This is a woman who plays a thousand roles before breakfast. I think the killer thing quite appealed to her.'

'But she denied it?'

'Big time. She said Symons was too pissed to manage a shag that Saturday night, let alone kill anyone. She also said that vegetarians try and avoid that kind of thing.'

'She's a veggie?'

'So she says.'

'And that's some kind of defence?'

'Definitely. She says veggies never kill people.'

'What about Hitler?'

'Good point, boss. Maybe we can bring that up in the next session.'

Houghton didn't share the ripple of laughter that went round the room. She and Nandy would be conferencing on the phone any time now. She had to know where this thing was headed next.

It was Suttle who broke the silence.

'We keep on at them both. That's the only option we've got.'

'We've nothing new to throw at them?'

'No.'

'So without a confession …?'

'You're right.' Suttle nodded. 'We're fucked.'

The next session began at half past four and lasted into the early evening. This time Suttle was monitoring the Donovan interview. Sitting beside Miller, watching the video feed, he knew the TIA had called it exactly right. Donovan was putting on the performance of her life. Not because she was trying to hide something but because she at last had an audience. She said she felt sorry for Kinsey. That last second and a half of his life, she said, would have been seriously crap. Exmouth Quays in the rain was a shit place to die. She hadn't the first idea why he'd done it, and if she'd ever suspected him of suicidal tendencies she might have put a lot more effort into keeping him happy.

The latter phrase appeared to offer at least the hint of an opening. Had this relationship of theirs been more substantial than she'd ever admitted? Might he have ended his life because she wouldn't commit to more than visiting rights? To both questions she answered with a flat no. Kinsey, she said, was an impossible man to get close to. No wonder his wife had done a runner.

In his heart Suttle knew she was right. At ten past seven he took a call from the TIA at Heavitree. After consultations with his lawyer, Symons had decided to go No Comment.

Within half an hour both interviews had been terminated. Det-Supt Nandy was waiting with Houghton in her office at Middlemoor. She'd obviously briefed him already. The atmosphere was grim.

'The PACE clock stops at five tomorrow morning,' he pointed out. 'The briefs will kick up if we insist on another session tonight, and to be frank I can't see what we'd achieve. We could try for an extension and start again tomorrow morning but D/I Houghton's right. We've got nothing left to fire at him. We're out of bullets. There's nothing left.' He paused. 'Jimmy?'

Suttle knew the question was coming. This was his party, his idea. He'd led them up this cul-de-sac. How did he propose to get them out?

'Are we talking fresh lines of enquiry?' Suttle asked.

'Yes.'

'There aren't any, sir. Not immediately. Not that I can see.'

'So what do you suggest?'

'I suggest we charge them anyway. And leave it to the jury.'

'You mean the CPS.'

'Of course.'

'Charge them with what?'

'Theft, obviously. Plus murder.'

There was a silence. Bold move. Two of the D/Cs exchanged glances. Rosie Tremayne was looking at her hands.

'But we have no evidence, Jimmy. All we have is supposition, which, if my memory serves me correctly, is where we began.'

'I still think he was killed.'

'By them? By these two?'

'Everything points that way. Motive. Opportunity. You said it yourself, sir. Other people are a mystery. No one really knows. What you see isn't necessarily what you get.'

'That's true. Do you think the CPS feel the same way? We need evidence, Jimmy. And we haven't got it. This is very nice, very tidy. But it doesn't *prove* they did it.'

'No, sir. It doesn't.'

'So what do we do?'

'I don't know, sir. It's your call not mine.'

He nodded. Suttle thought he caught a hint of disappointment in his face. *Maybe I've given up too easily*, he thought. Maybe Nandy was expecting more of a fight. Fat chance.

'Carole?' Nandy had turned to D/I Houghton.

'I suggest we go for an extension, sir. A night in the cells sometimes does the trick.'

'And what are we proposing in the way of fresh evidence? Mr Cattermole will need to know.'

Cattermole was the duty uniformed Superintendent. Without active ongoing inquiries, he wouldn't sanction a custody extension.

Suttle stirred. He was looking at Houghton.

'There's still one call I need to make,' he said.

'On who?'

'Pendrick.'

It was gone nine when Suttle made it down to Exmouth. The light was on in Pendrick's flat, and Suttle's finger on the bell brought him to the door. His lower face was still swollen from last night and when he led the way upstairs he seemed to have difficulty walking.

'Is this personal?'

'No.'

'What do you want then?'

'I need to talk about Kinsey. We made a couple of arrests last night, Tash and Milo Symons. We'll be charging them tomorrow.'

'For what?'

'Theft and murder.'

'Murder?' The word drew the faintest smile. 'You think they killed Kinsey?'

'Yes.'

'You can prove it?'

'We can get a result in court.'

'How does that work?'

Suttle walked him through the evidence: a hundred grand's worth of motivation and the key to Kinsey's door.

'But why? Why would they do it?'

'You know why they'd do it. Symons was jealous as fuck and they both wanted the money. A couple of minutes in the apartment? The two of them? No CCTV? Middle of the night? Job done.'

Pendrick was brooding. Suttle wanted him to say something. Anything.

'Well?'

'Kinsey was an arsehole. He deserved it.'

'What does that mean?'

'It means he's better dead. It means there's one less of his breed to fuck things up.'

'So we owe Tash and Milo a thank you? Is that what you're saying?'

'Definitely.'

'Are you surprised they did what they did?'

'I'm glad he's gone.'

'That wasn't my question. I asked you whether you were surprised or not.'

Pendrick's head came up. He held Suttle's gaze.

'Nothing surprises me any more,' he said.

Suttle was in Colaton Raleigh by half ten. He stopped for a beer at the pub up the road, brooding on the day's developments. He'd rarely felt so knackered. The last couple of weeks seemed to have emptied him of everything. He toyed with the pint for a while, then took a couple of mouthfuls and left it on the counter.

At the cottage the lights were off downstairs. He found a note from Lizzie on the kitchen table telling him there was food in the oven but he didn't even bother to look. Upstairs, he checked on Grace then went into their bedroom. Lizzie appeared to be asleep, her face turned towards the wall. Suttle got undressed in the bathroom, hanging his suit on the door ready for tomorrow morning. He sponged his face, brushed his teeth and spent a long minute eyeballing the image in the mirror. When he returned to the bedroom, Lizzie hadn't moved. He slipped into bed and turned his back on her. *Enough*, he thought.

Twelve

Lizzie waited until she heard the burble of the departing Impreza before she got up next morning. Suttle must have fed Grace first thing because when she went next door she found tiny gobbets of porridge on her daughter's nightgown. She took Grace back to bed, knowing she had to get them both out of the house for a bit. The thin curtains had never met properly in the middle and the broad blue stripe told her it was a lovely morning.

'The seaside, eh?' She gave Grace a hug.

They took a bus from the stop outside the village store. By half past nine they were in Exmouth. It was a five-minute walk to the seafront. The tide was out and the offshore sandbank was busy with gulls and oystercatchers. Heading east, Lizzie could feel a real warmth in the sun. Imperceptibly, her spirits began to rise.

Curiosity took her to the rowing club. To her surprise the gates were open, the door to the Portakabin unlocked. She parked the buggy at the foot of the steps and lifted Grace out. She wanted to sit her on one of the rowing machines, slide her up and down, pretend they were at the funfair. She mounted the steps and pushed at the half-open door.

After the blaze of spring sunshine, she stepped into the chill of the semi-darkness inside. She could hear someone on one of the rowing machines at the very back of the clubhouse, a steady rhythm, pull after pull, but it was seconds before she could make out a shape in the gloom. A face turned briefly towards her. The rate quickened, then fell back again.

Pendrick.

She knew she should leave. Then she changed her mind. Picking her way over the machines, she carried Grace towards him. He was still rowing, still pushing himself up and down the slide. She stopped beside the readout. Nearly twenty kilometres.

'How long have you been here?'

'Since seven. More than three hours.'

'Christ.'

He was still moving, his rhythm undisturbed. He didn't look up at her. Finally, she turned to go.

'Don't,' he said. 'I have to tell you something.'

'Please, no.'

'It's not that. I promise.'

'What then?'

'It's about this Kinsey thing. They've arrested Tash and Milo.'

'What for?'

'Theft ...' the sweat glistened on his swollen face '... and murder.'

'They killed Kinsey?' Lizzie was staring at him.

'No.' He shook his head. 'I did.'

'*You* did?'

'Yeah. I killed the man. It was me who did it.'

She took a tiny step backwards. *Mad*, she thought. Insane.

'Please,' she said. 'You're making this up. It's a story. You're trying to impress me. You're trying to get us back to wherever you want us to be. I don't want to know. There's no point. It's over.'

'I know that.'

'Then enough's enough. You needn't say any more.'

'You're wrong. I have to tell someone. You walked in.

You're here. All you have to do is listen.' At last he looked up at her. 'Will you do that?'

Kinsey, he said, had been getting under his skin for more than a year. The boasts. The money. The big fuck-off apartment. The way he went out and bought himself a crew. Everything. Then came the discovery that he was going to build at Trezillion. And not just Trezillion but other sites up and down the coast. These sites were almost holy. The man was into serious desecration. The man wanted to leave his scent, his smell, everywhere. Why? To make more money. He'd had a conversation about it, warned the man.

'What did you say?'

'I told him to drop it. I told him to go and build somewhere else.'

'And?'

'He just laughed. He told me I didn't know what I was talking about. He said the world had moved on. He told me that Cornwall needed people like him. He said it was time I got real.'

After that, he said, they barely talked at all. Whenever they were together, Kinsey made sure there were other people around – other guys, people like Andy Poole, people he could rely on. Pendrick looked up at her. He knew Kinsey was frightened of him because he could see it in his face.

'And did that make you feel good?'

'Yes.'

'And did he do what you wanted?'

'Of course not. You know that. You've seen those vile brochures he had done.'

Lizzie nodded. Pendrick was still rowing, still pulling hard on the machine: 20,762 metres.

'Is that enough to kill someone? A brochure?'

'Of course not. It was the girls as well. The Thai girls. He got them from an agency in Exeter. He'd boast about that too, in the boat. He'd tell us what they did for him, what he liked most. He had a special girl. He called her Blossom. Apparently she didn't speak a word of English and he liked that because he didn't have to talk to her. What that guy did was unforgivable.'

'To the girls?'

'To everyone. He screwed everyone. He couldn't stop himself. Guys like that don't deserve a life.'

On the Saturday night, he said, they'd all gone back to Kinsey's apartment. At first Pendrick hadn't wanted to be any part of the celebration but Lenahan had talked him into it. Bring a bit of class to the gathering. Give the wee man a shock. And so they'd all walked across to Exmouth Quays and piled into the lift and carried on drinking.

'It was me who first realised how pissed Kinsey was. He'd been drinking like a schoolgirl all night, knocking back the champagne – Christ knows how much he must have drunk. Then Tash arrived with the takeaway and he was shovelling that in too. There was no way he wasn't going to be ill. You could see it coming.'

When he started throwing up over the balcony no one else noticed. Pendrick went out there and got him to bed.

'Why? Why did you do that?'

'Because I'd made a decision.'

'About what?'

'About him, about Kinsey. I'd had enough. I was going to do it.'

'Kill him?'

'Yes. I didn't know how but that's what I was going to do.'

'Why?'

Pendrick's rhythm began to slow and for a moment Lizzie thought he was going to stop, but then he picked up again, ducking his head to wipe the sweat from his eyes.

'He had this laptop. He said it was in his bedroom. And before he started throwing up he'd promised us all a bit of a show. He called it his PowerPoint. I think he meant it as a joke.'

'You took a look at the laptop?'

'I did. I was using his en suite. He loved showing all this shit off. Granite walls. Jacuzzi. The laptop was on his bed. I fired it up and there she was.'

'Who?'

'Blossom. The Thai girl.'

'And?'

'You don't want to know. After that the guy hadn't got a prayer.'

'So you got him in from the balcony? This is later?'

'Yeah. I left him on the bed. All I wanted were his door keys.'

'Where were they?'

'In his trackie bottoms. I just took them. The state of the guy, I don't think he even knew they'd gone. Yeah, sweet ...'

He was speeding up now, pushing hard with his legs against the machine. Tash, he said, had organised the taxi. He'd been the first to be dropped off. He'd waited up until half two and then walked back to Exmouth Quays. He'd approached Regatta Court via the beach. It was pouring with rain and he hadn't seen a soul. The key to Kinsey's apartment also opened the main door to the block. Once inside the apartment, he'd gone into Kinsey's bedroom. Judging by the smell from the en suite, he must have been sick again.

'Was he asleep?'

'Spark out.'

'So what did you do?'

'I unlocked the sliding door to the balcony, went back to fetch him and just tipped him over.'

'Didn't he struggle?'

'Not really. He was still pissed, completely out of it.'

'And that was it? Simple as that?'

'Yeah. Call it waste disposal if you like. Afterwards I went back for the laptop and threw it into the dock. I was back home by half three –' he glanced up at her '– and I slept like a baby.'

By midday *Constantine* had finally hit the buffers. Milo Symons, while admitting the theft charge, had refused to answer any more questions about Kinsey's death, while Tash Donovan was asking her lawyer whether he could make any kind of case against the police for harassment. Why do these people keeping banging on, she kept asking him. Don't they understand about veggies?

By now, with Houghton's agreement, Det-Supt Nandy had decided to charge both Donovan and Symons with theft and release them on police bail. They'd have to attend the magistrates' court on Friday morning, where a decision would be taken about a possible referral to the Crown Court. With respect to any murder charge, Nandy was obliged to accept that lack of evidence put the investigative ball back in the Coroner's lap. *Constantine*'s MCIT squad had done its best to unearth evidence of foul play but had found nothing. In all probability, by accident or otherwise, Jake Kinsey had taken his own life. Case closed.

Houghton insisted on taking Suttle for lunch. They drove to Topsham, a flourishing village upstream from Exmouth, and went to a pub down by the river. It was a glorious day, warm enough to sit at a table by the water. Suttle insisted he wasn't hungry but Houghton ignored him. She knew his affection for ham, egg and chips. She even returned with two sachets of brown sauce.

'You look terrible,' she said. 'Is it Kinsey or something else?'

Suttle wouldn't answer. In one sense it was both. But how on earth could he explain that his wife had been off with a key witness?

Houghton wouldn't give up.

'Are you sleeping OK?'

'Yeah. Pretty much.'

'Grace all right?'

'She's sweet.'

'Lizzie?'

'Lizzie's fine.'

'So what happened to your hand?'

Suttle fought the temptation to cover his right hand. His knuckles were bruised from last night. He said he didn't want to talk about it.

'Some kind of fight?'

'Yeah. My fault.'

'And the other guy?'

'Don't ask.'

'It *was* a guy?'

'Yeah.'

'Not Lizzie?'

'No.'

The food arrived. They ate in silence. Suttle didn't want to talk about Kinsey or Donovan or Symons or any of the rest of it. He didn't really want to talk about anything. On every front his life seemed to have come to an end. Much like *Constantine*.

Houghton had other ideas. She told him that Nandy had been impressed.

'He might not show it, Jimmy, but he thinks you're the business.'

'Great. Didn't work though, did it?'

'That doesn't matter. What matters is you tried. He likes that. He loves people who answer back.'

'Is that how you got to be a D/I?'

'Partly.' She nodded. 'Yeah. He likes people who argue their case. You did just that. He can't fault you for running with it. And he can't fault you for effort.'

He eyed her for a moment. He felt immensely weary.

'Is all this meant to be some kind of compensation prize?'

'That's infantile, if I may say so. You're better than this, Jimmy.'

'Yeah? Am I?'

He held her gaze, then pushed the plate away. He said he

was grateful and he meant it, but she was right. He was going through a shit time and the worst of it was that he didn't know how it was going to end.

Houghton nodded, said nothing. A swan pushed through the reeds at the water's edge. She tossed it a fragment of roll. Then one of Suttle's chips. More swans.

'Crack on, Jimmy,' she said at last. 'That's the only option we've got.'

Lizzie was back at home when she got the call. It was Tessa from the rowing club.

'We have a bit of a situation,' she said at once. 'And I'm wondering whether you might be able to help.'

Molly Doyle, she said, had phoned half an hour ago after a conversation with the Coastguard. The club's single scull had been spotted by a fishing boat a mile off Straight Point. It was upside down in a worsening chop and there was no sign of the rower. Tessa had gone straight down to the club compound and found a pile of clothes inside the Portakabin. She was convinced they belonged to Tom Pendrick. He hadn't booked himself out the way he should have done, but the single's trolley was on the beach, awaiting his return.

'Why are you phoning me?'

'Because Tom might have mentioned taking the single out. Have you seen him recently?'

'I saw him this morning.'

'And he didn't mention it?'

'No. He was on the machine. He'd just done twenty K. Why would he go out rowing after that?'

'Good question.'

Tessa promised to keep her in touch and then rang off. Lizzie sat by the phone. All day she'd been on the point of putting a call through to Jimmy. Given what she'd inflicted on the man, it was the least she could do, but the more she thought about it, the more she realised she didn't know what to say. She imagined the squad must be close to arresting Pendrick. Hence this morning's confession. And hence, she assumed, his abrupt disappearance. The man had too much pride to hang around. Life had taken him to a very bad place. He'd settled his debts with Kinsey, and now, like his wife, he'd chosen the ocean to end his days. Full circle, she thought, reaching for the phone.

Suttle was still in Topsham when his mobile began to beep. He checked caller ID. It was Lizzie. For a moment he didn't want to talk to her but then he thought of Grace. Maybe something's happened. Maybe she needs the car.

'Hi.'

'Where are you?'

'Topsham.'

'We need to talk, Jimmy.'

'About what?'

'Pendrick.'

'There's nothing to say.'

'There is, my love. He killed Kinsey. How do I know? Because he told me.'

It took Suttle less than half an hour to make it to Chantry Cottage. An ugly situation had just got a whole lot worse. How long had his wife known about Pendrick? A couple of days? Longer? Had they been so close she'd decided to shield a killer? Why hadn't she told him before?

He found her feeding Grace in front of the TV. *The Good Life*. Bizarre.

'Just tell me what happened,' he said.

Lizzie told him about the conversation in the clubhouse. She tried to apologise for not contacting him earlier but knew it was pointless. Whatever she said, she was looking at serious trouble. In his current mood her husband was probably contemplating an arrest for perverting the course of justice.

'So where is he? Pendrick?' Suttle hadn't sat down.

'He's disappeared. He took the little single scull and no one's seen him since.'

She told him about the call to the Coastguard. By now she assumed they'd have the helicopters out and maybe the lifeboat.

'And what do you think?'

'What do you mean?'

'You know the guy. What's he up to?'

'I think he's had enough.'

'What does that mean?'

'I think he's out there somewhere, probably dead.'

'Why? Why would he have done that?'

'I assume he knew.'

'Knew what?'

'That you were close to arresting him.'

Suttle stared at her, then produced his mobile. Moments later he was heading for the patio, trying to get a signal to raise D/I Houghton. When he left the house he was still talking. He didn't say goodbye.

The club's single was towed back to Exmouth by the trawler skipper who'd made the initial sighting. Molly Doyle and Clive, the Club Captain, were on the dockside to manhandle it out of the water, lash it to a roof rack and take it back to the club compound. An exhaustive search of the clubhouse had discovered no sign of a note from Pendrick or any other clue that might shed light on his disappearance. Neither was there anything in the single to suggest what had taken him to sea.

The search for a body, alive or dead, continued after dark. Two helicopters with infrared gear worked slowly offshore from Straight Point, a couple of miles to the east, following the tidal drift. It was blowing a Force 4 by now and the sea temperature was a bare 13°C. The search was called off at 21.49, to be resumed at first light.

Thursday happened to be club night at the compound. News of Pendrick's disappearance spread quickly. At Lizzie's request

Tessa had driven up to Colaton Raleigh and taken her and Grace back to the club. In the absence of Jimmy, she wanted to be close to people. The thought of an evening alone in Chantry Cottage filled her with dread.

Rumours had been circulating for nearly a week now about Lizzie and Pendrick. No one knew that she was married, let alone that she was wedded to a detective investigating Kinsey's death, and she was touched by the number of near-strangers who offered her words of comfort. He may have made it ashore. He may still be out there. Don't lose hope. Not yet.

Past ten o'clock, still at the club, her phone rang. It was a voice she didn't recognise.

'My name's Dom,' it said. 'I live in the flat under Tom Pendrick's place.'

'You're the chiropractor?'

'The very same.'

He said he'd dropped by to pick up some paperwork and had found an envelope on his mat with her name and phone number on it. A couple of coppers had just been round and he understood that Tom, silly bugger, had gone missing. Maybe Lizzie ought to pop round and pick up the envelope. Sooner rather than later, eh?

It was Tessa, once again, who supplied the lift. Dom was a big man. He gave Lizzie a hug and kissed Grace and told her he was sure everything would turn out OK.

'He's wild, that Pendrick, but he knows the sea. He'll be back. I know he will.'

He gave her the envelope and wished her luck. Lizzie opened it in the car. Two keys, both Yale. Tessa was about to take them back to Colaton Raleigh but Lizzie told her to hang on. She got out of the car and crossed the pavement. The lock on the street door at number 50 was a Yale. Lizzie struggled with the first key but the second was a perfect fit.

Lizzie returned to the car and bent to the window.

'Here's fine,' she told Tessa. 'You've been brilliant.'

Suttle was at home watching the late-evening news when the text arrived. He spared it a glance. It came from Lizzie. She'd be staying in Exmouth overnight with Grace and would be back in the morning. He put the mobile to one side. On his return from Middlemoor, hours earlier, he'd found a note on the kitchen table: '*Gone to the club. Tess is sorting us out. No news yet.*'

No news yet? Suttle was beginning to wonder whether it was worth sustaining a relationship on notes and texts and a great deal of silence. When he'd got back to the office, late afternoon, Houghton had been waiting for him. He'd already given her the bones of Lizzie's news and now she wanted to know exactly what had been going on. Suttle had done his best. Through no fault of his own, his private life had overlapped with *Constantine* and finally been swamped. Lizzie, he said, had hooked up with Pendrick. He'd no idea how far the relationship had taken them both, but no way had it come to a clean end. At this point Houghton had nodded at his injured hand.

'Pendrick?'

'Yes, boss.'

'You've assaulted a prime witness? Who turns out to be the killer?'

'Yes, boss. A couple of good shots, if we're talking detail.'

'Pleased to hear it. So where is he?'

'I've no idea.'

The meet with Houghton had ended soon afterwards. Given the relationship with Pendrick, she wanted Lizzie interviewed under caution. If it turned out she'd been shielding Pendrick, she'd be in deep shit. As far as Pendrick was concerned, *Constantine* had no option but to wait. If his body was found, the file would go to the Coroner. If he'd simply disappeared, the file would remain open. As for Suttle himself, she had no choice but to remove him from the enquiry. Any further input to *Constantine,* she said, would be prejudiced by what she called his 'personal circumstances'.

'You're happy with that? We understand each other?'

'Perfectly, boss. I'll sort out the interview and look after the baby. Happy days, eh?'

Now he was watching the last of the national news. The local headlines followed. Pendrick's disappearance was the top story. Suttle found himself looking at footage from last year. A gaunt figure, barely recognisable, was climbing a set of stone steps at Penzance Harbour. A battered-looking rowing boat was secured to an iron ring beneath him. His hair was long, hanging in tangles around his bare shoulders, and in close-up his eyes seemed to have lost focus. The news coverage cut to a grainy shot of a helicopter sweeping seawards in the dying light, but what stayed with Suttle were the eyes. What had really happened out there in the Western Approaches? Had this man been nursing a serial grudge against the world at large? Had his poor bloody wife gone the way of Jake Kinsey?

Minutes later Suttle's mobile began to ring. It was Gina Hamilton. He got to his feet and went out onto the patio. Even here the signal wasn't great, but he got the gist of what she was saying. She too had been watching the news. So what was the real story?

'We got him,' Suttle said. 'He did Kinsey.'

'And you can prove it?'

'No problem.'

'How?'

'Full confession.' He stared into the windy darkness, his vision beginning to blur. 'Piece of piss.'

It took Lizzie nearly an hour to get Grace to sleep. Pendrick's bedroom was at the back of the flat. There were clean sheets on the bed and even a couple of neatly folded towels on the low table beneath the curtained window. Elsewhere, Pendrick had made a similar effort to tidy up. There were more towels in the tiny bathroom and a new tablet of soap in the shower tray. The kitchen was spotless, the draining board empty of washing-up. A note beside the electric kettle told her where to find tea bags and coffee, and there was fresh milk in the fridge. She might have stepped into a well-run holiday rental. All it lacked was a cheerful note about local must-see attractions.

With Grace asleep in the clean white spaces of Pendrick's bed, Lizzie went back into the living room. She'd half-expected another note – longer, more intimate – but there was nothing to explain the decision he'd taken. She'd absolutely no doubt about what he'd done.

He'd pushed his body to the limits on the rowing machine. He'd wheeled the tiny single down to the water's edge. He'd set off on an ebbing tide with the knowledge that the weather was about to get a whole lot worse. And somewhere out there, maybe at a time of his choosing, maybe not, he'd capsized the single and slipped away. An end like that, she realised, was totally in keeping with the journey he'd made. His wife had blazed the trail. And, after ridding the planet of Jake Kinsey, Pendrick had followed.

Might this be evidence of madness? She didn't think so. In awkward, uncomfortable ways Pendrick was a man who hung together, a jigsaw puzzle that made a kind of hallucinatory sense. His wasn't everyone's view of the world. In many ways it was savage, unforgiving. In others, she thought, it had an almost childlike naivety. He seemed to believe in the simple things – in getting by on very little, in taking people at face value – and when he realised that real life didn't work that way, that people rarely played by the rules, he'd decided to fold his hand and chuck it in. That's what had taken him to sea in the single. And this flat of his was pretty much all that was left.

She prowled around, trying to ignore her emotional investment in his story, trying to play the investigative journalist, not knowing quite what she was looking for. Leaving her the key this way was, she imagined, a kind of apology. Pendrick had brought sunshine and chaos to her private life. He hadn't understood that this thing of theirs was over and he'd made it infinitely worse by turning up pissed the other night. Any man could imagine the consequences of a scene like that, and access to his flat was his way of saying sorry. Thus the clean sheets and the readied towels. You might be hurting. You may need a place of refuge for a while. Make yourself at home.

His PC was on a table in the corner. There were file boxes beneath the table, each file neatly labelled. She knelt on the rug and started to go through the first box. This was stuff that went back years, letters to friends, photos from a thousand beaches, shots of Pendrick and the woman who'd shared all those adventures. Lizzie spread a handful of the photos on the rug. She was struck at once by how similar the woman was to herself – her own slightness, even her own smile. This must be Kate, she thought. No wonder he'd been so eager, so earnest, so committed. Déjà vu was too weak a word. In the sand dunes at Trezillion he must have been talking to a ghost.

She pulled out another box, extracted another file. This one was more recent. Inside she found an appointment slip for an SD clinic in Bristol. Mr T. Pendrick was due to attend on three dates in January this year. Beside each date was a pencilled tick. SD? Lizzie returned to the file, extracting a printout from the Internet: The web address was www.nhs.uk/conditions/erectile-dysfunction. She stared at it a moment, beginning dimly to understand. SD meant sexual dysfunction. Pendrick, poor man, couldn't get it up.

She sat back on her haunches, her gaze returning to the photos of Kate. Was this something that had happened to Pendrick recently? Or had it been casting a shadow for years? If the latter was true, she could only imagine the consequences. SD had never played a role in her life. Far from it. None of her boyfriends had ever let her down in that respect, and even a night on the Stella didn't seem to affect her husband's prowess. Pendrick on the other hand clearly had a problem.

She began to read. Physical causes of SD apparently included diabetes and nerve damage after prostate surgery. Psychologically, you could blame guilt, depression or some kind of unresolved conflict. She gazed at the list of triggers. As far as she could gather, it pretty much summed up the person that Pendrick had become. Guilt about Kate. Depression about the fate awaiting Trezillion and all the other Cornish coves. And the conflict with Kinsey, which, until a wet Saturday night a couple of weeks ago, had defied resolution.

She picked up a photo. It could have been one of a million beaches – the blueness of the ocean, the curl of faraway surf, hints of a palm tree in the corner of the frame – but what took her eye was the grin on Pendrick's face. It was natural, unforced, wholly genuine. This was a man who was happy in his skin. In the last hours of his life had he met that person again? Before he'd slipped under the waves had he found a kind of peace?

She thought about that last question, knowing she'd never be able to satisfy herself with an answer. Then she heard Grace beginning to stir. The tiny cry took her back to Chantry Cottage, and she shut her eyes, trying not to think about the wreckage of her private life.

After a while she got to her feet. Her mobile was in the bedroom. Grace, thankfully, was still asleep. She took the phone back to the living room and scrolled through the directory until she found the number she wanted. After a while she thought she might have got the time difference wrong but then came the familiar voice.

'Lizzie? How the fuck are you?'

'Crap, if you want the truth. We need help. Badly. And so do you.'

Thirteen

The search for Pendrick's body resumed at first light. By now there was no chance he was still alive. Exhaustion and hypothermia would have killed him long before the police chopper appeared once again over the boiling sea.

Suttle went to work as usual. The downstairs office, briefly busy after *Constantine* rose from the dead, was empty. A house fire in Seaton had taken the lives of two kids and their mother was gravely ill in a burns unit in Salisbury. Growing suspicions about the role of her estranged partner had triggered an MCIT investigation. Nandy, as ever, was blitzing the job, but Houghton had tactfully let Suttle sleep in.

'Appreciate it, boss, but there's no need. The last thing I want is time on my hands.'

Lizzie spent the day in Exmouth. She was in regular contact with Molly Doyle, who had the ear of the Coastguard, but by midday the search for Pendrick's body was called off.

Shortly afterwards, she took a call from a voice she didn't recognise. D/C Andy Maffett wanted to interview her with regard to a Mr Tom Pendrick. She parked Grace with Tessa and walked to Exmouth police station. With Andy Maffett was another detective called Rosie Tremayne. Offered the services of the duty solicitor, Lizzie chose to say no.

The interview, conducted under caution, lasted longer than

she'd anticipated. Lizzie kept the details of her brief relationship with Pendrick to a minimum, only too aware of the detectives' curiosity. Yes, she'd got quite close to the missing rower. Yes, he'd been more than helpful in all kinds of ways. And yes, he'd finally trusted her with the story of what had really happened to Jake Kinsey. Had she been surprised by his confession? Of course she had. Had she had grounds to suspect anything of the sort earlier? Absolutely not. Had she been shielding him in any way? No.

The interview over, Andy Maffett had fashioned her account into a formal statement which she'd signed. Warned that she might be recalled for a second interview, she had no choice but to say yes. Murder wasn't something anyone would take lightly. Of course she'd assist in any way she could.

Shaken, she'd returned to Tessa's house. The last thing she wanted was conversation and in her heart she wanted to hide away with Grace in the silence of Pendrick's flat but the premises had been sealed off by the police pending a thorough search. For a while she'd thought about contacting her husband but in the end she knew she wasn't up to hearing his voice. The last few nightmare days seemed to have grown darker still. At the police station she'd sensed that the two detectives wanted a lot more. Chantry Cottage, and now Tom Pendrick, had taken her to a very bad place indeed.

Her mobile rang at just gone seven. Gill Reynolds.

'How's life in the country?'

'Crap.'

Lizzie briefly explained about Pendrick. The man had wanted out. He'd taken a boat and gone to sea. By now, she said, he was probably dead.

'Christ. So how does that make you feel?'

'Terrible.'

She described the night that Jimmy had returned to find Pendrick at her kitchen table. Since then, she said, they'd barely exchanged a word.

'Bloody hell. So what happens next?'

'I wish I knew.'

'You have to do something, Lou. You have to have a sort-out.'

'I know.'

'Then do it. Just do it.'

'I can't. I don't know how to.'

'That's pathetic. I'm not hearing this. Of course you can. You've shafted that man, Lou. You've crapped all over him. You've got a child too. Think of Grace. Pull your bloody finger out, kiddo, and *do* something.'

'Yeah? Like what?'

The question disappeared into silence because Gill was too busy to talk any longer. In truth there *was* something Lizzie had done, but since making the call last night she'd heard nothing. It was a long shot, she knew, but just now she couldn't think of anything better.

He phoned around eleven when she was about to join Grace in Tessa's spare bed. There was comfort in hearing the voice she knew so well. He wanted directions to the cottage. He'd meet her there next day. She told him how to find Colaton Raleigh. She had to spell the name.

'What time?' she said.

'Midday.'

'That's great. I'm having to rely on buses at the moment.'

'To do what?'

'To get out to the cottage. It's the back of beyond.'

'You're not even *living* there?'

'No.'

'Fuck. So where's Jimmy?'

She looked at the phone, realising that she didn't know.

'Don't ask,' she said.

The following day was Saturday. It was raining when Suttle awoke. One look at the chaos of the kitchen convinced him he needed to get out. He toasted the last of the bread, piled the dishes in the sink, fed the cat and headed out into the rain. With no particular destination in mind, he pointed the Impreza west. After Exeter he took the A30 up to Okehampton. The word Bude on a signpost seemed to hold some promise but half an hour or so later he changed his mind. By the time he found Trezillion, the rain had stopped.

He parked behind the dunes and set out on foot. The wind was rising and the tide was in, pushing at the line of seaweed and assorted debris at the top of the beach. He skirted the dunes and found a path that led up onto a headland. From here, sitting among the rocks, he could look down on the nearly perfect crescent that was Trezillion. Any decent detective, he told himself, had to be able to get into other people's heads, other people's hearts. That was an early lesson he'd learned from Paul Winter. You have to *become* these guys, he'd always said. You have to see the world through their eyes. Only then can you be sure how to make life tough for them.

So what was Pendrick's story? And how come this place had meant so much to him? The answer seemed all too obvious. Anyone growing up here would have fallen in love with the place. That might explain the start of his quarrel with Kinsey. It might also account for bringing Lizzie out here. Pendrick had wanted to share an important bit of himself, just the way Suttle had once taken Lizzie back to the New Forest village where he'd spent his childhood years. That's what you did when you met someone you fell for. It was a kind of homing instinct, impossible to resist, and it meant that you'd stumbled over someone who really mattered.

He shook his head, not wanting to take the thought any further. Pendrick had brought Lizzie here because she'd suddenly become part of his life. More importantly, she'd gone along with him, conspired with him, borrowed the key and let herself into this secret place of his. He wasn't at all sure that he bought Thursday's story about Pendrick sculling off into oblivion, but in truth he didn't much care whether the man was alive or dead. Either way, it was too late. From where he was sitting, among a scatter of spring flowers in the spongy wetness of the turf, the damage had been done.

He got to his feet and headed away from Trezillion, following the cliff path. The next town of any size was Newquay. Maybe he could get a bus back from there to pick up the Impreza. Maybe he'd even be up for the return walk. But after half an hour he'd had enough. Trekking on for mile after mile seemed purposeless. He'd lost some inner sense of direction. He felt like a piece of debris, useless, inert, adrift in deep space. Increasingly depressed, he turned back towards the cove, his head bent against the first flurries of the returning rain.

For maybe a mile the cliff path zigzagged upwards. Then came a fork beneath an outcrop of black granite. A path less trodden led to the very edge of the cliff. The cove lay off to his right, the whiteness of the beach fringed by the sand dunes. That's where my wife wanted to make love to Pendrick, he told himself. That's where my marriage came to an end. The wind was gusting now, blasts of cold air off the ocean, and he felt the salty prick of moisture in his eyes. He took a step forward, then another, peering over the edge of the cliff. The sea boiled on the rocks below, surging back and forth. Easy, he told himself. A second or two of gathering terror and then nothing but darkness. For a moment he was perfectly still, telling himself that it would be for the best, that it would offer the kindest way out, but then he shook his head, thinking of Kinsey, of Pendrick, of Lizzie, of Grace, glad of the hot jolts of anger that flooded through him, an anger he could almost taste. He turned and headed inland, away from the cove and the roar of the incoming surf.

The path was steep. Minutes later, maybe a quarter of a mile inland, he found himself climbing through torn rags of grey mist towards a single tree bent almost double by the wind. His doubts had flooded back again. Had all this started way back, with his decision to go for Chantry Cottage? Had he bullied Lizzie into coming with him, into sharing this fantasy life he'd promised her? Should he have been a bit more cluey about the signals she was sending him, about her growing sense of lostness? Should he have been a better husband? A better dad? And just as important in another way, should he be making a bigger effort to get a word of warning to Paul Winter? A man he'd once revered? The questions hammered at his brain: three betrayals, three ways he seemed to have got life so comprehensively wrong. Maybe all this wasn't Lizzie's fault at all, but his.

He was still staring at the tree. The way it had shied away from the wind, the way it had given in to the elements, spoke of an implacable force beyond the power of resistance. But then he climbed a little closer, buffeted by that same wind, and stopped again, barely feet away. Despite everything, he realised the tree was still alive. On bough after bough he could see tiny green buds pushing through. Despite the wind, despite the salt off the ocean, despite the mountain of odds stacked against it, the tree was hanging on. Why? Because it hadn't – wouldn't – surrender. Because it had clung to a life of its own. Come back in a week or two, he thought, and it would be in full leaf. Climb up here on a glorious day in midsummer, with the temperature in the eighties, and he might pause a while to enjoy the shade it offered. He found himself grinning, suddenly alive again. The rain was harder now but he didn't care. He'd had enough of chasing the same old questions around and around. Guilt, in the end, took you nowhere. He checked his watch. Early afternoon. Perfect.

He was in Modbury within the hour. A petrol station on the edge of the town had pink carnations in a bucket outside the pay-booth. He bought three bunches and a bottle of Sauvignon. Minutes later he was parked across the road from Gina Hamilton's house. Her Golf was on the hardstanding. He stood at the front door for a second or two, dripping from the rain. She must have the radio on, he thought. Adele. Bless.

He rang the front-door bell, the flowers and the wine readied. When the door finally opened, he barely recognised her. Her feet were bare and she was wearing a pair of blue overalls, way too big. A crimson scarf was knotted over her hair and the brush in her right hand was threatening to drip white gloss all over the doormat.

She looked at him for a moment, then her eyes strayed to the flowers. If she was in any way surprised, it didn't show.

'You've come to give me a hand?'

'Sure,' he said. 'My pleasure.'

He left next morning at five past eight. Lizzie had been trying to get through to him all evening. Finally, he'd texted her back, asking if Grace was OK. 'Grace is fine,' came the reply. 'We have to talk.' But Suttle didn't want to talk. Not yet.

Then, in the early hours, came another text. 'Please meet us in the cafe at St David's Station. We're on the 09.28 to Portsmouth.' Suttle hadn't responded, rolling over and telling Gina it could wait.

Now he slipped into the Impreza and headed towards the A38. He was in Exeter by nine. Driving into the big car park outside St David's station, he wondered how Lizzie and Grace had made it over from Colaton Raleigh. The buses were hopeless on a Sunday. Had she got a taxi? Or had someone given her a lift?

He found her at a table in the far corner of the café. She looked pale and drawn. She'd gelled her hair too, and it didn't suit her. Her coffee mug was empty. Suttle asked her whether she wanted another. She shook her head.

'And you, young lady?'

Suttle had picked Grace up. She was wearing a dress Gill Reynolds had brought down from Pompey and already it looked too small.

Grace wanted cake. Suttle carried her to the counter. Already this little tableau felt surreal. His wife crouched over her empty coffee mug, staring into the middle distance. A rucksack and a bulging holdall on the floor beside Grace's buggy. A retired couple by the window having a quiet ruck about God knows what. Horrible.

Suttle carried the cake and a coffee back to the table and settled Grace on his knee.

'You'll need a hand with that lot.' He nodded at the bags.

Lizzie shook her head. She could manage. She'd always managed. It wouldn't be a problem.

'Don't be silly. I'll give you a hand.'

She shook her head again. She seemed close to tears. She glanced at her watch, fumbled in her bag for the tickets, anything to soak up the silence. Then, for the first time, she met his gaze.

'Is that all you've got to say?'

'Yeah.'

'You don't think we mean it? You don't think we're off?'

'Your decision, Lizzie. Not mine.'

'Going, you mean?'

'Yeah. And everything else.'

She looked at him for a long moment.

'You won't ever let this go, will you?'

'I've no idea. I haven't been here before.'

'But you won't. I know you won't.'

'How do you know?'

'Because all men are the same. Black and white. One strike and you're out.'

'One strike? Is that how you see it? Some kind of game?'

'Don't.' She turned away. 'This isn't helping.'

Suttle shrugged. If she wanted the satisfaction of a full-scale domestic, then he was happy to oblige. Otherwise there wasn't a lot to say.

'Your mum's, is it?' He broke off a chunk of cake and gave it to Grace.

346

'Yes.'

'So what's the story? What have you told her?'

'I told her the truth. I told her we're sick of living in the country. I told her we need a real home.'

'We?'

'Me. Does that sound selfish?'

'Yes, since you ask.'

'Thanks.'

'My pleasure.'

Suttle fed Grace more cake and then brushed the crumbs off her dress. A voice on the tannoy announced the imminent departure of the Waterloo train. Passengers for Portsmouth should change at Salisbury.

Suttle was nuzzling the warmth and softness of his daughter. At this rate, he thought, he'd be the one in tears.

Lizzie's hand was back in her bag. Then Suttle was looking at two pairs of keys on the table.

'Are they for me?'

'Yeah. They're both for the cottage.'

'You won't be back?'

'No. Not there. I'm through with it, Jimmy. I've had enough.'

'So it's over. Is that what you're saying?'

'That's your call. And in case you're wondering, I've no interest in where you might have gone last night. Yeah? Does that make any sense?'

Lizzie got to her feet. Suttle gazed up at her. For the second time in twenty-four hours he felt totally marooned, adrift in a world he no longer recognised.

He cradled Grace in one arm and picked up the holdall in the other. The guy at the barrier wouldn't let him through without a ticket. Suttle dropped the bag, kissed his daughter on the cheek, held her tight. He'd no idea when he'd see her again.

'Bye,' he said.

Lizzie had readied the buggy. Suttle strapped Grace in. They had three minutes to make the train.

'Be in touch, yeah?' Suttle said.

'You've got the number. You know where we are.'

Suttle nodded. He wanted to kiss her but he didn't. He wanted to say he was sorry, that he'd miss her, that it was all some gigantic fuck-up, but he couldn't find the words. She looked up at him, a strange expression on her face, her lips puckered, then she gestured him closer.

'Yellow Fiat,' she said. 'In the car park.'

Suttle found the Fiat minutes later. It looked brand new. It carried a Hertz rental badge and it was empty. He was still stooped beside the driver's window, looking for more clues, when he felt a hand on his shoulder. He straightened up, glanced round.

Paul Winter.

They drove out of the city, Winter visibly nervous, checking the rear-view mirror, braking at the last minute for turns that would throw anyone in pursuit. Suttle sat in silence, ambushed by a million questions. Was this why Lizzie had been so desperate to talk last night? Had Winter spent the night at Chantry Cottage?

They came to a stop in the middle of a trading estate on the outskirts of the city. The acre of car park outside B&Q was nearly empty.

Suttle was looking at Winter. The older man had put on a little weight since they'd last met and he seemed to have acquired an early tan.

'So how come?' Suttle asked.

'How come what?'

'How come you're here?'

'Lizzie belled me.'

'She's got your number?'

'Yeah. She's had it for ever. She sends me photos of Grace from time to time. That's me doing the family thing, if you're wondering. And something else, son. She didn't tell you because I made her swear she wouldn't. All right?'

Winter was angry. Suttle could see it in his eyes. He'd been flattered by Lizzie's invitation to become Grace's godfather and had never taken his duties less than seriously. Hence, Suttle assumed, the enormous risk he was taking.

'She told you about the Pompey situation?'

'Yeah.'

'Dave Fallon? The Spanish bounty hunter?'

'Yeah. She phoned me.'

'And?'

'We're on the move. It's under control.' He didn't go into details.

'So what else did Lizzie tell you?'

'Pretty much everything, as far as I can judge. You're living in a shit hole, son. You should have sorted it out.'

'I know.'

'So why didn't you?'

Suttle stared out through the windscreen. He didn't have an answer. This was like talking to his dad, he thought.

'Did she tell you about a bloke called Pendrick?'

'That's all bollocks. The woman was upset. She'd been upset for months. When that happens, all bets are off. You should have noticed, son. Then there wouldn't have been a problem.'

Suttle nodded. Winter was probably right.

'It's crazy down here. The job's non-stop. There aren't the bodies to go round any more. This isn't Pompey. You work your arse off and then some.'

'Great. Except you happen to have a wife. And a daughter.'

'I know.'

'And that matters?'

'Of course it does.'

'Then sort it, son. Get a fucking grip.' His hand was in his jacket pocket. He produced a bulky white envelope. When he tossed it across to Suttle it landed in his lap.

'What's that?'

'Money.'

'I don't want money. I don't need it.'

'Wrong again, son. You need to get out of that khazi of a place, you need to find somewhere fit to live in, and you need to start behaving like a human being. That little girl loves you. And so does your daughter. So take a few decisions, eh? And make it happen.'

Suttle had never heard Winter like this, so forceful, so aggressive. Twenty-plus years in CID had made him the master of ambiguity, of the hidden threat, of the carefully prepared traps that littered every conversation. Not this onslaught.

'Do I get a say?'

'Of course you do, son. But do me a favour, yeah? Don't tell me you've been betrayed. Don't bang on about this guy Pendrick. Lizzie was out of her head. And that was down to you.'

'My fault, then.'

'Yeah. Fucking right. So like I say, get a grip.' His eyes hadn't left Suttle's face. 'Are you listening or do I have to start all over again?'

Suttle wouldn't answer. He fingered the envelope. It felt like a lot of money. Winter was still watching him.

'Euros, if you're wondering. High-denomination notes.'

'Where did you get it from?'

'None of your business, son. Sell the place. Buy somewhere half-decent. Then she'll come back.'

'How do you know?'

'Because I'm not stupid. Because I watch as well as listen.' He held Suttle's gaze a moment longer then checked his watch. 'I'm off back to Heathrow in an hour. Where can you get something to eat in this town at ten in the morning?'

Suttle took him to a hotel back by the station. They ordered a full English each, and prior to its arrival Winter raided a neighbouring table for a bottle of HP sauce. There were plenty of very good reasons for living in Croatia but breakfast evidently wasn't one of them. Even Misty, he said, was starting to pine for a proper plate of bacon and eggs.

'How is she?'

'Barking mad. It was my birthday last week. You know what she bought me? A set of salsa lessons. Nightmare.'

The thought of Winter stepping onto the dance floor with the high-kicking Misty Gallagher put a smile on Suttle's face. He wanted to know about her daughter, Trudy, the third member of Winter's little ménage. A car accident last year had broken her neck and left her with serious nerve damage. How was she doing?

'Fine. She's got a boyfriend, and you know what he does for a living?'

'Tell me.'

'He's a cop. Mad about her. Nuts. But you know something? He's another one who can't see further than the end of his dick.'

'You think I'm like that?'

'Only you know, son.'

'That wasn't my question.'

'OK, so what were you up to last night?'

'I was with a woman called Gina Hamilton.'

'Shagging?'

'Yes.'

'OK, was it?'

'Very nice, since you're asking.'

'She's a D/I, right?'

'Yes.'

'Divorced?'

'Nearly.'

'And what else?'

'Neurotic as hell.' Suttle was grinning this time. 'Stuffed animals everywhere. Just like Misty.'

The waitress arrived with breakfast. Winter attacked his black pudding with relish. A tiny comma of HP sauce attached itself to the corner of his mouth.

Suttle wanted to know more about Croatia. In a year or so it'd be joining the EU. After which Winter was back in the firing line for a European Arrest Warrant.

'You're right, son. Unless Dave Fallon gets me first.'

'So what's the plan?'

'Serbia. They've got proper gangsters there. Misty thinks she can pull some real animal who can sort out the likes of Dave Fallon. It's a neat idea. I just hope he's good with salsa.'

Suttle had no idea whether he was joking or not and knew – in any case – that it didn't matter. This brief glimpse of the old Winter had revived something deep inside him. They'd finished breakfast. Winter mopped his chin with a napkin and Suttle accompanied him back to the Fiat.

Winter wanted to know how to get onto the motorway north but Suttle had something else on his mind.

'You want out, don't you?' he said.

'Out of where, son?'

'Croatia. Serbia. Abroad. Wherever.'

'What makes you think that?'

'I've been watching. Like you always told me to.'

Winter shot him a look, then extended a hand.

'Glad to hear it, son. Take care of her, eh? And Grace too.'

Winter turned to go but Suttle called him back. He was holding the envelope. There was no way he could take this money.

'Leave it then.'

'Where?'

'Here. Any fucking where. It's not for you, son. It's for them.'

Three weeks later Lizzie was back behind her old desk at the Pompey *News*. The editor had agreed to let her work three regular days a week plus freelance payments for supplementary features she put together in her spare time. This was a blessing for her mum, who found Grace a bit of a handful, and it also permitted Lizzie to kid herself that very little had really changed. She still got her daughter up every morning. She still put her to bed every night. The only difference was that now she had more to think about than dripping taps, elderly neighbours and incessant rain.

Suttle, meanwhile, banked nearly £37,000 in euros. That same afternoon he wrote a cheque for exactly the same amount and sent it to Lizzie. He'd talked to her a couple of times on the phone, prior to nonsense conversations with his daughter, and had managed to avoid a row. Soon, he promised Grace, he'd be down to Pompey to take her out for a treat or two. Whatever else happened, he explained sternly, she wasn't to forget him.

His relationship with Gina Hamilton, meanwhile, appeared to have stalled. Performance reviews had given way to some kind of operational involvement in a long-running corruption case and she was working all hours. For his own part, Suttle was equally under the cosh. A pensioner couple had been found battered to death in their Sidmouth bungalow and to date no one had a clue who'd done it.

Late one night, as knackered as ever, Suttle lifted the phone to Gina Hamilton. Still numb from losing his daughter, he'd begun to hate the silence of Chantry Cottage. Most television these days was for the brain-dead, and conversations with the cat were a poor substitute for real life.

'I miss you,' he said.

'Yeah?'

'Yeah.'

'Really?'

'Really.'

'Be honest, Jimmy. I know exactly what you're missing.' She laughed. 'Me too, as it happens.'

*

Three weeks later, for the first time, Lizzie had a girlie night on the town with Gill Reynolds. Gill had forgiven her for walking out on Chantry Cottage and they were friends again. They went to a bar in Gunwharf, a minute's walk from Paul Winter's old apartment. Lizzie had banked the cheque from her estranged husband and was quietly checking house prices in Southsea. Jimmy would, in the end, turn his back on the West Country. Of this she was quite certain.

For a Friday night the bar was unusually empty. Gill had just booked a holiday in Sri Lanka, a fortnight she intended to share with her latest conquest. This was a guy she'd been dating for less than a month, but already she knew that she'd stumbled on someone who would change her life.

'He's really bright, Lou.' She sucked the last of her vodka and Red Bull. 'And the good news is he loves me.'

'Married?'

'Yeah. For now.'

'Kids?'

'Two.'

'So how's he going to explain a couple of weeks in Sri Lanka?'

'No idea. I've already bought the tickets, though, so there has to be a way.'

It was at this point that Lizzie's mobile began to ring. Not recognising the number, she ignored it. Moments later it rang again. Same number. This time it was a text with an accompanying photo. Gill had gone to the bar for refills. Lizzie stared at the text. For a second or two it made no sense, a message from a distant planet, just random nonsense. Then she forced herself to look again, to piece it together and try and understand. 'She's a beauty, I promise you. Any time you fancy it. XXXX'

Lizzie's finger strayed to the attachment. She opened the photo. It was Pendrick. He looked thinner and somehow younger. He was standing in the cockpit of a sizeable yacht.

The yacht was anchored in some kind of lagoon. Pearl-white sand. A fringe of palm trees. Not a soul on the beach. Pendrick was grinning the way she recognised from the photos she'd found in his file box. And he was blowing her a kiss.

Lizzie stared at the image, at the beach, at the nut-brown figure so carefully posed against the view. This was a face that she barely remembered, from a time she wanted to forget. So far, the police had shown no interest in calling her back for another interview and for that she was deeply grateful.

'Lou?' Gill was back with the drinks. She'd seen the photo. 'Who's that?'

Lizzie didn't answer, shielding the phone. Gill wasn't having it.

'Show me, Lou. Gimme, you old slapper.'

Lizzie shook her head. The image of Pendrick still hung on the tiny screen. She gazed at it a moment longer, telling herself to get a new mobile, then her finger found the delete command and the face was gone.

Acknowledgements

New series. New setting. New police force.

My thanks to Paul Netherton, Russ Middleton, Antonia Weeks, Jez Capey, Alan Barnsley, Mike West, Jane Williams, Larry Law and Jacquie Cox, all of whom opened doors, shared impressions, explained procedures and generally briefed me on the realities of criminal investigation in Devon and Cornwall. And a special thank you to Steve Carey who was extremely generous with his time and his long experience at the cutting edge of CID in south-west England. Top man.

My son Jack guided me through the netherworld of video gaming and, with his partner Hannah, masterminded a memorable stroll through the badlands of Harehills in his adopted city of Leeds. Rob Williams, a good friend, shared his memories of moving into a near-derelict country bungalow in a damp fold of the Otter Valley, an account which sparked Chantry Cottage. Mia Marchant-John from Regatta Court gave me an extensive tour of Jake Kinsey's extraordinary apartment, while Richard Soper offered a thought or two about the realities of life in Exmouth Quays. Most important of all, Deb Graham shared her memories of growing up in Exmouth – a recent past that has shaped a town I've grown to love. Sadly, Deb died suddenly this year and, as a consequence, this book is dedicated to her memory. An inspirational woman, much missed.

I also owe a substantial debt of gratitude to Dr John Maskalyk, whose book *Six Months in Sudan* is a must-read for anyone interested in what happens when one culture collides head-on with another. Eamonn Lenahan grew out of those pages and sharpened what I always felt to be the real thrust of this book: that we in the West live in a bubble of our own making and may be neither the wiser nor the richer as a result.

To everyone at the Exmouth Rowing Club, another sincere thank you. Offshore rowing, to be personal for a moment, has transformed our lives. Lin and I and our fellow Vulcaneers (don't ask) are the luckiest guys.

This is a step away from the Faraday series and represents an act of faith on behalf of my editor, Simon Spanton, my agent, Oli Munson, and – fingers crossed – my readers. Faraday's was a very different journey. Where this one may lead is anyone's guess.

Love crime fiction?

Visit

THE MURDER ROOM.COM

Discover, discuss and download some of the world's greatest vintage crime novels.

Read the classic crime novels that inspired the modern-day greats, released for the first time in ebook.